The Truth of Yesterday

The Truth of Yesterday

Josh Aterovis

P.D. Publishing, Inc.
Clayton, North Carolina

ISBN-13: 978-1-933720-81-4

9 8 7 6 5 4 3 2 1

Cover design by Josh Aterovis
Edited by: Verda Foster/Danielle Boudreaux

Published by:

P.D. Publishing, Inc.
P.O. Box 70
Clayton, NC 27528

http://www.pdpublishing.com

Acknowledgements

Thanks to Robert, Richard, Linc, and Gary for all their help in the process of rewriting *The Truth of Yesterday*; Barb and Linda for giving Killian a safe a nurturing home; and Alec Weinberg and Jared Nunn for modeling.

We are all liars, because
The truth of yesterday becomes a lie tomorrow,
Whereas letters are fixed,
And we live by the letter of truth.
The love I feel for my friend, this year,
Is different from the love I felt last year.
If it were not so, it would be a lie.
Yet we reiterate love! love! love!
As if it were a coin with a fixed value
Instead of a flower that dies, and opens a different bud.
~ DH Lawrence ~

We like to think of life as a story, complete with a nice, neat beginning, middle, and end. Real life is seldom that orderly. We often forget just how powerful the past can be. After all, it's over and done with, so how can it affect the present? The truth is, while the past may be over, it is seldom done — especially in matters not properly dealt with. It has a way of twisting our perceptions, our feelings, and even our reality. Things we thought long behind us can suddenly be very much before us.

Our past influences every waking minute. It defines who we are today, whether for good or for bad. It has the power to affect the future in ways we can't begin to understand. Like echoes returning from a great distance or ripples in a pond, the past can come back to haunt us: torturing us with what might have been, taunting us with unrealized potential, terrorizing us with truths we tried to ignore, tormenting us with losses too great to absorb.

We each, in our own ways, try to move on from the past. Some of us attempt to do so by closing our eyes in the ostrich approach: if I can't see you, then you can't see me. Others try to outrun it. Some of us manage to convince ourselves it never happened. There are as many methods of avoidance as there are pasts to avoid. In the end, however, if we live long enough, the past will catch up to us. If we aren't careful, we may live just long enough for it to do so...and no longer.

Chapter 1

I sat slumped in my chair, eyes on the clock, counting the seconds until I was free. While the professor droned in the background, I'd stopped listening half an hour earlier. Luckily for me, he wasn't saying anything of real importance. This class was a waste of time. The professor had a love affair with the sound of his own voice, and we students were mere voyeurs. I could have simply read the book, showed up for the tests, and done just as well. Unfortunately, attendance counted as much as test scores for this professor, so I had to make an appearance.

Finally, the class ended, and I was the first person out the door. I was supposed to meet Micah, my boyfriend, on the other side of town. He'd told me he had something he wanted us to talk about. I had no idea what he had in mind, but that phrase alone was enough to strike fear in my heart.

Or maybe I was just overreacting. It didn't have to be anything serious.

I started my car and checked the dashboard clock. If I hurried, I could swing by my office, check my messages, and still have no problem meeting Micah on time, as long as the roads weren't too congested. Despite being only a small city on the Eastern Shore of Maryland, Salisbury did have its share of traffic woes.

I made it to the office with no great delays. I parked my car in the small lot next to the building and I ran up the stairs to Novak Investigations. Shane Novak, the private investigator I worked for, was out on business for the afternoon. As his assistant, I mainly did a lot of paperwork, but I also got to help out on some of his cases. I'd even been assigned one of my own recently, which was why I'd wanted to stop by the office.

I sat down at my desk and jiggled the mouse to wake up my computer. I left it on during the week in case Novak needed to look something up. The first thing I did was turn on some music. I hated being in the office when it was empty and silent as a tomb.

"I didn't think you were coming in this afternoon," someone said behind me a few moments later.

I jumped and spun around. "Oh, hey!" It was Novak. "I didn't think you'd be here, either. I just wanted to check my messages."

"I finished up early, so I decided to get some work done while it was quiet." He gave me a meaningful look.

I made a face at him and turned off the music. "Don't worry, I'm not staying long. I wouldn't have even known you were in if you hadn't snuck up on me."

Novak chuckled. "I didn't sneak up on anybody, and you're fine. I'm just giving you a hard time. Since you're here, why don't you give me a quick update on the Knox case?"

My mentor was referring to my first official solo job. He was keeping close tabs on my progress, but I wasn't complaining. I was a little nervous about being out on my own, even though it was a fairly run-of-the-mill, cheating-spouse case. A woman came into the office the week before and asked to speak to Novak. When I wanted to know what about, she replied, "I think my rat-bastard of a husband is cheating on me. If he is, I want proof so I can file for divorce and sue him for every damned penny he has."

You'd be surprised how often we hear variations of that statement. Or maybe you wouldn't.

"Well, I've been doing surveillance on Mr. Knox. As you know, his wife thinks that if he's having an affair, then it's happening either at work or when he goes away on business trips. I've been following him back and forth to work every day, and so far he's been a good boy. He hasn't taken any side trips, unless you count the grocery store one night and the liquor store another."

"What about when he's at work? Or when you're at school? How can you be sure he isn't cheating then?"

"I thought of that. I'm paying the receptionist to alert me if any women come to see him regularly or if he leaves unexpectedly."

Novak raised one eyebrow. "Nice thinking, but how do you know you can trust her? What if she's the one having the affair with Knox?"

"She didn't seem to like Mr. Knox very much. That's what gave me the idea of making the offer to her in the first place. I was asking questions about him, and I could tell she didn't care for the guy. Every time I said his name, you'd have thought she smelled something bad. When I asked her what she thought of him, she told me he was smarmy and had a reputation for being a ladies' man. I asked her if she'd like to make a little extra cash, and she jumped at the chance. Actually, she seemed sort of excited to help."

"So what's the deal? She calls you if he does something suspect?"

"Or texts me, whichever is easier. She might not always be able to call if there are people around."

Novak shook his head. "You young'uns and your texting." He turned to go back into his office. "Keep up the good work, kid."

I glowed. His praise didn't come often, so when it did, I tried to soak it in.

I flipped open my phone to check the time and almost fell off my desk chair. If I didn't hurry, I'd be late for my date with Micah. I'd check my messages tomorrow when I came in to work. They could wait.

Fortune smiled upon me, and traffic was light on my way to the diner where I'd agreed to meet Micah. So light, in fact, that with my rushing I managed to arrive a few minutes early. I didn't see Micah's car in the parking lot, so I went in, got a booth, and ordered a soda while I waited.

"Somebody joining ya, or you ready to order?" The waitress, a middle-aged woman with a chipped front tooth and greasy grayish-brown hair falling out of a half-hearted ponytail, stared at me with a blank expression. Maybe she'd had a rough day. Or a rough life.

"I'm waiting for someone." I gave her a small smile so she wouldn't hurt me. She didn't return the gesture as she stalked away without another word. She wouldn't be winning any personality contests in the near future.

I was just beginning to get a little concerned that Micah wasn't going to show up when I saw his silver Civic pull into the lot. I watched him unfold himself from behind the steering wheel and turn to face the restaurant. He stood by the car for a minute, just staring into the windows, almost as if he was posing. I waved, but was pretty sure he didn't see me.

He shook his head as if to clear his thoughts and moved quickly across the parking lot, where I lost sight of him. He reappeared inside a few seconds later and quickly spotted me.

"Hey, Killian," he said, sliding into the booth across from me. He brushed his floppy brown hair out of his dark eyes and smiled.

My heart skipped a beat. He was so gorgeous. "Hey, I was beginning to think you were standing me up." I grinned to let him know I was only teasing.

"Yeah, sorry about that," he said distractedly. "I got hung up with the story I'm working on right now. I told you they finally gave me one with some real weight, right?"

"Yeah. The county council thing." Micah was a reporter for the local newspaper. "It's about time you got a real story, especially after all the attention you attracted with your piece about Amalie's House."

He shrugged. Amalie's House was a pre-Civil War mansion turned bed and breakfast, run by my surrogate father, Adam, and his partner, Steve. The place came complete with its very own ghost. When the inn had opened, Micah wrote an account of the haunting. The article received a huge response — almost all positive — leading Micah to start a weekly series on local haunted hot spots. As a result, he was also getting more respect around the paper. He'd told me the day before about being assigned his first big story, the possibility of major corruption and payoffs in the county council. He was as excited as I'd ever seen him about his work.

Sitting across from me in the diner, though, he seemed withdrawn and preoccupied. I wondered if something had gone wrong. I hoped the newspaper hadn't taken the assignment away already and given it to their star reporter, a jerk named Walters. "Is everything okay at work?"

"Oh, yeah, things are going great. That's why I was late. The council member who we think is up to his eyeballs in graft made the mistake of firing his secretary last week. She's just dying to blow him out of the water. I was on the phone with her, and she was talking so fast I could barely write it down quickly enough. Of course, everything will have to be verified. I've really got my work cut out for me on this one, but it could be huge."

"That's great." So it wasn't the story he was upset about. While I figured he'd tell me in his own time, I was not known for my patience. "What are you ordering?"

"I think I'll just get a burger." He hadn't even glanced at the menu.

The waitress was once more approaching our table. "Ready to order?" Her tone suggested she was half hoping we'd change our minds and leave.

"I'll have a hamburger — lettuce, tomato, and ketchup, no pickle," Micah said.

Between the tension I was sensing from Micah and our waitress's dour mood, I suddenly didn't have much appetite. "I'll just have a house salad."

"Drinks?"

"Water is fine with me," Micah said.

I held up my still-full glass. "I'm good."

She made the proper notes on her little pad and moseyed off toward the kitchen.

After she left, an awkward silence fell between us. Micah sat looking down at his hands twisting nervously in his lap. I found myself getting more and more worried since that sort of behavior was so out of character. Finally, I couldn't take it anymore. "So, what's wrong? What did you want to talk about?"

"Hmm? Oh, it'll wait until the food gets here."

"Why? You afraid I'll lose my appetite if you tell me now?" I tried to keep my voice light, but inside I was tensing up like crazy.

"It's not that." He looked away, suddenly entranced by the giant fish tank near the door.

"Micah, what's going on? Are you breaking up with me?"

He turned back to face me, his eyes wide. "No! At least...I hope not." He sighed. "Killian, where are we going?"

"Huh? What do you mean?"

"Our relationship. Where is it going?"

"I...I don't understand what you're asking."

"Killian, we've been dating now for several months, but I feel like we're not getting anywhere. I've tried to be patient, but how much can a guy take?"

"Is this about...sex?" I was eighteen and, for all intents and purposes, a virgin. I'd only had one other boyfriend, with whom I had never gone all the way. Micah had said from day one he didn't want our relationship to be about sex, and, to his credit, he'd never pushed me.

"No, this isn't about sex." He sighed. "You know it's not about sex. And you know what this is really about. I need more from you than mere companionship, someone to go to dinner with or to the movies or out dancing. I want intimacy, and I'm not just talking about sexual intimacy. I feel like you're constantly holding me at arms' length. I want to be closer to you. No, I need to be closer to you. I need you to let me in."

"Micah... I... Wow!"

"I told you it should have waited."

"No, I..." I paused and took a deep breath. "Look, Micah, I don't know what to say. I thought we were doing fine."

"We are. We're doing just fine. But that's the problem. I don't want to just do fine. I want to do great. I want to be completely satisfied in our relationship."

"And you're not."

"No, I'm not. I feel like there's a part of you — a big part — that I've never even seen. Although I've caught hints and brief glimpses, and those are what have kept me around, I rarely get to see the real Killian. I want to know you completely and totally, but you have to trust me and let me in."

"I thought I was..."

"Did you?"

Before I could answer, our charming waitress appeared at the table with my salad and Micah's burger. "Enjoy." She plopped the platters down in front of us unceremoniously and stomped away.

I looked at the limp, dreary salad and realized I'd completely lost my appetite after all. Micah was apparently experiencing a similar predicament. I pushed the salad to one side.

"Killian," he started again, "I care about you. I really do. I even...I would even say I love you. I've never known anyone like you. You're so smart and funny. I enjoy being with you, and God knows you're never boring." He worked up a weak smile. "And, of course, it doesn't hurt that you're one of the cutest guys I've ever met." The smile slowly disappeared. "But I can't live like this. I can't keep going on in this limbo unless I know there's a reason to hope for something more."

I stared down at the table. "I care about you too. I've loved spending time with you and getting to know you."

"But?"

"There's no but."

"So...what are you saying? You'll let me in?"

"I...I don't know what you mean."

He sighed and ran his hand through his hair. "Sometimes—"

"Sometimes what?"

"Sometimes I feel there's something coming between us still. Or someone."

"What do you mean?"

"He's still here, between us, almost like he'd never left."

"What? Who?"

"Asher. That's what this is all about, isn't it? You can't let go, can't move on."

I blinked. "Asher? How'd he get into this?" Asher was my ex-boyfriend. We'd broken up months ago, and he'd moved away when school started. I didn't understand why Micah would bring him up after all that time.

"I think you still have feelings for him."

"That's not..." I stopped with the word "true" still on my tongue. Was he right? If I was honest with myself, I had to admit Asher was at least part of the reason I hadn't been moving faster with Micah. I'd been hurt pretty badly after our breakup, and wasn't at all eager to rush into another situation where I'd be that vulnerable again. Micah was right when he said Asher was coming between us, just not in the way he thought. "I'm sorry."

"Me too. Sorry won't fix this, though."

"That's not what I meant. Look, I don't have feelings for Asher. Trust me. I'm definitely over him. The thing is...he hurt me. A lot. He was my first love, and he broke my heart when he dumped me for somebody else. I just—"

"You're afraid I'll hurt you?"

I nodded.

"I can't promise I won't. I wish I could, but nobody can make a promise like that. All I can tell you is that hurting you is the last thing in the world I'd ever want to do."

"So...how do I fix this? How do we fix it?"

"You have to move on, Killian. You have to be willing to take a risk with me."

"What do you mean by risk?"

"Moving to the next level is going to require a certain amount of risk for both of us. We both risk getting hurt, risk losing what we have. All love involves risk. You have to decide if what we have, or what we could have, is worth that risk. Do the benefits outweigh the potential costs? I've decided that for me they do, but only if you're willing to commit to this just as much as I am."

"I..." I stopped, at a loss for words. My brain was going a mile a minute trying to keep up, but I was starting to feel overwhelmed. What if I didn't have an answer for him right that moment? Would he walk away and never look back?

Luckily, Micah responded to my unspoken question before I could launch into a full-fledged panic. "You don't have to tell me right now.

That wouldn't be fair. I don't want to put you on the spot." He pulled out his wallet, selected a twenty, and tossed it on the table. "Take your time and think about it. Be sure you know what you want, and then call me. I won't call you. If I don't hear from you in a reasonable amount of time, I'll know you decided it wasn't worth the risk, and I'll try to understand." He stood up and looked down at me sitting with what I'm sure must have been a stupefied expression.

"Micah, wait..."

"For what?"

"What's a reasonable amount of time?"

He forced another smile. "I want you to have time to think about this, about what I'm asking of you. There's no real timetable. I'm not giving you a deadline or anything. I hope I'll be talking to you soon, but if not, no hard feelings. I'll always love you." He turned and walked out the door.

I watched him through the plate-glass window as he crossed the lot once more, climbed into his car, and drove away without ever once looking back. I was still sitting there several minutes later when the waitress came back.

"Can I getcha anything else?" she asked disinterestedly, as if our food wasn't still sitting completely untouched on the table and my dinner partner hadn't just walked out on me.

"I, uh, think we're done here." I slid out from the booth. "Keep the change."

"Do you want a doggie bag?" she called after me.

"No thanks," I said. Whether she heard me or not I didn't know and didn't particularly care.

I was sitting in my room that night with a school book open in front of me on my desk, ostensibly studying. In reality, I can't begin to tell you the first thing about the chapter I was supposed to be reading. My conversation with Micah kept replaying over and over in my mind. I wondered what I could've said differently, and what I was going to do about what he'd said.

I liked Micah. I really did. It wasn't entirely out of the question that I could fall in love with him...if I let myself. And that was the problem. Micah was right. I had been holding a part of myself back from him. The more I thought about it, the more I wondered if he was also right about the reason. Maybe I wasn't as over Asher as I'd led Micah — and myself — to believe. I still missed him. If I was honest, I knew I did. It had been months since we were a couple, and we hadn't been happy even before that. Still, he had been my first boyfriend, and I'd loved him. I think somewhere in the back of my mind I always thought we'd get back together. I had been thrown for a loop when he announced he was moving away.

I wasn't sure I was ready to do what Micah asked. Could I take the next step and put myself at risk? It hurt so much when Asher left, more even than when we'd broken up. I'd lost so many people in my life I guess in some ways it was only natural for me to eventually begin building up defenses to keep others away. It wasn't entirely intentional either. I knew it wasn't fair for me to expect Micah to keep coasting along uncertainly, but I wasn't sure if I was prepared to open myself up the way he wanted. I was afraid to allow him in for fear I'd lose him; however, it looked like I was about to lose him anyway.

I slammed the book shut and let my head drop onto the desk with a thud. "What am I going to do?" I moaned out loud.

"Why do you always have to make everything so hard?" a familiar voice asked from behind me. I snapped my head up and around so quickly I felt something crack in my neck.

"Ow!" I yelped. "Damn it, Seth. You scared the crap out of me."

My deceased friend reclined on the bed, arms behind his head, and feet crossed at the ankles. He wore what I was beginning to think of as his uniform: faded jeans, heavy black shoes, and a clingy black shirt. His expression was one of benign amusement.

Unfortunately, it was not uncommon for me to see dead people, especially Seth. I had been his friend before he was brutally murdered. Actually, I'd been his one and only friend. He was the only openly gay kid in our school at the time, a fact that made him terribly unpopular with the in-crowd. He was the one who started me on my own coming-out journey.

After Seth's death, when my biological father found out I was gay and kicked me out, Seth's dad Adam, who was also gay, was the only person I'd known to turn to. He'd taken me in without a second thought and become more like a father to me than my real one ever had. Of course, Adam didn't know his dead son had a bad habit of showing up in my bedroom unannounced.

"What? No hello?" Seth grinned at me from his perch on my pillow. "No 'Gee, Seth, it's been a long time, how've you been?'"

"You're dead. I don't have to ask how you've been. I wish you wouldn't just appear like that. And what is it with people sneaking up on me today?"

He sat up and pulled his long limbs into a cross-legged position. "Oh, quit being such a drama queen. I didn't sneak up on you. I was just lying here. For God's sake, you're never happy unless you have some sort of crisis going on."

"That's not true." My protest came out whinier than I had intended.

"Okay, so maybe it was a little harsh, but you do make mountains out of molehills. Shall I list examples?"

"Please don't."

He shrugged and grinned, satisfied he'd made his point.

"So where have you been the last few months? I'd pretty much convinced myself you were just a stress-induced hallucination. When was the last time I saw you? At the barn?"

"Yes, at the barn. I got in a little trouble over that, broke a few rules. I guess you could say I'm on probation."

"Probation? What rules?"

"I've told you there are certain rules I have to obey if I'm to be allowed to come here."

"Yeah, yeah, yeah. I meant what rules did you break?"

"Oh. Well, that's another rule. I can't tell you what the rules are, remember?"

"You just like being mysterious."

He stuck his tongue out at me. "No, there really are rules. Although I have to admit, this whole mystical-entity thing does appeal to me. Look, we're supposed to help out by dropping enigmatic hints, no direct advice. And we're never allowed to interfere with the Pattern. When I gave you the strength you needed to escape from those ropes, I crossed the line."

"You gave me...what? The Pattern? What are you talking about?"

"Pretend I didn't mention that, okay? If I keep this up, you'll never see me again. Anyway, I didn't come here to enlighten you about how this all works."

"Why did you come?"

"You need me."

"I do?"

"Yes."

"Oh."

"I'm here to help you figure out what to do about Micah."

I rolled my eyes. "It's like having my very own fairy godmother."

"Fairy something, anyway."

"Seth..." I said warningly.

"Right, so as usual, you've gotten yourself into a quandary over something that should be simple."

"Simple for you, maybe."

"It should be simple for you. Do you like Micah?"

"Yes. You know—"

"Do you care about Micah?"

"Yes, but—"

"Do you love Micah?"

That one stopped me cold.

"Killian, do you love Micah?"

"I...I don't know."

"Yes, you do. Quit hiding and face the truth. If you don't stop being an idiot you're going to lose him forever."

Hearing his words so closely echo my thoughts from earlier caused my stomach to lurch. I didn't want to lose Micah.

"I do love him."

"Then tell him so, and then let him help you get past your fears and insecurities. He'll work with you if he knows there's something to work for. If you don't give him anything, though, what reason does he have to stay?"

I stood up and started pacing. "I don't even know why he'd want to stay with me. I mean, I'm a freaking mess. I'm scared to let someone I care about love me, I'm hung up on my old boyfriend, and I'm sitting in my bedroom talking to a dead guy."

"Hey, leave the dead guy out of this. Micah wants to be with you because he loves you. Asher is a part of your past now. He'll always be a part of you, but you have to let him go."

I stopped pacing and faced Seth. "What if I can't?"

"Can't what? Let Asher go? You can."

"You sound so sure."

"That's because I am sure. I know you, Killian. I know you can do this. Deep down you know you can, too. You're scared, and it's okay to be scared. Just don't let the fear control your life."

I sighed and sat on the edge of the bed, near Seth but not too close. He looked as if he'd be as solid as I was, yet I was always afraid if I touched him I'd go straight through him. "You're right. I have to stop being an emotional cripple. It's time to move on. I'll call Micah now." I jumped back up and reached for my cell phone.

He grinned. "That's the spirit. No wait, that's me." He cackled at his own awful pun.

I groaned. "Are we finished here?" I hit Micah's speed-dial button.

"Almost. Just one more thing. Since you're confronting your fears about Micah, don't you think it's also time you confronted your fears about your Gifts?"

I froze with my finger on the Send button. "What?"

"Your Gifts. You haven't forgotten them, have you?"

"No, despite the fact that I've been valiantly trying."

Gifts. That was what my friend Judy called my unwanted abilities to see spirits and sometimes catch glimpses of the past. I called them a curse.

"Why are you so scared of them, Kill? You have them for a reason."

I snapped the phone shut and set it back on the desk. "Yeah, well, I didn't ask for them."

"You didn't ask to be blond either. Or have blue eyes. Or to be gay."

"This is different."

"No, it's just another facet of who you are, and the sooner you deal with it, the better."

"I'm doing just fine without them, thanks."

"We'll see."

"What's that supposed to mean?"

He stood up and stretched, his body twisting in an almost feline manner. "Don't worry your pretty little head about it."

"No, tell me!"

"Sorry, I can't."

"You can't just say something like that and not explain."

"Sure I can. I'm enigmatic, remember?" He seemed to be taking entirely too much pleasure in my squirming. "Now, as much I'd love to, I can't sit here and argue with you about your Gifts all night. I have to go."

"Seth...please." I frowned. "There. I'm begging. Are you happy now?"

Seth's goofy grin faded. "I'm sorry. Really. I'm not just being a jerk. I can't tell you what I meant, but you'll find out soon enough. Just believe me when I say you're going to need to deal with your Gifts sooner or later...and the sooner the better."

"You're scaring me."

He broke into a smile again. "Don't be scared. Just deal with them already. I'm going to leave now and let you call Micah."

"Wait! When will I see you again?"

He shrugged. "Who knows? When you need me."

"Seth...wait..."

"Can't. Sorry." He flashed me one more goofy smile, and then he was gone.

It's very disconcerting to have someone simply vanish right before your eyes.

Chapter 2

Micah wasn't home when I called, so I left a message on his machine saying I wanted to talk to him. I thought about being somewhat more informative, then decided that news of the sort I had to share would be better delivered in person.

Micah didn't return my call until the next day. That morning, I'd tailed Mr. Knox, the allegedly unfaithful husband, to his job as a salesman for a seafood-distributing company, checked in with my friend at the receptionist desk, and finally gone to the office to finish a little paperwork before my first class at 11. Micah agreed to meet me at my house that evening so we could talk.

The rest of the day went by in a blur. I barely paid attention in class, and I almost forgot to follow Mr. Knox back to his house. All I could think about was Micah. I was so excited to give him my decision I couldn't focus on anything else.

After I got home, I changed my clothes twice while waiting for him to show up. I finally settled on a dark-blue, form-fitting, long-sleeved shirt that I knew Micah loved because he said it brought out my eyes. I completed my outfit with a pair of jeans he always claimed made my butt look nice.

"You're acting like it's your first date," Kane commented from his place in front of the computer as I gave myself a last once-over in the mirror.

My honorary little brother was quite the expert on dating. He'd had more girlfriends at sixteen than most people had in their entire lives. He'd recently broken up with the girl he'd gone out with all summer, saying he had to keep his options open now that school was back in session. Attracting girls was not a problem for him. He had bright green eyes and shaggy blond hair that he wore in a disheveled fashion, which seemed to drive the girls wild.

"I'm as nervous as if it were," I said.

"Why be nervous? Anyone with half a brain can tell he's crazy about you."

"Is that how you were able to tell?"

Kane clutched his hands over his heart. "Oh, that hurt...right here."

Being the mature older brother I am, I stuck my tongue out at him and left to wait downstairs.

Of course, Micah chose to arrive the moment I had to use the bathroom. The doorbell rang, and seconds later I heard Kane clattering down the stairs.

"I'll get it," I yelled, knowing from experience that if Kane answered, it would only lead to embarrassment for all involved, but mostly for me.

"From the bathroom? Don't be stupid. I've got it."

I heard the door open and swore under my breath.

"Hey, Micah," Kane said. "Good thing you got here when you did or Killian would have tried on everything he owns."

"Argh!" I howled. I washed my hands and burst from the bathroom to find Micah standing on the front steps. He looked fantastic in a dark-gray, ribbed turtleneck sweater and black pants.

"You could have at least invited him in," I said.

"Like you gave me time. Anyway, I'm going out. Tell Dad I'll be home by ten o'clock."

"Okay, be careful." For all our bickering, we were actually pretty close, and I often caught myself being protective of him. He threw me a look and loped off toward the old truck Adam had bought to use at the B&B. He let Kane drive it when they didn't need it.

I turned back to Micah, who was still standing just outside the door.

"Um, come on in."

He stepped into the hall where we stood awkwardly for a few seconds, neither of us quite sure what to say.

"Do you want to go to my room so we can talk?" I finally asked.

"Sure."

He followed me upstairs and into the room Kane and I shared, where the uncomfortable silence returned.

"I thought about..." I started at the same time Micah began, "You said you wanted..."

I giggled, and Micah smiled. It was what we needed to break the tension.

I started again. "I thought about what you said, and I realized you were right. I wasn't giving you all of myself, partly because I wasn't completely over Asher. And it was also because I was afraid of being hurt again. Then I remembered what you said about risk." I took a deep breath. "Micah, I love you."

I watched his face intently for his reaction. I saw something flash in his eyes, but I couldn't identify it before it was gone.

"What does that mean?" he asked guardedly.

"It means I've decided to take the risk and try to make this work. It means you'll have to help me if you want to make it work too, but I'm willing to try."

"What about Asher?"

"You mean, am I over him? Not completely. Not yet, anyway. Who knows? Maybe I never will be, but he's a part of my past now. I have to move on, and I'd like to move on with you. I do love you. I realized that last night. I was scared to death at the thought of losing you."

"That scared you more than the possibility of getting hurt?"

I nodded. "I was afraid to let you in because I was afraid I'd lose you and I'd just get hurt again. Then I realized I was going to lose you by not letting you in. That would have hurt just as much...because I was already in love with you."

"Are you really in love with me, Killian?"

I paused barely long enough to see the vulnerability in his eyes. "Yes, I am."

He drew in a shaky breath and slowly released it. "Good, because yesterday when I said I could fall in love with you, that wasn't exactly the truth. The truth is I already have."

I threw myself into his arms, and we tumbled backwards onto the bed. I kissed him firmly on the lips, and without hesitation he started kissing me back. He rolled us over so he was on top. After a few minutes, he gently pulled away and lifted himself up onto his elbows so he could look me in the face.

"God, you're so beautiful, Killian. I could just stare at you all night. You know, this is exactly the way I hoped it would happen, but I was too afraid to believe it actually would."

"Oh, ye of little faith," I teased.

"It's not going to be an easy road, though. You know that, right?"

"I never thought it would be. You're going to have to be patient with me. I doubt I can drop all the walls at once. I might need your help."

"We'll work on it together. You know you're not the only one with walls though, right?"

"You too?"

He shifted his weight off me and onto the bed. I cuddled into his side, my head on his shoulder. His fingers played with my hair. I didn't think he was going to answer at first, but finally he took a deep breath. "I think everybody has walls to some degree — if they've lived at all, anyway. Some are worse than others. From my experience, it seems gay guys have more walls than most. I guess we have to start building our defenses sooner than other people."

I twisted around so I could see his face better. "You've told me about being abused by your neighbor and how you reacted by having sex with a lot of people, but you've never mentioned falling in love. Am I the first person you've ever loved?"

Micah softly stroked the side of my face. "No, I fell in love once before, when I lived in DC. We lived together for a while."

That was news to me. "Why'd you break up?"

"I moved here, he stayed in DC. Neither of us wanted to do the long-distance thing. We made a mutual decision to just call it quits. We both agreed we'd run our course and there was no sense in waiting to break up until things got ugly. At least that way we could stay friends."

"Did you?"

"For a while. Then the phone calls and emails got further and further apart. Eventually, we just stopped talking. About the same time I met you, actually."

"Do you still love him?"

"I'll always love him, but I'm not in love with him anymore."

"Are you over him?"

He thought for a moment. "Yes. I don't think I really was before I met you, but I know I am now. I never expected my relationship with him to be a forever thing."

"What about us? Are we a forever thing?"

He stared into my eyes for several seconds before answering. "I don't know. I guess that remains to be seen. Any other questions, sir?"

"What? You know everything about my past. I'm just trying to learn more about yours."

"You know everything that's important. You know I love you. You know I want to be with you. What more do you need?"

"Um, how about a written guarantee? Completely satisfied or my money back."

He threw his head back and laughed. "I'll satisfy you, you little brat." He jumped up, straddled my waist, and began to tickle me.

I laughed, wiggled, and writhed under him as I gasped for breath. "Stop!" I finally managed to shout. "Stop! I'm gonna pee!"

He collapsed on top of me where we both panted and giggled.

"If anyone walked in right now they'd never believe you were only tickling me."

"Um, we're fully clothed. I realize you're a little inexperienced, but you do know you start by getting naked, right?"

I shoved him off and punched him in the arm. "Not funny."

He sat up and reached into his pocket. "I have something for you."

That caught my attention. "What is it?"

He pulled out a small, gray jewelry box.

"Oh, is that what I felt? You mean you weren't just happy to be lying on top of me?" I didn't take my eyes off the box.

"Oh, I was quite happy to be there. I'm sure what you felt was the real thing. I bought this to give you no matter what you decided. If we broke up, it was something to remember me by. If we didn't, then...well, here."

I took the box gingerly and held it in my lap, half afraid to open it. "Always prepared. You'd make a good boy scout."

"Except for the fact that I'm gay. Open it, please."

I looked down apprehensively at the box. What if it was a ring? I wasn't ready for that. I tentatively pried open the lid and felt all my anxiety drain away. Nestled against the plush cream lining was a beautiful rainbow pendant on a delicate silver chain. The pendant was an inverted, stained-glass triangle framed in silver.

"I went with silver because you don't seem like the gold type," Micah said softly. "It's a pride necklace."

"It's beautiful."

"I hope you like it. I've never seen you wear much jewelry, but I noticed it in the store and..."

"I love it." I leaned forward and kissed him on the lips.

"Want me to put it on you?"

"Please."

He took the box from my hands and freed the necklace. After fiddling with the clasp until it opened, he moved behind me on the bed and put the chain around my neck. The pendent lay perfectly in the hollow at the base of my throat.

"Stand up so I can see," he whispered in my ear.

With a little shiver, I did as he asked.

"You look incredible." He gave me a seductive smile.

I draped my arms around his shoulders. "So do you."

"It's a shame to waste all this sexy. What do you think about hitting the Inferno?"

The Inferno was a gay dance club located on a back road in the last place you'd expect to find a club of any sort, let alone a gay one. We'd been there a few times, and I'd been delighted to discover that I loved to dance and was actually pretty good. While I was technically underage, Micah knew the bouncer, a bulldog of a drag queen named Carmen, who allowed me entrance without a word.

I jumped at the chance to go dancing. I left a note for Adam telling him where Kane and I were so he wouldn't worry.

If you didn't know what you were looking for, you'd never suspect the Inferno was anything other than a warehouse. From the outside, it was quite unremarkable: an unassuming, two-story, cinder-block building with no paint on the walls, no windows to speak of, and surrounded by a few straggly pine trees and acres of fields. A small, inconspicuous sign above the large black metal door was the only indication you'd arrived at the right place. Well, that and the gravel parking lot full of cars. It was a Friday night and the joint was jumping.

On one side of the door stood a tall, broad-shouldered, bald man who appeared to be looking for an excuse to bash in someone's face. I'd never heard him utter a word in all the times I'd been to the club. On the other side, under an overhang, was a podium with a high barstool behind it. On the stool sat Carmen.

No one who had ever met Carmen was likely to forget her. She was very large, for one thing, easily topping out at six-feet six without her heels — which must have added at least another three inches — and built like a tank. Her square face would never be described as pretty, or even attractive. She compensated for her lack of looks with an abundance of makeup and hair big enough to have its own zip code. That night, the wild wig she had chosen was approximately the same shade of pink as Pepto-Bismol. Her silver-sequined, ankle-length dress was a few sizes too small. Her trademark mirror-ball earrings dangled from her ears. Although I couldn't see her shoes, I knew from previous visits that I could have used them as skis. The ensemble was pulled together by a pink feather boa draped around her broad shoulders.

While the Eastern Shore wasn't the most liberal part of the state — rednecks and country bumpkins abounded — no one ever feared any trouble with Carmen and her silent sidekick on duty. I'd heard she kept a large pistol somewhere on her person and she knew how to use it. I didn't doubt the rumors for a second, not that she'd ever need the weapon with Mr. Tall, Dark, and Ugly on the scene.

"Well, well, well, if it isn't my favorite boys," she said, waving a large, red lollipop around.

"You say that to all the boys," Micah replied with a grin.

"You know it, honey. So Micah, darling, are you still running around with this baby?"

"He has a name, Carmen."

"I know your name, don't I, Killian baby?" She waved the lollipop under my nose. I noticed it was shaped like a penis.

"Hi, Carmen."

"The baby speaks. He's a pretty one, Micah. I have to give you that. Just be sure you hide him if the big bad police ever happen to show up."

"I promise." Micah held up three fingers. "Scout's honor." He slipped his arm around my waist and pulled me into the Inferno, where the sound of Carmen's laughter was quickly drowned out by the cacophony of sound.

The club's name was quite fitting. The noise may have been the first thing to hit you as you entered, but the heat was close behind. For some reason, it was always hot as Hades inside the building. I suspected it was meant to encourage guys to take their shirts off...as if they needed any encouragement.

Once our eyes adjusted to the dim lighting, a smorgasbord of sights and sounds awaited us. Multicolored strobes flashed, laser beams sliced through the haze like lightsabers, and fog machines created such a miasma we almost had to feel our way along the dance floor. A mass of male bodies was gyrating, bumping, and grinding to the heavy beat of the dance music blasting from every angle. Sweat and glitter sparkling on the dancers' skin created a dizzying and mesmerizing effect.

The décor was simple: an industrial look with lots of concrete and shiny black metal. Chimney-like columns spaced at regular intervals around the room spouted flames — not real ones, but a gauzy material illuminated with red and orange lights from below and blown upward by fans. Spiral staircases led to a wide, metal-grid catwalk that went around the whole room and overlooked the dance floor. Tiny pedestal tables sat near the walls, each with four stools bolted down around it.

I was in awe of this place. It was so foreign to anything I'd ever seen before. Everywhere I looked there were guys kissing, touching, dancing, and laughing. It was euphoria.

"Ready to dance?" Micah yelled into my ear, the only way I could possibly hear him over the din.

"Hell, yeah!"

A few hours later, we slipped out the door into the fresh, cool air. Although the party was still going strong inside, I was completely exhausted. Dancing is strenuous exercise.

"With all that heavy breathing you two should at least be naked," Carmen said lazily.

"Don't you ever want to be inside?" I think it was the first thing I'd ever said to her besides hello.

"In there? Are you kidding?" She snorted. "Honey, I'm way too old for all that foolishness. I'd throw out a hip or something. No, I'm content to just sit here and breathe in the ambiance of youth and beauty."

"Oh, come on." Micah scoffed. "We both know you could dance circles around most of those guys in there. You're healthy as a horse."

"And just as big." She produced a cigarette from her cleavage and lit up. "Now you boys run along. It must be past the baby's bedtime."

"Yes, mother." I shot her a grin and started for the car.

"Sassy one, isn't he?" Carmen yelled. "Keep an eye on him, Micah."

Micah chuckled as he trotted to catch up to me. "Did you sneak one of my drinks again tonight?" He was referring to the first time he'd brought me to the Inferno, when I'd been so nervous I'd fortified myself with his alcoholic beverage before hitting the dance floor. "I've never seen you so playful with Carmen."

"Nope, all I drank was the bottled water you got me. I just figured if she was going to dish it, she could take it. Hey, remember our first date when you promised me if I went out with you again you'd tell me who Carmen really was?"

"I did?"

"Yeah, you did."

"Well, I lied."

"No fair. You promised."

"You're the detective. You figure it out."

"I hate it when people tell me that."

I was at the office again the next day, plugging away at the stack of paperwork that kept building up on my desk, when Judy swept in as only she could. Judy Davis was a slender, attractive woman with a deceptively ordinary appearance. She wore her straight, blonde hair cut off bluntly just above her shoulders and tucked behind her ears. She looked as if she'd come from working in her garden, which she probably had. She took a great deal of deserved pride in the tiny, but exquisite, flower gardens she had created in just the few short months she and her nephew Jake had been living in their small house.

"Hi, Judy," I said. "Novak is out on his case." She and Novak, a widower, had been dating for a few months, and she occasionally dropped in unexpectedly to see him.

"I know. Actually, I'm not here to see Shane. I'm here to see you."

"Me?"

"Yes, you. I need to talk to you about Jake."

For a brief time, back before Asher and I had started dating, Jake and I had almost become boyfriends. I'd ended up choosing Asher, while Jake and I remained just friends. We were barely even that these days, though, so I couldn't imagine why Judy was there to see me about him. After his entire family had been killed, he'd gone to live in California with Judy. They'd only recently moved back to Maryland.

"What about Jake?"

"Well...hang on." She grabbed one of the chairs that sat against the wall and dragged it over to my desk. She settled into it and took a deep breath. "I'm worried about him. I think he may be doing drugs."

"Oh, well, I really wouldn't know. We don't talk that much anymore."

"I didn't expect you to know. That's why I'm here. I want you to find out."

"Huh?"

"I want to hire you to find out what's going on in Jake's life."

"Hire me?"

"He won't talk to me. I've asked him, but he won't say a word. I know things have been hard for him since Tom and Janice died, but we've always been able to talk — at least we could before we came back here. I'm beginning to think moving was a mistake."

Tom and Janice were Jake's parents. Janice was Judy's sister.

"Wait a minute." I was still confused. "What about Novak? Why don't you just hire him?"

"I think that would make things just a little too awkward. I mean, I'm seeing Shane, and there's already enough tension between the two of them as it is. Shane thinks I let Jake get away with too much. He's almost eighteen, though, so I can't baby him anymore."

"But you can hire me to follow him around?"

"Oh, don't sound so judgmental, Killian. If he'd talk to me, I wouldn't have to do this. He's my responsibility now. I'm worried sick about him. I've been having...feelings...premonitions — whatever you want to call them — that he's in danger. I don't know what sort of danger and I need to find out. Please, will you do this for me? As a favor? Not that I won't pay you."

Judy was the one who first insisted I had Gifts. She was a psychic of sorts. While she didn't have a crystal ball or read tea leaves — at least as far as I knew — she did occasionally get "feelings" about things, and she was almost always right. She also had premonitions sometimes: little glimpses of the future — rarely enough to actually be helpful, but creepy nonetheless. While I had no problem with Judy's Gifts, I would have appreciated her keeping them to herself. I had some serious doubts when it came to my own.

I also had doubts about investigating Jake. "I don't know..."

"Please, Killian. It would mean a lot to me."

"I just don't feel comfortable following my friend around. I mean, I'm not even that good at this. I'm still learning."

"Poppycock. Shane says you're a natural, the best he's ever seen even without training. I know you can do this, and I know you'll do it well, because you care for Jake, too. If he's involved with drugs or something else illegal, his life could be in danger. If you refused to help me and something happened to him, how would you feel?"

Great. There was a guilt trip too. Could her visit get any better? She was right, though. I knew if anything happened to Jake after I'd turned her down, I'd never forgive myself.

I sighed. "Okay, I'll do it."

"Thank you, Killian. But there's one more thing."

"What's that?"

"I want you to keep this quiet."

"Of course."

"I mean, from Shane."

"You don't want me to tell Novak?"

"No. Not yet. Let's see what's going on first."

"It's not good to keep things from the person you're dating." Or from your boss, I thought, but didn't add. I didn't like the idea of trying to hide an investigation from Novak.

"Killian, darling, as much as I appreciate your concern, I don't need relationship advice. I mean that in the kindest possible way. I know you don't like keeping things from Shane, but you'll have to trust me that it's best for now."

"Fine." At least I understood why'd she'd come in to talk to me while she knew Novak would be out.

"Please don't be upset with me. You'll understand later."

"Whatever. How do you want me to start? Stalk him?"

She sighed. "He gets out of school at two-thirty. I don't know where he goes afterwards. He doesn't come home some nights until eight or later. There've been a few nights he didn't come home at all. When I ask him where he was, he just tells me not to worry about it. If I get angry, he tells me to mind my own business. I grounded him, but it didn't faze him in the least."

"Can't you take his car away from him?"

"I could, but he'd just find another ride. At least this way I know he's doing the driving. If he is into drugs, I have to say I've never seen him high or out of control when he gets home."

"So what makes you think drugs? You said earlier that it could be something else illegal. Like what?"

"I don't even know. I simply had a feeling it involves drugs. I have no real evidence besides his erratic behavior, which could, I guess, be nothing more than typical teenage rebellion."

"Then what makes you think it's not just that? Is there anything besides coming home late?"

"He's been buying a lot of stuff recently and I have no idea where he's getting the money from — certainly not from me."

"Stuff like what?"

"Electronics. Clothes. I don't know what else. That's just what I've noticed."

"Is there anything more?"

"Just the gut feelings I mentioned. You know, I've come to trust my Gifts, Killian. Speaking of which, how are you coming with yours?"

"I'm not. Back to Jake..."

"Killian, you know you really should learn more about your Gifts. I think they're very strong."

"I'm not interested."

"But you have to be. They can be dangerous if left untrained, or they can be a marvelous tool if you know how to use them. You were given them for a reason, you know."

"You sound like Seth," I said crossly.

"Is he still coming to visit you?"

"I hadn't seen him for a few months, but he showed up the other night."

"Relationship problems?"

"Actually, yeah. But he also said I should deal with my Gifts. As I told him, though, I'm doing just fine without them."

"Are you?"

"Yes. I am. Now, is there anything else I need to know about Jake?"

She signed but gave in. "You know what he drives, right?"

"A dark-blue Jeep?"

"Yes. That's all I can think of right now." She stood up and pushed the chair back to its original position. "You'll let me know as soon as you have something?"

I looked into her eyes and recognized the pain and fear that she was making an effort to hide. I nodded. "Yeah, I'll keep you updated."

She bit her lip in a most un-Judy-like fashion. "Thank you."

made it sound as if finding something she'd filed herself on her own desk was a major accomplishment.

"Maybe we will." I laughed, but it got me thinking what a good idea it would be to hire somebody as our secretary or receptionist, since it would free me up a lot.

The phone rang just then. Before answering it, she handed me what turned out to be a fax from a hotel in Washington, DC, confirming Knox's reservations for that Friday night through Sunday morning. I pulled out my notepad to jot down the pertinent information.

Sharla hung up just as I finished. "Thanks," I said, giving the fax back to her. "Now, if he leaves unexpectedly during the day or if you suspect something fishy, you remember what to do, right?"

She grinned broadly. This was her favorite part. "Sure do. I send you a text saying he's left." She made a face. "I still wish you'd let me be a little more creative. Can't I say something like, 'The chicken has flown the coop'?"

I laughed again. "You watch too much TV, Sharla. If you really want to say 'the chicken has flown the coop', go ahead. I'll know what you mean." She clapped excitedly.

I pulled a twenty out of my wallet and slid it across the counter.

Sharla slid it right back at me. "Keep it this time. I'm having too much fun to get paid. I feel like I'm one of Charlie's Angels."

"Except you're cuter than any of them."

She beamed. "And it's about damn time they had a black one."

I was leaving my last class of the day later that afternoon when I remembered that I needed a particular program for one of the courses I was taking. Knowing I didn't have it on my computer at home, I made a side trip to look for it at the campus bookstore, where it would be much cheaper with my student discount.

I found the disc and went to the checkout area, choosing the shorter of the two lines. When I noticed my clerk, I was doubly glad for my selection. He was cute in a slightly awkward sort of way. He had full, red lips and short, light-brown hair. Behind his small, wire-rimmed glasses, his eyes were an indeterminate color. I studied them while he waited on the person in front of me, trying to figure out what color they were exactly. I had just decided they were hazel when I realized he was staring back and had said something I'd missed.

"Huh?" I tried not to blush.

"I said, 'Can I help you?'" He seemed to be fighting back a smile.

I handed him the disc and gave in to the blush.

As he rang me up, I noticed his gaze kept straying to the rainbow pendant around my throat. "Nice necklace," he said after giving me my total.

"Thanks. It was a gift." I started to add that it was from my boyfriend, but for some reason the words wouldn't come out.

"Have you heard of Haven?"

"Um, not really." It sounded familiar, but I couldn't quite place it.

"It's the gay/straight alliance here on campus. We meet on Thursday nights. You should come sometime."

I felt my blush deepen and wondered why. I wasn't ashamed of being gay. I'd been out for several years and had actually helped Asher start a GSA at our high school. Maybe I just wasn't used to being so easily identified as gay by a complete stranger.

"Um, thanks."

The guy smiled. "My name's Noah. I'm the vice-president. The meetings start around eight in the student lounge in Wicomico Hall. It's really informal. We usually have between twenty and thirty people show up. We'd love to have you come."

"Thanks, maybe I will." My inexplicable awkwardness was fading, and I found myself a little intrigued. With nobody waiting behind me, I decided to ask him more about the group. "So what does Haven do?"

"Well, we're partly a support group, but we also sponsor a lot of educational and awareness stuff on campus. We put on events a couple of times a year — during Gay and Lesbian History Month and for National Coming Out Day in October."

"That was last week, right? I really didn't pay much attention, because I had some other stuff going on."

"Yeah, that's over for this year." Someone came up behind me, and Noah greeted the customer before turning back to me. "Hey, I'd like to talk to you more about this if you're interested." He grabbed a piece of scrap paper, scribbled something on it, and handed it to me. "This is my dorm room and cell phone number. Call me sometime."

I took the slip with a promise to give him a ring and started walking away.

"Oh, hey," he called. I turned around to find him holding out the disc I'd just bought. "You forgot this."

I grinned sheepishly and took it from him. "Thanks."

"Oh, and what's your name?"

"Killian."

He smiled and focused on his next customer.

"You're with Micah," I told myself firmly. I chanted it like a mantra all the way back to my car.

I was cutting things close getting to Jake's high school before it let out for the day, but I arrived just in time. I parked in a visitors' space at an angle with a good view of the student lot. While Jake and I were the same age, he'd taken so much time off from school to recover from injuries — both mental and physical — received when his family died, he'd fallen behind and had to be held back a year. He was a senior, which put him one grade ahead of Kane.

I was once again trying to justify following someone who was supposed to be my friend when I spotted his Jeep leaving the lot. Quickly pulling out a few cars behind him, I made sure to keep at least one vehicle between us at all times. Unlike Knox, Jake did know what I drove, so it was even more important than usual to make sure I was discreet.

I tailed Jake to a mall on the far side of town. Maybe he was just doing a little shopping. I followed him inside, making up an excuse as I went, in case he spotted me. That was another lesson from Novak: always have a cover story prepared. Unless they are pathological liars, most people have trouble coming up with a convincingly innocuous explanation on the spur of the moment. If Jake did see me, I'd tell him I was looking for a new jacket now that it was starting to get cooler.

I shadowed him around for about an hour, somehow managing to avoid being noticed. The only things I learned were that he had an affinity for tight clothing, shopped for lotion at Bath & Body, and knew practically every kid in the mall.

I was just about ready to give up when I noticed a sudden shift. He began to behave in a very suspicious manner, throwing quick glances over his shoulder and generally acting extremely guilty. Although I was able to stay hidden by ducking into stores and jumping behind racks of clothes, my spy tactics were drawing attention and making it rather hard to keep a good eye on my quarry. At first, I thought maybe he had sensed me following him, but quickly realized he was up to something.

I slipped behind one of the large potted palms in the middle of the mall and watched him through the fronds as he took one final glance around, then turned suddenly down the hall leading to the restrooms. I cursed under my breath. There was no way I could follow him in there without his seeing me. I watched from my tropical hiding place while several other guys came and went, all different ages and types, until Jake finally reappeared after about fifteen minutes. My curiosity raging, I trailed him as he made directly for the exit. Part of me wanted to take a look around the men's room, but I knew that was probably useless. Following Jake made more sense.

Back out on the road, I soon realized he was heading for home. I glanced at the clock and remembered I had to get over to Knox's building soon so I could trail him home as well. What an exciting job I had, following people around while they shopped and drove home. I tailed Jake until he turned into his driveway. As I went by, I hoped and prayed he wouldn't glance up at his rearview mirror and see me pass, or if he did, that he wouldn't recognize my car.

I almost missed Knox. A few seconds longer and he would have been gone. He was leaving a little early, but I arrived just in time to fall in behind him. Traffic was light, letting us make good time back to his house. I parked and watched him walk up to the side door.

Since he was going to DC that weekend, I would be as well. I'd have to call Mrs. Knox the next day to see what she knew of the business trip, then speak to Novak about making the arrangements. He would have to approve any trips. I wished I could talk to him about Jake, but I had made that promise to Judy. With a sigh, I started the car and drove home.

"I think you should go," Adam was saying as he washed and rinsed the dinner dishes while I dried and put them away.

We were discussing the GSA on campus. "I won't even know anyone there," I said, still not completely over my adolescent shyness.

He handed me a plate. "You'll know that guy Noah."

"No, I met him once in the bookstore. That does not equate to knowing someone."

"You said he seemed nice."

"He was nice."

"Cute?"

"What does that have to do with anything? I'm dating Micah."

"Doesn't mean you're blind. It was just a question, Kill. From your response I take it he was cute though, huh?"

I sighed. "Yes, he definitely was. Why do you think I should go? I mean, what's the point?"

"Well, first off, it never hurts to have more friends. Secondly, you probably have something to offer. Some of these kids may be struggling with issues you've already dealt with, like figuring out whether they're gay and coming out. Plus, you know how I like to support these sorts of things. If Haven is involved with education on campus and in the community, it's a great cause."

I had to admit he was right. I had been interested when Noah was telling me about it. I just needed a little nudging. I knew I'd probably call Noah later that night or the next day.

I glanced over at Adam and wondered if he missed his partner on nights when Steve was at the B&B. It had to be hard living in two different places. If they had guests, one of them always stayed at Amalie's House while the other stayed with me and Kane. Technically, we were old enough to take care of ourselves, but Adam liked to keep the family together as much as possible.

Business was still a little slow, so some nights, we were all together at the beach house. Kane occasionally stayed over at the inn. I had only spent the night there once and didn't plan to do so ever again. During renovations, we'd discovered the house was haunted. Although we'd thought the problem was settled, we were apparently wrong. There had been a few incidents since the grand opening.

I called Mrs. Knox the next day between classes and learned that she knew all about the business trip. She wanted me to follow him. An all-expense-paid trip to DC sounded great to me, especially since it was only a three-hour drive. I wondered why Mr. Knox was taking the commuter plane, but I guess if your company is willing to spring for the tickets, it's better than driving.

After school was over for the day, I went to the office to talk to Novak. I found him at his desk typing away on a report. He stopped when I stuck my head in.

"What's up, kiddo?" Novak was a retired police detective, and he looked the part. You could tell at a glance that he used to be in law enforcement or the military. He wore his iron-gray hair in a buzz cut and kept his body fit and lean, but it was more than that. There was something in the way he carried himself. Although his age was hard to guess, I knew he had to at least be in his late fifties, and it wasn't impossible that he was even older. When his wife died soon after he retired, it hadn't taken him long to realize he wasn't cut out for sitting around the house. That was the beginning of Novak Investigations.

"There's a new development in the Knox case," I said, still in the doorway.

"Sit down and fill me in." He swiveled his executive desk chair around to face me. Novak's office was a comfortably eclectic space. The first things you couldn't help noticing were the bookcases, which took up one whole wall. Made in all different heights and woods, they were filled to overflowing with books. There were law books, phone books, atlases, maps, and a set of encyclopedias that was easily older than I was. One case was reserved for his collection of hardcover detective novels, many of which were signed and/or first editions.

In the center of the room sat his desk, a huge expanse of scarred golden oak. I always figured the office must have been built around it, since there was no way that mother could have fit through the door. Its top was usually completely clear, unless he's working on a case. Then it was apt to be quite cluttered with files, papers, photos, and more. Behind the oak behemoth stood a daunting procession of battleship-gray filing cabinets, each one meticulously labeled and locked. Two large leather armchairs faced his desk.

For the most part, I liked the room. There was one exception, however: the odd, ugly, humpbacked sofa he kept on the wall opposite the bookcases and under the room's lone window. I know furniture is incapable of harboring ill will, but I'd swear that sofa is evil. It seemed to crouch malevolently off to one side, its carved claw feet gripping the floor for traction, waiting for some poor, unsuspecting soul to make the fatal mistake of sitting on it. Then, moving with a swiftness that belied its ungainly size, it would devour the hapless victim whole, before perhaps spitting out a shoe.

I moved quickly toward an armchair while carefully avoiding looking at the sofa. Luckily, I reached my chair unmolested.

I quickly filled Novak in on what little progress I'd made with the Knox case thus far. I ended by mentioning the proposed DC trip.

"Will it interfere with your school work?"

"No, Knox isn't checking in until late afternoon, and his flight leaves him just enough time to get there. I only have morning classes on Fridays, so I should have no trouble driving up there before he arrives."

"Have you been to DC much?"

"Not really."

"Damn. I'd go with you if my case weren't so close to busting wide open. I can't afford to leave. Do you know anyone who's familiar with the city?"

"Micah used to live there."

"Do you think he'd be willing to go along with you? We can hire him as a consultant if we need to."

I smiled. "I bet he'll be willing to go without the monetary incentive."

Novak chuckled. "I'd imagine you're right, there. Ask him, and let me know what he says. If he can't go, I don't want you going. You don't know the city well enough to be running around on your own."

As much as I liked the idea of having Micah along, I felt I had to defend myself. "I don't need a babysitter."

"I didn't say you did. I just believe you should have a guide who's familiar with the city. That is, if you think you can work with your boyfriend along and not get too, ahem, shall we say...distracted?"

I blushed. Novak didn't have any problems with my being gay — in fact, he'd told me that his grandson was gay — but it still seemed odd to hear him make comments like that. "I think I'm professional enough to not get distracted."

Novak let out a guffaw. "Kid, there's never been a man born yet who was professional enough to not get distracted by sex. Tell you what, though, you do your job well enough, and maybe we'll work something out so you have some free time. Deal?"

"Deal," I said, my face burning.

Chapter 4

Thursday was uneventful. Mr. Knox drove to and from work without deviation from his usual schedule, my classes were boring for the most part, and I was pretty much caught up on paperwork at the office.

I was in my room later that night, supposedly studying, but Micah came over unexpectedly. I was sitting at my desk, while he sprawled across my bed. I'd just finished filling him in about the latest developments of my case — if you could really even call them developments.

"So anyway, I have to go up to DC this weekend to see if Mr. Knox behaves himself while in our nation's capital, and I was hoping you could come with me."

Visibly tensing, Micah sat up and shook his head. "Uh, no. I don't think I can do that."

I frowned. "Are you busy?"

"No. I mean, I don't have any plans. I just don't think I should go."

"Why not?"

"I just don't think it's a good idea." He seemed extremely uncomfortable.

"If you're suggesting I won't be able to do work with you along..."

"It's not that."

"Look, it was Novak's idea. He said if I didn't have a guide with me, somebody who knows the city, then I can't go."

"I'm sorry, Killian. You'll have to find someone else."

"Like who? I don't know anybody in DC. I don't get it. You don't want to go with me?"

"Don't be silly. Of course I do...if it was anywhere but..."

"Anywhere but what? DC? I don't understand."

He took a deep breath. "I lived there the whole time I was in college. Believe me, I'm in no hurry to go back."

"But that's exactly why I asked you, because you've lived there. You know the city. I don't. I've only been there a few times, and never alone. Besides, it was only to go to the zoo or the Smithsonian or somewhere like that. I can barely figure out the Metro, let alone find my way around in a car."

"Look, Kill, not all of my memories from that time are good ones. In fact, I have some pretty unhappy associations with DC. If you were going anywhere else, I'd be thrilled that you'd asked me."

"What kind of unhappy associations?" My curiosity was suddenly piqued. I could actually see him close off before my eyes. Obviously, I wasn't the only one with trust issues. "Okay, I can see you aren't going to tell me, so I'll withdraw the question and save you the trouble."

"This isn't a courtroom, Killian, and you're not a lawyer," Micah said quietly. "You can't withdraw a question and expect it to be stricken from the record. You're right, though. I'm not ready to talk about it yet. I promise I'll tell you sometime, just...not right now."

"Skeletons in the closet," I whispered, remembering a conversation we'd had when we first started dating.

"What?"

I shook my head. "Never mind."

He frowned, and we fell into an uneasy silence. Suddenly, he glanced down at his watch. "Oh, hey. Didn't you say something about a meeting you had to go to tonight?"

I drew a blank at first, until I remembered the gay/straight alliance. I'd mentioned it to Micah the day before when we were talking on the phone, and he'd thought it was a great idea.

"You mean Haven?"

"Is that the GSA thing on campus?"

"Yeah."

"Did you ever call that guy?"

I'd explained about meeting Noah, leaving out my attraction to him. It was just a physical attraction, after all. No sense in bringing it up — at least, that was my justification. "No, I never called him."

"Well, call him now. See if they're still meeting tonight."

"You just want to get rid of me so I won't sulk about the fact that you're keeping secrets from me."

"I'm not trying to get rid of you, and I'm not keeping secrets. I'm just not ready to talk about it."

"You're not ready, or I'm not ready?"

"Does it make a difference?"

"Maybe."

"Oh, for... Are you going to call that guy or not?"

With an exaggerated sigh, I swung around to the desk and rummaged through the clutter for the slip of paper with Noah's number. I found it under the sticky bottom of a glass mug, which held a thin film of something that might have once been hot chocolate. Purposefully keeping my back to Micah, I picked up my phone and dialed. I was just about to hang up when someone answered.

"Yo," a male voice practically shouted into my ear. Whoever he was, he sounded quite winded.

"Oh, um... Is Noah there?"

"Yeah, hang on," he panted. I wondered what I had interrupted. I heard the guy's muffled voice calling Noah. "It's for you. Why didn't you just answer it? I had to run all the way from the shower. I thought you'd left or something."

I guess that answered my question.

"Sorry, I was playing my guitar and had my headphones on," someone — presumably Noah — said. A second later, his voice came on the line. "Hello?"

"Noah? Hi. This is Killian. We met in the bookstore..."

"Oh, hey. With the pride necklace, right?"

"Right." I couldn't help smiling at his remembering me.

"You're the cute little blond. You're calling about Haven?"

I blushed at the cute-blond remark and almost stuttered when I answered. I was suddenly glad I'd kept my back to Micah. "Yeah, are you meeting tonight?"

"Sure are. You thinking about coming?"

"Maybe."

"Oh, come on, no maybe's. Say you'll be there. It's a great bunch. I know you'll like them. Are you shy?"

"A little."

"I used to be really shy too, so I understand. How about if I meet you in front of the main doors at Wicomico Hall and we can walk in together? That way I can introduce you."

He wasn't leaving me much room to back out. I gave a mental shrug and accepted. "Okay, what time?"

"The meeting starts at eight, so why don't you get there at, like, a quarter of?"

"Okay."

"Great. See you then, Killian."

"Sure thing."

We hung up, and I took a second to pull myself together before turning back toward Micah. "I'm supposed to meet him in front of Wicomico Hall at quarter of eight."

He glanced at his watch again. "Then, you'd better get going. It's at least a forty-five-minute drive from here."

I nodded and stood up the same time Micah did. He moved toward me until he was standing so close I could feel his body heat — almost touching, but not quite. I slid my arms around his waist and pulled him against me, my lips finding his. After we kissed for a minute, he slipped gently away.

"I'm sorry about, well, you know."

I gave him a half-smile. "You'll tell me when you're ready. Or I'm ready, whichever it is. Don't worry about it. I'll live."

He wrapped me in a tight hug. "I love you, Killian. Don't ever doubt that."

"I love you too." My voice was muffled by his shoulder.

He backed away, then leaned in to give me one last quick kiss before we walked downstairs together.

I stuck my head into the living room, where Steve was reading a book. It was his night at home, and he was taking full advantage of being away from the B&B. He was about the same age as Adam and just as handsome — in a darker, more solid way. He had been a successful architect until he gave up his practice to open Amalie's House.

When I told Steve where I was going, he sent me on my way with a wave and an absent-minded smile. Realizing how distracted he'd been lately, I wondered if he wasn't feeling weighed down by the possibility the B&B might fail.

Micah stopped me at the front door. "Hey, I have to use the bathroom. Will I see you tomorrow?"

"Yeah. Definitely. I'll call you when I get home." I gave him another quick peck on the lips and left.

During the drive to school, I thought about Steve and the B&B. I knew he'd sunk a sizable fortune into buying and restoring the old house — a fortune he had partly inherited and partly saved from his successful business. Except for a small safety net he'd invested, nearly all his money had gone into the project. It struck me that he was probably sweating this out a lot more than I'd realized.

Of course, there was also Amalie. As Adam had said, she wasn't helping. I sighed deeply and resolved to talk to Steve soon. If he really was as upset about the ghost as Judy and Adam seemed to believe, then maybe I'd have to reconsider going back to the house. As much as I wanted to avoid that at all costs, my family was more important than my fear...and I had to admit I was afraid.

Any further contemplation was cut short by my arrival at school. In my distracted state, I must have been driving considerably over the speed limit and was lucky no cops were out.

Although I was somewhat early, I decided to head on over to Wicomico Hall anyway. As I approached, I noticed several people standing and talking in the illumination of the old-fashioned light posts. One of them was Noah, who'd obviously shown up early, too. When he looked over and caught my eye, he immediately broke into a smile. He said something to the guy he was chatting with and walked toward me.

"Hey, Killian. I didn't know if you'd come or not."

"I came." I had an amazing talent for stating the obvious.

"Well, good." To his credit, he said that without a trace of sarcasm or teasing. "Let me introduce you to some people." He led me back to the others gathered in the lamplight: two guys and a girl.

"Everybody, this is Killian." They all turned to face me wearing polite smiles. "This is Peter." He indicated the short, pudgy guy he'd been talking to when I'd arrived. Peter had straight, mousy-brown hair, almost no discernable lips, and dull brown eyes. All in all, he was pretty average, probably not someone you'd look at twice. "Peter is the co-president of Haven. The other co-president is Val. She'll be here eventually. She's always late."

Noah pointed to the second guy. "This is Ray, he's the secretary. That's Tanya." Ray and Tanya waved cheerily. Ray looked like a tiny bundle of energy. He was constantly hopping and bouncing from one foot to the other, or dancing to music only he could hear. He looked Hawaiian or Filipino: small with a dark complexion, straight black hair, and huge, dark eyes. Tanya was a little on the heavy side. Her pale blonde hair was spiked with blue tips...to match her eyes, I guess.

Noah grabbed my elbow and pulled me toward the doors. "Come on. I'll show you where we meet. See you guys inside in a few minutes."

"I'm never going to remember all the names," I said as we entered the building.

"Don't worry about it. We'll probably do one of those lame introduction games tonight where everybody has to say their name, major, and what shampoo they use or something like that. Peter seems unusually fond of them." He shrugged. "I guess they serve their purpose. You know, I assumed from your necklace that you were gay, but I never really asked. Are you?"

"Would I be here if I wasn't?"

He shrugged again. "Well, it is a gay/straight alliance. I just figure it's never safe to assume anything. So you are?"

"Yeah. I am."

"And should I assume from the necklace that you're out?"

"Pretty much. I mean, my family and friends all know. I don't make any effort to hide it. I came out in high school. I had a boyfriend, and literally everyone in the school knew we were a couple after my ex announced it at an assembly."

He stopped in his tracks. "You're kidding!"

I laughed. "Nope. I swear."

"Man, that's cool. I was out in high school too, but not on that level. I just told some friends and left it at that. So you mentioned your ex. Are you seeing anyone now?"

I glanced over and noticed him look at me from the corner of his eye. Was his interest merely polite conversation, or was there something more behind it? I decided that clearing the air up front might save us both trouble. "I dated the guy from high school for about two years, but we broke up senior year. I'm seeing someone else these days."

"That's cool." His tone was casual, but I thought I saw a flash of disappointment. While we were talking, he'd led me down the hall and into a rec room complete with pool tables, table tennis, a couple of arcade games, and other distractions. At the back of the room, there was a glass partition that sectioned off a lounge area with tables, couches, and chairs. A flat-screen TV hung on one wall. Two girls shared one of the sofas, a slim black guy lay sprawled on the floor, and a burly white guy slouched in a chair.

"This is where we meet," Noah said, swinging open the door.

The conversations broke off as we entered. "Hey, Noah," the burly guy called, echoed by the others.

"Hey, guys, this is Killian," Noah said. "That's Olivia and Felicia on the couch, Anthony on the floor, and Everett in the chair."

I wasn't sure which of the girls was Olivia and which was Felicia, but they were similar enough in appearance that I doubted I could have told them apart anyway. They were both average-size, with short, dark-brown hair, brown eyes, and not a hint of makeup. They both wore glasses and shapeless, baggy sweatshirts over faded jeans. They almost looked like twins, but something about the way they were sitting made me think they might be lovers.

Anthony waved. "You can call me Tony." He had the thin, lithe body of a dancer and sharp, chiseled features that made him look like an ebony statue come to life. I waved back.

"Ooh, fresh meat!" Everett's smile let me know he was only joking. The way he dwarfed his chair, it was easy to see that he was a giant, but a gentle one if my initial impressions were accurate — and they usually were. He had curly, reddish-brown hair with a matching goatee and greenish-blue eyes.

Noah waved a finger in the big guy's direction. "Careful, Ev. He's taken."

"Figures. All the good ones are either taken or straight."

I sat in the center of one of the other couches with Noah to one side of me. Another group of students made their way across the rec room in our direction, the ones I'd met outside plus several additions. As more and more people arrived, the names were no longer getting connected to faces. A few I recognized from my classes, but I didn't know any of them by name. I was actually kind of surprised to learn they were gay, but then I remembered that just because they came to these meetings didn't necessarily mean they were. As Noah said, it was a gay/straight alliance.

Peter called the meeting to order, and, as predicted, started one of those annoying games in which everyone had to announce their name, major, and favorite type of underwear. The women overwhelmingly favored bikini panties, while boxers held a slight lead among the men.

As for the guy/girl ratio, it was fairly even. One of the attendees might have given the girls a narrow majority if my initial guess about his gender was wrong — which was a very real possibility.

Peter was just about ready to begin the meeting proper when a very pretty Hispanic girl burst in to join us. She was on the short side, with long, glossy black hair, beautiful brown eyes, and pouty red lips. She was wearing a tight sweater and even tighter jeans that showed off her shapely figure. A black leather backpack was slung over her shoulder.

"And Valora makes her grand entrance, as always," Ray said under his breath while writing something in the notebook on his lap. If he hadn't been sitting on the other side of me, I probably wouldn't have heard him.

"Sorry I'm late," she said in a lightly accented voice.

"It's okay, Val," Peter said with a grin. "It's not like it's unusual. We were just getting ready to start."

"Cool, then I didn't miss anything?" She settled gracefully into a spot on the floor next to Tony.

"Well, you missed the introductions. What kind of underwear do you wear?"

Val blinked in surprise for a second. "That question sounds funny coming from you, Petey," she said and everyone laughed. "Shall I assume this was part of the introductions?"

"Yep."

A small, sexy smile curled up the corners of her full lips. "Then, if you must know, I wear a thong." There were a few wolf whistles before she continued. "If we're having introductions, does that mean we have someone new?" She scanned the group — now about twenty-five or thirty strong — and quickly picked me out. "Aha, I haven't seen you before, have I?"

I smiled. She was the kind of person I liked immediately. "Probably not. My name's Killian. This is my first time here."

She giggled. "You make it sound like an AA meeting. Hi, my name is Valora and I'm a lesbian." She giggled again. "I'm only teasing. Don't turn all red on me. You can call me Val."

"Val is the co-president," Noah reminded me.

"Can I move on now?" Peter asked impatiently. Val arched an eyebrow and leveled an icy glare in his direction that didn't seem to faze him in the least. I decided Val was the people person, while Peter was the administrator. They probably made a good pair.

"God forbid we should get off schedule. Yes, you may get on with your agenda now," Val said. Peter stuck his tongue out at her, and she reciprocated, then they both broke into wide grins.

"They're always like this," Noah whispered. I tried not to shiver as his breath tickled my ear.

The meeting itself was rather unremarkable. I was a little lost for most of it, as they were mainly discussing the success of their National Coming Out Day celebration. They also talked about plans they already had in the works, including a Halloween costume dance that didn't appeal to me at all. I still had unpleasant memories of the last one I'd attended a few years before.

The official meeting ended promptly at nine, but most people hung around and chatted in small groups. Noah invited me to stay too, and since I figured it was a good way to get to know them, I did. I ended up surrounded by Noah, Val, Peter, Tony, and Everett. Val had moved to the couch next to me in the spot vacated by Ray. They all seemed very interested in the new guy.

"Well, what did you think of your first meeting?" Val asked me.

I shrugged. "It was okay."

"Only okay?" Noah sounded disappointed.

"Well, I didn't really know what you were talking about most of the time. It'll be better once I get more involved."

"Then you'll probably be back?" I thought I detected a note of hope in his voice.

"Probably."

"Can I ask a personal question?" Val said.

"Would saying no even slow you down?" Peter teased.

"Nope," she shot back with a grin. "So, are you Noah's new boy toy?"

Noah quickly jumped in before I could answer. "He's dating someone, Val."

"Yeah, I met Noah at the bookstore earlier this week. He saw my pride necklace and invited me."

"The campus bookstore?" she asked.

"Yeah."

"You go to Stinky?" she asked with surprise in her voice. Stinky was the affectionate nickname given to Pemberton University due to its initials.

"Yeah, I'm a freshman."

"Damn, I'm sorry. I thought you were like sixteen and Noah was robbing the cradle."

I laughed. I was used to being mistaken for a lot younger than I was. Sixteen was actually an old estimate for me. Maybe my looks were finally starting to mature. "No, I'm eighteen."

"Still a baby," she said.

"How old are you?"

"Twenty-one."

"And you?" I asked Noah.

"Twenty."

I looked to Peter.

"Twenty-one," he said.

"Nineteen," Everett volunteered.

"Twenty," Tony called from the floor, where he was now doing some sort of stretching exercise.

"Oh, I guess I am the baby of the group, then," I said.

"Just of us here now," Peter said. "I doubt you're the youngest in the whole group. I know there are other eighteen-year-olds."

"Besides," Everett said, "you're probably more mature than most of us anyway."

"Speak for yourself," Val shot back quickly.

I grinned. "I have a question. How many of the people who attend the meetings are gay?"

"Most of us," Noah said. "There are maybe three or four straight girls. Everybody else is at least bi."

"Most straight people, especially guys, are too scared to come because they're afraid their friends are going to think they're gay too," Peter said.

"And we all know how horrible that would be," Val said sarcastically.

"But that's one of our goals," Noah went on. "We're trying to change the way people look at being gay so it's not such a negative thing."

Val grimaced. "It's slow progress."

"But at least it is progress," Everett said. "Almost everybody knows I'm gay, and the vast majority just don't give a shit."

"That's because you're a big ol' white boy." Tony unwound his body from the pretzel in which he'd twisted himself. "They're afraid you'll bash their skulls in if they say anything." Everett opened his mouth to protest, but Tony wasn't finished. "Not that you would, and I'm not saying that everybody has a problem with it secretly, but there's definitely still a lot of prejudice and bigotry on this campus. Try being gay and black. That's two strikes against you. And it was even worse back home. Black women might not have much problem with you being gay, but the brothers? Damn. You don't stand a chance."

"The Latino community is probably even worse," Val said. "I grew up in a mostly Puerto Rican neighborhood in Baltimore. I've seen plenty of guys get the shit kicked out of them just cuz they weren't macho enough. They get called names like faggot and cocksucker, and most of the time they aren't even gay. Imagine how the poor guys who really are gay feel. They gotta hide it or get out of there. I never let anyone know I liked girls until I was in college — not even my best friend. I dated guys all through school and just pretended I didn't put out cuz I was a really good little Catholic." She shrugged. "I'm probably going to hell now. Think I need to confess?"

"Nah, you're too far gone for help now," Peter said.

"What about you?" Val asked him. "You had any problems with people knowing you're gay?"

"Outside of my family, you mean? Not really. I'm not remarkable enough to draw much attention. No one cares which way I swing," Peter answered.

"Oh, stop with the pity party," she said. "What problems did you have with your family?"

"Just the usual. Mom flipped out, Dad disowned me, and my brother acts like I'm dying of AIDS."

"That's the usual?" Noah asked. "Then I'm glad I'm unusual. My parents were a little shaken at first, but they educated themselves, and they're okay with it now. Or, if not okay, at least they're trying."

"Then you're one of the lucky ones." Peter sighed. "My parents are better now, though. They've had a few years to deal with it, but it was ugly at first."

"My mom still don't know," Tony said.

"My dad doesn't, but I think my mom knows," Val said. "At least she's stopped asking me if I'm dating any nice boys at college."

"I'm another one of the lucky ones, I guess," Everett said. "My whole family had no problem with it at all, but then we're a pretty liberal bunch, and they'd assumed I was gay since I was a little kid. What about you, Killian?"

"My family? Well, my real dad freaked out, beat me up, and kicked me out of the house. This was right after a gay friend of mine was murdered, and I was stabbed at the same time." I almost cracked up at the stunned expressions on everyone's faces. "The dad of the murdered kid took me in, and I've lived with him and his partner ever since. My mom ended up divorcing my dad and moving to Pennsylvania. I stayed with Adam and Steve and Adam's other son, Kane."

Noah's jaw was somewhere around his knees. "Wow!"

"Yeah," Val said. "I think you win the hard-knock-life award."

"Hands down," Tony seconded, while Peter and Everett nodded.

I laughed. "I didn't know it was a competition."

"You're right, it's not," Noah said.

"Well, it's getting late, and I still have work to do," Peter said.

Everett sighed. "Me too. I was just putting it off as long as possible."

"You know," Val said thoughtfully, "I'm really glad you came along tonight, Killian."

I blinked in surprise. "You are? Why?"

"Because I've known some of these guys for several years and this was the first time we've ever sat down and talked about our lives like that."

I shrugged. "It had nothing to do with me."

"Sure it did," Noah said. "If you hadn't been here we wouldn't have gone off on that tangent. See? You're already making positive changes in the group. Now you have to come back."

I laughed. "Fine. As long as nothing else comes up at work, I'll be back."

"Where do you work?" Noah asked, as everyone stood up and started gathering whatever things they had brought.

"Uh, well, actually I'm a private investigator." That time I had to laugh at the way everyone froze in place and turned to look at me in shock.

"For real?" Tony's eyes were wide.

"Yeah, for real."

"Whoa. You're just full of surprises, aren't you?" Everett said.

Val chuckled. "Well, we hope to see you next week, Mr. PI."

The group quickly scattered in different directions, leaving me alone once again with Noah.

"Walk you to your car?" he asked.

I shrugged. "If you want."

"I do."

We left the building making small talk. Once we reached my car, I could tell he had something to say. "Spit it out."

"Huh?"

"Whatever it is you want to say."

"Oh. Am I that obvious?"

"Yup."

He took a deep breath. "So, uh, how seriously are you dating this guy? Do you go out with other people?"

"No, we're seeing each other exclusively." I felt bad shooting him down, but he seemed to expect my response.

"And I can tell you're not the type to fool around, so let me just say that, if anything ever happens and you break up with him, give me a call, okay? In the meantime, friends?" He held out his hand.

I smiled. "Friends." We shook on it.

He held on a little longer than necessary, then slowly backed off a few steps before turning and jogging away. I watched him go before climbing into my car. If I weren't with Micah, I'd be all over him. It was very good for Micah that I wasn't the type to fool around because I was actually finding myself a little tempted with Noah.

Chapter 5

When I got home, the first thing I noticed was Micah's car still parked next to Steve's. Had he ever left? Had he been there the whole time I'd been gone? A quick peek at my watch told me it had been almost three hours. What could that mean? I jumped out of my Mustang with a nervous flutter in my stomach, took the three steps up to the porch with one leap, and let myself in.

I found Micah in the living room with Steve. They glanced up and smiled when I appeared in the door. At least they didn't seem surprised or uncomfortable to find me standing there, as I imagined they would be if they'd been talking about me.

"We were just talking about you," Steve said.

Oh. "Is that good or bad?"

"Mostly good." Micah gave me a grin and a wink while patting a spot next to him on the sofa.

I settled at his side, then looked from him to Steve. "Were you here the whole time?" I asked Micah.

"Yeah. I stuck my head in to say bye to Steve, and we started talking. You know what they say about time flying when you're having fun."

"So, what all did you talk about?"

"You want him to recap three hours of conversation?" Steve asked in a teasing voice.

I shrugged. I had a feeling everything wasn't being said.

"Well, the *Readers Digest* version is that I've decided to go with you to DC."

I practically bounced off the couch. "Really?"

"Really."

"Oh, my gosh! That's great! Oh, thank you so much. I'd better go call Novak. And then I need to pack."

"Whoa, slow down," Micah said. "When are we leaving? I still have to make arrangements with work and all."

"Is tomorrow around noon too soon?" I was hoping beyond hope it wasn't.

"I think I can swing it. Go talk to Novak."

I practically flew from the room.

Novak had so much faith in my abilities to convince Micah that he'd already booked us adjoining rooms in the same hotel as Knox. Micah and I firmed up our plans, then he left to go home and pack a bag while I went upstairs to do the same.

I was extremely excited. Not only was I getting ready to follow my first case on my own into the city, but this would also be Micah's and my first time away together. I had a feeling it would be a weekend to remember.

"Wow!" We had stepped into the lobby of the hotel where Knox — and Micah and I — would be staying. I tried to keep my mouth from dropping open. Places like this made me realize that, at heart, I was little more than a country bumpkin.

I'd never been in such a luxurious hotel before. Tall, white columns rose from the brightly polished white marble floor to meet a high, vaulted ceiling from which enormous crystal chandeliers were suspended. The wainscoting was rich, dark wood that I thought might be mahogany, above which original oil paintings hung on silk-covered walls. The furniture arranged around the lobby on thick oriental rugs all appeared to be authentic antiques, or if not, then high-quality reproductions.

"One thing's for sure," Micah said. "This guy you're following has expensive tastes."

"At the very least he doesn't mind spending the company's money." I started across the expanse of marble toward the young woman behind the desk. "Hello. I believe you have two rooms reserved under the name Kendall."

She flashed me a smile and typed on her computer for a minute, then looked up. "Are you Mr. Kendall?"

I nodded and tried not to giggle. I couldn't remember anyone ever seriously calling me Mr. Kendall before.

She looked at the screen again, then back to me. "Did you say two rooms?"

"I thought so..." I said a little uncertainly. Wasn't that what Novak had told me? I suddenly wasn't sure.

"We only have you down for one room, sir."

"Oh...I..." That was unexpected. "Is there an adjoining room available?" I hated the desperate tone creeping into my voice. I was glad Micah was wandering around looking at the artwork and not paying attention to my check-in process.

She hit a few more keys before shaking her head. "I'm sorry. There's a large business convention going on and all our rooms are pretty much booked up. I hope it won't be a problem."

I took a deep breath. I wanted to argue, but at the same time I didn't want to make a scene. More than anything, I wanted to get out of the lobby before Knox showed up. Traffic had been heavy on the Beltway, and we were running later than I'd planned.

I'd completely forgotten about the convention. Mrs. Knox had mentioned it was the reason her husband was leaving town. At the time, I'd been relieved that my job would be easier, seeing as he'd be less likely to leave the hotel. Suddenly, though, I was cursing the damned event.

I'd never spent the night with Micah before and hadn't planned on that trip being the first time. I felt my stomach clench.

"Mr. Kendall?" The woman was looking at me with a worried expression. "If it's a problem, I can get my manager. I don't know what he'll be able to do, though. As I said, we're booked up through the whole weekend and—"

"It's fine," I said through gritted teeth. "It won't be a problem."

She smiled apologetically. "Are you sure?"

I nodded, so she started clicking away on her keyboard. A few seconds later, the printer spit out a form, which she handed to me. "Just sign right here, and I'll get your key cards for you."

After I signed, she handed over two keycards in a little envelope along with my receipt. It was all being charged to Novak's company credit card and would in turn be billed to Mrs. Knox. If she was wrong about her husband's philandering, she'd be looking at a large bill for nothing. Then again, maybe her peace of mind would be worth it.

"I'm truly sorry for the inconvenience," the desk clerk said again, her attention already turning to the wealthy-looking couple walking up behind me. While she put on a good act, I somehow doubted her sincerity.

I looked around for Micah. When he saw my expression he frowned. "What's wrong?"

"There's a slight change of plans," I said grimly and started for the elevator.

"What's going on?"

I stabbed the button for our floor. "We have to share a room." By that point, I was so tense I was no longer noticing my lavish surroundings.

Micah looked at me silently for a second, then chuckled. "Is that all? You had me scared for a minute there." When I didn't respond, he cocked one eyebrow. "It's not the end of the world, you know."

"I just...I wasn't ready for this."

"Ready? Ready for what?"

"I just mean I wasn't prepared. I thought we had two rooms..." My voice trailed off.

"Killian, I'm not going to jump you as soon as the door closes. Give me a little credit here. I think I can control myself that much."

I blushed but didn't say anything.

He sighed. "Maybe there are two beds."

There weren't.

"It's not that bad." He was starting to sound a little insulted. I looked dubiously at the lone queen-size bed. "Look, if it would make you feel better, I'll get another room."

"They're all booked up." I was still standing just inside the doorway clutching my suitcase in front of me like a shield.

"Then what do you want? Should I go find another hotel? I can't go home. We drove up here together."

"I don't know what I want."

"Do you ever?" His question, and its unspoken implications, stung like a slap in the face. "I didn't mean that," he said quickly. "It's just...you're the one who wanted me along so badly. I mean, would it really be that horrible to share a bed with me?"

I took a deep breath. "You're right. And I do want you along. I'm sorry I'm being such a jerk. It just caught me by surprise."

"Maybe we can get a rollaway bed."

"And put it where? No, we don't need a rollaway bed. I'm being stupid. We can share the bed."

"Are you sure?"

"Yes, I'm sure."

"I promise I'll stay on my side." He gave me a teasing leer. "Unless you invite me over to your side, anyway." He waggled his eyebrows at me.

I managed a weak smile in return, but it was enough. The worst of the tension was gone, although my stomach was still knotted up in a tight little ball. "I'd better go back downstairs so I can keep an eye out for Knox." I was secretly glad for the excuse to get out of the room and pull myself together.

Micah and I had already discussed how the surveillance would work. We both knew this was a business trip for me, which meant I had to do my job. I was going to watch for Knox to check in and keep an eye on him after that. If he started to leave the hotel, then Micah would step in as my guide. It wasn't a perfect plan. If Micah took too long to reach the lobby when I called up for him, we could lose Knox. Still, it was the best we could come up with. We were afraid that two of us lurking around the lobby would be too conspicuous.

I grabbed a book out of my suitcase and went back downstairs. After ascertaining from the helpful desk clerk that, much to my relief, Knox hadn't checked in yet, I picked a chair that afforded me a clear view of the main door and the front desk while keeping me mostly out of sight behind a large potted plant. I settled in and pretended to read.

It was about an hour before Knox entered and made directly for the desk, followed by a bellhop pushing a luggage cart laden with two large suitcases and a garment bag. How much did this guy need to pack for a weekend?

His check-in apparently proceeded much more smoothly than mine had, because he'd accepted his keycard and was getting on an elevator in no time. I made myself wait where I was until the door closed behind him, then went over and pretended to push the UP button. While I "waited" for the elevator to arrive, I watched to see which floor Knox stopped on — the one above Micah's and mine.

As soon as I knew where to go, I pushed UP for real. Almost immediately the other elevator slid open. The ride was agonizingly slow and I was almost frantic by the time the doors opened. I was just in time to see the bellhop carrying the last of Knox's bags into the room. I hesitated for a second, but Knox didn't reappear before the bellhop emerged tucking a five-dollar bill into his pocket.

I made note of Knox's room number, then cased the hallway looking for a place where I could unobtrusively keep an eye on him. Luckily, about halfway along the corridor in the opposite direction from the elevators was a small alcove with two chairs, a tiny table, and a lamp. While it wasn't ideal, it would have to do. Chances were fairly good that, if Knox came out of his room, he'd head for the elevators and not toward me. As long as none of the other folks on the floor noticed me hanging around and reported me to security, I'd be okay. I checked my watch as I settled into one of the chairs. It was a little after four.

Stakeouts have to be one of the most boring things I've ever experienced. They're definitely the worst part about being a private detective. You can literally spend hour upon hour doing nothing but staring at a door. I had a book with me, but feared I'd get so into the story that I'd miss the moment when Knox finally made his move. As a result, I could only give the book half my attention, which was very unsatisfying for someone who likes to read as much as I do.

It was just before six when Knox stepped out of his room. He'd changed from his traveling clothes into a business suit. Pulling the door shut, he strode off down the hall toward the elevators without looking in my direction.

I remained where I was until the elevator doors closed, then watched the lighted numbers descend to L. Knowing I didn't have time to wait for the elevator, I ran for the stairs. The last thing I wanted was to lose him that early in my surveillance. I raced down the steps two at a time and was panting when I reached the bottom.

I took a deep, calming breath and hoped I had composed myself somewhat before I entered the lobby. Scanning the room as casually as possible, I felt my stomach drop. Knox was nowhere in sight. I crossed the room as quickly as possible without running, cursing under my breath with every step, and looked outside. Still no sign of him.

Then I remembered the convention. It was being held in the building itself. Didn't weekend conferences often start on Friday evening? I quickly ducked back into the hotel and caught a bellboy by the sleeve. "Excuse me. Can you tell me where the conference rooms are?"

I thought the bellboy was around my age, but had the misfortune to bear a more-than-slightly simian appearance. In his uniform, he looked like an overgrown organ grinder's monkey. Instead of jumping up and down while demanding a quarter, though, he smiled politely and gave me directions.

I thanked him and hurried off, not quite at a jog, but not far from it. I rounded the last corner and came to a screeching halt. To my vast relief, my quarry was standing not too far from me talking to another man in a suit. Luckily, Knox's back was to me, and I was able to survey the area before slipping back around the corner.

It was going to be harder to keep an eye on him in the conference room. Not only was there no convenient alcove setup, but there would be people coming and going constantly. More importantly, I probably looked fairly shifty standing at the edge of the corner with my back pressed against the wall. I forced my body into a more casual stance, as if waiting for someone to come along.

What was I going to do about Knox? I peeked around the corner again and watched while he and the man he was talking to seemed to finish up their conversation. They shook hands and moved toward one of the conference-hall doors.

"Can I help you?" a voice asked from behind me, causing me to jump guiltily. I spun around to find someone from the hotel staff glaring at me the way one might look at a pile of offending doggie doo that had somehow managed to situate itself under one's foot. The man facing me was a little above average in height with stiffly gelled dark hair and beady eyes that glared down his long, thin nose.

"Um, yes..." My mind raced to come up with a cover story. Damn it! I'd forgotten Novak's first rule of private investigation. "Is this the, uh, place where the, er, conference is being held?" Weak, but it would have to do.

The man arched an eyebrow. "Yes, indeed it is. Are you a participant in the conference?"

"Oh, um, yes. I'm staying here too," I added just to be safe. I showed him my keycard, which did seem to make an impression. I could almost read his mind: at least I hadn't crept in off the streets.

"Could I be of assistance to you? Show you to the correct conference room, perhaps?" He paused meaningfully and then sprung his trap. "Which conference are you here for?"

Crap! There was more than one? Or was it a trick question? I hadn't even thought to check to see what conference Knox was attending. Had Sharla or Mrs. Knox told me? No, I didn't think so.

"The, uh, one for sales," I replied lamely.

"Ah, yes. That one." He seemed a little disappointed that I'd come up with an acceptable, if not particularly intelligent, answer. Being thought dim was preferable to being thrown out peremptorily on my rear, however.

"It's right this way. Follow me." He walked briskly past me and around the corner.

I couldn't very well refuse — not if I wanted to get out of this while attracting as little attention as possible. I held my breath, stepped around the corner, and much to my relief, Knox was nowhere in sight.

I decided to risk a question. "Are there other conferences going on this weekend?"

My guide gave me an irritated look. "No, this is the only one."

So it had been a trick question. I could tell he didn't appreciate having to admit it. He ushered me through one of the doors, and I was immediately grateful for the low lighting inside, most of which was focused on a man standing behind a lectern at the front of the room. Clearly, the first meeting had already begun.

"If you haven't registered and received your name badge yet, please don't forget to do so as soon as our introductory session is over," the man was saying. At least my lack of plastic-coated ID wouldn't be too obvious. I took a seat in the back row.

As my eyes adjusted to the dimness, I scanned the room for my quarry. I spotted his sandy-blond hair about halfway toward the front. At least I could keep an eye on him now, even if it did mean sitting through a few boring speeches.

And boring they were. By the time eight o'clock rolled around, I was struggling just to keep my eyes from slamming shut. When the speaker stopped for a break, I slipped down in my seat while Knox walked by. I couldn't believe in just thirty minutes they would actually be starting back up for yet another two hours. I wanted to cry at the very thought.

I texted Micah to let him know what was going on, then stood up and stretched before making my way out into the hall with the last of the stragglers. I found Knox at the registration table picking up his name badge. Registration was a casual affair at this point, most people having already signed in, and the remainder of the badges and conference kits were simply sitting on the table.

That gave me an idea. I decided a little camouflage couldn't hurt, and as soon as Knox moved away from the table, I sidled over and found a blank badge and a marking pen. I quickly scribbled a fake name on the badge and clipped it to my shirt. I'd be Tom Smith for the night. Picking up a kit, I moved into a corner out of the way and waited. Knox never left my sight.

The rest of the session offered nothing to recommend it. I was approaching a comatose state by the time the last speaker finished up, until the polite applause as he stepped off the platform startled me into full alertness. He was replaced a moment later by the man who'd been giving directions when I first entered.

"That's all for this evening," he said, sounding about as awake as I felt. "We'll see you all back here in the morning at eight-thirty. And don't forget the complimentary continental breakfast."

I groaned inwardly as everyone stood and moved toward the doors. That meant I'd have to be up early so I could keep an eye on old Knox. God only knew when I'd be getting to bed tonight.

I watched Knox walk past, waited while a few more people went by, then stood and followed. Finding a group of men talking among themselves about their plans for the rest of the evening, I pretended to join them. When Knox disappeared around the corner, I extricated myself from the group and trailed after him. He went directly to the elevator and up to his floor. With a resigned sigh, I ran back up the stairs and arrived just in time to see his door closing.

I took my post again, sitting in one of the rather uncomfortable chairs in the alcove, and prepared to wait. Two hours later, when it was becoming increasingly obvious that Knox was in for the night, I decided to risk returning to our room. I would just set the alarm clock early enough to be back in what I was beginning to think of as my own private alcove long before Knox arose in the morning. I wasn't exactly thrilled, but what choice did I have? It was all part of the job.

I rode the elevator down to our floor and let myself into the room as quietly as I could in case Micah was asleep. Once my eyes adjusted to the near darkness, I could make him out in the bed, arms thrown over his head, the blankets pushed down to his waist leaving the band of his boxers showing. My eyes slowly traveled up his chest, silvered by the light, so that he looked eerily like a white marble statue — handsome and perfect. I felt my breath catch in my throat. His face was still and peaceful. I was so struck by his beauty that I felt my throat close up. I was supposed to sleep with that?

I felt a hint of panic rising once again in my chest and fought it down. What was I so scared of? I loved Micah, didn't I? I knew I did. And I knew he loved me. So what was my hang-up?

Objectively, at least part of it was simply the fact that I was a virgin. I had no idea what I was supposed to do or how to do it. I didn't want to act like an idiot. I wanted it to be perfect and wonderful and just the way it always was in the stories. The matter wasn't helped by the fact that I knew making love to Micah would break down the last of any walls I was managing to keep up between the two of us. Once those walls were gone, I'd be completely vulnerable — something I hadn't thought I'd ever want to be with another person. Suddenly, as I stood there watching him sleep, I wasn't so sure anymore. Being vulnerable with Micah was actually starting to sound almost inviting — especially if that involved being naked with him under those sheets.

I pushed the thought quickly out of my head...or tried to anyway. I'm working, I reminded myself sharply. I promised Novak I wouldn't let myself be distracted by having Micah along.

That was all well and good, but I felt a stirring in my groin just looking at him. I turned quickly and set the alarm clock for an ungodly hour. I slipped out of my clothes and into the sheets, ignoring my erection as best I could. Micah never stirred. Either he was in a very deep sleep or he was still mad at me from earlier. I couldn't blame him if he was. I'd acted like a royal prick.

I rolled onto my side so I could see his face. I wanted to reach out and touch him. I wanted to feel his body next to mine, skin against skin. I wanted to kiss him. I wanted to shake him awake and make love to him. I didn't do any of those things though. I just lay there and watched him sleep until my eyes refused to stay open any longer.

All too soon, I was awakened by the rude blaring of the alarm clock. For a few confused seconds I couldn't remember where I was or why my alarm was going off when the room was still pitch black. Then I felt Micah stirring at my side, and it all came back to me.

I fumbled with the clock, finally managing to turn it off. I so did not want to get up. I forced myself into a sitting position with my legs dangling off the edge of the bed while I tried to wake enough to think clearly.

"What time is it?" Micah asked.

"Too early."

I was trying to summon the energy to stand when I felt his hand slide across my back, warm and slightly rough. A shiver rippled through me and suddenly I was very awake.

"I didn't even hear you come in last night."

"I didn't want to wake you."

"I wish you had." I felt him sit up, and a second hand joined the first in its exploration of my back.

"I should go. I need to make sure I'm in place before Knox leaves his room." I didn't move. I felt paralyzed by his touch.

He ran his hands up my sides and over my shoulders, causing another chill to course through me. He leaned in so close I could feel the heat from his body as his hands traced down my chest.

"God, Killian, you're so beautiful." His lips brushed my ear, echoing my thoughts about him from just a few hours ago.

When he began to kiss my neck, it was like fire spreading through my veins. I heard a little whimper and realized it had come from me. He gently pulled against my shoulders, drawing me against his body. I melted into him, all thoughts of work completely gone. I was lost in the moment.

I tipped my head so I could look into his eyes. Even in the near darkness, I could see the love there...and the hunger. His lips met mine, and I twisted to face him. The kiss started out as a soft pressure, but quickly turned passionate. Micah shifted and slowly lowered me to the bed before covering me with his body, our lips never separating.

I felt something poking me in the side and realized it was Micah. I was undoubtedly doing some poking of my own. Meanwhile, Micah's hands were all over me, sliding up my sides, down my legs, across any skin he could reach. I'd never had an experience anything like it. I was electrified. My breath was coming in gasps now.

Micah slowly pulled back, his eyes staring deeply into mine. "I love you."

"I love you too." The words came without hesitation.

He leaned in for another kiss, but this one ended quickly as he moved his lips down and began kissing my throat. He found a soft spot just under my ear, and my body arched beneath him in response. He spent a few moments there, and just when I couldn't take any more, he slowly moved his lips down my neck, across my chest, and down to my stomach. My mind was whirling through the clouds, but it was brought quickly back to earth when I felt Micah's fingers creep under the band of my underwear.

"Micah," I gasped, panic in my voice as I grabbed his wrist.

"What is it, Killian?" he asked in a tortured voice. "You know I love you, and I know you love me. What's wrong?"

"I...I'm scared."

The look in his eyes softened as his hand gently stroked my cheek. "I promise I won't hurt you." His voice was so sincere I couldn't doubt him for a minute.

"It's not that, not anymore..."

"Then what is it, baby?"

I felt so stupid, but I had to say it. "It's just that I...I don't know what to do."

The sweetest smile spread across his face as he leaned in and kissed me softly on the lips. "Don't worry about a thing, my beautiful boy. I'll show you everything you need to know."

Chapter 6

Wow!

That was about the only coherent thought I could muster for a while, following what had turned out to be the most amazing experience of my life. Of course, I wasn't particularly trying to be coherent. I was simply basking in the afterglow of our lovemaking.

"Wow!" I thought again, except I must have said it out loud the second time.

Micah chuckled. "I wish you'd stay that easy to impress," he said.

My head was resting in the hollow between his shoulder and his neck, his arms wrapped around me, our legs intertwined. "Just make me feel like that every time, and I'll stay impressed," I murmured into the soft skin at the base of his throat.

He stroked my back gently, causing goose bumps to rise — among other things. "You can't be ready to go again already."

"Tell him that." I tried not to blush and failed miserably.

"Hey, I'm not complaining, but I'm not as young as you are. I need a little time to recover."

"Oh, yeah, you're so ancient. You're what, five years older than I am?"

"Around that."

I sat up and looked down into his eyes. He was just as beautiful in the golden, early-morning sunlight as he'd been in the moonlight. "Okay, old man, I'll give you time to recover. You get ten whole seconds before I ravage you. Ten, nine, eight, seven, six..."

"God." He grabbed me and pulled me down on top of him. "I've created a monster."

"...five, four, three..."

"Is this what our relationship is going to become now?"

"...two...hey, you asked for it, mister...one." I swung my leg over him and leaned down to cut off his retort with a deeply passionate kiss. His response was almost immediate. "See? Now that wasn't so hard — or should I say 'difficult' — was it?"

Micah choked down another laugh. "Don't you have work to do?"

"Oh, shit!" I yelled, sitting up so suddenly the room actually spun for a second. I frantically tried to find the clock. Finally, realizing that one of the pillows had been thrown over it at some point, I uncovered it and let out a yelp. "I'm late!" I leapt off the bed and began running aimlessly around the room searching for clothes.

Micah sat up and watched me with obvious amusement. "Killian, calm down."

Did he have to sound so maddeningly reasonable? "Calm down? Easy for you to say. You're not the one who probably just blew his whole case." I couldn't believe how much time had gone by since the alarm went off. How could I have been so careless — especially after I'd promised Novak not to get distracted? I was furious with myself.

"You don't know that you've blown anything," Micah said, then with an evil grin, added, "Except me, of course."

I stopped in my tracks long enough to glare at him. Grin still in place, he slipped from the bed, picked up my pants, and held them out to me. "You're a great detective, Killian. If this guy's cheating, I know you'll catch him at it one way or another."

I took a deep breath. I needed to calm down so I could think. Suddenly, an idea began to form in my devious little mind, a way to salvage the situation. If Knox was busy with the conference until noon, that was the perfect time to search his room.

I dressed quickly and started for the door. Micah caught my arm on my way by him and gave me a quick kiss on the lips. "Good luck, Kill. I love you."

I stopped long enough to give him a real kiss goodbye. "I love you too." I yanked open the door and paused again. "I'm sorry I'm running off after..."

He smiled. "It's fine. Just go."

I took the stairs two at a time and practically burst onto Knox's floor. The hallway was completely empty...and that was when the fatal flaw in my plan hit me: I didn't have the first clue about how to get into his room. Maybe I could take his keycard somehow or sneak in while the cleaning crew was busy. Of course, those things probably only worked in movies and novels. Novak had never given me any lessons on breaking and entering. Being a retired cop, he generally shunned such lawless tactics. I, on the other hand, had no such qualms. "Whatever Gets the Job Done" was officially my new motto. If only I had the knowhow.

Since I was alone in the hall, I approached Knox's door for a better look. It appeared tamperproof, at least to my amateur eyes. I wondered how anyone broke into modern hotel rooms. They must have some sort of Bond-type gadget: a card that deciphered the door code or something. I tried the handle on the off chance it was open. No such luck.

I pressed my ear against the panel thinking maybe someone was inside. To my complete and utter surprise, the door swung open as soon as my ear touched its cold surface. I almost stumbled into the arms of a brassy blonde woman standing on the other side. She wore a white fluffy robe knotted around her slim waist and a pissed-off look on her face.

I straightened up quickly and tried desperately to think of some reason why I might have been jiggling her door handle. Once again, I was caught without a cover story. If my first solo case were an exam, I'd be flunking badly.

"Hang on," she said into the cell phone she had pressed against one ear. She eyed me up and down. "Do you work here?" Her voice was a high-pitched whine.

Relief swept over me. "Yes." She'd saved me the trouble of coming up with an excuse. Taking a closer look at her, I suspected I'd found the proof I needed that Knox was cheating. I'd met his wife, and this, quite definitely, was not Mrs. Knox. The woman standing before me had to be his mistress, but I needed to make sure.

"Well, for Christ sake, do something!" she shrilled.

"Um, what exactly do you need?" I asked hesitantly while my mind ran ahead full-tilt.

She heaved a monumental sigh meant to express her dissatisfaction with the service. It succeeded in ruffling my hair and alerting me that she hadn't brushed her teeth since getting up.

"I told them down at the front desk that the damn toilet was overflowing. Now will you quit standing there like a dolt and do something?"

"Um, I'm not the plumber." I thought quickly. "He's been called. They just sent me to see if I could help with anything. Want me to take a look?"

"I want you to do something!"

I stepped around her and started for the bathroom while she trailed after me grumbling into the phone. "I swear, as nice as this place looks, you'd think they'd have better help."

"Did this start after your husband left?" I asked as casually as I could.

"Ha," she said into the phone. "He wants to know if it started after my husband left." Then to me: "I don't have a husband."

"Oh, I'm sorry. I just assumed the man who rented the room..."

The toilet was indeed overflowing. A small lake had formed on the tiled bathroom floor and was starting to seep through the dam of towels she'd piled in the doorway. I wasn't sure what I was supposed to do now that I was there.

"No, it didn't start after the bastard left. It started before. He just told me to deal with it. Now you deal with it." She turned away and continued her conversation on the phone while I made a show of stepping gingerly into the water and wiggling the handle on the commode. Niagara Falls kept flowing.

"I know!" she yelled in response to something the person on the other end of the line said. "He's married, alright, but not to me. Oh, no. I don't have the moneybags Old Fort Knox has, the bitch. Why am I so stupid? I've been going along with him for two years now — putting up with his sudden calls asking me to meet him for a weekend, putting up with his sneaking me in and out of his rooms while he's gone, putting up with not seeing him for weeks at a time, knowing that he's with her. But do you think he ever does anything for me? No. I'm just the other woman who's supposed to come running whenever he calls. I'm just supposed to sit around waiting for him to come back. I'm just supposed to deal with the fucking toilet when it overflows, while he runs off to his little conference. I can't even have him for one day. Is that too much to ask? Is it?"

While she was working up a full head of steam, I noticed her purse sitting on the counter. A quick check confirmed her back was to me, so I leaned over and opened the bag. Pulling out her wallet, I flipped it open to her driver's license. She was Camellia Ledbetter. With a name like that, I'd want to get married too. She lived in DC, so he must have seen her only when he was away on "business trips".

I dropped the wallet back in and noticed an envelope addressed to her. It had been ripped open and its contents removed, so I grabbed it and stuffed it in my pocket. When another glance confirmed I had avoided detection, I shifted my faux-attention back to the toilet.

"You're damned right it's not fair!" she was shrieking. "I'm still an attractive woman. I could find someone else, someone who'll marry me. Hey, why aren't you doing anything?"

It took me a second to realize that last bellow was directed at me. "I think we should wait for the plumber," I said.

"Then what the fuck are you doing here? What good are you? And why aren't you in uniform?"

She was just noticing that now? Since I'd gotten what I needed — more than I needed actually — it was time to make my exit. "You called so early I didn't have time to put my uniform on," I said glibly. She gave me a confused look as she tried to work that one out. "Why don't I go see if the plumber is here yet?" I made a beeline for the door.

The elevator was opening just as I passed. I glanced in at a hotel staff member with a plumber in tow. I felt a rush of adrenaline when I realized what a close call that had been.

I trotted down the stairs to our room feeling flushed with the pleasure of my accomplishment. Letting myself in, I found a surprised Micah sitting up in bed, clutching the sheet to his chest, his eyes large and round.

"Killian!" He sighed, dropping the sheet to reveal that he was as naked as the day he was born. "You scared the hell out of me. I thought you were the cleaning lady, and here I am still naked."

"Sorry." My apology was somewhat unconvincing on account of the giggles.

"You certainly seem to be in a better mood," he said.

"I should be. I just closed the case!"

"What? That's great!" He jumped up and grabbed me in a huge bear hug. "I told you you're a great detective."

"Actually, it was just dumb luck. I came really close to missing it altogether."

"But you didn't, and that's what counts. I'm going to order a celebratory breakfast." He sat me down and started for the hotel phone.

"Let me call Novak first." I was eager to tell him of my first big success on my own.

"Don't you think it's a little early?"

"Are you kidding? Novak rises before the sun."

A little smirk spread across Micah's face. "Hmm... If I remember correctly, he's not the only one."

I grinned back as I pulled out my cell phone and called my boss. He answered on the second ring.

"Guess what?"

"Hello, kid," he replied evenly. "You know, most people start their conversations with a salutation of some sort, such as hi, hello, hey, yo, or even wassup."

"Hi, hello, hey, yo, wassup. Now guess what."

"You closed the case?"

"Oh," I said as I deflated.

"Sorry, I guess you wanted to pop the big news. Let's try that again, shall we? I don't know, Killian, what?"

"It's not the same now," I said.

"Well I still don't know the details."

That brightened me a little. "He is cheating on his wife."

"You know that for a fact?"

"Yes. I even managed to get an envelope with his mistress's name and address on it. Plus, I talked to her myself. It's been going on for some time now."

"She told you that?"

"Yes. Well, she thought I was there to fix the john, but—"

"To fix the... Never mind. I probably don't want to know. Great job, kid. I knew you had it in you."

"It was dumb luck actually. I didn't even know she was in the hotel at first. Knox snuck her in while he was in the conference. If I hadn't, er, overslept this morning, I probably never would have realized she was here. I just happened to be outside the room when she opened the door and I practically fell in."

"Still, you had the presence of mind to act when the opportunity presented itself. A good seventy-five percent of our trade is blind luck."

"Well, whatever it is, I did it. I'll be home this afternoon, I guess. You want me to come in and type up the report tonight, or will tomorrow morning be soon enough?"

"Actually, didn't I promise you some free time if you finished up this case quickly?"

"Oh, yeah." I'd almost forgotten in all the excitement.

"Why don't you stay one more night? Have Micah show you the city. I'll even pay for the room. Consider it a little bonus for a job well done."

"Are you serious?"

"Yep. You earned it, and besides, this is the first case you've closed on your own. You deserve a little celebration."

"Oh my gosh! Thanks so much, Novak."

"Don't thank me. Just keep up the good work."

"Oh, I will."

"I don't doubt it. Now go have fun. And, Killian?"

"Yeah?"

"I hope you get to sleep in tomorrow morning, too." I could hear the wink in his voice as he hung up. I felt my face burn bright.

"What did you get all excited about?" Micah asked, coming out of the bathroom in a robe. "And why is your face so red?"

I waved off the second question and just answered the first. "Novak said we could stay another night, on him, as a reward for finishing up the case so quickly."

Micah's eyebrows flew up. "Really? Wow, that's pretty damned nice of him."

"Tell me about it. He said to have you show me the city." He frowned a little, and I quickly rushed on. "Oh, come on, Micah." I said. "I don't want to stay in the hotel room all day and night. Show me stuff I've never seen before."

He gave me a sexy smile. "I could do that right here in bed."

"Or we could go out and then come back for that."

"You're not going to give up, are you?"

"Nope."

He sighed. "Fine, I'll give in now and spare us both the bother."

"Woohoo!" I jumped into his arms, wrapping my legs around his waist.

"Don't get too excited. We don't even know what we're doing yet."

"What is there to do?"

He shrugged. "There're museums, shows, clubs..."

"I don't want to go to a stuffy old museum, not this time anyway. I've done that already. I want to go somewhere I've never been before. I want to have fun. I want to celebrate."

"A club, then?"

I stuck out my bottom lip. "We can go to a club at home."

Micah laughed. "The Inferno is about as much like the clubs here as a kitten is to a full-grown tiger."

My eyes lit up. "Oh, really?"

"Really. We have all day to decide what we're going to do. Now, what do you want for breakfast?"

I smiled slyly. "You."

"Holy sea of men, Batman," I yelled to Micah as I stood at the railing overlooking more writhing bodies than I'd ever seen in one place in my entire life.

Micah laughed. Or, at least, he appeared to be laughing. The noise level was so high any sound he might have made was lost completely. I didn't even know how on earth he'd heard me. The music was pounding so hard the walls actually seemed to vibrate with the bass line. The lighting was low, and between that and the smoke machines, the atmosphere was much murkier than the Inferno's, which had been my only previous experience with a gay club. You could fit four Infernos into that place, and there were easily six times as many people crowded inside. I could already feel a trickle of sweat down the middle of my back.

"Quit gawking," Micah shouted in my ear. "Someone's going to mistake that open mouth for an invitation."

I snapped my jaw shut and took another look around. The club, called Michelangelo, was known as the premier gay club in the DC area. In the center of the dance floor was a huge white statue that looked remarkably like Michelangelo's famous David except for one small detail. Or, not so small, actually. This David was sporting a very impressive erection. Over his head, a huge disco ball hung from the ceiling, which was painted in a parody of the Sistine Chapel. There were still naked folks lounging about on clouds and such, but they were all hard-bodied men in this interpretation, and some were doing more than just lounging.

There were two dance floors on different levels — a smaller one downstairs and a huge one on the second floor. We'd gone in through a glitzy entryway, showed our IDs — since DC clubs were 18 and over — paid the cover, and Micah whisked me down a hall crowded with men. He'd led me up a flight of stairs to a balcony overlooking the larger dance floor. I was still in culture shock. I'd never felt like such a hick before.

"It's a little tacky," Micah shouted, "but lots of fun. You ready to dance?"

I looked out over the masses down below me. "As I'll ever be."

He led me back down the stairs, and plunged into the sea of bodies. It was at least an hour later before we broke free for a much-needed breather. I'd been groped, grabbed, and fondled more in that hour than in the rest of my life combined. Micah clutched my wrist and started pulling me back down the hall. I couldn't help noticing that he really seemed to know his way around.

Suddenly someone going the other way grabbed Micah's arm and let out a high-pitched squeal. "Oh my Gawd!" He had a Middle-Eastern look: olive complexion with dark, almost black eyes under heavy eyebrows, and a hawklike nose. His black hair hung to his shoulders in soft curls. He was very striking, not someone who would be easily forgotten.

"What are you doing back in town?" he yelled. "We've been looking for you. Are you here because you heard?" He was gripping Micah's arm as if he thought my boyfriend might bolt at any second.

Actually, judging by the look on Micah's face, that was entirely possible. He had the same expression in his eyes as the raccoon we'd found in the garage when I was a kid. Dad had cornered it and shot the poor thing with the very pistol I'd later use to put down a serial killer who was hoping to make me his next victim. I'd cried about the damn raccoon for hours.

"I'm sorry," Micah said, trying to shake the guy off his arm. "I think you must have mistaken me for someone else."

Hawk Nose hung on like a leech. "No fucking way, honey," he said. I decided he was on something. I didn't know much about drugs, but his eyes were strangely unfocused and his words slurred ever so slightly. "I'd know you anywhere."

"Well, I don't know you," Micah said. He snatched his arm away, sending his cling-on stumbling, and yanked me off down the hall before Hawk Nose could recover his balance. I almost had to run to keep up with Micah.

He pulled me into a lounge with plush red chairs and sofas arranged around the room. There were more guys in there. It seemed there was no shortage of male bodies no matter where you went in this place. Most of the ones in here were occupied with at least one other person, some with more than one, but there were still plenty of hungry eyes following us as we made our way across the floor.

"I'm not sure whether to be flattered or frightened," I shouted to Micah. The volume level was a little lower in there, so I didn't quite have to scream.

"What do you mean?" He pushed me gently into a recently vacated chair and straddled my legs.

"All those guys staring at us."

Micah snorted. "They stare at anything with a dick."

"Gee, thanks. You really know how to make me feel special."

He laughed. "I didn't mean it like that. You would definitely be of special interest to most of them. You're what's known as a twink."

"Twink?"

"It means you're young, hot, and blond. The last isn't necessarily a requirement, but it helps."

"Hot, huh?"

"Oh, definitely. Very, very hot. If you ask me, you're the hottest one here."

I wrapped my arms around his neck and pulled him closer to me. "I might have to argue about that."

"Oh yeah?"

"Yeah, because I happen to think that you're the hottest one here."

"How about if we call it a tie?"

I pretended to think it over. "I suppose I could live with that."

He leaned in and gave me a deep kiss that started a familiar tingle in my crotch.

"Keep doing that and I'm going to want breakfast again."

"They have a room for sex too, you know." He smirked salaciously.

I felt my eyes grow wide as Micah started laughing. "You were kidding, right?"

"Actually, no, I'm not. Maybe I'll show you later. Hey, I have to go pee. How about you?"

"No, I'm fine," I said absently. My mind was still on the room Micah had mentioned. I didn't know if I wanted him to show it to me. In fact, I was pretty sure I didn't.

"Okay then, don't move. I'll be right back." He leaned in and kissed me again, then jumped up and started for the door.

Watching him cross the room, I realized I wasn't the only one interested in his progress. It made me feel good to be with someone other people seemed to find as attractive as I did. They could look as much as they wanted...provided they didn't touch. I was admiring his tight butt as he vanished through the door.

While I was still looking in the direction he'd gone, I noticed Hawk Nose slip out behind him. I sat up sharply, debating whether I should follow, when I felt a presence behind me.

I spun around and looked up to find an angel hovering over me. Not really, of course, but that was my initial impression. He was backlit by a bright spotlight, making his halo of reddish-blond curls seem to glow like fire. His white satiny shirt only enhanced the illusion. As he moved around to stand in front of me, I realized he was quite real and, to my surprise, didn't look a day over fifteen. He was a little shorter than I was, with a pale, creamy complexion and rosy-red cheeks that were as smooth as a baby's bottom. He had the biggest pair of blue eyes I'd ever seen and perfect little rosebud lips. His hair hung in ringlets all around his face. In short, he looked like a Renaissance painting come to life.

"You're with the guy who just left, right?" he asked.

"Huh?"

"The guy who just left, the one Razi followed out? Is he your man?"

"My man?" I glanced back towards the door again, still trying to decide if I should stay put or go after him.

"Your boyfriend. Is he your boyfriend?"

I turned back and focused on him again. "Who is Razi?"

He snapped his fingers in front of my face. "Dude, are you on something? Try to focus here. Razi's the one who grabbed your boy in the hallway just now. He's sure he knows him. Is he your boyfriend?"

"Yeah." I shook my head. I was having trouble following this conversation. "Who are you?"

"Tad."

"Tad who?"

He made a face. "Tad Young if you must know. I'm with Razi."

I looked him over. "Speaking of 'tad young', aren't you a tad young to be in here?"

He rolled his huge blue eyes. "Like I haven't heard that one before. Why does it matter to you how old I am? Besides, you don't look much older."

"I'm eighteen."

"Oh, well okay. Anyway, Razi thinks he knows him. What's his name?"

I suddenly wasn't so sure I should say anything more. "Why should I tell you?"

"Is it Micah?"

I looked at him sharply.

"It is, isn't it?" He grinned, revealing perfect white teeth. "Razi was right."

"Who is this Razi, and how does he know Micah?" I wondered why Micah had pretended not to know him.

Tad, if that was his real name, shrugged. "I think they used to work together."

"Where?" I was suddenly interested. I knew next to nothing about Micah's life here in the city.

Tad evasively shifted his eyes away and shrugged again. "I don't know."

"Yes, you do."

"Why don't you ask Micah?"

"Because I'm asking you," I snapped.

"Sheesh. Excuse me for living. I should have never come over here." He turned and started walking away.

I was on my feet in flash. I grabbed his elbow, making him turn to face me. "Hey, I'm sorry. Let's start over, huh? I'm Killian."

He smiled. "Hi, Killian. You've already made fun of my name, so we don't need to go there again."

"I apologize."

"It's cool. I'm used to it."

"Is that your real name?"

He looked at me suspiciously for a second, then nodded slowly. "It's short for Thaddeus."

"So where did Micah and, uh, Razi work together?"

"Look, I don't know for sure, so I probably shouldn't say anything."

I pleaded with him with my eyes.

Heaving a sigh, he gave in. "Razi said he used to be in the business."

I frowned. "What business?"

Tad gave me a measuring look. "You're not from around here, are you?"

"Will you just—"

"Okay, don't get your knickers in a knot. The same business Razi is in."

"Which is?"

He looked around, as if to make sure no one was listening, then leaned toward me conspiratorially, slipping an arm around my shoulder. "The escort business."

It suddenly seemed as if the room retreated, all the noise rushing away into the distance. I felt flushed, hot and cold at the same time. So that was Micah's big secret, the one thing he couldn't trust me enough to tell me. It all made a sudden, horrible sense. Micah used to sell his body for sex. He'd been a prostitute.

Tad yanked his arm back suddenly, as if he'd been burned. The crowd came flooding back into focus as he hurried away. I started to call after him when I felt someone slip his arms around my waist from behind. I jerked my head back to find it was Micah.

"Who was that?" Although his voice was falsely bright, his eyes staring after Tad were troubled and distant. "Was someone trying to pick you up? I knew I shouldn't have left you alone."

I pulled away from Micah's embrace and turned to face him. "That was Razi's boyfriend," I said, matching his faux-cheerful tone as his eyes flew wide open in surprise and his mouth turned down sharply with dismay. "You remember Razi, don't you? You used to work together, after all."

Chapter 7

"We need to talk."

"You think?"

"Killian, it's not what it seems."

"Oh, my mistake. Then, you weren't lying to me about having been a hooker?"

"For God's sake!" he hissed between clenched teeth. He looked around. So far no one was paying us too much attention, although a few heads were beginning to turn as my voice climbed in volume. "I never once lied to you. I always said there was stuff in my past I wasn't ready to talk to you about. You knew that. Well, now it's not a secret. Can you understand why I wasn't exactly eager to trot that little piece of information out on our first date?"

"Our first date, maybe, but we've been seeing each other for months. When were you going to share it with me? Never?"

"I was going to tell you this weekend."

"Oh, please. You expect me to believe that?"

"I was. Ask Steve."

"Steve? What does he have to do with this? He knows?"

"It's what we were talking about the other night. He thought you would be able to handle it if I told you the truth. I was planning on telling you everything while we were here."

"Steve found out before I did?"

"Will you stop twisting my words? I needed someone to talk to about this, someone objective." He looked around again. "Can we not discuss it here? I'd rather continue in private."

"Fine. Let's go." I stormed out the door without bothering to see if he was following me.

An angry guy fighting back tears as he crashed through the hallways must not have been too unusual for Michelangelo's, since I hardly garnered any attention during my dramatic exit. By the time I made it to the parking lot, I was unable to hold myself together any longer. I leaned against a pole and let the sobs come.

Micah must have been right behind me the whole time, because he was at my side in a second. He placed a hand on my arm, but I jerked away from his touch. "Killian, please. I'm sorry. I'll explain everything, I promise."

"Just get the car."

He reluctantly backed away a few steps before turning and jogging off.

"Men," a husky, smoke-and-acid-filled voice said from behind me.

I turned to find a tall, rail-thin black man leaning against the wall, a long cigarette between his fingers. While details such as his age and general description were lost, thanks to my bleary eyes, I registered effeminacy from his stance and the way he spoke.

He took a drag from the cigarette and released the smoke with his words. "What did he do, baby? Did you catch him with another guy?"

I shook my head in confusion.

"He'll explain all right. He'll have an answer for everything. I know his type. They think a handsome face can get them out of anything. Don't stand for it."

"I..."

"Well don't worry your sweet little head about it. A pretty boy like you could have any guy in this place. You remember that. Oh, and also remember that all men are dogs."

"I don't—"

A car pulled up behind me, and Micah called out, "Killian?" saving me from trying to think of a suitable reply. I turned almost gratefully to climb in.

"Remember!" the guy shouted after me. "Dogs!"

"What was that about?" Micah asked as I slammed the door.

I just turned my head away and stared out the window. Although I was in control enough to know that a hysterical attack wasn't going to help anything, I had a lot I wanted to sort out before we got back to the hotel.

After making a couple more unsuccessful attempts to start a conversation, Micah lapsed into a tension-filled, uneasy silence that lasted until we were alone in our room. "Are you finally ready to listen to me?" he asked as soon as the door closed behind him.

"Now you want to talk?"

"Killian, you're angry, and I can understand that."

"You're damn right, I'm angry. I can't believe this."

"What are you so mad about? Because you didn't find out before this or because of the way you found out?"

As angry as I was, I had to admit that was a good question. Would I have been this upset if he'd told me himself? The answer was obviously no. I was pissed off because I'd heard it from some glitter boy at a club. If he'd really discussed it with Steve — and that would be easy enough to verify — then maybe he had intended to tell me over the weekend.

With rational thought came a sudden deflation. I felt the anger drain out of me as if someone had pulled a plug. I wasn't ready to stop being mad, though, damn it. The self-righteous indignation served as a sort of shield against the other things I was feeling. With that gone, I was left with a terrible sense of vulnerability. This man to whom I had given my body that very morning used to do the same thing for money. I was extremely uncomfortable with the idea, to say the least.

My thoughts must have been written clearly on my face. "I think I need to explain," he said, sitting heavily on the edge of the bed.

He patted a spot next to him, but I took the one chair in the room instead. I wasn't ready to be that close to him yet. "What's to explain? You used to be a...a...hustler."

Micah rubbed his face wearily. "It's not like that, Kill. You don't understand."

"You sold your body, right? How hard is that to understand?"

"I wasn't a hustler. It's not like I was standing on a street corner picking up tricks."

I shrugged. "Does the terminology really matter?"

"Yes. Yes, it does. There's a big difference."

"Well, for God's sake, please educate me."

"I was an escort."

"I don't—"

"Hustlers work on the street. They're usually runaways — drug-addicted, disease-riddled kids who get picked up by random johns and just barely earn enough to survive...or more likely support their habits."

"So...what? You only fucked rich guys for money? I'm still not seeing a big difference."

"It wasn't like that..."

"Then what was it like, Micah? You believe just because you, what, got a phone call instead of waiting on a street corner it somehow makes what you were doing better?"

He took a deep breath. "I think I'd better explain everything."

"I don't really want to hear any more, thanks."

"Please hear me out, okay? Please?"

I started to refuse again as the voice of the guy from the club echoed in my head: *"He'll have an answer for everything."* What could it hurt, though? The situation couldn't get much worse as far as I was concerned, and — who knew — maybe Micah's explanation would help me understand. That seemed about as likely as my sprouting wings, but I decided I had nothing to lose. "Go ahead."

He sighed and stared down at his hands in his lap. Once I'd given my grudging consent, he didn't seem to know where to begin. He took a few more deep breaths and started haltingly. "I told...I told you that my parents were pretty supportive of me when I finally came out to them. I never had problems there, but we didn't have a lot of money, especially after the legal stuff with the guy who abused me and all my counseling bills. They used almost every dime left to pay for my first semester of college. I had some scholarships, academic stuff, but they didn't amount to much. I got a job at a pizza joint, but it still wasn't enough. The shift hours started interfering with my school work, causing my grades to suffer. I lost my scholarships. I didn't know what to do. I was desperate but too proud to ask for help.

"I'd pretty much decided to drop out when this guy I knew from school started flashing cash like he'd hit the lottery. Since he was in the same boat I was, putting himself through college and just barely scraping by, I realized something was up. I figured he was selling drugs."

When Micah rubbed his face again, I could tell we were reaching the hard part. "I'd managed to be pretty discreet up till then about being gay. Hardly anyone knew, which was how I wanted it. Toward the end of the semester, though, when I figured I wouldn't be back for the next one, I just didn't care anymore. Word got around that I was queer, and the next thing I knew, the guy with all the cash shows up at my room one night. He told me he had an offer I couldn't refuse. When I insisted I wasn't interested, he pulled out a wad of cash and asked, 'Don't you at least want to know where all this comes from?' By that time, I figured what the hell. I'd at least hear him out.

"He told me how he'd been recruited for a local escort agency. He said it was a classy setup. You got paid big bucks to keep lonely gay guys company, and you didn't even have to sleep with them if you didn't want to...although you made a lot more in tips if you did. He said they would accommodate my school schedule, and I could take home more in a single week than I made all month at the pizza place. If I was interested, he could get me an interview."

Micah paused and looked up to gauge my reaction. On the inside, my guts were twisted into a knot that I didn't think would ever unravel. However, my expression must have been neutral at the very least, because he seemed satisfied with what he saw and continued.

"You have to remember that my attitude towards sex then wasn't what it is now. I'd been abused as a kid and even with all the hours of counseling I'd logged, I'd still not worked through everything. I told you about that on our first date. So...what the guy was suggesting...it seemed like the perfect solution to all my problems. I asked him to set up the interview. Within a few days I was talking to some guy, and a week later I was hired."

He stopped and seemed to wait for me to make a comment of some sort. I didn't know what to say, so the silence stretched out until he began talking again, as much to fill the void as anything.

"It wasn't even that bad. They'd call me with a job. If it fit my schedule, I'd take it. I went to theaters, museums, art shows, concerts, dinners at fancy restaurants — places I would never have gone to on my own."

He took a deep breath. "And yes, I slept with some of them...most of them. I didn't have to, and I never did anything I didn't feel completely comfortable with. And the money...the money was unreal.

There was no way I could have made that kind of cash any other way. It paid for school and left me plenty to spend however I wanted. You get used to that kind of lifestyle pretty quickly.

"Even after I met someone..." His words faltered as his eyes blazed with raw pain for a brief, unguarded second. I knew there was something he wasn't telling me. That was a fresh sting I'd seen, not an old ache. He recovered and went on. "Even after I met someone, I stayed in the business. I stayed in it until I graduated."

At that point, he seemed to run out of words. Whatever had hurt him appeared to have knocked the spirit out of him.

"What is it?" That was the first time I'd spoken since he'd started his explanation.

"What is what?"

"Something's wrong. I mean besides us. I can see it in your eyes, especially when you mention the person you met."

The reaction was there again this time, but not quite as strong. He looked away.

"Don't keep more secrets from me." My voice was soft, but the pain I still felt was clear in my voice.

"While I was working for the agency..." he began roughly. He cleared his throat and continued. "While I was working for them, I met someone. His name is...was Paul." I noted the past tense. "He was another escort. We became friends and then..."

"Lovers?"

He nodded. "We moved in together. I'd dated a few other people, but none of them could handle the fact that I was an escort. It was different with Paul. He understood. He was in the business too. We were happy together."

"Did you love him?" I asked, even though I wasn't sure I wanted to know. Actually, I could plainly see the answer.

He nodded.

"What happened?" I asked, unable to help myself.

"Things started falling apart during my last semester. I knew I was going to have to move on soon, find a job, grow up. I wanted to do that together with Paul, but he wasn't ready. I started seeing a counselor again. She was good — better than any of the ones I'd had before. She agreed with me that I needed a change — I needed to escape and, more than anything, I needed to stop relying on sex as a tool to get what I wanted. I'd used it when I was younger, trying to find love, and now I was using it for profit. On some level, I already knew that, and the gradual realization was the source of my restlessness. Hearing it from someone else simply made it clearer.

"When I graduated, I had several job offers. Two were particularly attractive: one for a weekly in Washington and the other for a daily paper on the Shore. Paul pressured me to take the job in DC and stay with him, but I wanted out of the city and away from the business. We fought about it, talked about it, cried about it... In the end, I accepted the daily and moved to Salisbury. I asked Paul to come with me, but he said no. He wasn't ready to leave the city...or the business. Neither of us wanted to pursue a long-distance relationship with all its associated baggage. Besides, too much had been said by that time. So we just broke up."

"This is the guy you told me about?"

He nodded.

I was quiet for a minute, processing everything I'd learned. It was clear Micah still had strong feelings for this guy, for Paul. Where did that leave me? "Do you still love him?"

Micah's face sank into his hands. "Of course." His voice was muffled, but I had no problem understanding him.

I drew a shaky breath. "Do you want to go back to him?"

His head shot up with a confused expression. "What?"

"I can see how much it hurts you to talk about him. Do you want to go back to him?"

"Why would you think...?" He shook his head. "Killian, I let go of Paul and moved on a long time ago. I'll always care about him — he was my first love — but I wouldn't have said I loved you unless I meant it. I wouldn't have pursued a relationship with you if I didn't think I could give you one-hundred percent. It's like you and Asher."

"Then, what's that pain I see in your eyes every time you mention him?"

His mouth opened and closed a few times silently. I thought he was going to start crying, but he somehow managed to pull himself together enough to attempt a halting answer. "The guy at the club? Not the kid who was talking to you, the other guy, the kid's boyfriend?"

"Razi?"

A look of distaste flickered across his face. "Yeah, Razi. He used to work at the agency too, but he left to go out on his own. Most guys do eventually. You get all the profits then. For some reason, Paul always had a soft spot when it came to Razi. I never cared for him, but Paul insisted there was something more to him than just the slick exterior, something inside worth sticking around for. The news Razi thought I'd heard..." He stopped and gulped a few times before he could go on. "Razi thought I was back in town because Paul was killed a few days ago."

"Oh!" I felt a rush of relief at that revelation, followed almost immediately by shame. "I...I'm sorry." I knew I was blushing hotly even though there was no way Micah could have read my thoughts and known how callous they were.

"I don't expect you to feel bad," Micah said, making me feel worse. "It's not like you even knew him."

"Still, he meant something to you."

"But not to you. Look, I imagine you have a lot to sort out. I'm going to take a walk and leave you to your thoughts."

I started to protest that it wasn't necessary, but clamped my mouth shut when I realized how much I really did want to be alone for a while. Instead, I simply nodded, and he let himself out.

I threw myself down on the bed to allow myself a few minutes of wallowing in self-pity. In one short night, my new fairytale romance had soured into more of a twisted Brothers Grimm tale...and it seemed grim indeed. My Prince Charming turned out to be nothing like the man I thought he was.

Then the dragon of rational thought once again reared its ugly head, forcing me to admit that nothing had actually changed. Micah was still the same guy I'd been dating for several months, the same one I'd given my virginity to just that morning. He hadn't changed. The only thing different was that I knew more about him.

Still, hissed that nasty little part of me, he did hide his past from you, even if he didn't outright lie about it.

In all fairness, the reasonable side of me argued, he did tell you there was a part of his past he hadn't revealed to you yet. And he was going to do it this weekend.

The simple fact of the matter was, though, that no matter how good a reason Micah felt he had for turning tricks, it still made me very uncomfortable. I knew my attitude was possibly due to my having grown up sheltered in a small town. While Maryland was a fairly liberal state, the Shore was still rural and conservative for the most part. It had been remote from the rest of the state until halfway through the twentieth century when the bridge connecting the peninsula to the mainland was built. In many ways its people were still isolated and distant from the western shore of the Chesapeake Bay and the urban areas around Annapolis, Baltimore, and DC.

Was my discomfort something I could overcome? I didn't know, at least not yet. I needed more time to figure things out.

Did I still care about Micah? That much at least I was able to answer: Yes, I did. And with that thought, the pain inside me welled up again.

By then, I was physically and mentally wiped out. My rational mind finally gave up and let my emotions take over in a torrent of self-indulgent tears. By the time I'd cried myself out, I was well on my way to slipping into a restless sleep.

I awoke with a start when Micah let himself into the room. I glanced at the time and saw it was two o'clock in the morning.

"Where've you been?" I struggled to sit up, my mind still fuzzy from being awakened so abruptly.

"In an all-night coffee bar down the street. You weren't the only one who needed to think. I'm sorry I woke you up."

"S'okay."

He started undressing, and despite myself my heart began to beat just a little faster. "What are you doing?" I asked stupidly.

"Getting ready for bed," he said in a drained voice that didn't leave much room for argument.

I argued anyway. "You're sleeping here?" What can I say? I'm not at my best when I'm awakened in the middle of the night.

"No, Killian, I thought I'd sleep in the hallway. Yes, I'm sleeping here. And, don't worry, I won't lay a finger on you." He pulled back the blankets on his side of the bed and slid under the covers before turning his back purposefully to me.

I stared at his back for a while, almost wishing he would lay a finger on me. While part of me wanted him, another part was disgusted by my desire. Finally, my exhaustion overcame my warring emotions, allowing me to fall back into a fitful slumber.

I woke up to a morning dreary enough to match my mood. The sky was leaden and heavy with the promise of a downpour before the day was out. Micah wasn't there, but a note he'd left on the desk informed me he'd gone for breakfast and would bring me something back.

I was just getting out of the shower when Micah returned carrying a small paper sack. "I got you a bagel with cream cheese." He couldn't quite meet my eyes as he set the bag on the dresser. "I hope that's okay."

"It's fine. Thank you." I turned away to get dressed.

I sensed him move up behind me and then felt his hands on my waist. I tensed up under his touch.

"Micah..."

His hands fell away. "So what's going on? Are we breaking up?"

"No." I kept my back to him as I pulled on my clothes. "I mean...I don't know right now. I need more time to figure things out."

"Figure what out, Killian? Do you love me?"

"I... Yes."

"And I love you. What's to figure out?"

"It's not that simple, and we both know it." I turned to face him. "If it was as easy as just saying those three words, I'd still be with Asher and you'd still be with Paul."

Hurt flashed in his eyes at the mention of Paul's name. At least I thought that was the source of the pain until he spoke. "It always comes back to Asher, doesn't it?"

"What? Wait. That's not what I meant."

"What did you mean, then?"

"You said yourself just last night that, while you would always love Paul, you'd moved on. That's how it is for me when it comes to Asher. I loved him, but that wasn't enough to make it work. Same thing with you and Paul. If it wasn't enough for them, how do we know it's enough now?"

He sighed and knuckled his eyes. "Just tell me what to do to make this right."

"I don't know. I don't think there's anything anyone can do. You can't just wave a magic wand and fix everything. It's going to take time, and I don't even know if it'll be right then."

"What is the problem exactly? That I didn't tell you? I'm sorry, Killian, but at least everything's out in the open now. There are no more secrets. We can rebuild the trust."

"That's not even it. Not really. I'm still a little hurt at the way I found out, but I know that wasn't really your fault. It was just totally shitty timing."

"Now you know why I didn't want to come to DC. But if that's not the problem, what is?"

"I'm just having a lot of trouble with the whole idea of you being an escort."

He sat down heavily on the bed. "But I explained all that to you."

"I still just..."

"It's a part of my past. I can't change what happened, and I wouldn't if I could. I'm not ashamed of what I did, you know. It put me through college, and it's a big part of who I am today. I wouldn't be the same person if I hadn't gone through all that. I was good enough for you to fall in love with me. Why am I not I good enough for you to stay in love?"

I was fighting tears again, but I'd be damned if I'd fall apart in front of him. I pulled myself together and took a deep breath. "We're not going to get anywhere right now. I think we should just go home. I need a few days to work through all this on my own."

"Oh, great. You're asking for the infamous break. Everybody knows that's the death knell for a relationship."

"Micah, I'm not breaking up with you. I'm not even asking for a break. I just need a few days to figure out what I do want. This is a lot for me to take in. I mean I'm just a kid from the boonies. Give me a chance."

"You sell yourself short, Killian. Just don't sell us short too." He picked up his suitcase and yanked open the door. "I'll be waiting in the car."

I sighed and zipped up my bag. After a cursory look around the room to make sure we weren't leaving anything, I started to follow. I was halfway down the hall before I remembered the bagel. I just might need the sustenance for the long ride home.

Chapter 8

The drive home felt every bit as long as I'd feared it would. Micah and I didn't arrive until late morning, and we barely spoke the entire time. When Micah dropped me off, I just mumbled, "I'll call you soon."

I wanted to talk to Steve, but Kane was the only one home. He told me both Steve and Adam were at the B&B. Something had happened over the weekend, but he didn't say what, and I didn't ask. I was in no mood to deal with anyone else's problems.

I was also in no mood to sit around the house doing nothing. I drove to the office only to find it empty, but since it was Sunday that wasn't such a surprise. I typed up my report, relying heavily on my notes because my mind wasn't exactly at peak performance. Afterward I was left with nothing to do except fret. I dropped the report on Novak's desk and went home.

Neither Adam nor Steve had returned yet, so I shut myself in the room I shared with Kane. He could tell I was in a bad mood and quickly cleared out — for once without asking a bunch of nosy questions. I spent the rest of the night feeling sorry for myself and trying to figure out what to do about Micah.

The next day, I forced myself to go to class, although later I couldn't recall a single thing we'd discussed. After school, I stopped by the office. As far as I could tell, Novak hadn't been in yet. My report still sat where I'd left it the night before. I played games on my computer until it was almost time for Jake to get out of school for the day. I wasn't sure if following him would do any good, but it sure beat sitting around the office doing nothing.

Once at the high school, I parked in almost the exact same spot I'd chosen the time before. As I sat and waited for the final bell to ring, my mind began to wander. Of course, the first place it went was directly to Micah.

I still couldn't believe Micah had once been an escort. He'd told me about his troubled childhood, about the much older neighbor who had seduced him and kept him quiet with mental abuse. He'd explained how it had affected his self-esteem and his view of sex, and as a result, how he'd slept his way through practically the entire male population of his school. He'd also assured me his views of sex had changed as he'd gotten older, and he never wanted his relationships to be based solely on sex again.

None of that information had prepared me for the big news, however. I still couldn't help wondering if Micah really would have told me if Tad hadn't spilled the beans first.

The dismissal bell rang, registering vaguely at the back of my mind.

I was much more consumed with the question of how knowing about Micah's past would affect me. Being an escort had shaped his character. As he'd said, he wouldn't be the same person I knew if that hadn't happened. I'd fallen in love with him, so obviously I liked how he was. Still, the idea of him having sex with someone for money horrified me. I couldn't deny that.

I was so caught up in my thoughts I completely missed Jake's leaving the school. In fact, I didn't notice anything until his Jeep drove past. I cursed as I quickly started my car and pulled into the line of vehicles waiting their turn to get out of the lot.

I was furious with myself for being so careless. I should have been paying more attention instead of getting lost in my own head. Novak always warned me never to allow my personal life to interfere with my investigation, yet that was exactly what I had done.

My frustration grew as the kid in front of me took forever to merge into traffic. I couldn't figure out if he was busy texting or just being overly cautious, but either way I almost popped a blood vessel waiting for him to go. I finally managed to get out of the parking lot, and the chase was on. Jake had a considerable lead, but I quickly made up for the lost time — while simultaneously venting my frustration — by driving like a maniac until he was once more in sight. It was just plain luck that he hadn't turned off the main road. If he had, I'd have lost him for sure.

I fell a few cars back from him as Novak's training took over, leaving my mind free to go back to worrying. Why did his having been an escort during college bother me so much? Was it just because I'd grown up so sheltered? I had to admit I could be a little prudish. If I loved Micah, though, his past shouldn't matter. At least, that's what I'd always heard. Therefore, if it did matter, did that mean I didn't love him?

How could I know if I truly loved him? I knew I enjoyed being with him. I missed him when we weren't together. I was undeniably attracted to him. Was that love? What was love?

I'd loved Asher, and probably always would, but it was so difficult to define. What I felt for Micah was different from what I'd felt with Asher. Did that mean I loved Micah less, or was it different every time? And if I did love Micah, didn't that mean I should be willing to accept him as he was, checkered past and all? Why was I having such a hard time with this? It wasn't as if he'd been a killer-for-hire or done something that actually hurt anyone. While the morality of being an escort could be argued, it all depended on whose moral code you were using. It was a perfectly legal business in many countries and even some parts of the U.S. More importantly, he wasn't doing it anymore. I was pretty sure I wouldn't be able to handle dating someone who was still working as an escort. I was too insecure for that.

Maybe insecurity was what it all came down to. Was Micah comparing me to all those other guys he'd slept with when we were in bed? If so, I was sure I couldn't even begin to measure up. I hardly knew what I was doing. Why was Micah even interested in me? I was just some inexperienced kid from nowhere. He was a talented, bright, gorgeous, sophisticated man. What if he got tired of me one day? What was keeping him from leaving me for somebody better?

I was so caught up in that train of thought I didn't even notice when Jake turned off. I just suddenly realized he was no longer in front of me. I had no clue when I'd passed him or where. I let loose with a string of curses as I pounded the steering wheel in anger.

I fumed for several minutes before I could even begin to calm down. I took a deep breath and tried to relax. It was not turning out to be a good day. Clearly, I wasn't focused enough to do any surveillance. Maybe I wasn't focused enough to do anything. I thought about just driving home and locking myself in my room again. Jake was definitely gone, and I had no idea where.

I pulled into a gas station to turn around when a sudden thought occurred to me. I might not know where Jake was going, but I was pretty sure where he wasn't going. We had been driving in the opposite direction of his house when I lost him. That made it the perfect time to search his room, assuming I could manage to stay focused on the job at hand and not allow my thoughts to distract me again.

When I arrived at Judy and Jake's house, I was pleased to see that my hunch had paid off. Jake's car was nowhere in sight. Better yet, Judy's van was parked in the driveway, so that meant she was home.

As I got out of my car, Judy opened the front door. "Hi, Killian. I thought I heard somebody pull in. You haven't found anything out."

It was a statement not a question, but I answered it anyway. "Not yet. I was hoping I could search Jake's room while he isn't here."

She nodded and ushered me inside. "I hate doing this, but I can't stand by and do nothing. I know something's wrong. I just don't know what. It's killing me."

The anguish in her voice was so strong it stopped me in my tracks. I turned to face her and found myself hugging her spontaneously. "I'll find out what's going on, I promise."

"Please do."

I entered Jake's room with a twinge of guilt. While it was one thing to snoop through a complete stranger's personal belongings, it was quite another to be doing it to a friend. I felt as if I was violating a trust between us.

It looked like a typical teenage boy's room. A few posters were plastered on the walls, one advertising a gay teen movie and a couple of others for various bands. Clothes were scattered wherever they'd landed when Jake had removed them. A dirty plate sat on the floor and, nearby, a toppled-over glass with a dried skim of milk inside. A musty smell pervaded the space, reminding me of an empty locker room.

The room itself was on the small side, with most of it taken up by a double bed, a dresser, a desk, a bookcase, and an entertainment center that held what appeared to be a brand-new, large, flat-screen TV, DVD player, and all the latest game systems. I whistled softly at the electronics. Judy was right. That stuff had definitely cost a bundle. Where had Jake gotten the money to buy it all? I realized that was what Judy hired me to find out.

Where to start? I surveyed the room and chose the desk. I began opening drawers and sifting through the contents, trying to leave as little sign that I'd been there as possible. I hadn't done many room searches, but I'd assisted Novak a few times.

I couldn't help smiling as I remembered my first search the previous summer. I'd found a stash of illegally filmed videos showing some local officials in compromising positions at a sleazy motel. The manager had been taping them with hidden cameras for his own pleasure. The fact that it also netted him a lucrative income blackmailing the folks on the tapes was just icing on the cake. We'd called in the cops, and he was promptly arrested. Last I'd heard, he was in jail — where he belonged.

My search of Jake's desk, however, turned up nothing more than a few bad test grades and a single marijuana roach all the way at the back of the bottom left-hand drawer. God only knew how long it had been there, and it was hardly the kind of problem I suspected Judy was worried about. Hell, for all I knew, it was Judy's. She struck me as the type to indulge in a bit of the herb on occasion.

With the desk out of the way, I moved on to the dresser, which contained nothing except clothes. I'd never realized Jake was such a label whore. Almost everything bore the name of an expensive brand, and it was all new, some items with the tags still attached. I almost fell over when I saw the prices. How could he afford to shop at these places? I was beginning to understand why Judy was so worried. The deeper I dug the more questions I had.

In the closet I discovered more new clothes and a few boxes of outgrown toys and games. Dust bunnies large enough to pose a threat to small pets had set up camp under the bed, but they were unchallenged for the space. When I peeked beneath the mattress I found nothing. Next, I carefully searched the bookcase, checking behind the books and feeling along under the shelves. The only thing I learned was Jake favored science fiction and seldom used the set of encyclopedias on the bottom shelf. The dust was so thick down there it made me sneeze.

Unless I had missed something, which was entirely possible, nothing was left but the entertainment center. It had only a few places where something could be hidden, mainly a small cabinet with doors at the bottom and a carved wooden box on one of the shelves.

When I opened the cabinet doors, a small avalanche of magazines, DVDs, and photographs tumbled out — a motley assortment of gossip rags, entertainment newsmagazines, recent movies, and gay porn. I set the magazines aside after shaking each one upside down to make sure there was nothing slipped between the pages. All that fell out were subscription floaters, although there were enough of those to paper the walls. I opened each DVD case, even taking the discs out to be sure nothing was tucked behind them. Everything appeared normal.

Finally, I went through the pictures more carefully in case there was a clue in any of them. Most were of people I didn't know. Since the backgrounds often included palm trees, I deduced they had been taken while Jake was living in California. Towards the bottom of the pile, I started recognizing some of scenes, a few old photos from Sheridan family gatherings, birthdays and holidays mostly. Seeing them still alive caused a dull ache.

The next few almost made me forget why I was there. One must have been taken when I'd briefly dated Jake's twin sister, Gilly. In the picture, Gilly and I were in the foreground, my arm tossed casually around her shoulder, while her older brother Todd glared from behind us. I stared at it for a while before moving on.

Then came some snapshots taken at the huge Halloween bash the Sheridans had thrown right after Gilly and I broke up. One showed Jake, Kane, Asher, and me mugging for the camera in our costumes. It wasn't a night I was all that eager to remember.

The last photo in the pile was the one that really got to me. I had no idea when it was taken or who had taken it. It had a candid feel, as if the subjects were unaware anyone else was around. In it, Seth and I were walking down the hall at school, our heads bent in towards one another as if we were talking. Seth's face held a familiar half-smile at whatever I was saying.

I hadn't even known there had ever been a picture taken of us together. Although for a moment I was terribly tempted to slide it into my pocket, I knew I couldn't risk Jake's noticing it was gone. I reluctantly returned it to the pile and, after making sure I hadn't missed anything in the cabinet, shoved everything back in. Considering the way it all had just slid out, I wasn't too worried that he'd notice if anything was in the wrong place. I shut the doors on the mess and tried to shut the picture out of my mind as well. If only one were as simple as the other.

That left only the carved wooden box to look through. Lifting its lid, I found nothing but a few more photos of Jake and Judy, some discarded movie stubs saved as keepsakes, and a cheap silver ring of the sort they sold on the boardwalk — all of it about as exciting and incriminating as air.

Then, for some reason, I took everything out of the box and picked it up. It was surprisingly heavy, and a suspicion rose in my mind. I shook it and heard a shuffling sound despite the fact it was empty — or at least appeared to be empty. A second, closer look showed the outside to be a lot deeper than the inside.

When I turned it over, I discovered the bottom was rigged to slide out. It was a snug fit, but I was able to move it with my thumbs far enough to get my fingers in to push it open. When I saw what was inside, I almost dropped the box. There was a huge wad of cash made up of hundred-dollar bills. How on earth had Jake gotten so much money?

That wasn't the only surprise. There was a ticket, which at first I thought was another movie stub, but on further inspection proved to be for an event that hadn't yet taken place. It was for the well-publicized AIDS Benefit Ball, a chic, high-society function I'd read about in the paper. They were expecting everyone from the governor on down to be in attendance, and tickets started at $300 a piece.

Under the ticket was a clipping from a newspaper, the grainy image of an elegant man shaking hands with an older gentleman whom I recognized as a state senator, even though half of his face was cut off. The other guy, the obvious focus of Jake's interest, I'd never seen before. Who was he, and why did Jake have a picture of him hidden in this secret compartment?

I studied the picture for a little longer, then replaced it and the other contents and slid the bottom back into place. I carefully set the box down in the outline left in the light coating of dust on the shelf. When I was finished, you would have never known the box had been touched.

I moved to the doorway and paused to scan the room as critically as possible, finally deciding that if there were any more secret hiding places, they would have to stay hidden. So far, I'd managed not to leave any signs I'd been there, and I didn't want Jake to suspect his room had been searched. While I couldn't imagine what it could be, some sort of innocent explanation could exist for everything. If so, I didn't want to alienate my friend or cause problems between him and his aunt for no reason.

I found Judy sitting at the kitchen table with a mug of hot tea steaming in her hand. She pushed another mug in my direction. "Sugar?" she asked.

I took the chair next to her. The tea was so strong I had to add several spoonfuls of sugar before I could drink it. We sat and sipped in companionable silence for a few minutes.

"You didn't find anything definite, but you found some things that concern you." Judy seldom asked questions unless they were for your benefit. It was eerie at times, but you eventually got used to it.

"I found a joint in one of the desk drawers." I decided to start small and work my way up to the big stuff. She waved that aside. As I'd suspected, it wasn't high on her list of concerns. "I also saw that he'd bought an awful lot of rather expensive clothing over the last few months."

"In the last month, actually."

"Do you have any idea where he got the money?"

"No. None. He doesn't have a job, at least not a legitimate one."

"Did you ask him where the money came from?"

"Yes. He told me to mind my own business and stormed off."

I frowned. "Same thing with the electronic equipment?"

"You mean the TV and all? Yes. He just showed up with it one day. He wouldn't say where that came from either, only that it was a gift."

"A gift? From who?"

"Like I said, he wouldn't tell me anything. That's why I came to you."

I took a deep breath. "Do you know the carved wooden box on the entertainment center?"

She gave me a confused look. "I've seen it. Where it came from I have no idea. It's one more thing that just showed up one day. It was the least of my worries, so I didn't pay much attention to it. Why?"

"There's more to it than meets the eye. It has a false bottom that slides out. He had some things hidden in there."

Her eyes sharpened. "What kinds of things?"

"A wad of money that probably equals about six months of my salary, if not more, a ticket to the AIDS Benefit Ball, and a newspaper clipping of a man I don't recognize."

Judy frowned. Obviously, it wasn't what she'd been expecting. "What in God's name is he doing with a ticket to AIDS Benefit Ball? Those things are harder to come by than plutonium."

I shrugged. I didn't have any clue.

She thought a moment, then asked, "What did the man in the picture look like?"

"Distinguished." I realized it wasn't the most vivid description. I thought a moment. "He had dark hair and was tall and slim." I shook my head in frustration. "Hang on."

Going back to Jake's room, I retrieved the clipping and took it out to Judy. "Recognize him?"

She stared at the picture for a moment before shaking her head. "Never seen him before in my life. But..."

"But what?"

"As soon as I saw him, I got a bad feeling about him."

I stared intently at her face. Her eyes were troubled. "What kind of bad feeling?"

She shook her head. "I don't know. Just...I'm sensing death."

"Do you mean he's dead?"

"I don't know. Possibly, but I doubt it. Unlike yours, my Gifts have more to do with the future than the past."

I ignored her last statement. "Then, what do you mean you're sensing death? Is he going to die?"

"Maybe. Or someone close to him. I'm not sure. And I could be wrong."

"Possibly? Maybe? You aren't sure? What good are these Gifts if they can't be more helpful than that?" I said.

Judy's shoulders slumped, and she rubbed her forehead. I could see the tension in her face. "I'm sorry," she said softly.

"No, I am. That was uncalled for."

"That's just not how Gifts work. They don't give you easy answers anymore than cars can transport you instantly to wherever you want to go. They're tools. You have to learn how to use them. In this case, I have no idea what the feeling I got when I looked at that picture meant. Just keep it in mind. It could come in handy later."

I nodded and went to put the picture back in the box. When I returned to the kitchen, Judy's elbows were resting on the table, her head in her hands. I hated to see her look so dispirited.

I sighed. "It could all be something completely innocent."

She looked up, and a single raised eyebrow spoke eloquently. "Trust me. I've racked my brain trying to think of an innocent explanation for all this, and nothing has occurred to me. Where is his money coming from? How can he afford to buy all these clothes and expensive equipment? And now I have even more questions. How did he get a ticket for the Ball, and why would he want one? And who the hell is that man in the picture?"

I couldn't stand to see her so upset. "You hired me to find the answers to those questions, and, damn it, I'm going to find them."

She gave me a weak smile. "Finish your tea."

Typical Judy, I thought. As I drained my cup, I sputtered and picked something off my tongue.

Judy calmly reached over, took my mug, and peered into it.

"Don't tell me you read tea leaves."

She glanced up at me and smiled a little. "Not often, but I picked it up from a woman who lived in my neighborhood back in California. She claimed to be of Gypsy descent." She shrugged. "Who was I to argue? She also read tarot and palms. Fascinating woman. I'm not nearly as good as she was. My Gifts really lie in other areas, but I'm not bad. Or so she said."

"So what do mine say?"

She studied the bottom of my mug for a while before answering. Her face lost all expression, and when she spoke it was in a voice so low I had to strain to hear her. "You're fighting battles on many fronts. Some are within, but others come from without. Some are battles you shouldn't even be fighting, and whether you know it or not, many of the battles are intertwined. There is even one on the horizon that you haven't begun yet, and what you decide about it could greatly affect the others."

I sat for a moment, not sure what to say. "That's a lot of battles." My weak attempt at a joke fell flat. "You got all that from some tea leaves?"

She looked up and smiled tightly, a smile that didn't reach her eyes. "Most of it." She stood up and rinsed the mug out in the sink before turning back to face me. If possible, her eyes were even more troubled than before. "I'm worried about you."

"Why? Because of these battles you're talking about?"

She nodded.

"I'll be fine," I said with more bravado than I actually felt. The truth was, her predictions left me feeling very unsettled. I was wondering what the battles could be. The situation with Micah was one that jumped to mind, and it was probably the internal one she mentioned. What could the external ones be, though? My investigation of Jake? And what was this mysterious future battle? I hated these vague predictions. I never knew what to think of them. One thing I did know: I most certainly did not like all this talk of battles. It sounded awfully violent.

Almost as if she were reading my mind, Judy spoke up. "I'm worried because there's a feeling of death running through all your battles. Not necessarily yours," she added quickly as I felt the blood drain from my face. "Although...it is within the realm of possibility."

I took a deep breath and tried to force a carefree smile. "That's pretty vague, you know. It's not outside the realm of possibility that we could all die tomorrow. I mean, we could die anytime. I could get hit by a drunk driver, or lightning could strike me when I walk outside. No one has any guarantees."

"No, but we can increase our chances of dying by acting foolishly."

"Am I acting foolishly?"

"I don't know. Are you?"

"I don't think so."

"One of the battles you're facing is your refusal to acknowledge your Gift. That's foolish."

"Oh, great, here we go again. Haven't we been over this enough?"

"Obviously not. You still haven't acknowledged it."

"I have acknowledged it. I admit it's there. I just want to ignore it. Isn't that my choice?"

"Sure, and it's also the choice of a natural artist not to draw if they so choose, or someone with a beautiful voice not to sing if they wish, but if they make that choice they're throwing away a beautiful gift that could have been of benefit to others."

"It's not the same."

"Oh, but it is. You were given this Gift for a reason. It's a part of you. You can choose not to use it or to ignore it, but it's still there. By choosing not to use it, you're denying a part of yourself just as people who won't admit they're gay are denying a part of themselves. But unlike choosing not to sing or draw or admit that you're gay, ignoring this Gift could have dire repercussions."

I felt a chill go down my spine. "What kind of repercussions?"

"What you have is essentially an untrained Gift. Whether you like it or not, you have the ability to see things other people can't. You have the ability to communicate with those caught between this world and the next. And that's just the Gift we know about. It's very possible that if you have one, you may have others."

"But how can that have dire repercussions? If I choose not to use my...Gift — and I use the term loosely — what could happen?"

"There is some purpose behind your Gift, something that only you can accomplish. And before you ask, I don't know what that purpose is. I sense it's of great importance, but I don't know more than that."

"Does it involve the battle on the horizon?"

She paused. "No, I don't think so. I think that's a separate issue. I think whatever this purpose is, it's in the distant future. Your decisions now, however, will affect it greatly."

"You mean if I decide to ignore the Gift?"

"The path you choose affects your destination."

I frowned. "That sounds like a fortune cookie."

"But it's very true. The decisions you make now will affect when and how you face your purpose."

"How do I know if I'm making the right decisions?"

"You don't. Not until it's too late to change them."

I suddenly felt very small and insignificant. I didn't like the idea that there was some destiny out there with my name on it — that my life was somehow out of my control. Of course, I still had the choice to ignore the Gift, if you call that a choice. Accept it and fulfill my destiny — whatever that might be — or ignore it and possibly screw up not only my own life but others' as well.

I remembered something Seth told me a long time ago, before he was killed. He said I was at a crossroads then, something he felt was significant because my middle name, Travers, means crossroads. He said that the path I chose would affect the rest of my life, and that there was only one right path for me. I'd thought then that I had chosen the right path, and that was the end of it. I was beginning to realize now that life was really a succession of crossroads, and you had to constantly and consciously choose what path you took. Although there was still only one truly right course, it seemed they all eventually led to the same place. Whichever one I chose would apparently decide how prepared I would be when I got there, or maybe even if I got there at all. One wrong choice and I could wind up dead. Hadn't Judy said that the feeling of death had permeated my fortune? She couldn't be sure it wasn't mine.

I don't know how long I sat there lost in thought before Judy spoke up again. "You can't let yourself be paralyzed by indecision and fear. You have to keep making decisions and fighting your battles. It's entirely possible that the purpose I sense is only within yourself. That wouldn't make it any less important, you know."

I shook off the dark mood I'd been slipping into and gave her a tentative smile. "Obviously, I need to give this a lot of thought."

She smiled, and her eyes showed relief as her whole body relaxed. "It's a good sign that you're willing to think about it at least."

"It doesn't seem like I have much choice."

"You always have a choice, Killian."

"What about you?"

"What about me? I have choices as well."

"No, I mean, what did your tea leaves say?"

Her smile faltered a little as she reached almost reluctantly toward her mug. She examined the dregs, and her smile faded away completely. She was so still and quiet I didn't want to move or make a sound for fear of breaking the spell. Finally, she carefully set the mug down and looked up. I couldn't read the expression in her eyes. It was almost as if she had closed shutters behind them, hiding her emotions from view.

"Well?"

She shook her head slightly. "Don't worry about it."

"But—"

"No, I think that was a message meant for me and me alone. You'd better go before Jake comes home." She grabbed her mug and rinsed it out before I could say another word, almost as if she were trying to wash away whatever it was she'd seen at its bottom.

I stood slowly. Then, taken by a sudden urge, I spun around and grabbed Judy in a tight hug.

She was surprised at first, but quickly returned the hug just as fiercely. "Go," she said after a moment, gently pushing me away. She turned quickly back to the sink, but not before I saw unshed tears flashing in her eyes. What had she seen in that mug that could have caused such a reaction? I wasn't at all sure I wanted to know.

Chapter 9

I sat in my room that night, alternately brooding about — what else? — Micah and my so-called Gifts. The truth was I didn't want to deal with either of them. Generally, my defense system can be best described as the Ostrich Syndrome. I stick my head in the sand and hope the problem goes away. I have to admit this approach seldom works. Actually, it only allows the problem to turn around and bite you on your own exposed ass.

I should know. I've been bitten more than once. Where Micah was concerned, we clearly needed to talk. I just wasn't ready. As for the Gifts, Judy was right. It was vital that I learn how to control them. That didn't mean I had to like them. And what if it just opened the floodgates to more psychic abilities? What would be next? Would I start reading tea leaves too? Would I tell fortunes at carnivals? Or maybe I should shoot for the stars and hope for my own infomercial on TV. People could call in to have me tell them their fortunes for the low, low price of $2.95 a minute.

On second thought, maybe that would be preferable to dealing with the dearly departed.

Someone knocked on my door, causing me to jump a little. "Come in," I called, but no one entered. "Hello?" Still nothing. With a sigh, I got up to check, but the hallway was empty.

"Very funny, Kane," I said. I shut the door and turned back to the bed, only to practically jump out of my skin.

"A bit on edge, aren't we?" Seth asked. He was lying on his side, head propped on one hand, his lips twitching with barely suppressed laughter.

"I suppose that was your idea of a joke."

He shrugged a shoulder. "Well, you said you don't like it when I just appear unannounced, so I knocked this time."

"Admit it. You love scaring me."

"Hey, it's one of the perks of being a ghost."

"If you weren't already dead..."

"Be nice. I came to talk to you."

"And that's supposed to make me want to be nice?"

Seth rolled his eyes expressively and sat up. "Seriously, Killian, we need to talk."

"About what? If this concerns my so-called Gifts, I've already had one lecture about them today. I don't need another."

"Oh, well, I was going to bring that up, but it's not the main reason I'm here. While we're on the subject, though, have you made up your mind about them yet?"

"No, I haven't, and I don't intend to be rushed on this, either."

"Who's rushing you?"

"You, Judy, Adam..."

"It's only because we care."

"I wish you cared a little less."

He frowned. "You don't mean that."

I sighed and sat down next to him on the bed. "No, I don't. Not really. It just gets kind of frustrating sometimes. I feel like I don't even have a choice in the matter."

"Of course you have a choice. We all have choices. Every minute of every day we make choices. And you even have choices within the choices. If you decide to accept your Gifts and learn to use them, what you do with them is still up to you."

"Is it? What about 'My Big Purpose' Judy was talking about?"

His eyes shifted away. "Oh, that."

"Yeah, that." I looked at him closely. "Do you know what it is?"

He shrugged.

"You do, don't you?"

He cleared his throat uneasily. "I've told you before I can't talk about it."

"Oh, for God's sake..."

"Exactly."

That stopped me. Rather hard to argue with deity. "Well, can you at least tell me how long I have to get ready?"

He shook his head, still not meeting my eyes.

I fought down my aggravation. I understood it wasn't Seth's fault. It wouldn't be fair to take out all my frustrations on him. Then another thought occurred to me. "Is this mysterious purpose why you started coming to see me?"

He jerked around to look me in the eye. His surprised expression was all the answer I needed. "W-why would you ask that?"

It was my turn to shrug. "Not too many people get personal visits from their dead friends. If the rules are being bent for me, then there must be some pretty significant reasons behind it."

Seth seemed to be searching for a way to answer me without saying too much. "Not very many people have your Gifts, either."

"And we're back to that."

"It all comes back to that eventually." He sounded apologetic.

"You said that wasn't the main reason you came. What was?"

"This thing with Micah..."

I groaned. "I should have known."

"It's not like that," he said defensively.

"Oh really? So you're not going to tell me not to make snap judgments? You're not going to recommend I talk things out with him? And you're not going to suggest I give him the benefit of the doubt?"

"Ha! You don't know me as well as you think you do. I was also going to say it wouldn't hurt to educate yourself before you made any decisions."

I stuck my tongue out at him and then frowned. "Educate myself?"

"Yes. About escorts."

I made a face. "Why would I want to do that?"

"Because, before you go pulling some sort of holier-than-thou shtick, it might be a good idea if you knew what you're condemning."

"I'm not condemning anything."

"Aren't you?"

"No, I'm not." A pause. "Am I?"

He gave me a look that clearly said, "Figure it out for yourself."

"Why is everything always so hard?" I asked plaintively. He opened his mouth to answer, and I rushed on, "And please don't say I make it hard."

He closed his mouth with a snap and grinned at me. "Then I don't have any other answers."

I grabbed a pillow from behind me and threw it at him. I was more than a little surprised when it went right through him.

"Neat trick, huh?" He gave me a self-satisfied smirk. "Oh, quit gaping. It's really not attractive."

"You know," I said slowly, "I almost forget sometimes that you aren't really here."

"Oh, I'm here. You just forget that I'm not really alive."

"Why is it that you don't bother me, but Amalie does?"

He thought a minute before responding. "Well, you knew me. The fact that we were friends may make it easier. Plus, she and I aren't quite the same thing. Amalie's not here by choice the way I am. She can't just leave whenever she wants to and go back to the other side. She's full of pain and anger, and you can't help sensing that."

"What do you mean, I can't help sensing it? Can anyone sense it?"

"Not...exactly."

"Is it because I can see her?"

"No..." He dragged the word out.

"Is it because I can talk to her?"

"No..."

"Oh, great? Is this another Gift?"

"Possibly."

"Possibly? It either is or isn't. So which is it?"

"I shouldn't have said anything," he said sheepishly.

"Well, you did, so explain what you meant."

"Have you ever heard of empathy?"

"It's kind of like sympathy, right?"

"Close, but not exactly. They both have to do with feelings. With sympathy, you might feel sorry for someone because of something that happened to them, or even relate to them because you've experienced something similar. Empathy goes beyond that to actually feeling another person's emotions, experiencing them for yourself as if they were your own."

"I have that?"

"To some degree. It's part of what makes you such a good investigator."

"How would that help?"

"It usually makes it very easy for you to read other people, to understand their true intentions and judge their character — the way you just get an instant impression about someone."

"Or the way I can sometimes just know someone is lying to me without really knowing why?"

"Yeah. Most of the time it's probably not even something you do consciously. It's pure instinct. It's a part of who you are."

"That seems like it could be a useful Gift."

"They're all useful, Kill. They're tools, just like anything else. Empathy can also be a handicap, though. It can sometimes cloud your judgment. You get so caught up in someone's pain or loss that they can manipulate you, maybe without even trying to."

"Like with Caleb." I'd known instinctively there was something wrong about him, but I'd let his story of abuse and his pain overshadow that...and almost ended up dead in the process.

"Right. Understanding your Gifts, both their strengths and their weaknesses, could help you to avoid similar situations in the future."

"Do I have other Gifts?"

"I don't know."

I gave him a skeptical look.

"Really, I don't. I only knew about the empathy because it's a pretty obvious one, and it's already manifested itself clearly."

"Oh." I was disappointed.

He grinned.

"What?"

"At least I've got you interested now."

"Did you do that on purpose? You manipulated me, didn't you?"

"I honestly didn't."

I had the suspicious feeling that even if Seth hadn't been the one manipulating our conversation, someone somewhere was pulling some strings, and I didn't like the feeling one bit.

Seth stood up. "Well, I've done what I came here to do. I guess I'd better be going."

"Wait," I called, sitting up suddenly.

"What?"

"I still have questions."

"That's what Judy's for."

"Well, don't just vanish. Do you have any idea how creepy that is?"

"Nope." He gave me a broad wink, and then simply wasn't there anymore.

"Jerk!" I yelled at the thin air.

The bedroom door swung open to reveal a rather startled-looking Kane. "What did I do now?"

"I wasn't..." I started to say I hadn't been yelling at him, but realized he would just want to know who I had been yelling at then. It would be difficult to explain that his dead brother had been the subject of my tirade. I tried to think of an excuse, but nothing came quickly enough.

"You know," Kane said with an injured expression, "you're the one who's been a jerk lately. You're always in a bad mood, and I'm really getting sick of it. You're not the only one with problems, you know."

I suddenly felt like the biggest asswipe in the universe. I'd been so caught up in my confusion I hadn't even noticed that Kane was hurting. "Kane, I'm sorry. You're right. I've been selfish and moody. I really am sorry."

He looked somewhat mollified but just gave a noncommittal shrug. He wasn't ready to let me off the hook that easily.

"You want to talk about it?"

"Do you really care?"

"Of course I care. You're my little brother." I patted the bed next to me, the very spot Seth had just vacated.

With a sigh of relief, he shut the door and came to sit next to me on the bed. "It just seems that everything's been going wrong lately."

"Like what?"

"Jen broke up with me, Jake's been acting weird, and it feels like our family is being torn apart."

"Whoa." I didn't even know where to start. I decided to get what I thought to be the easy one out of the way first. "What happened with you and Jen?"

"I dunno. I thought everything was fine, and then suddenly she just dumped me."

"Were you serious about her?"

"No, not really"

"So, it's just a matter of you not being used to being the dumpee instead of the dumper, huh?"

"I guess."

"Is this gonna hurt your rep as the school stud?"

He blushed but looked perversely pleased. "Not really."

"Then what's the big deal?"

"Well, when you put it like that, it's not a big deal at all. She just hurt my feelings. I mean, I didn't even like her that much. I was probably going to break up with her soon anyway."

"So that's what this is all about. It's not even about being dumped. You're just mad because she dumped you first."

He grinned sheepishly. "Okay, yeah. You make me sound so shallow."

I laughed, then quickly turned serious. "What's this about Jake?" It was professional interest, but I tried to keep my voice from betraying more than brotherly concern.

"Well, you know how when he first came back we hung out a little? We weren't best friends or anything, but we did stuff together, and we at least talked. Now, I hardly ever see him anymore, and when I do, he doesn't say a word to me. I started asking around, and all his friends say he's been acting the same way with them. He's either completely ditched them, or he avoids them."

I frowned. Things kept looking worse and worse. What had Jake gotten into? "Do his friends know what's going on?"

Kane shook his head. "Nobody seems to know anything. A couple of them said it was gradual, some said it happened all at once, but whatever's going on, he's done a great job of keeping it secret."

I sighed and decided to bring Kane in on Judy's request. "Judy's worried too."

Kane's eyes widened. "She doesn't know what's going on either?" He had a tendency to think of Judy as some sort of all-knowing oracle. His expression clearly said if she didn't know, then all hope was lost.

"Kane, how could she know? She's another one Jake isn't talking to. He hardly even comes home anymore. In fact, she's so worried she hired me to look into it."

His jaw dropped. "You're investigating Jake?"

"Yeah." I suddenly felt guilty all over again.

Kane blinked a few times, then his expression changed from shocked to thoughtful. "I guess if he isn't telling anyone what's going on, he didn't leave a lot of choice to those of us who care about him."

I was a little surprised by his reaction and didn't know quite what to say.

"I mean, it sounds to me like he's gotten involved with something he doesn't want anyone to know about, right?"

I nodded. "Any ideas?"

He thought for a moment and then shrugged. "Sex? Drugs? Rock and roll? Who knows? He's not dropped any clues as far as I can see."

"I might have found a few clues today, but I still don't know what they mean." I told him about the contents of the box's false bottom.

"Maybe he's selling drugs," he said.

"Then what's the deal with the AIDS Ball, and who's the guy in the picture?"

"Maybe he's hoping to do business at the ball."

I gave him a doubtful look. "With who? The governor?"

"I don't know how this stuff works. Do I look like a drug dealer?"

"What exactly does a drug dealer look like?"

"Good point."

"And that still doesn't answer the other question. Who's that guy?"

"Maybe he's Jake's supplier."

"He didn't look like a supplier. He looked like a politician or somebody important."

Kane frowned. "You don't think he's been hired to kill that guy, do you?"

I couldn't help but burst out laughing. "You think Jake's an assassin?"

Kane grinned. "It sounds pretty stupid when you say it."

"Trust me. It sounded just as stupid when you said it."

"Well, if he's not selling drugs, and he's not a killer-for-hire, where else could he be getting his money?"

"That's not all he could be selling," I said slowly.

"You mean...?" Kane's eyes grew wide. "You think he might be selling his body?"

Micah's story about the ready cash available to escorts came unbidden to my mind. "It's possible. But we shouldn't jump to any conclusions until we know more. I've barely begun to look into this."

"Too bad you can't get into the AIDS Ball. It would be interesting to know why he's going."

I felt a bulb light up over my head. "Who says I can't get in?"

"Kill, there's no way you can afford those tickets."

"No, but Novak has contacts coming out the wazoo."

"Sounds painful. Do you really think he can get you in?"

"I don't know, but I'll find out tomorrow. In the meantime, would you do me a favor? Can you keep your eyes and ears open at school? Listen for any gossip or rumors going around about Jake. Sometimes there can be just enough truth in those to set me in the right direction."

"No problem."

"And Kane, I don't have to tell you to keep quiet about this, right? I mean you can't tell anyone."

"No duh, Killian. I'm not a dumb little kid anymore. I'm not that much younger than you, you know."

"Sorry. You know I'm really proud of you."

"Actually, I didn't know that."

"Really?"

"Yeah, really. We're not as close as we used to be. None of us are."

"Is that what you meant when you said you felt like the family is falling apart?"

"Yeah. I hardly ever see Steve anymore. He's at the stupid B&B so much. And Dad's almost as bad. When they're here, they're so busy they don't have time to spend with me. Now I sound like a little kid, and right after I just said I was so grown up..."

"No, you don't sound like a little kid. I know what you mean. And I've been just as bad. I've been so busy with school and work and...Micah that I haven't spent any time with you."

He nodded. "I know."

"Well, now that I realize what a jerk I've been, we're going to spend more time together. You should talk to Adam and Steve, too."

"They don't need any extra stress right now." He suddenly sounded very mature indeed. "Especially after what happened the other night."

"What did happen, anyway?" I suddenly felt guilty for not having asked sooner.

"Amalie," he said, as if that answered everything.

"What about her?"

"It was the first weekend they've had almost every room full, and she decided to make an appearance."

"Oh no. Did everyone see her?"

"No, it was just one couple, but they raised bloody hell. They had everyone in the whole house completely freaked out. Dad was there because it was such a big crowd, so between him and Steve, they managed to calm everyone down for the most part, but several couples still left...and demanded their money back."

"Great. Poor Steve. He's been stressed out enough as it is."

"I know. That's why I don't want to say anything right now. I'll wait until things settle down there."

"What if things don't settle down?"

He shrugged. "Then I'll suffer in silence." He stood up and started for the door. "I'm a big boy, remember? I can live without my daddy."

I sighed and flopped back onto the bed. Just what I needed: more guilt about not using my Gifts. It seemed the Powers That Be were conspiring against me, and I was quite certain I wasn't happy about it at all.

My plans to ask Novak about the AIDS Ball were postponed the next morning. As soon as I walked through the door, I knew it was going to be one of those days. The tiny reception area that held my desk and two hideous orange chairs was filled to overflowing. A woman I had never seen before was perched nervously on the edge of one of the chairs, clutching her purse like a shield.

Another woman I recognized as the wife of the philandering Mr. Knox was busy yelling at Novak — apparently over some of the charges on her bill. This was a common-enough occurrence. If you came back with good news, they were only too happy to pay, but come back with bad news...

The other occupants of the room were our delivery guy from UPS and a man from one of the insurance companies that Novak did some work for from time to time. He'd been in often enough that I should have known him by sight, but he was so nondescript I could never quite remember what he looked like from visit to visit. He was the type of person you forgot as soon as he was out of sight — or maybe even before.

It was about four-too-many people to fit comfortably into the already claustrophobic space. I dealt with the UPS guy first, signing for the package so he could leave. Then I ushered the insurance agent into Novak's office to wait there. By the time I'd done that, Novak had somehow managed to calm Mrs. Knox down and even gotten a check out of her.

Once she was gone, Novak disappeared into his office, leaving only the small birdlike woman on the chair. She looked rather frightened. I got the impression she would have bolted long ago if there hadn't been so many people between her and the exit. Even after it was just the two of us, she kept darting little glances in the direction of the door, as if she were still debating flight.

"Can I help you?" I asked, causing her to jump a little.

"Um, I, uh, don't know..." She peered longingly at the door.

"Are you looking for a private investigator?"

Her pale-blue eyes shifted to me for a brief second, but quickly slid away again. "Maybe."

She was not the most definite creature I'd ever met. "Would you feel more comfortable talking directly with Mr. Novak?" Sometimes people who had matters of a sensitive nature didn't want to spill their guts to someone they assumed to be the secretary...and who looked like a kid, besides.

She nodded timidly.

"What's your name? I'll let him know you're here as soon as he's available." She'd seen him go into the office with the insurance agent, so she knew he was busy at the moment.

Her eyes grew large at the seemingly simple request. "I, uh...I'd rather not. Maybe...uh, maybe this wasn't a good idea."

She made a move to get up, and I quickly smiled soothingly — at least, I hoped it was a soothing smile. She was still looking at me as if she half-expected me to leap across the desk at her.

"If you'd rather not give your name, that's fine. It happens all the time here."

"Really?" She lowered her bottom back to the chair, although she still stayed perched right at the edge, where a sudden getaway would be easier should the need arise.

"Really," I assured her. She seemed to relax the slightest bit, until the door flew open again, and she flinched as if expecting an attack.

It was Micah.

"Hey," I said in surprise. "What are you doing here?"

He gave me a funny look that I couldn't quite read. "I came to talk to you."

"I..." I glanced toward the woman, who was trying desperately to pretend she wasn't there. "I'm not sure I'm ready to talk."

He sighed. "Relax, Killian. I'm not here to talk about that."

"Then what do you want to talk about?"

"I want to hire you."

Chapter 10

"W-what?" I must have heard him wrong. "What did you say?"

"I said," he spoke slowly, over-enunciating each word, "I want to hire you."

"To do what?"

He sent a meaningful look in the direction of the room's other occupant, who was staring at the purse in her lap as if it was the most fascinating thing she'd ever seen.

Before I could come up with a suggestion, the door to the inner office swung open and the insurance company representative came out, followed closely by my boss. "We appreciate your work, Mr. Novak," the agent said. "As always, you completed the assignment ahead of schedule and to your usual standards of excellence. We'll be in touch when we find ourselves in need of your services again."

"Let's hope for your sake that isn't too soon," Novak said genially.

The plain little man let himself out while Novak cast a curious glance in the direction of his next visitor.

"This lady is waiting to see you privately."

She smiled gratefully at me as she followed him into his office.

As soon as the door closed I turned back to Micah. "Well?"

He took a deep breath. "I want you to look into Paul's murder."

I sat for a second staring dumbly back at him. "You want me to investigate the murder of your ex-boyfriend?" I asked slowly, making sure I had this right.

"Yes."

"You don't think that's asking a lot?"

"I don't know. Is it? If Asher was murdered, wouldn't you want to know the truth? I need to find out what really happened to Paul so I can move on completely."

"I thought you already had."

"This is different. Now it feels like unfinished business."

"What about the police?"

He grimaced. "Apparently they aren't trying very hard."

I frowned. "What gives you that idea?"

"I know people back in the city, people in positions of authority. I called them to verify what Razi had told me. It seems the murder of a known male escort isn't very high on the police's list of priorities. There's no family demanding justice, and the public couldn't care less. There's enough crime in the city that something like this tends to get pushed to the back burner, especially if it isn't an open-and-shut case. They just don't have the manpower on the police force."

"So you want me to find out who killed him?"

He nodded. "I'll hire you as if I were any other client."

"I don't know if I'm the right person for this, Micah."

"I think you are. You've done this before. More than once, even. Everyone says you're already one of the best."

"That was on my home turf, so to speak. They were all local. I'm familiar with the area. I don't know anything about the city."

"You might not know the city, but I do. I'll help you."

"What if you don't like what I find?"

"Then I'll deal with it. At least I'll have the truth."

I shook my head. "I wouldn't have any idea where to start."

"I do. I know names, friends, people at the agency, places he hung out. I even have a key to his apartment — assuming he didn't change the locks after I left."

I was running out of arguments. Despite myself, I was becoming interested. Up until the Knox case, everything I'd done had been local. If I was any good as an investigator, I should be able to solve a case anywhere. This would be the perfect test of my skills.

Then there was the part about Micah's being able to have closure. If I wanted to try and make things work with him — which I had to admit I did — helping him find it might be necessary. I still wasn't certain we could work things out, but I was pretty sure we wouldn't have a chance if he was obsessed with the fate of his ex-boyfriend.

I sighed. "Tell me what you know."

Relief flooded Micah's eyes. "Thank you, Killian." His voice was filled with sincerity. He grabbed one of the chairs and pulled it closer to the desk.

"Don't thank me yet," I muttered.

He took a deep breath. "Let's see. I don't know that much, really. He was still working for the same agency we were with when we met. It's a pretty well-respected business as far as such things go, with a reputation for being reliable and discreet. The owner's name is Neal. I've talked to him on the phone, although I never actually met him. He tends to keep a low profile."

As he spoke, I was jotting everything down in the little notebook I kept with me at all times. One of the first things Novak ever taught me was never to trust my memory.

"So far as I'm aware," he continued, "he's not dated anyone seriously since I left. He was friends with that guy we saw at the club, Razi. He was pretty cozy with one of his neighbors, a really nice girl named Sabrina. He had a few other casual friends but not many. He was kind of shy when he wasn't working. He was a favorite with guys who like the sweet, quiet type.

"He was...Razi found him in his apartment." Micah broke off, and his eyes unfocused as he tried to continue. "When no one heard from him for a few days, Razi went by and...I guess he had a key, too. He called the police. They showed up and did their thing. I don't really know the details, just what he told me the other night. Paul...was strangled. I, uh, do know that. And the apartment was trashed — stuff broken and tossed around."

"Do the police have any theories?"

He blinked and focused on me, almost as if he'd forgotten I was there. "Um, not that I'm aware of. Razi said at first they thought he'd walked in on a robbery, but they kinda dropped that theory when nothing seemed to be missing."

"You do understand that if it turns out to be some botched random break-in, I'll never be able to figure out who it was."

"Yes. I understand, Killian. Just please..."

I took a deep breath. "Tell me more about Paul."

"How do you mean?"

"What was he like? Was he secretive? Who would he be most likely to confide in?"

He thought a minute before answering. "He wasn't exactly secretive, but he kept a lot to himself."

"What's the difference?"

"It wasn't that he would intentionally hide stuff from me, he just wasn't one to open up. Although he didn't talk about himself much, he was a great listener. You'd find yourself telling him your whole life story, spilling your guts. He'd take in everything you said and somehow make you feel better. It was only later that I realized he never did the talking. He never spilled his guts to me."

"So he wouldn't confide in anyone?"

He shrugged. "If so, I don't know who. He sure never confided in me."

"I know I asked this before, but I want you to really think about this before you answer. What if I find something you don't like? What if he was involved in something illegal — er, besides just being an escort? What if he wasn't who you thought he was at all? Are you sure you want me to do this?"

"Yes. I'm sure. No matter what you find, at least I'll know the truth."

I nodded. That was the answer I was looking for. "Then I'll talk to Novak about it."

"Novak?" he asked with a confused expression.

"I work for him. I can't just take a job. I have to get his approval."

"Oh. Well, okay. When?"

"When I get the chance, Micah. He's with someone right now."

"Oh, yeah. Will you call me as soon as you find out?"

"Yeah," I promised wearily, suddenly wondering if I was doing the right thing even thinking about this.

"Thank you, Killian." He stood up and pushed the chair back to its place before turning to me again. "You can't imagine how much this means to me."

I appeared to be committed now whether I liked it or not. And the more I thought about it the less I liked it. Could I truly be objective? I wasn't acquainted with anyone involved except Micah, whose participation would be peripheral at best — or so I hoped. On the other hand, Paul was Micah's ex, the guy he'd once lived with, made love to, been in love with. Even assuming I could be objective, my argument that I didn't know the city was still valid. Someone familiar with city life would have an edge on a country boy like me. Someone who knew something about the escort agency would be even better.

A little voice inside my head argued that I'd have Micah for those things. He'd lived in the city for years, so he knew it as well as anyone, and he definitely was familiar with the escort agency.

No, it wouldn't be that easy. I wasn't sure I wanted Micah along as I investigated his dead former lover. It would be hard enough without having to see his emotional turmoil at every turn. Unfortunately, I didn't have any other contacts in the DC area, and without one, I couldn't take the case.

However, Micah would be crushed if I refused. It would probably be the end of any chance we had at anything. I was beginning to feel like a fox cornered by the hounds.

Then the thought occurred to me that Novak might not approve of the idea of my going off to DC on my own to chase a murderer. In fact, he might even forbid me to go. Maybe there was a way out of this yet.

Novak was in the office with the mysterious woman for what seemed to be an unusually long time. When the door opened at last, I thought she looked just as uneasy as she had when they'd gone in. Whatever had taken so long didn't seem to have helped with her nerves.

They crossed the room without speaking, and Novak held the door open for her.

"Thank you," she said in a small voice.

"You're welcome, and try not to worry," Novak said.

She cast him a look that clearly spoke her feelings about the chances of not worrying. Then she turned and scurried off, seeming to draw in on herself as she went.

Novak closed the door and turned to me. "Busy morning."

"That's an understatement. Do you have a minute to talk?"

"Sure, let's go in here."

I followed him into his office and took one of the leather chairs. He closed a case file that was open on his desk and slid it into a drawer. That struck me as a little odd, since I usually typed the files for him from his handwritten notes.

"Is that lady who just left a new client?" I knew from experience there was no point asking about the file straight out.

"Yes, I'll be handling her case."

"I don't have any cases right now," I said — at least none he knew of.

"This is a rather delicate situation."

"What do you mean?"

"I'm afraid I promised her complete confidentiality."

"Even from me?" I was a little offended.

"Yes, even from you." He stopped and grinned. "And don't go acting like you're the injured party here." He paused dramatically. "How's your investigation of Jake going?"

My mouth fell open. "How'd you find out about that?"

Novak laughed. "You think I'm not aware of what's going on under my own nose? I wouldn't be much of an investigator if I couldn't keep track of what my own employees were up to."

"You followed me?"

"No, nothing that dramatic. I knew something was bothering Judy, and I knew you were up to something besides your assigned case. I asked Judy point blank what was going on and, when she confessed her concern about Jake, it was clear she was holding something back. I put two and two together and came up with you. I didn't know for sure until just now, though."

"You aren't mad?"

"Why would I be mad?"

"That I took the case without talking to you? Or that I took the case at all?"

"I wish you'd talked to me first, but I know how persuasive Judy can be. And if you're worrying that I'm bothered about her asking you instead of me, don't be. I understand her reasoning and agree one-hundred percent."

"You do?" I asked with no small relief.

"Yes, absolutely. Things are dicey enough between Jake and me as it is. If Jake found out I was following him, the whole situation would just go all to hell."

I frowned. "Not that it'll be much better if he finds out I'm following him."

"Still, better you than me. So what did you want to talk about?"

"A couple of things, actually. Since you know about Jake, it'll make the first one that much easier." I told him about my search of Jake's room and my discoveries.

When I was finished, he thought for a minute. "Well, what you found could have several different explanations, but I don't like any of them. You still haven't told me what you wanted to talk about, though."

That was Novak, always going right to the point. "The two things that bother me the most are the photo and the AIDS Ball ticket. They don't fit in with the theories I have. I can't do much about the picture, but I could do something about the Ball."

"And what would that be?"

"I could attend."

Novak cocked an eyebrow. "And just how do you propose to get a ticket at this point?"

"That's what I wanted to talk to you about," I said with an impish grin.

He pushed back in his chair. For a minute I thought he was going to tell me there was no way, but then his expression grew thoughtful. "I might be able to do something. I'll look into it and let you know."

"Great!"

"Don't get your hopes up. That thing is not easy to get into."

"I know."

"No, you have no idea. Anyway, what else did you want to talk about? You said you had several things?"

"Well, actually, there's just one more thing..."

Something in my tone must have set off Novak's internal alarms. "And what exactly would that one thing be?"

"It has to do with Micah."

"Will you stop beating around the bush and get to the point, kid?"

"Well, Micah's...um, old roommate..."

"Meaning ex-lover."

I tried not to blush. "Right. Ahem. Well, Micah's ex...boyfriend was murdered last week. He lived in DC."

"And what does that have to do with you?"

"Micah wants me to look into the murder."

"No."

"What?" I was surprised at the firmness in his curt answer, even though I'd been half-hoping that would be his response.

"A murder is a matter for the police. You don't need to go sticking your nose into it."

"You didn't mind it when we were looking into the murder of Caleb's dad." Why was I arguing? He'd given me the answer I wanted. Why couldn't I just leave it alone?

"That was a different set of circumstances. The police were at a standstill in their investigation. It even seemed they were chasing the wrong guy. Plus, they welcomed our assistance."

"Maybe the DC police would welcome the assistance, too. They're really overworked, and besides, they aren't even trying to solve this case."

"How do you know so much about the police in DC?"

"Micah has contacts. They told him the murder of a known escort wasn't high on their list of priorities."

Novak nodded as if that made sense. "An escort, huh? And he's Micah's ex?"

I blushed again, but thankfully, he didn't seem to expect an answer.

"Why you? Wouldn't a PI from the city be a better choice?"

"That's what I said, but Micah really seems to want me to do this."

"But you don't know DC at all."

"Micah does. He said he'd help."

"That would make a big difference. How familiar is he with the escort business?"

"Uh, very," I said, trying not to blush yet again.

"That would put you at a distinct advantage." He seemed to be thinking for a minute. "There's only one major problem left."

"What's that?"

"You don't have a license yet. Micah can't hire you."

"Oh." I hadn't even thought of that.

"There is a way around it," Novak said.

"There is?"

"Micah can hire me, and I'll assign you the investigation."

"We can do that?"

"It's the same as what we did with the Knox case. You'll just report everything back to me. You'll need someone to hash things out with anyway. And if you get in over your head, I'll step in and help."

"That's pretty much a given," I said.

"Don't sell yourself short, kid. You're a good investigator. A little more time and you'll be a great one."

I flushed with pleasure at his praise.

"So I should tell Micah it's a go?"

"Sure. Just type up the contract and have him sign it. You can begin right away."

"Great." I jumped up and started for my desk in the outer room.

"One more thing," he called, stopping me at the door. "I know I said I'd help you if you got in over your head, and I will, but the new case I just took could be demanding a lot of my time. Don't plan on using me as a crutch. You'll be on your own for the most part."

I gulped a little, but nodded. "Okay."

Novak smiled. "You can do this, kid. Don't worry."

I left his office flattered at his faith in me, though more than a little miffed at myself. Why had I argued him into this? Of course, it hadn't really taken that much arguing. I was suddenly suspicious. Was Novak trying to get me out of his hair? And if so, could it have something to do with the mysterious, birdlike woman who was now his client?

I decided that fretting about it wouldn't serve any purpose at all, and I could certainly make better use of my time. I started off by calling Micah to get all the information I could from him: names, addresses, and details he hadn't told me before. While we were speaking, it occurred to me once again that having Micah along on the interviews would probably be more of a hindrance than a help. He was definitely too close to this, too emotional. People would be less likely to talk in front of him, to say things about Paul that he might not want to hear. At the same time, I didn't know my way around the city as well as he did. I had no idea how to find any of the places on my list.

When I posed the question to Micah, he agreed it would probably be best if he didn't go along to interview people. He didn't have any suggestions for a solution.

Novak unexpectedly provided the answer while I was still talking to Micah. "Good news, kid. I just got off the phone with an old buddy of mine who transferred to the DC department. He confirmed what you said about the police not being overly interested in this case. He also offered to give us a hand in exchange for a few favors."

"What kind of help?" I asked with more than a little suspicion. "And more importantly, what does he want in return?"

"You get more like me every day." Novak chuckled. "You don't have to worry about his price. It involves a few tins of Fisher's caramel corn and our combined weight in Dolle's saltwater taffy." The caramel corn and taffy were both world-famous treats available from the boardwalk in the nearby resort town of Ocean City, but not in the DC area where Novak's friend lived. "Those gifts will buy you a personal guide to the city."

"Huh?"

"My friend, Louis Silver, has a daughter around your age who's driving him crazy wanting to become a cop. He thinks her partnering with you for this investigation will cure her of that idea without placing her in any immediate danger."

"How will that cure her?" I was confused. My early experiences playing junior detective had only solidified my desires to become a PI.

"Once she sees how boring a routine investigation is, he thinks she'll change her mind. Plus, this case has the added bonus of being somewhat unsavory. He said she's been a little sheltered, and exposure to the darker side of the city might scare her off."

"Darker side? He was an escort, not a street prostitute."

Novak waved off my arguments. "The only difference is how much they get paid."

"Spoken like a true ex-cop," Micah's voice growled into my ear. I realized he'd been listening to the whole conversation over the phone.

"Well, what's my guide's name, and how soon is she available?" I asked, ignoring Micah for the moment.

"Her name is Christina, and Louis has to talk to her first. He's supposed to call back later this afternoon. He seemed to think she'd be ready to go when you are."

"I hope so. I'd like to get started tomorrow, if possible."

"We'll see what Louis has to say."

After promising to give Micah a heads-up as soon as I knew what was going on, I finished my paperwork so I'd be free for the rest of the week. It was mid-afternoon before Novak's friend phoned to say his daughter was all for the arrangement and could start the next day. We agreed that I'd park outside DC at one of the metro stations and meet her in the city.

With that settled, I called Micah back and told him the plan. *Well, I thought as I hung up, I've committed myself now. There's no turning back.*

What had I gotten myself into? A murder investigation in a city I knew nothing about?

I did have a new partner, though — a strong-willed girl from the sound of it. I'd partnered with girls in an investigation twice before, and neither arrangement had turned out well, to say the least. The first time had been with Jake's sister, Gilly, who'd pretended to be my girlfriend while I tried to figure out who killed Seth. Except, even though we'd agreed up front that we'd be dating in name only, she'd developed a crush on me, which turned to anger and hurt when I couldn't return her feelings. It had complicated things greatly, and in the end, she was just one more victim for a serial killer.

The next girl I worked with turned out to be a serial killer. I definitely hadn't had much luck with female partners in the past. This was going to be an uphill battle all the way.

The thought of a battle made me recall Judy's ominous predictions. Could this be one of the conflicts Judy mentioned in our tealeaf-reading session? Or was I just being paranoid after all her talk of battles and death? I could only hope I was being paranoid.

Chapter 11

Visions of medieval combat filled my dreams that night: horrible scenes of unkempt, empty-eyed men slashing, chopping, and clubbing each other on a bloody battlefield. Needless to say, I awoke the next morning less than refreshed. Rolling out of bed with a groan, I stumbled to the bathroom. It was not an auspicious beginning to the first day of my investigation into the death of Micah's ex.

I was supposed to drive up to DC that morning to meet Christina, my new partner in crime. The way I was feeling, though, I wondered if that was the wisest course of action. It was as if I'd been fighting in the dream battle myself — and judging by the state of my head, I'd been hit by a flying flail.

I felt a little better after a shower, enough so I decided to go ahead with the original plan. I forced down a slice of toast even though I wasn't hungry, then set off in my little black Mustang that I affectionately called Shadow.

The drive up Route 50 could never be described as exciting...or, for that matter, even interesting. The land of the Eastern Shore is astonishingly flat. While some of it is incredibly beautiful, those bits don't, for the most part, touch that particular stretch of highway. The highlight, as usual, was the huge span of bridge that crossed the Chesapeake Bay.

I arrived at the New Carrolton Metro station by late morning. Since that was the first stop on the line, the train was almost empty and I had no trouble finding a seat. While we thundered along the tracks, pausing every few minutes to allow more commuters to board, I thought idly about my responsibility to my Gifts. Although I still wasn't especially happy about them, I finally knew I had to face and accept them the best I could, whatever they might be. I owed that much to Steve and Adam.

I sighed. That meant I had to meet up with my old pal Amalie again. I could think of a few things I'd rather do — such as have all my teeth extracted. I wasn't even sure what I was supposed to do. Talk to her? How did I do that? Did I ask her to sit down over a cup of coffee? Would it be the way it was with Seth? My heart started racing just thinking about it.

As the train rumbled into the underground tunnels of the Metro system, the bright sunlight was suddenly cut off, and the scene from *Ghost* where Patrick Swayze is chasing the other dead guy through subway cars suddenly came to mind. I quickly decided to think about something else.

Of course, the next thing that came to mind was Micah. What was I going to do about him? I was pretty sure I wanted to make our relationship work. He was a great guy. So what if he had a checkered past? I'd known that from the beginning. Why, then, was the whole escort deal still bothering me so much? The even bigger question was: Why the hell was I looking into the murder of his ex-boyfriend? It occurred to me for the first time that maybe I was doing this because I wanted to know more about the guy Micah used to love — and, on some level, always would.

I didn't like where that line of thought was going, so I decided to run over my game plan for the day. I wanted to find Razi and talk to him first. He'd given Micah his business card. It was minimalist, to say the least, bearing only his first name in large, bold letters and his phone number beneath. I was planning to call him, remind him who I was, and with any luck, get him to either meet me or tell me how to find him.

After that, I wanted to take a look at Paul's apartment. I had Micah's old key in my pocket and could only hope it still fit the lock. If not, I wasn't sure what I would do, but I'd come up with something. I also hoped Christina would be willing to go along with whatever I said and not try to run the show herself.

I was supposed to get off the Metro at the Smithsonian station and rendezvous with Christina at the base of the Washington Monument. She'd said I would recognize her because she'd be dressed all in black. How cheery. The way things were going there'd probably be a convention of Goths at the monument when I got there.

When we pulled into the cavernous underground station, its arched ceiling honeycombed to muffle the roar of the trains and the crowds, I allowed the flow of people to carry me toward the escalator leading to street level in the center of the Mall. The Capitol building sat at one end of it, and my goal — the Washington Monument — at the other. Museums lined both sides: the buildings of the Smithsonian, the National Gallery, and many more. I wondered why it had been so long since I'd been there. DC really wasn't that far from where I lived. I guess I just took it for granted.

When I reached the base of the towering obelisk, I started around its perimeter looking for a girl dressed all in black. It didn't take long to find her. Before she noticed me, I stopped a moment to look her over. She was about my height, thin but wiry. She was wearing a loose-fitting, long-sleeved black T-shirt, baggy black cargo pants, and black combat boots. Her hair was dyed black, cut short, and worn spiked. All that black made her skin look even paler than it really was, and it was pretty pale to start with. What's more, she didn't appear to be wearing a scrap of make-up. She looked like one of the dead people with whom I was supposed to be able to talk. She did not inspire confidence.

I gave a purely mental sigh and approached her. As soon as she saw me moving in her direction, she locked a pair of steely gray eyes on me. "Are you Killian?" she asked in a low voice as soon as I was close enough to hear her.

I nodded. "You must be Christina."

"You can call me Chris."

"Hi, Chris." I smiled my biggest smile, but her sober expression didn't waver. "I'm impressed you recognized me."

"Well, your boss said to watch for a pretty little blond boy. He didn't mention you were gay, but if he had, it would have made it even easier."

I blinked in surprise. "I'm gay?" I repeated stupidly.

She blinked back at me. "You didn't know?"

I fought the urge to let loose a hysterical giggle. "Um, yeah, I knew. I meant, how did you know?"

She shrugged. "I have a good sense about people."

"Do I act gay?"

She frowned. "How does one 'act gay'?"

We were not getting off on the right foot. I gathered my wits about me and started over. "Forget I asked that. I'm glad you're helping me out on this case. I really appreciate it."

"No problem. My dad thinks this will make me change my mind about becoming a cop, among other things."

I wondered at the other things, but thought it best not to ask.

"I'm old enough to make my own decisions, though," she said, "and I've wanted to be a cop as long as I can remember." She shrugged again. "How old are you anyway? You look younger than me."

"I'm eighteen."

"We're the same age then. You in college?"

"Freshman year."

"Me too. Where?"

"Pemberton U." She started at me blankly, so I added, "It's on the Eastern Shore. What about you?"

"George Mason."

Thoughts of Asher swept through my mind — George Mason University was where he'd ended up going — but I tamped them down quickly. What were the chances she'd know him?

"Okay, enough chitchat," she said suddenly. "Time to get to work. You're the boss. What's the plan?"

I gave another mental sigh, this time of relief. At least she was willing to let me keep control of the investigation and follow my lead. I'd been worried that she'd be the controlling type.

"I need to try this number and see if I can get him to meet with me," I said, producing the card. She looked it over and gave me a look with a raised eyebrow.

"Let me guess. Judging by the lack of specified occupation, this Razi must be in the sex-for-hire business."

I was impressed. The girl was sharp. "Escort."

"Close enough," she said flippantly. "And before you get too impressed, Dad told me the case had something to do with a dead prostitute, so it was an obvious deduction. That's pretty much all I know, though, so why don't you give me a quick rundown of exactly what you're trying to do."

I did, briefly explaining Micah's involvement with Paul and how he'd found out about his murder, adding everything I knew about Paul from what Micah had told me. I was about to mention how the police were refusing to do more than a cursory investigation before I remembered that her father was on the city police force. I stopped in midword as her expression darkened.

"Don't stop," she said. "Not that it matters. I can figure out the rest. The police don't have any interest in catching whoever killed the fag, right?"

"Something like that."

"Figures. That's why I want to be a cop, to stop shit like that from happening. It's disgusting."

I was startled by the vehemence in her voice but tried not to let it show. Instead, I pulled out my cell phone and punched in Razi's number. I was just about to end the connection when someone finally answered.

"'ullo?" It sounded as if I'd woken him up.

"Is this Razi?"

"No."

I waited a beat. "May I speak to him?"

"He's not here."

The voice was vaguely familiar, and I realized it must be the kid from the club. What was his name? "Is this Tad?"

A pause. "Who's this?" the voice suddenly sounded more awake, and more than a little startled.

"Do you remember last week at Michelangelo? I was with the guy Razi knew. You talked to me in the lounge."

"Um...it's a little hazy."

I was going to have to work for this. "My name is Killian. My friend's name is Micah."

Another pause. "What do you look like?"

"Blond hair, blue eyes, a little taller than you."

"Still nothing."

I gritted my teeth and took a deep breath. "You told me that my boyfriend used to be an escort."

"Oh. Yeah. Now I remember. You're cute."

I bit back a sharp retort and took another deep breath instead. "Thanks," I managed. "Look, it's very important that I speak to Razi. Do you know when he'll be back?"

"Not really. He's on a job. What do you need to talk to him about?"

"It's kind of personal. I'd rather tell him about it."

"Does it have to do with your boy? What's his name? Mikey?"

"Micah, and no...not exactly."

"Oh. Well, does it have anything to do with Paul?"

"You knew Paul?"

"Kinda. I wasn't around that long before he was killed, but I met him a few times."

Novak always told me being flexible was the most important attribute of a good investigator. It would probably be useful for an escort, also, but that was beside the point. It was time to change my plans slightly. "Could I talk to you?"

He was quiet for a minute. "I dunno."

"I'm not going to cause trouble. I promise. It's really important."

"Why?"

"Micah wants to know what happened to Paul."

"He was killed."

"We know that. He wants to know why."

"I don't know that."

"But you might be able to help me figure it out."

"You? Shouldn't that be up to the— Shit! You're not the cops, are you?"

"Me?" I laughed. It was somewhat forced, but I didn't think it was noticeable, especially to someone who didn't know me. "No way. I'm a private investigator."

"Aren't you a little young?"

"Well, I'm technically still in training, but I've already helped solve three murders." I saw Chris's head snap up at that remark, her eyes widening with a new respect for me. "Besides, the cops don't give a damn about Paul. To them, he's just another gay escort, and as far as they're concerned, the city's better off without him. If I don't find out who did this, no one ever will."

There was dead silence on the other end of the line and, for a minute, I thought he'd hung up. Then, finally, he spoke. "Okay. If I give you directions, can you find me here?"

"Yes," I replied without hesitation. I signaled to Chris to get her attention. "I'm going to repeat the address back to you so I'm sure I have it right, okay?" I spoke for both of their benefits. I wanted Chris to pay attention so that she could tell me if she knew where the address was, and I wanted Tad to know why I was repeating everything. Chris nodded her understanding. I was beginning to think we might work well together after all.

"Okay." Tad rattled off an address, which I repeated right back. Chris nodded. She knew where it was.

"Got it," I said. "You'll be there for a while?"

"I'm not going anywhere."

"Okay, good. I'll see you soon then. And, Tad? Thanks."

"Yeah. You might want to hold your thanks until after you talk to me. I told you I didn't know him that well."

"Every little bit helps."

"We'll see." He broke the connection.

I turned to Chris as I put the phone away. "And we're off."

"We'll take the Metro." She stalked off purposefully in the direction I'd come from, leaving me to scamper behind. "It's not a great neighborhood," she said when I caught up to her.

"Dangerous?"

She looked at me out of the corner of her eye. "Everywhere in the city is dangerous — or it can be. Where we're going is only dangerous in a different way. Keep your eyes open and stay near me."

I must have given her a startled look, because she broke out in the first genuine smile I'd seen. "My dad's a cop. I've had every type of self-defense training you can imagine. I may not look all that dangerous, but, trust me, I am."

Something in the tone of her voice made me inclined to believe her.

We got our fare cards figured out and boarded the train. We would have to backtrack to L'Enfant station and switch from the Orange Line to the Green. The trip wasn't really that far, and we didn't talk much. I was preoccupied, thinking about how Chris had known right away I was gay. Did I really act so stereotypically gay that people could tell just by looking at me? I'd never thought about it before, but for some reason it bothered me. For one thing, it would make me less effective as an investigator because I'd be more memorable if someone happened to notice me.

"Gaydar," Chris said abruptly.

I gave her a blank look.

"That's how I knew you were gay when I saw you."

I eyed her warily. I had the eerie feeling she'd been reading my mind.

"I've been sitting here thinking about it," she said, "and I decided that if we're going to be working together, we need to trust each other, right?"

I nodded.

"I'm gay too."

"Oh." I frowned. I wondered if my own gaydar was malfunctioning.

"I don't usually tell people. Not that I'm in the closet or anything. I just don't advertise it. That's the other reason I suspect Dad wanted me to work with you on this. He thinks if I see the dark side of the gay culture, as he puts it, then I'll decide to be straight. I've tried to tell him it's not like prostitution is only a gay thing, and being gay isn't a decision anyway, but he's older, set in his ways. Besides, it's not like I don't already know all about this stuff. You can only be sheltered so much when you grow up gay in the city." With that she hopped up and started toward the door. "This is our stop," she called over her shoulder.

I hurried to join her just as the train came to a halt. After we left the station, Chris took her bearings.

"Where do we go now?" I asked.

"I'm not sure."

"But I thought—"

"I know it's this general area. Don't worry, I'll find it." She dashed back into the Metro station, leaving me gaping after her. She reappeared a minute later and headed off confidently down the street. I scrambled after her with a feeling I'd be doing that a lot.

"I got directions," she said when I fell into step next to her.

"Yeah, I figured that," I said.

She walked as if she knew exactly where she was going, her ground-eating stride causing me to trot along. It seemed as though I had to take two steps for every one of hers. At that rate, it didn't take too long to find the address Tad had given me. Like most of the buildings in this area, it was run down and a little shabby.

Chris stopped at the main entrance. "He's on the second floor?" she asked.

"Yeah."

"Okay, so what's the plan now? Do I go in with you or do I stand guard?"

I shrugged. I hadn't really thought that far ahead.

"There're advantages to both. If I go in with you, I might pick up on something you miss, but if I stay outside, then I can get help if something goes wrong."

I didn't even want to think about the sorts of things that might go wrong. However, I'd been in situations without backup before, and I knew how important it could be. "Maybe you should be lookout." I was a little worried she wouldn't be happy with that, but she just nodded.

"I'll follow you up to the second floor and keep out of sight until you're in the room, then I'll stay near the door. If anything goes wrong, you just scream like a banshee, and I'll get help."

I smiled weakly and crossed my fingers that we wouldn't have to put that plan into action. I led the way up the dingy stairwell. Chris stopped just out of sight, according to plan, while I rapped on the metal door.

"Yeah?" came a muffled response from the other side.

"Tad? It's Killian Kendall, we talked on the phone?" There was a pause long enough to allow him to peer through the peephole before he released the locks. The door opened a few inches, still attached to the frame by a thick chain.

"Are you alone?" Tad asked. From the two-inch slice of him in view, he was bare-chested and tousle-headed.

"Um, yes," I fibbed.

The door shut for a second, then reopened just wide enough to allow me to slide in. Tad quickly hooked the chain back in place and shot the locks home. I began to feel a little trapped and fought a rising sense of unease.

He turned to catch my uncomfortable expression. "I've lived here less than a month, and I've been mugged twice and beat up once," he said in a carefully casual voice. "I'm a little concerned with security. I hope you don't mind."

"I, uh, guess I can't blame you." I tried not to stare at him. He was wearing nothing but a pair of workout shorts, and I got the impression that he'd only pulled those on to be polite. His body was pale, slender, and taut with just the slightest hint of definition. His reddish-blond curls were springier than the last time I'd seen him, making the halo effect even more striking. Once again, I was struck by his ethereal beauty.

"You can sit down." He curled up on the couch in the center of the room, folding himself onto the cushions with a cat-like grace that I envied. I felt like a Neanderthal as I plopped self-consciously into an overstuffed leather chair.

Tearing my attention away from him, I took in the room. It was elegantly sparse, with lots of black and chrome. Not much to offer in the knick-knack department. In fact, there was very little real personality to the place. It occurred to me that Razi had either rented the apartment already decorated or given some interior designer free rein. There was a slight hint of incense hanging in the air, a spicy scent that conjured up images of exotic bazaars and teeming streets.

I turned my attention back to Tad to find him studying me with the same care I'd given him and the room.

"You don't look like a detective," he said.

"I'm a private investigator," I said, playing the semantics game. "What do you think a detective should look like?"

He grinned. "Fatter, older, and uglier."

I laughed. "Then I guess I should be flattered that I don't look the way you expected."

His eyes sparkled with humor. "Do you go to Michelangelo's very often?"

"Last week was my first time."

"What did you think?"

"It was fun, but it kinda got ruined."

The sparkle faded. "Oh, yeah. Sorry about that."

I shrugged. "Well, that's what I'm here to talk about."

"So shoot."

"You said you'd met Paul?"

"A couple of times."

"What was he like?"

Tad thought a moment before answering. "Quiet. He was friends with Razi, but they're really different. Razi is loud and intense and likes to be the center of attention. Paul would rather sit in a corner and just watch everything. You'd forget he was there sometimes. But everybody seemed to like him."

"Somebody didn't," I said before I could stop myself. He frowned. "Sorry. What did he look like? I never met him." The question wasn't really relevant to anything, but I was curious. It would also help Tad loosen up if I started with questions that were relatively easy to answer.

"He had blond hair with blue eyes and was pretty small and...I dunno...quiet somehow. He was really cute if you took time to look at him, but most of the time if there were a lot of people around, you just kind of missed him somehow."

I was struck by how much his physical description could have fit me. Apparently, Micah liked a type. "Do you have any pictures of him?"

"I don't think so."

"Can you tell me anything about him besides that he was quiet? What kind of a person was he?"

"I didn't know him that well. I know Razi thought a lot of him. Razi doesn't have many guy friends. I think he feels threatened by them, like he sees them as competition. He didn't feel that way about Paul." He fell silent, and I allowed him a minute to think. "Paul was always really nice to me. He seemed...concerned about me, always asking how I was doing and telling me if I ever needed a place to go I could stay with him. And it wasn't in a creepy sort of way, you know? I didn't get the feeling he was hitting on me. It was like he genuinely cared. I think him and Razi might have even fought about me." He stopped as if he'd said more than he'd intended.

That caught my attention. "Fought about what?"

"Um..." I could tell he was searching for something to tell me, probably a lie. I decided to head him off.

"How do you know Razi? Is he your boyfriend?"

"I guess you could say that."

"What would you say?"

He shrugged. "Razi took me in when I didn't have anywhere else to go. I was living on the street, sick, hungry... He took me to the doctor, fed me, and let me stay here."

"He sounds like a saint."

Tad made a face. "Not exactly. In exchange, he gets sex whenever he wants it."

I raised an eyebrow. "You're okay with that arrangement?"

"It's better than the streets. And let me tell you, Razi knows what he's doing. So I guess it's not all that bad."

"Are you gay?"

He seemed surprised by the question. "What?"

"Are you even gay?"

"Yeah." I could tell he was still so surprised by the blunt question that he'd answered truthfully.

"How'd you end up on the street?"

He looked away. "Does that matter?"

"Maybe. You never know what will matter."

At first I didn't think he was going to answer, but finally, without ever looking in my direction, he began to speak in a low voice. Once he started, it was as if a dam had burst, the words flowing out of him until he'd spilled the whole story. "I grew up in this little dinky town in Virginia. My mom died when I was born, so it was always just my dad and me. I think in some ways he blamed me for her death. We weren't very close.

"I've known I was gay for a while now, probably since I was twelve or thirteen. I used to fool around with my best friend whenever he spent the night at my house or I stayed with him. I don't know if he was gay too or if he just liked to fool around. We never really talked about it. That all stopped within a year or so, but I still liked guys. Then I met someone online. He was a little older than I was and lived here in DC. We started dating, but I was keeping it all a secret. He would drive to see me while my dad was at work, or we'd meet somewhere and spend some time together when my dad thought I was with friends. Then one night my dad came home from work early — I don't even know why — and he caught us...well, you know. It was bad. I thought he was going to kill us. My boyfriend — and I use the term loosely — bolted so fast I barely even saw him go. He left me to face my dad alone, and I never heard from him again. My dad beat the shit out of me. He never touched me after that night, but I could tell he hated me. He hardly even spoke to me. It was horrible living there.

"Finally, I just couldn't take it anymore. I left. I spent a few nights with a friend, a girl from school, but her parents said I couldn't stay. I didn't know where else to go, but the guy I'd been dating lived here, so I hitchhiked to the city. It was stupid. I didn't have a clue where to look for him once I was here. I've never been so scared in my life. Every night I thought I was going to be killed — and I was half-hoping I would be. Then one night I was begging for money outside a restaurant over on the Circle — you know, Dupont Circle? There are a lot of gay people around there. Sometimes, a few of the guys would give me a little money if I did certain things for them, or let them do certain things to me.

"The next thing I know there's this guy telling me to come on. I figured he thought I was a hustler, which I guess I pretty much was, and he was taking me home for the night. I decided not to argue, since a warm place to sleep sounded pretty good about then — no matter what I had to do to get it. It was Razi. He brought me here and told me to sleep on the couch and if anything was missing when he got up, he'd hunt me down and cut off my dick. I didn't know what was going on. I didn't sleep at all that night, I was so scared. He got up the next morning, cooked me breakfast, then took me to the doctor, and after that, shopping for clothes. I've been here ever since."

"He just took you in?"

"Yeah. Just like that. For a few days I kept thinking I'd wake up and it would all just be a dream...but then he started asking for his payment, and I knew it wasn't."

"Did he hurt you?"

Tad blushed. "Not so I minded."

"Did you feel forced?"

He shrugged one shoulder. "I knew it was what I had to do if I wanted to stay here. He never said it in those exact words, but I knew. And it's not just sex. I also clean the apartment, wash the dishes, do the laundry, make appointments, and some other stuff."

"Did Razi ever try to contact your father?"

"He never even asked me my story."

"What about Paul?"

He seemed suddenly wary. "What about him?"

"Did he ask you for your story?"

He seemed to be trying to decide whether or not to trust me. He made up his mind and nodded. "He's the only other person besides you that I've ever told. I don't even know why I told you."

"Is that what Paul and Razi fought about?"

He shrugged again. "Maybe. I don't really know."

Obviously, that was as much as I was going to get out of him at the moment. If Paul was the stand-up guy everyone kept telling me he was, then he probably disapproved of Razi's payment plan, and might even have wanted to contact Tad's father. I doubt Razi would have been willing to give up his personal houseboy.

"How old are you again? Fifteen?"

He nodded.

"And how old is Razi?"

His eyes snapped to mine and grew round with fear. "You can't turn him in. Please! You can't do that. I know it's not great, but I'm fine. Really. It's better than living on the street, and I don't want to go back to my dad. I know that's what they'd do. I can't go back."

"Maybe they'd put you in foster care."

He sat up straight, his back rigid. "Like that would be so much better. Look, I'm almost sixteen. That's the age of consent, right? So in just a few more months, it won't even be illegal, technically."

The panic in his voice was wearing me down quickly. I hated to hear him sounding like a terrified little kid.

"Is Young even your real last name?"

His startled look gave me all the answer I needed, but he answered anyway. "What difference does it make? There's no way I'm telling you now. You'd just go to my dad or turn me in. I swear, if I have to go back, I'll run away again, and maybe this time there won't be any Razi to take me in. Or...or...I'll kill myself."

"Tad," I said before he could go into full-scale hysterics. "I won't turn him in, I promise. At least not until I know what's going on. I have to admit I'm not really comfortable with the whole situation, though."

"It's not really any of your business," he said stiffly.

"I'm sorry." Realizing I'd done a great job of ruining any sense of rapport we'd been building, I tried to reverse the damage. "You know, my dad beat me up too when he found out I was gay, and then he threw me out of the house."

Tad relaxed the slightest bit, and I could see the curiosity in his eyes. "Where'd you go?"

"I was lucky. I had someone to take me in. He was my friend's dad, and he's gay too."

"Your friend or your friend's dad?"

"Both, actually."

"Oh wow. That's so cool. I wish I'd had somebody like that. It must be great living with your friend and all."

"It probably would have been, but my friend was murdered. That's kind of why I got into this sort of thing."

"Oh. I'm really sorry."

It was my turn to shrug. "It's been a couple of years now. It doesn't hurt quite as much as it used to."

"What about your mom?"

"She left my dad not too long after that. She moved away but let me stay with Adam — that's my friend's dad who took me in."

"You still live with him?"

I nodded. He'd almost relaxed completely now, curling himself back into his feline pose. I was about to ask another question when a loud knock came at the door. Tad apparently was not only like a cat in his movements, but also as nervous as that famous long-tailed cat in a room full of rocking chairs. When he heard the knock he almost leaped right off the couch.

"Tad? You in there?" a voice called from the hallway. "Let me in."

"Shit," Tad said, giving me a startled glance. "I thought you'd be gone before he got home."

"Will he be mad that I'm here? After all, I did come to talk to him."

"I don't know," Tad said, looking toward the door as another pounding knock sounded.

"Just go let him in. I won't tell him anything we talked about." The boy cast me a grateful look and headed uncertainly toward the door. In the best-case scenario, it was time for the second interview of the day. In the worst, Chris and I would be testing out our emergency plan very soon.

Chapter 12

When Razi blew through the door, I was afraid it was going to be the worst-case scenario.

"Damn it, Tad, I don't know why you have to lock this place up like fucking Fort Knox. I feel like I'm in jail. And there's a creepy girl lurking around in the hallway. Do you know what that's about?"

His verbal barrage came to a screeching halt when he spotted me standing awkwardly by the chair. Immediately, his expression changed into a semblance of pleasantry. "Hi, I remember you. You're Micah's little friend, right?"

I tried not to bristle at the condescension in his voice. "My name's Killian."

"Like the beer." He was wearing obviously expensive clothing — dark slacks with a high-quality, white, button-down shirt open at the collar, and very pricy leather shoes. His black hair was pulled back into a pony tail at the nape of his neck.

He looked me over in a way that left me feeling like a prize steak on the butcher's counter. "To what do I owe the pleasure of your company?" He spoke English with only the slightest hint of an accent, but his careful pronunciation made me think it wasn't his native tongue.

I kept my gaze evenly on his, not wanting to let him know how uncomfortable he made me. "I'm a private investigator." His eyes widened in surprise for a second, but his polite mask quickly slipped back into place. This guy was an excellent actor. I would have to watch every nuance. "Micah has asked me to look into Paul's murder."

"Paul Flynn?"

I nodded.

"Is that why you were at Michelangelo? I thought you were dating Micah."

"I was — I am — dating Micah. He didn't even know Paul was dead before he ran into you."

"Oh. Well, what do you want with me?"

"I'd like to talk to you. You were a friend of Paul's; you knew what his life was like, and you were the one who found him."

He shrugged with purposeful nonchalance. "I doubt I can tell you anything useful."

"Can we sit down?"

"Oh yes. Please excuse my horrible manners. Sit down."

I took the chair I'd been sitting in before, and Razi took Tad's place on the couch. When Tad made a move to sit down next to him, Razi shot him a look that I couldn't quite interpret. Tad seemed to have no such trouble. He paused for just the slightest second, then cast a quick glance in my direction before leaving the room.

"Now we can speak in private," Razi said. "I hope you weren't here too long with just him. He's not the most fascinating conversationalist."

I shrugged. "We were fine. I like him. He's a nice kid." Razi's eyes narrowed slightly at the word "kid", but he didn't comment. "Is he related to you?" I asked innocently, as if I hadn't just received the whole story of how Tad had ended up with him.

Razi arched an eyebrow. "Do we look related?"

I shrugged in answer. "I've known siblings who didn't look anything alike."

"We'd certainly be disparate siblings. No, we're not related. He's a friend. I'm doing him a favor. He needed a place to live, so I let him stay here in exchange for cleaning the place and a few other small favors."

"That's really kind of you." I hoped I was keeping the sarcasm out of my voice.

Something of it must have slipped through, though, because his eyes narrowed again. The rest of his face remained set in its carefully bland expression. "I know what it's like to be in his position."

"Really?"

"Yes, but that has nothing to do with the subject at hand. You came to talk about Paul."

It wouldn't be as easy to weasel information out of Razi as it had been with Tad. Tad was younger, naïve, and innocent in many ways — and, more importantly, looking for someone to trust. Razi was older, more experienced, and obviously a lot more suspicious. I was having a hard time guessing his age. The closest I could guess was in his twenties, but he had the type of hawkish features that make it hard to pin it any closer than that.

"Yes, I did. How well did you know him?"

"He was one of the very few people I called friend."

"What was he like?"

"Nice. Kind. Good. Those words may sound empty, but they describe Paul very well."

"He was an escort?" I didn't mean anything by the question, but I could tell Razi took it wrong. His body stiffened, and his jaw tightened.

"Yes, he was an escort. That doesn't make him any less nice, kind, or good. Paul had his reasons. He had his story."

"What do you mean?"

"We all have stories. Most of us get into it for the money. Some of us need it more than others. Paul was a senior in college when he decided to come out to his parents. They were very religious and didn't take it well. They cut off all his support, leaving him to finish out the year as best he could. One of his friends was in the business and got him an interview. He was perfect. He had this sort of innocence about him that the clients just loved. He was successful enough that he stayed in it even after he graduated. You make more money on your own with no middleman, so most guys go solo eventually. They don't usually stay with an agency. Paul did."

"Why?"

"I guess he wasn't the ambitious type. He said he was earning a good living without having to do anything but show up for his appointments." He shrugged. "Who can argue with that?"

"What about his family?"

"What about them?"

"You said they didn't approve of his being gay."

"That would be putting it mildly. More like they totally flipped out — told him he was a sinner and going to hell, the whole works. They wouldn't have anything to do with him for a long time. When Paul's father died, he had to find out from the newspaper. That was really hard on him. He went to the funeral, but no one would even acknowledge his presence. Then a few weeks later his mother called. Pretty soon, he started going to see her every once in a while."

"How was that?"

"I don't really know. Paul didn't talk about it. He was very reserved. He never actually told you how he was feeling. Sometimes it was obvious, like when his father died, but most of the time you never knew what was going on in his head."

"Do you know if the rest of his family was still antagonistic?"

"I have no idea. For all I know they were still preaching at him every time he went over there. Even so, I think he would have put up with it if it meant seeing his mother again."

"Did you ever meet his family?"

He let out a short bark of laughter. "You must be joking. No, I was the last person Paul wanted to introduce to his family. They were rather racist as well as religious zealots."

"So you don't actually know if any of them were unbalanced or anything?"

"Are you suggesting one of them killed him? I don't think so. It seems to me like they would have done it a long time back if they'd wanted him dead."

"How long ago did his dad die? Maybe his showing back up again sent someone over the edge."

"It was a couple of months ago, maybe six at the most."

"So it's possible, then."

"Perhaps." He didn't seem convinced.

"Do you have any other ideas? Did he have any enemies?"

"Paul? No. Everyone loved Paul."

"Everybody keeps saying that, yet obviously someone didn't like him."

A slight frown tugged down the corners of his mouth. "Perhaps it was just a random burglary gone wrong."

"I thought the police pretty much discarded that theory."

"They did, but then they don't really care much either way. As far as I'm concerned, it's still as valid a theory as any."

"You found him, right?"

"Yes." His eyes shifted away.

"Can you tell me about that?"

He took a deep breath. "It's hard to talk about."

"Take your time."

"I hadn't heard from him for a few days. That wasn't unusual lately, but if he didn't call me, I'd generally call him after about three or four days just to check in. When he didn't answer his phone, I started getting worried. Finally, I just decided to go over. I had a key so I could feed his fish when he was going to be away for a few days. He had this huge fish tank with all kinds of exotic fish.

"I let myself into his apartment. It was trashed — completely and totally trashed. All his paintings were off the walls and destroyed. He loved art. His fish tank was shattered. Every table had been tipped over, lamps smashed. It was horrible."

His eyes had unfocused as if he were seeing it all again. "And in the middle of all the mess was Paul. He was just lying there, as if he was a doll someone had simply thrown away. I knew he was dead as soon as I saw him. I've seen dead people before."

I took note of that last comment. I was pretty sure he hadn't realized what he was saying, but I wondered what it meant. "I know this is hard, but can you describe the body? What position was he in? Was there blood? That sort of thing."

He took a ragged breath. "It wasn't a peaceful death, that I can tell you. It wasn't one of those cases where the person just looks like he's sleeping. I don't know if you've ever seen a strangling victim. I hadn't. Not before that. It's horrible. I...I'll never be able to forget it."

I let him sit in silence for a few minutes to collect himself before asking my next question. "Did you notice anything missing?"

"Nothing that I could say for sure. He collected coins, some of them quite rare and expensive. Although the collection was scattered across the floor, it looked to be all there. Paul wasn't a big jewelry person, but what he did have was still in the bedroom. His TV, stereo, computer, nothing appeared to be gone."

"So that's why the police ruled out burglary?"

"You'd have to ask the police. They don't confide in me."

"If you don't think his family could have killed him, who do you think did?"

"I don't have any ideas."

"None at all? What about coworkers? Did he have another job?"

"No, he didn't need another job. He was making more than enough doing what he was doing."

"What about other escorts? Clients?"

He shrugged. "Anything's possible."

"Do you know how I could get in touch with any of them?"

"Sorry."

"Sorry you don't know or sorry you won't help me?"

Another shrug.

"What about the guy who owns the agency? Neal, right?"

"I don't know."

"You used to be with the agency, didn't you?"

"Yes."

"And you don't know how to get in touch with Neal?"

"We don't exactly send Christmas cards, you know?"

"Why are you avoiding my questions?"

"I'm answering your questions."

"They're non-answers. Don't you care about finding out what happened to Paul?"

"Paul is dead. Nothing you do is going to bring him back." His voice was hollow.

"What if he was murdered by a serial killer who preys on escorts? You could be next."

"We lead risky lives. We meet strangers for a living. We all know that every appointment could be our last. We try not to think about it, but we know it. I know it. Paul knew it. You accept the risk and do your job."

"So that's it? This is just one more risk?"

"Pretty much."

"You have no intention of helping me find out what happened to him, do you? You don't give a damn about Paul."

He looked me squarely in the face, his black eyes flashing. "The only way you can survive this business is to not give a damn. No one gives a damn about you. Not the police — we're scum to most of them. Not the clients — it's strictly business. And not the agency, if you work for one — you're a replaceable commodity. Nobody gives a damn about Paul."

"Micah does."

He snorted. "How nice. I'm sure Paul would appreciate that if he were still alive, especially since he never heard from Micah after he left. What good does Micah's concern do Paul now?"

"We can find out what happened to him and make sure he gets justice."

"Justice? What a joke. There is no justice — not for us. Go away, little boy. I can't help you."

I stood up with a sigh, figuring that was all I was going to get out of him. I had a feeling he knew more than he was saying, but this wasn't the time to press it. I started toward the door to let myself out. Tad hadn't relocked all the bolts when Razi came home, so I didn't need assistance.

I paused as a thought struck me and turned back to Razi, who was still sitting on the sofa. "What's your story?"

He looked up, surprised, as if he hadn't expected me to still be there. "What?"

"Earlier you said you all had stories. I know Paul's. I know Micah's. What's yours?"

He looked away. "My story is my own. Leave now, please."

I watched him for a second more, then let myself out.

Chris waited until I reached the stairwell before falling in beside me. "Well?"

"I didn't find out much. Especially not from Razi."

"Is he the one who went in after you were already inside?"

"Yeah. He knows more than he's saying, but whatever he knows, he sure isn't telling me."

"He wouldn't say anything?"

"Nothing I didn't already know or couldn't find out from Micah. Well, nothing directly. I did discover things weren't very good between Paul and his family, but Razi doesn't seem to think they could have had anything to do with the murder. Not that his opinion carries much weight. I want to meet them myself."

"Do you see this Razi guy as a possible suspect?"

"Well, Razi says they were friends, and both Tad and Micah back that up. Still, he might have had a motive. He's got a sweet setup now with Tad. According to the kid, Paul didn't approve of their – for lack of a better word – relationship. He said Razi and Paul had a fight about it."

"What do you mean?"

"Tad's a runaway. He was a street kid on the fast track to becoming a hustler when Razi took him in. It wasn't exactly out of the kindness of his heart. The kid cleans and sleeps with Razi in exchange for food and a roof over his head. If Paul was threatening to find Tad's father, Razi might have tried to stop him."

"You don't sound very convinced."

"That's because I'm not. He's hiding something, but I'm pretty sure he didn't do it. Actually, if we're talking suspects, as much as I hate to say it, Tad makes a better one."

"The kid?"

"Yeah. He had a lot more at stake if Paul decided to look up his dad. I have the feeling Tad would do pretty much anything to avoid going back to his father."

"Do you really think he's a killer, though?"

I sighed. "I'd hate to think it. I like him. But I've been fooled before."

She looked over at me. "You're going to have to tell me a few of these stories sometime."

"Sometime before this is over," I said.

"Back to Razi, did you learn anything else from him?"

"Not much. He has some history he doesn't want to talk about. Actually, he has a lot of stuff he doesn't want to talk about. If everyone is like him, this isn't going to be easy."

We came out onto the street and stopped. "Where to now?" she asked.

"I guess we can try and find Paul's apartment, see if the key Micah gave me still fits. I hope the place hasn't been cleared out yet."

"Probably not that quickly. The police investigation isn't closed, so I doubt they've released the apartment. It would look pretty bad if they had. What's the address again?"

I gave it to her and she nodded. "That's a better part of the city, close to Dupont Circle. It's a really nice area. He must have been making good money to afford to live there."

"It's not like Razi's place was a dump. Apparently money is not an object when you're a successful escort."

"Back to the Metro, then."

"Killian," a voice called from behind me. I turned around to see Tad running towards us. He'd thrown on a T-shirt and a pair of sandals but still looked completely disheveled.

"Tad?" Chris asked under her breath.

"Yep."

"Razi's in the shower," Tad said, out of breath. "I only have a minute, but I didn't want you to leave without saying bye. He didn't say anything to me after you left, but he was in a pretty bad mood. Did he seem mad that I let you in?"

"He's hard to read. Why?" I was suddenly concerned. "What would he do if he was mad? Would he hurt you?"

Tad grimaced. "I hope not. I don't really know. He's never actually been mad at me before. Annoyed, maybe, but not mad. I just don't want him to kick me out."

I felt bad for the poor kid, and even worse that I might have caused more trouble for him. I pulled out my wallet, found one of my cards, and scribbled my cell phone number on the back. "If he hurts you, call me. I'll come get you personally."

Tad blinked in surprise, and for a second, I thought he might cry. "Are you serious?"

"Very. Even if you just decide you want out of your arrangement, call me."

He frowned. "I owe him. He saved my life. And besides, where else would I go? I'm not going back home."

"What if your dad wanted you back? Maybe he's changed his mind since you left. He might have realized how much you meant to him."

"You don't know my dad," he said. "I'm not going back. I don't care what anyone says."

"Well, I won't make you do anything." I didn't want him to be afraid of contacting me just because he thought I might hand him over to his father. "Will you call me if you need me?"

He looked at the card in his hand, then slipped it in his pocket before giving me a lopsided grin. "I dunno. Maybe, maybe not. No promises."

"It doesn't have to be this way, you know."

"It's not that bad, really. Better than the streets. Better than home." He shrugged. "It could be worse."

"Maybe it could be better."

He looked at me for a minute without saying a word, but his expression spoke volumes. It was obvious he was torn between what he felt he owed Razi and wishing things could be different. His eyes shifted to Chris, as if noticing her for the first time.

"I'm his assistant," she said quickly.

"You guys won't turn me in, will you?"

I sighed. "No, I won't turn you in."

He looked to Chris, who shrugged. "Hey, I only do what he tells me to do."

He seemed satisfied and started backing toward the building. "I need to get back up there before he finishes his shower."

"You'll probably be seeing me again," I said. "And remember, call me if you need me."

He grinned. "Okey-dokey." He spun around and ran back into the building.

I stood staring after him.

"Cute kid," Chris said. "Shitty deal." She glanced over at me, noticing my frown. "What are you thinking?"

"I wish there was something I could do for him."

"There's hundreds more where he came from," she said sadly. "I've heard that at least thirty percent of all teenage runaways are gay kids. At least he has food and a roof over his head."

"But for what? He's essentially a sex slave."

"You gave him an option. That's more than he had yesterday. If he decides he wants out badly enough, he'll call you."

"He's just a kid. He has a family somewhere who doesn't even know where he is."

"He made it pretty clear he didn't want to go back to them. Are you going to break your word and turn him in?"

"No, I won't do that. I just wish there was something more I could do. Besides, I don't even know his last name. Or, for that matter, if Tad is even his real first name."

"Okay, let's start moving. We can talk while we walk, unless you're too blond to handle that."

I laughed, breaking my melancholy mood. "I think I can handle it." We turned once more toward the Metro station.

"Good. So what's next on the agenda?"

"I'd like to check out Paul's apartment. I want to get as much done as I can while I'm here."

"Are you going back tonight?"

"That was the plan."

"Well, if you need a place to stay, you can crash at our place."

"Thanks," I said with a pleased smile. I was starting to like Chris. She was turning out to be a good partner.

The trip to the Dupont Circle stop took about twenty minutes. From the station, we walked another twenty minutes to find Paul's address. Just as Chris had said, it was in a very nice neighborhood. The streets were lined with stone and brick-faced townhouses, each with its own tiny patch of lawn, most filled with flowers. Paul's building was actually a brick apartment block tucked between two sections of townhouses.

You had to be buzzed in, so we just stood nearby and waited for someone to come or go. It wasn't long before a woman with two small dogs came out. We slipped in behind her before the door could close. She never even noticed.

Paul's apartment was on the third floor. We took the stairs, but Chris stopped me at the second-floor landing. "Okay, here's the plan. If someone heads for the door, I'll call you on your cell phone. I don't like staying out here and leaving you to go in alone, but I know we need a watch. I almost panicked when Razi showed up. I was ready to break the door down if you yelled or anything. It was hard not knowing what was going on."

"I don't know what else we can do without your being very conspicuous. As it was, Razi noticed you. If he hadn't gotten distracted by my being there, he might have called the police. We don't want someone doing that."

"Well, if they do, I'm pretty sure I can get out of it because of my dad. Still, it would be a pain we don't need."

"Right, so I think we'd better just stick with the plan where you come to the rescue should I need it. And don't forget, cell phones work both ways. I can call you too if there's any trouble."

"Okay, but I don't like it," she said. "And I'm only going along with this because I don't have a better idea. We have to work out something better before we do this again."

I gave her a smile and climbed the rest of the stairs to the third floor. There were only four apartments. It was easy to identify Paul's door, the one with police tape across it. The others were closed and blank. There was no way to know if anyone was behind them.

I took a deep breath and fished out the key Micah gave me. If it didn't work, I wouldn't have to worry about any of this. I slid the key carefully into the lock, which clicked and released when I turned the key. Pushing the door open slowly until it was just wide enough for me to squeeze through, I ducked under the tape and quickly shut the door.

The room smelled of damp carpet and mildew and was so dark I couldn't see a thing after the bright light of the hallway. I fumbled along the wall for a light switch, but before I could find one, I heard the door handle rattle behind me.

I froze in place, praying it was just Chris. The door swung open suddenly, flooding the room with enough light to temporarily blind me.

A dark figure stood in the doorway. "Don't move. I have a gun," a harsh voice ordered.

Chapter 13

This was definitely not good. I froze where I was and slowly raised my hands. Getting caught was not part of my plan. Assuming I survived long enough, Chris and I were clearly going to have to work out a better way for her to warn me.

As my eyes adjusted to the light, I began to get a better look at my challenger. To my great surprise, it turned out to be a small, slender Asian woman with long, glossy, black hair. And in her dainty little hands was a deadly-looking pistol, aimed directly at my chest.

"Who the hell are you and what are you doing here?" she said in a surprisingly deep and husky voice. She didn't sound at all the way she looked. "And don't think for a minute I don't know how to use this thing."

"My name is Killian Kendall," I said as calmly as I could manage. "Are you a police officer?"

"I'll ask the questions, thank you. What are you doing in Paul's apartment?"

She'd said Paul's apartment, I noted, so she was most likely not a cop. Hadn't Micah mentioned something about a neighbor of Paul's that he was very close to? What was her name?

I wondered if I should lie and say I was a friend of Paul's or tell the truth. I decided that, in this case at least, the truth was the best policy. "I'm a private investigator looking into the murder of Paul Flynn."

"You seem a little young to be a private eye."

"I can't help that."

"Who hired you?"

"Micah Gerber. He asked me to see what I could find out about Paul's murder, since the police don't seem to be taking a great interest in it."

"Micah?" she asked warily, the gun wavering ever so slightly.

"Yes."

"How do I know you're telling the truth?"

Good question. Just then, the name I was searching for surfaced. "Are you Sabrina?" When her eyes widened, I took that as a yes and went on. "Micah said you were a good friend of Paul's. Maybe you can help me find out who killed him."

The gun dropped a little farther, but I kept my hands in the air. I wasn't about to risk my life with any sudden moves.

"How'd you get in here?"

"Micah gave me a key."

That seemed to be what she wanted to hear. The gun dropped to her side, and she stepped back from the door.

"Will you help me?" I lowered my hands very slowly, keeping them in her view.

"I'll talk to you, but I think we should go to my apartment. If someone comes along, I don't want to be standing here with Paul's door wide open. It wouldn't look good."

There was no arguing with her logic.

In the hallway, I risked a quick glance toward the stairwell and saw a wide-eyed Chris peeking around the corner at us. I motioned surreptitiously for her to remain hidden.

The door next to Paul's was standing open. Sabrina stepped to one side and motioned with the gun as if to say, "After you." She wasn't going to give me the chance to get behind her — a smart move on her part had I been someone dangerous.

Entering her apartment, I found myself in a large open space that served as both living and dining room. Straight ahead was the kitchen, and off to the right was a closed door that I assumed led to a bedroom. The place wasn't large, but Sabrina had decorated it tastefully with a blend of antique furnishings and Asian art.

"Have a seat," she said casually, as if she entertained guests at gunpoint all the time. Then again, for all I knew, perhaps she did.

I perched gingerly on the edge of her scroll-back Victorian sofa and watched her expectantly. She sat across from me on an uncomfortable-looking carved wooden chair. Seeing her clearly for the first time, I realized how beautiful she was. Her features were delicate and refined, making her look remarkably like a finely sculpted china doll.

Then she spoke and ruined the effect. "Would you like a drink?"

"Er, uh, no, thanks." It wasn't a question I had expected.

"So Micah asked you to find Paul's killer?" She fiddled with the gun in her lap.

"Yes. Um, do you think you could set the gun down? It's making me a little uncomfortable. I promise I'm not going to hurt you, but if it makes you feel better, you can set it on the table right next to you where you can grab it if you need to."

"Oh." She looked down at the gun in surprise, as if she'd forgotten she was holding it. "This?" She aimed the gun at my chest and pulled the trigger before I could react. I flinched, but nothing happened. "It's not real," she said. "I bought it at a women's safety conference I attended a few years ago. It's just meant to scare people. I don't like real guns."

I stared at her in disbelief. "What would you have done if I'd attacked you?"

She blinked as if the thought had never occurred to her. "Hit you with it?"

"Do you even know any self-defense?"

"Yes. What does any of this have to do with Paul?"

"It doesn't have anything to do with Paul, but if you're going to run around pointing a toy gun at people, you'd better be able to take care of yourself."

"I don't make a habit of it," she said defensively. "I heard someone going into Paul's apartment and knew it wasn't the police. Now can we get back to the subject at hand, please?"

"You're right, I'm sorry. It's really none of my business."

"It's okay..." She gave me a hesitant smile. "I guess I sort of made it your business when I pointed it at you. For the record, I'm a second-degree black belt in Taekwondo. So anyway, Micah hired you? Do you actually know him or did he just hire you?"

"I know him. We've been dating for a few months."

Her mouth formed a little "o" of surprise. "So...wait...you're dating Micah and you're investigating the murder of his ex-lover?"

I gave her a wry grin. "That about sums it up."

"Wow. Either you're a better person than I am, or you guys have a weird relationship."

"The latter, most likely."

"Wow. How is Micah?"

"He's...good. I guess. He's been shaken up by Paul's murder. I don't think he was completely over him."

She frowned. "Did you know Paul?"

"No, I'm not from around here. Can you tell me about him?"

"Where do I start?" She sighed. "He was a sweetheart. I miss him so much. I keep thinking I'm going to run into him in the hall. It hasn't really sunk in yet that he's gone."

"Were you good friends?"

"Yes, very good friends. We talked pretty much every day, and I don't just mean in the hallway. Sometimes he'd call me at work just to chat." She paused. "I really miss him. He was a good person. He was a good person. He didn't deserve to die — especially like that." She broke off and visibly tried to regain her composure.

"I talked to Razi Akiba earlier today. Do you know him?"

Her expression changed as if she'd bitten into something rotten. "Oh, I know him, alright."

"I take it you don't like him?"

"No, I don't."

"Any particular reason?"

She thought a moment before answering. "I'm not really certain. There's just something about him I don't trust. I always got the impression that he was using Paul, although I couldn't quite explain why or for what. I know he tried to break Paul and Micah up when they were still dating."

"He did? Did Micah know?"

"Well, I never told him. I talked to Paul about it, but he wasn't concerned. He said they had a solid relationship and it didn't matter what Razi said or did. It was well before Micah started talking about wanting to get out of DC."

"Why did he try to break them up? Did he want to date Paul?"

"That's what I thought at the time. As far as I know, though, when Micah left the city and Paul was available, Razi never made a move. It always struck me as strange. If he was so hot for Paul, why didn't he go after him when he was single?"

"Maybe he's the type who's only interested in what he can't have."

"He does strike me as that type, but still..."

"Or maybe Razi was dating someone else by then."

"That's possible. I certainly don't keep up with his love life. I don't really spend much time in his company. Only if it was one of Paul's rare get-togethers."

"After Micah left, did Paul date anyone else?"

"Not seriously. He always said he was so busy with work that he didn't have the time or energy to date socially. I thought maybe he was still hung up on Micah."

"So there's no angry, jilted ex-boyfriend out there?"

"Not that I'm aware of."

"Did he have any enemies?"

"No. That's what's so scary about all this. It seems so random, and yet, the way he died... It seems like a murder with a lot of...passion behind it. Do you know what I mean?"

"Passion?"

"Yes, strong emotion. Somehow, it doesn't feel — what's the word police use? Premeditated? There are so many ways to kill someone if you just want to get rid of him — poison, shooting, a planned accident. Strangulation seems like such a heat-of-the-moment thing to do. It's a very personal way to kill. The victim is actually in your hands as his life leaves him."

I shuddered at her words. "You sound like you've given this a lot of thought."

"Oh, I have. Trust me. I've lain awake almost every night since it happened, wondering what it was like for poor Paul in those last seconds, trying to figure out why on earth someone would want him dead. I just don't understand."

"And you probably never will. Most murder is senseless. There's no way you can understand it."

"I just wish I could do something."

"You can. You can answer my questions and tell me everything you remember."

"I'll do my best."

"Great. Were you in a position to know who came to his apartment?"

"I didn't spy on him or anything, but yeah. Living next door to him and being friends, I saw people come and go. The walls are paper thin in this building, so even if I didn't see them show up, I could hear when he had someone over."

"Who came?"

"He didn't have many friends. Besides Razi, mostly just...well..." She broke off and seemed unsure of how to continue.

"I know Paul was an escort," I said, just in case that was the hang-up.

It must have been, because she relaxed slightly and went on. "Besides Razi, it was mostly just his clients. He did in-calls and out-calls."

"Meaning?"

"In-calls are when the clients come to you, out-calls are when you go to them."

"So a lot of clients came here?"

"I don't know about a lot."

"But some came here?"

"Yes."

"Did any come more than once?"

"You mean like regulars?"

"I guess so, yeah."

"I'm sure there were regulars, but I just didn't pay that much attention. It wasn't really any of my business, you know?" She paused thoughtfully. "Still, there was this one guy I did seem to see fairly often. I assumed he was a client, although I don't know that for a fact."

"Can you describe him?"

She screwed up her face in concentration. "He's kind of hard to remember. He wasn't strikingly handsome, but he wasn't ugly. He was just kind of ordinary."

I groaned silently. Ordinary people were the hardest to describe. People tended to take less note of them, and what they did notice could apply to nearly anyone. Exactly like Novak's insurance rep, the one I could never remember. I made a stab at it anyway.

"What color was his hair?"

She frowned. "Brown? Gray? I'm not really sure."

"Eyes?"

"I have no idea. I'm not being very helpful, am I?"

I smiled but didn't answer. "Was he tall or short? Fat or skinny?"

"I can answer those at least. He was average height and weight."

Of course he was. "Did you notice any distinguishing features? Any moles or scars? A particular piece of jewelry?"

She shook her head. "I'm sorry. I simply didn't pay attention."

"Are you even sure it was the same guy each time?"

"Yes, I noticed that much. It's just hard to describe him."

I gave up and went on to the next question. "Did you ever see anyone else who stood out? Maybe they didn't seem to belong here or you saw them repeatedly?"

"The only thing I can think of is, the last couple weeks Razi's been showing up here with this kid — a pretty boy, curly red hair, big blue eyes. He looks like he's thirteen or fourteen at the most. I don't know where Razi got him. Probably bought him off some crack whore."

"We've met. His name is Tad. He was a homeless kid that Razi took in."

She raised an eyebrow. "At what price? Razi never does anything out of the kindness of his heart — if he even has one."

I shrugged. It wasn't my place to go into that with Sabrina. "Did Paul confide in you much?"

"I don't think Paul confided in anyone very much. Still, he probably told me more than most."

"A few people I've talked to said he seemed a little different recently, more withdrawn and almost secretive. Did you notice that?"

"Now that you mention it, yes. It didn't exactly register at the time because I was busy. My sister was getting married, and I was the maid of honor. I hadn't thought about it at all, but he no longer invited me over very often, and we definitely didn't talk as much."

"Do you have any idea why? Was something bothering him? Do you think he was hiding something?"

"I honestly don't have any idea," she said. "I was so caught up in my own life that I didn't even notice anything different. My God, what kind of friend am I? What if Paul was killed because I couldn't be bothered to notice something was wrong?" Her voice was escalating to the point that I was afraid she'd burst into tears any moment.

"You can't blame yourself for this," I said quickly — and, I hoped, convincingly. "We still have no idea what happened. Maybe it had nothing to do with why he was withdrawing. For that matter, we don't even know for sure he was withdrawing. Perhaps his life got busy at the same time yours did. It might have been totally unrelated to his murder. We don't have enough information yet to make any kind of educated guess. Besides, even if it was connected in some way to his murder, he could have come to you, and I'll bet you would have dropped everything to help him, right?"

She sniffled a bit and nodded. "You're right. I would have."

"See? You don't have any reason to blame yourself for Paul's death. The only person to blame is whoever killed him. And you can help me catch whoever it was."

"I can?"

"Yes. Can you think of anyone, no matter how remote, who might have wanted Paul dead?"

"I can't. I'm sorry, I just can't think of anyone."

"What about Razi?"

She shook her head. "No. He's a sleaze ball through and through, but if he was going to kill someone, I don't think it would be as direct as strangling. He'd be more the type who'd poison you slowly. Or maybe stab you in the back."

"So you don't have any ideas?"

"None at all."

I sighed. I wasn't coming up with an abundance of suspects so far. Or motives, either, for that matter. I needed to get back to the physical evidence.

An inkling of an idea began to form. "You've been in Paul's apartment, right?"

"Many times."

"Would you walk through it with me? You can tell me if anything is missing. Razi said he didn't think so, but you'd know better than I would."

"But we shouldn't be in there. It's a police crime scene."

"The police don't seem very eager to solve this crime. We might discover something that would help me find Paul's killer. Besides, they're done with it by now."

"What if we get caught?"

"I have a contact on the DC police force," I said, hoping it was true.

She was quiet for what seemed like an eternity. I could almost see the wheels turning in her head. Finally, she took a deep breath and looked into my eyes. "Fine. Let's do it."

We crept out of her apartment like a couple of cat burglars after she checked to make sure there was no one in sight. I caught a glimpse of movement in the stairwell, so I knew Chris was still on duty, for whatever that was worth. I unlocked the door again and Sabrina quickly slipped in, with me close behind. As before, the first thing I noticed was the unpleasant odor. In addition to mildew, I also detected a faintly rotten smell.

"Ugh," Sabrina said under her breath. She knew where the lights were, so this time there was no fumbling around in the dark.

She gasped as the room was revealed. After a quick glance around, I couldn't blame her. It was a disaster scene. I'd never seen anything quite like it. The layout was a mirror image of Sabrina's apartment. Paul's decorating taste even had an Asian flare as well, but from what I could piece together from the debris, his had a little more Indian influence. That was before the tornado hit, though. What we were seeing was the aftermath. The room had been deliberately and maliciously demolished, item by item. Razi's description of the chaos didn't even begin to cover it.

The beautifully embroidered cushions that had covered the wooden-framed couch had been ripped to shreds, their innards strewn across the floor. Ceramic and glass shards covered the parts of the floor not hidden by the cushion stuffing. Art that had once hung around the room — much of it original oil and watercolor paintings — had been torn off the wall and destroyed. Even the TV sitting on the entertainment center had its screen shattered, its insides exposed and looking strangely vulnerable.

A fish tank on a wrought-iron frame stood against one wall. Its front had been smashed, causing its contents — including several now-dead fish — to wash across the floor. The thick, wool Persian rug and the carpet underneath had absorbed the water and now emitted a sour mildewed scent. Between that and the fish, at least I'd identified the sources of the unpleasant odor.

"Oh my God," Sabrina whispered.

"Is this the first time you've been in here since it happened?" I spoke in a low tone. It seemed somehow inappropriate to raise my voice. I almost felt as if I were in a mausoleum.

She nodded.

"I don't even know where to begin..." I hoped I didn't sound as overwhelmed as I felt.

"How did the police find anything? Wouldn't they have to collect all this as evidence or something? They always do on TV."

"I don't know. Maybe they aren't done in here after all. Don't touch anything."

"I already touched the light switch," she said, a hint of panic entering her voice. "I should have never agreed to this."

"Calm down. I'll fix it." I pulled my sleeve down over my hand and carefully wiped the light switch clean. "There. If you have to touch something, make sure you put your shirt over your hand. And for God's sake, don't take anything."

"I'm not touching anything else. I think we should leave."

"We're here now. We might as well look around."

"I'm not moving."

"Can you tell if anything's missing?"

"How should I know? How can you tell anything in this mess?"

"What did he have of value?"

She took a deep breath. "His electronic equipment." That was all plainly visible on the entertainment center and amidst the rubble on the floor. "His art collection." Also readily identifiable. "And his coin collection."

Razi had mentioned that, making a point of saying it had been left. "Where'd he keep it?"

"In the bedroom."

I started making my way carefully across the room, glass crackling under my feet. As I passed the kitchen, I noted the destruction continued in there. All the dishes had been pulled from the cabinets and shattered on the floor.

"This couldn't have been quiet. The whole place is wrecked. You said the walls are paper thin. Why didn't anyone hear something?"

Sabrina's shoulders drew up. "I must have not been home." She sounded defensive.

"I didn't just mean you. What about the other neighbors?"

"Mrs. Gupta across the hall is legally deaf. She wouldn't have heard if the killer was smashing dishes in her own kitchen. When she watches TV I can hear it as clearly as if I were sitting next to her on her couch."

"And the other neighbor? There are four apartments on this floor."

"That's Kent. I don't know what he does, but he's away on business more than he's home. You could ask him, but chances are good he wasn't here when Paul was..." Her eyes skated across the wreckage and she shuddered.

"How about the apartment beneath us?" I said. "If anyone had been in, they would have had to hear a lot of bumps and crashes when all these things hit the floor."

"You're probably right, only I have no idea who lives there."

I made a mental note to check in with Mrs. Gupta, Kent, and the person downstairs before I left.

Moving on to the bedroom, I carefully opened the door using my shirt again. I reached in to turn on the light, but before I could find the switch, my breath caught in my throat. A feeling of complete and utter terror overcame me. I couldn't breathe. I tried to scream, tried to gasp, but my lungs wouldn't work. It felt as if a pair of strong hands gripped my throat. I clawed at my neck and stumbled back from the door. My chest began to burn, and the room started to fade into black.

In the background, I vaguely heard Sabrina yelling something, but the words wouldn't penetrate. It was as if she was calling from far in the distance.

Suddenly, just as quickly as it had begun, it was over. I gasped in great gulps of air as I slumped against the doorframe.

"What the fuck was that?" Sabrina's voice veered wildly toward hysterical.

"I don't know," I gasped. "I couldn't breathe, it felt like—"

"What? What did it feel like?"

"Like I was being strangled."

Her eyes grew wide and she took a step back. "That's not funny."

Still struggling to catch my breath, I lifted my eyes to meet hers. I knew she could tell I wasn't kidding, but she wasn't ready to give up that easily.

"Is this some sort of fucked-up joke?"

I shook my head. "No. I couldn't breathe. It felt like my throat was closed off...exactly like being strangled."

She looked through the open door into the dark bedroom, her eyes full of fear. "That...that's where they found Paul's body." Her voice was tight with rising panic. "What the hell is going on?"

I only wished I knew.

Chapter 14

What had just happened? Had I somehow experienced Paul's death, or had it just been my imagination? The thought that I might have actually felt Paul dying was terrifying. And to what purpose? The police had already determined he'd been strangled. Then again, who said there was a purpose in any of this? I only knew I needed to talk to Judy...and soon.

Sabrina brought me back to the moment with a frightened whimper. "I want to leave."

I looked up. She was slowly backing away while keeping a wary eye on me as if I had suddenly sprouted a second head, a tail, and horns. I nodded and started to follow her. Before I had taken two steps, however, I felt as if I'd been lassoed and was being pulled toward the bedroom. The sensation wasn't so much physical as psychic. I stopped in midstep and slowly turned back toward the doorway. The feeling grew stronger.

"What are you doing?" she asked in a shaky voice.

"I...I have to go in there."

"No! You can't!"

"I...need to."

"I'm not going with you."

"Fine. Stay here." I took the few steps through the door and stopped again. With my body blocking most of the light from the other room, the bedroom was left in deep gloom. It almost seemed as though the shadows were alive — or as if something or someone was hiding in them. There was a definite feeling of pain and anguish within the room. It stopped me in my tracks as effectively as a wall. I couldn't make myself take another step.

Then, without thinking, I reached for the light switch. Somehow, I wasn't surprised when my hand went directly to it with the surety of someone who lived there. It was behind the tall armoire that stood a few inches from the wall by the door — not the sort of place you would notice or expect to find a switch. I wondered fleetingly how I seemed to know exactly where it was, but as light filled the room, all other thoughts fled, along with the awful feeling of death.

The bedroom was as neat as the front rooms were chaotic. For a moment, I was surprised it hadn't been trashed like the rest of the apartment. Then I realized it probably had been, and the police had gathered everything up as evidence.

Thanks to the lack of mess, it didn't take long to see that if the coin collection had been on the floor, it was gone now. I wondered where Paul had been killed, where his body had lain until Razi found him.

No sooner had the question fluttered through my mind than I had the answer. I staggered a little as the room seemed to shift out of focus before slowly sharpening once more — only this time it was as if I were viewing a double-exposed photograph. Over the image of the room as it appeared now, I saw a fainter, ghost image as it must have looked when Razi found Paul. Drawers were yanked from the dressers and dumped all over the floor — clothing was strewn about everywhere. The mattress was shoved off the box spring, and the bedside table had been knocked over, shattering the ceramic lamp that had stood on it. Coins preserved in little cardboard squares lay scattered. In the midst of it all, lying on the far side of the room, between the bed and what I assumed to be a closet door, was Paul's body.

The effect was quite dizzying. I shook my head and squeezed my eyes shut. When I reopened them, the ghost image was gone, the scene back to normal. I sighed. Just what I needed: another manifestation of my gifts.

I moved slowly about, edging my way along the walls to avoid the place where Paul had lain. I was sure the police had thoroughly searched the room, so why was I drawn to it? I didn't even attempt to think about what — or who — had attracted my attention.

"What?" I said aloud in a low croak that I barely recognized as my own voice. "What am I supposed to see? Why did you drag me in here?" There was no answer. "Look, Paul...or whoever you are, if you want me to understand why I'm here, you're going to have to help me out."

Nothing happened for a moment. I was just starting to feel really silly for talking to an empty room when I heard the slightest hint of noise behind me. It sounded like the soft rustle of material against material.

Not at all sure it was any sort of clue, I turned to face the antique armoire by the door. It was an enormous piece of furniture, almost reaching the ceiling, with a set of double doors on the front. It must have been a bear to move in. I approached it carefully and reached out to open the doors. It was completely empty. I frowned.

Then I heard the sound again. Now that I was closer, I realized it was coming from the top of the wardrobe. I looked around for something to step up on so I could see the top, but there was nothing in the room. I went back out into the living room in search of a suitable item.

"What are you doing now?" Sabrina asked.

"Is there anything I can stand on?"

She looked at me for a second, then shook her head slightly. "I have a step stool in my apartment." Her tone was wary but resigned.

"Do you think I could use it?"

"Why not? Anything to get this over with faster." She cautiously slipped out the door and returned a minute later carrying a small folding stepladder.

"That's perfect. Thank you." I took it from her and went back into the bedroom.

The first thing I thought when the top of the armoire came into view was that Paul must have been a meticulous housekeeper. There was no sign of the thick dust or cobwebs one would expect to find in such an out-of-the-way place. The top was slightly inset with a two-inch rim around the edge. A small block of wood, about one-by-three inches, was attached on each side of the top.

Almost like handles.

It was as if a light bulb lit up over my head. Back when Steve and Adam were buying antiques for the bed and breakfast, I remembered Steve talking about how some of the old pieces had hidden compartments built into them: desks often had secret drawers, chests had false bottoms, and — most relevant for me — armoires had faux tops.

I grabbed the blocks of wood and lifted. Slowly but surely the top began to slide upward. Once I had it off, I found myself staring down into a four-inch-deep cavity, cleverly camouflaged from cursory examination. No one would ever realize there was a difference in height between inside the cabinet and the outside unless he knew what to look for. I would never have noticed if I hadn't seen the blocks of wood.

The cavity held a single letter-sized envelope, which must have been pretty important if Paul had gone to all that trouble to hide it. I picked it up and discovered it wasn't sealed, just tucked into itself. When I lifted the flap, a key fell out and bounced on the carpet below.

After retrieving the key, I looked inside the envelope and found a single sheet of paper. It was a handwritten letter, dated about a month earlier: "I never thought when I bought this armoire that I'd have any use for the secret compartment on top, and up to a few weeks ago I didn't. If you've found this, then one of two things has happened. Either you were looking for it — in which case, congratulations — or I'm not around anymore and you're probably the new owner of this beautiful piece of furniture. If it's the latter, feel free to throw this away. It's no longer of any use to me. If it's the former, then you've got what you wanted. I hope you're happy. Sincerely, Paul Flynn."

I was more confused than ever. It seemed Paul felt his life was in danger, but from whom? And why hide the key? Why was keeping it safe so important?

I examined it closely. It was small, silver, and oddly shaped, with no markings on it whatsoever. What was I supposed to do with it now? I hadn't noticed anything in the apartment that could be unlocked. Could the killer have removed whatever the key went to?

"Killian," Sabrina called from the other room. "I think we've been here too long. We have to go."

She was right. We had been there for a while. "Coming," I said. "Let me put things back."

I quickly replaced the letter in the envelope, and after a moment's hesitation, folded it and slid it and the key into my pocket. I dropped the top of the secret compartment back into place. Once again using my shirt as a cleaning cloth, I carefully wiped the armoire free of my fingerprints — or so I hoped. Then, grabbing the stepladder, I returned to Sabrina.

"Did you find what you were searching for?"

I paused for a second, then shook my head. "No luck."

She gave me a suspicious glare. "You were in there a long time. What were you doing?"

"Just looking around. I thought you were ready to go."

"I am. You're avoiding my question. Why did you need the ladder?"

"I wanted to check everywhere, and the armoire was too tall for me to see on top of it. Okay? Hold the short jokes, please. Let's get out of here."

My subterfuge seemed to work, or at least she gave up. She cracked open the door and peeked into the hall. Apparently, the coast was clear because she squeezed out with me right behind her.

Once we were safe in her apartment, I turned to face her. "I appreciate your help, Sabrina. I know it wasn't easy for you."

"If it helps find Paul's killer, then it was more than worth it. But...what...what happened in there?" She almost seemed as if she wasn't sure she wanted to know the answer.

"What do you mean?"

Her eyes narrowed. "You know what I mean. When you said you felt like you were being strangled. What happened?"

I shrugged, hoping I appeared nonchalant. I had avoided the subject while I searched the room and wasn't quite ready to tackle it there in front of Sabrina either.

"Are you some sort of psychic?"

"What? Why would you think that?" I was unnerved by her guess.

"It seems like the only explanation."

"Maybe I just have an overactive imagination."

"I saw you. You weren't imagining anything. You looked...you looked like you were being choked, except there was no one else there."

A shiver raced up my spine. "I don't know what was going on, and I'm telling you the truth. Nothing like that has ever happened to me before. I don't understand it any more than you do. Now, I really appreciate your help, but I have to be going."

She put a hand out and caught my arm as I turned to leave. "Can I at least have your card? In case something else turns up?"

I fished one out and handed it to her. I knew it was unprofessional of me, but I wanted to put as much distance between myself and the whole unsettling experience as possible. I let myself out of Sabrina's apartment without another word.

I found Chris sitting in the stairwell, head propped on her hands, looking eminently bored. As I appeared at the top of the stairs, she glanced up, relief written plainly on her face. I expected to hear recriminations about taking so long, but before I could say a word, she bounced to her feet. "I'm so sorry."

I was confused. "Sorry for what?"

"I was so busy watching the stairs it never occurred to me that someone would come out of their apartment and ambush you. When I saw the gun I almost shit my pants."

I gave a halfhearted chuckle. "You and me both. It turned out to be a fake, though."

"Fake gun? That seems dangerous."

"That's what I said. Anyway, she was Paul's neighbor and friend."

"Great. So she was helpful?"

"Yes and no."

"Explain, please."

"I found something. Paul wrote a letter and hid it with a key. I'm pretty sure it's what the killer was after. The way he tore the place to pieces, it seems obvious he was looking for something: probably the key."

"And you found it?"

"Yes."

"But the killer couldn't?"

"It was very well hidden."

"Where was it?"

"Um...in a secret compartment in the top of an armoire."

"An arm what?"

"It's a big piece of furniture, like a wardrobe. People kept their clothes in them before they started building closets. Paul was using his for other purposes."

"How in the world did you think to even look in there?"

"I, uh, had a little help," I said. "But the point is, I don't know what the key goes to."

"What about the chick with the gun?"

"Sabrina? What about her?"

"Would she know what the key is for?"

"I didn't tell her I found it."

"Why not?"

"I don't know. I guess I felt that the fewer people who know the better. Besides, I'm not sure I trust her completely."

"Oh. Good point. So what did the key look like?"

I fished it out of my pocket and held it out in the palm of my hand.

The color drained from Chris's face. "Killian! You removed evidence from the scene of a crime."

"What was I supposed to do? How can I find out what the key goes to if I leave it in there?"

"We could have told the police and let them handle it. It is an ongoing murder investigation, after all. Being in there in the first place is bad enough; taking stuff is more than even I can get away with."

"Well, it's too late now. I already took it."

"You have to put it back."

"It's too risky. I'd have to explain to Sabrina why I was sneaking back in there without her and she's already suspicious of me as it is."

"Hello?" She leaned over and knocked lightly on my forehead. "Is anyone home in there? You've now tampered with evidence. That's a criminal offense. You have more to worry about than what Sabrina thinks of you. We have to let the police know about the letter and the key. What did the letter say, by the way?"

I reached into my pocket again, and Chris smacked her forehead. "Please tell me you didn't take that, too."

I grinned sheepishly and produced the offending object.

Chris sighed heavily. "Holy fuck! What were you thinking?"

"I, uh...guess I wasn't."

"Clearly. We've got to get back in there now."

"And then what?"

"We call the police."

"And say what? 'Oh, by the way, I just happened to be snooping around Paul Flynn's pad today, and you won't believe what I found in the bedroom.'"

"It doesn't have to be like that. We can make an anonymous tip."

"Again...and say what?"

"We can say we're concerned friends who know Paul had a hidden compartment in his armoire-thingy. We can tell them we think there might be evidence in it. Or we can just let my dad know, and he can handle it."

"Then I'll never learn what the key is for."

"We can find out. My dad knows people."

I hated to admit it, but I was beginning to think she might be right. "Only one problem. Even if we tell the police, there's no guarantee they'll do anything. It's not like they've been exactly on the ball with this case. That's the whole reason I was hired in the first place."

"So what do you propose then?"

"I stick the letter and the key back in my pocket, find out what the key goes to, and take it from there."

"What about the police?"

"They don't know the key exists so it's not like they're looking for it. They missed it when they did their search."

"They didn't have the help you did," she said meaningfully, letting me know I hadn't done as good a job of distracting her as I'd hoped. "What if you turn up something that you can take to the police? How will you explain the key then?"

I thought for a minute. "I'll just tell them I was given the key with an anonymous tip."

She raised an eyebrow. "You mean you'll lie?"

"It's not a complete lie..."

She narrowed her eyes and gave me a stern look. "We're not done talking about your 'anonymous tipster', but we can't stand here in the hallway and yak all day. If we're done here, why don't you come back to my house with me? We can discuss this further there. My dad wanted to meet you anyway."

"Actually, I should check in with some of the neighbors first, if that's okay."

She shrugged. "Sure. I'll just wait here." She patted the wall. "I'm starting to really like hanging out on staircases."

I laughed and returned to Paul's floor. Ignoring Sabrina's door, I went to the one directly across the hall. According to Sabrina, this was Mrs. Gupta's apartment. I knocked and waited a minute. When no one answered, I knocked again, a little louder this time, remembering that Mrs. Gupta was hearing impaired. I heard some shuffling through the door and, a few seconds later, the sounds of locks being undone.

The door swung open to reveal a bent, frail woman wearing a brightly colored sari. Her face was deeply creased, and her steel-gray hair was pulled back into a bun. Despite her age, her eyes were sharp and sparkling, and they quickly gave me a once-over. From her expression, it appeared she found me lacking. "What do you want?" She had a heavy, melodic accent.

"I'm looking into Paul Flynn's murder." I spoke slowly and much louder than usual to be certain she would be able to hear me. I wasn't sure how deaf she was. "I'm hoping you can answer some questions for me."

Her frown deepened. "You do not have to yell. I have already talked to the police."

I lowered my voice sheepishly. "Yes, I know, but I've been hired by a concerned friend. Were you home the day Mr. Flynn was killed?"

She glared at me, and for a moment, I thought she was going to refuse to answer. "I do not get out much, so I am sure I was."

"Did you hear anything unusual — loud crashes or shouting, perhaps?"

She shook her head. "I did not hear anything. I probably had my TV on."

"And you didn't see anyone suspicious?"

"No. Nothing. I cannot help you." She shut the door.

I sighed and turned to the last door: Kent, the traveling businessman. If he was away as much as Sabrina said, I doubted he'd be home, but it was worth a knock. As I suspected, no one answered. I pulled out a business card and jotted a quick note asking him to contact me at his earliest convenience, then stuck it in the door jamb.

I rejoined Chris in the stairwell. "Going down. This is the last one. I want to check the apartment under Paul's."

She grinned. "You know where to find me."

I knocked on the appropriate door. No one answered, so I tried again, a little harder. I waited about a minute and tried one more time.

A few seconds later, a middle-aged woman in a frumpy, ill-fitting pantsuit stepped out of the neighboring apartment. "That one's vacant," she said peevishly.

"Oh. I'm sorry. I didn't know. Can you tell me how long it's been empty?"

She gave me a funny look. "Several weeks, at least. They're doing some renovations before they rent it out. They were almost done and then the ceiling got some water damage so they had to replace that too. What's it to you? You want to rent it?"

"No, no. I'm looking into the murder of Paul Flynn. He lived in the apartment right above this one."

"I know who he was. You don't have a murder in your building and not know about it. That's where the water damage came from."

She had a point. "Sorry. Of course. Were you home the day he was killed?"

"I'm in and out. I'm a realtor. Why?"

"Did you hear anything from upstairs?"

She frowned. "Like what?"

"Loud crashes? Dishes breaking? Shouting?"

"No, nothing like that."

"Anything at all?"

"Nope. Are we finished? I have a client I need to call back."

I nodded. "Yes. Thanks for your help."

She disappeared back into her apartment without another word.

I left to get Chris, but she met me halfway. "That didn't go so well."

I rolled my eyes. "Not at all. Complete waste of time. I guess we're done here. Until I can find out how to get in touch with Paul's family or the guy that owns the escort agency Paul worked for, I don't really have anywhere else to go."

"So we're off to see my dad?"

"Um, sure." I was somewhat nervous. Chris's father sounded a little authoritarian, and authority figures tended to make me uncomfortable. A psychiatrist would probably say it was leftover baggage from my father. I would say they'd probably be right.

"Don't worry," she said, reading me like a book. "Dad's just a big teddy bear."

"Teddy bear. Right."

"Really." She looped her arm through mine and started dragging me down the stairs.

From the Metro station, it was a short trip to the neighborhood where she and her dad lived with her twelve-year-old brother. Her mom had passed away a few years previously from cancer, she'd told me on the ride. Their home was a two-story brownstone townhouse like the ones I'd seen in Paul's old neighborhood — perhaps not quite as nice, but still well-kept and very welcoming.

Chris let us in. "Dad?" she yelled at the top of her lungs.

While we waited for an answer, I took in the entryway. It was wainscoted in dark wood, whose rich patina could only have come from years of polishing. Above the paneling, the walls were painted white. A mirror hung over a small table by the door, and in the corner stood an old-fashioned, brass coat tree bearing an assortment of outerwear, including a police uniform jacket. A hallway laid with a carpet runner gave access to the rear of the house. A staircase led up to the second floor. Doors opened to the right and left at the front of the hall and again farther down.

"In here," a man replied from the room to our left.

Chris stuck her head in. "I have Killian with me."

"Well, don't make him stand in the hall. Come on in and have a seat."

"I didn't want to interrupt if you were busy." She entered the room, motioning me to follow.

Mr. Silver's den was cozy if a bit shabby. A ratty old sofa faced a big-screen TV, while an equally beat-up recliner stood off to one side. Chris's father sat at a large wooden desk against the front wall, under the window overlooking the street. He was a big man, tall and broad-shouldered with the beginnings of a beer belly. His short dark hair was peppered with gray, and his pale blue eyes seemed tired but kind. He pushed away a stack of papers and smiled a warm greeting in my direction.

"I welcome the interruption. The problem with being a policeman is there's too much damn paperwork. You must be Killian."

I shook his outstretched hand and smiled in return. "Yes, sir. And trust me, Mr. Silver, there's plenty of paperwork in the private-investigator business, too."

He laughed. "I don't doubt it. And none of this 'Mr. Silver' business. Call me Louis. Have a seat."

I sat next to Chris on the sofa.

"So how'd the first day on the case go, Christina?"

"It went okay, I guess. I mostly just stood around waiting."

He smiled indulgently. "I told you most investigative work is hurry up and wait."

I almost laughed at how much he sounded like Novak when he said that.

Chris continued, "Still, Killian learned quite a bit, so it was worth it."

"I couldn't have done without you," I hastened to assure her. "You were a huge help."

She laughed. "I don't know about that, but thanks."

Louis turned his attention to me. "I'm not really familiar with the case aside from what I've read in the paper and the little Shane told me over the phone. Why don't you fill me in?"

I quickly sketched out the details for him, including my interviews that day — leaving out, of course, my search of the apartment and finding the key and letter. When I finished, he nodded thoughtfully. "Sounds like you're doing a good job. Shane was right about you." His face suddenly creased into a big smile. "So how is old Shane Novak these days?"

"He's good."

"Is he keeping busy?"

"Busier than he'd like, according to him, but in all honesty, I don't think he'd have it any other way."

He laughed. "You're right about that. He was one hell of a cop. You've got a good teacher when it comes to learning the investigative process."

"You don't have to tell me."

"How about the home front? Has he moved on after his wife's death?"

"You're one to talk, Dad," Chris said.

"Hush," he said, but his eyes were warm. "That's my business. I'm prying into Shane's right now."

I laughed. "I don't think he'd mind. He's been dating someone for a little while now. Her name is Judy."

"Have you met her?"

"Oh, yes. I introduced them."

"She's a good woman?"

"The best."

"Good for him. He deserves it."

"If the inquisition is over," Chris said, "I'd better show Killian how to find his car so he can head home."

"You're welcome to stay here tonight," Louis said.

"Thank you, but I'd really like to get back to Salisbury."

"The offer stands anytime you need it. Shane says you're a fine young man, and that's all the recommendation I need."

I blushed at the compliment and nodded awkwardly. Chris saved me from further embarrassment by grabbing my arm and dragging me toward the door.

"It was nice to meet you," I called out at the last minute as I remembered my manners.

"You too, Killian," he called back.

Just as we were walking out the door, a skinny kid with dark hair and eyes exactly like Chris's came down the hall.

"Hey, Chris," he said, eying me over.

Chris stopped with a small sigh. "Hello, Kevin. I don't have time to talk right now. We have to go."

"You aren't even going to introduce me?"

"Kevin, Killian. Killian, Kevin."

"Is he your boyfriend?" Kevin asked in that annoying singsong voice kids use. "What happened? Decide to switch teams?"

Chris merely dragged me out and shut the door firmly behind us.

"That was my twerpy little brother," she said in an aggrieved tone.

"Hey, I have one too. I can't tell you how many times he's embarrassed me in front of people. And it's usually at the door, too."

She laughed. "He's not so bad, really. It was hard on him when Mom died."

"I'm sure it was hard on all of you."

She shrugged. "I was prepared — or as prepared as you can be for something like that. She'd suffered a long time. At least she's not suffering now."

I nodded, and we walked the rest of the way to the station in silence. When I turned and prepared to say goodbye, Chris surprised me by inserting money into the fare-card machine.

"What are you doing? I can find my own way now. You don't have to come with me."

"I know I don't have to. I want to. I have a few questions for you."

"What kind of questions?" I had a sinking feeling I already knew the answer.

She finished getting her fare card before facing me with a look of resolve. "Earlier today we both agreed we couldn't be partners unless we were honest with each other. You avoided the issue when I asked earlier, but now I want to know about this help you got finding the key — and you're going to tell me the whole story if you want me to keep working with you."

Chapter 15

I sat staring at Chris while trying to decide what to say. She'd caught me off guard by demanding the whole story. After thinking about it for a few minutes, though, I decided it would be best to tell her everything. If she was going to be my partner in this investigation — and I really hoped she would be since it seemed we worked well together — then she had a right to know. What if I had another one of my "psychic friends" moments and she was there? She needed to be prepared. If she couldn't handle it or chose not to believe it, that was up to her, but at least she'd understand what was going on.

So I told her. I started by giving her the back story about Seth and his murder, and how he had started coming to see me. Then I filled her in on Amalie and what Judy had told me about the Gifts — and how I'd been reluctant to use or even acknowledge them. I finished up by explaining everything that had happened in Paul's apartment.

To my surprise — and relief — she just nodded and said, "Okay."

"Okay?"

"Yeah. It's no biggie."

"No biggie? Dead people talk to me, or at least they communicate with me, and all you have to say is, no biggie? Don't you care?"

She gave me a withering look. "Why should I care? A good investigator uses whatever tools he has available. I can't even pretend to understand these, uh, Gifts you have. I do know I'm very glad I don't have them. But as long as you do, you should use them. I mean, hell, the results speak for themselves. You found that key, and there's no way you would have ever found it otherwise, right?"

I nodded.

"Then what's the big deal? You have a unique ability. I don't envy you for it, but it could definitely have its uses. My advice, unsolicited as it is, would be to get all the training you can for those Gifts. Maybe you'll be able to control the, er, attacks like the one you had in the apartment when you felt like you were being strangled. At any rate, the better you understand them, the more helpful and the less scary they'll be."

"You know, that's pretty much what Judy and Seth have been saying all along, but hearing it from you seems to makes more sense."

She laughed. "Well, at least something makes sense."

The Metro pulled into New Carrolton station just about then, and we said our goodbyes.

Our conversation gave me a lot to think about on the long drive home. It was the first time I'd laid everything out like that for someone else, and Chris was only the second person I'd ever told about Seth. I'd never even mentioned him to Micah, and I wasn't sure I ever would. There was just something about Chris that I trusted instinctively. She had a down-to-earth quality about her, a certain practicality that I found comforting.

More importantly, I realized, while explaining it all to Chris, I'd made up my mind to do what Judy had been bugging me to do for months now: get training for my Gifts. It was a scary thought, since it meant I'd have to face them in order to train them...and I really didn't want to do that.

As much as I didn't want to, though, I knew I had to. Things seemed to be escalating, and it frightened me. I'd never experienced anything like the strange feeling I had in Paul's apartment. Was it a new Gift or just an extension of the ones I already knew about? Had all my Gifts manifested themselves, or would more be working their way to the surface?

I arrived home around eight to an empty house, which suited me just fine. As much as I loved Adam and Steve, I wasn't ready to go into an explanation of my strange business trip. I was still too shaken by what had happened.

I went up to my room and stood by the phone, debating about whom I should call first — Novak or Judy. Novak could wait for morning, I decided. I needed to talk to Judy right away.

I breathed a sigh of relief when she answered on the third ring.

"Are you busy right now?" I asked.

There was a slight hesitation. "Not really."

"I need to talk to you."

"Is it about...?" Her voice was filled with tension.

"Jake? No, this is personal."

"You want to talk now?"

"Yes, please. If it isn't too much trouble."

"No, I don't suppose it is. Do you want to come here, or would you rather I went there?"

"Well, I just drove home from DC, so I'd rather you came here, but it doesn't really matter."

"No, that's fine. I'll be over shortly." She hung up without saying goodbye. I had the feeling I was interrupting something, but she was too polite to say so.

True to her word, Judy was knocking on the front door in no time.

"Thank you for coming over," I said as I let her in.

"You're welcome. Now, do you mind telling me what this is all about?"

"Something happened today that I need to discuss with you."

"In DC?"

"Yeah," I said slowly. "How did you know I was in DC? Oh...your Gifts?"

She laughed. "You told me on the phone, you goof. Look, before we get started, can I make some tea?"

"I can do that," I said while blushing furiously.

We went into kitchen, where I rummaged through the cabinet. "I don't think we have any tea leaves. Just regular tea bags."

Judy leaned against the counter with an amused expression. "That's fine. I wasn't planning on doing any readings. I just want tea. Now tell me what happened today in DC."

I got out a tea kettle and started filling it with water. "I'm investigating a murder. I don't know how much Novak told you..."

"He didn't tell me anything. He rarely discusses work with me."

I put the kettle on the burner, then sat down at the table and took a deep breath. "There was this guy who was strangled in his apartment. I was in there looking around, and when I opened the door to the bedroom where he was murdered...something happened."

"Wait, do I need any background information?"

"Um, I don't think so. Except, the police don't seem to be too interested in solving this case. The man killed was an escort. You know what that is, right?"

She arched an eyebrow. "Sweetie, I wasn't born yesterday. I would hope I know what an escort is. My question is: how did you stumble onto this case? It's in DC and, as far as I know, you don't frequent escorts. For that matter, how'd you get in his apartment?"

"Okay, so maybe you do need a little background." I sighed. "The man killed, his name was Paul. He was a...friend of Micah's." I knew my pause told her more than I'd intended, so I rushed on. "That's how I got involved, and that's why I had a key to his apartment."

"Okay, got it. So you were in his apartment. You opened the door to the room where he was murdered and something happened. What was it?"

"I...I don't know how to describe it except...I think I experienced his murder."

Her eyes widened. "What do you mean?"

"I mean...it felt like someone was strangling me. I couldn't breathe. I couldn't scream. I could feel the fingers digging into my throat."

Judy stared at me in wide-eyed silence until the kettle began to whistle, startling us both. She turned off the burner as I jumped up to grab a mug for her and, after a moment's thought, one for myself too. A nice, hot cup of tea suddenly sounded very comforting.

With our tea in hand, we sat down at the table again. Leaning back into my seat, I continued, "And that's not all."

"There's more?"

I nodded and inhaled the scent of steeping tea. "The person who was with me, Sabrina — she was Paul's neighbor and friend — wanted to leave, but I felt really drawn to the bedroom. She wouldn't go in with me, so I went in by myself. The room had been cleaned by the police, but I saw some sort of double image of what it looked like right after the murder. And then...I don't know why I did it, but I asked...I asked Paul to show me what he wanted me to find."

Judy calmly added a spoonful of sugar to her mug, stirred, and took a sip. "And did he?"

"Sort of. There was a noise from an armoire."

"Which you don't think was a coincidence."

"No, as much as I'd like to, I don't. And then..."

"There's more?"

"In the top of the armoire I found a secret compartment containing a letter and a key."

"What did the letter say?"

"Just that Paul thought he was in danger, so he was hiding the key."

"And what does the key go to?"

"I have no idea. That's not the point."

She laughed. "I'm sorry. I was just caught up in the story. The point is, you're exhibiting new aspects of your Gifts, and it's upsetting you."

"You're damn right it is. I felt like I was being strangled."

"But no physical harm came to you, right?"

"Not unless you want to count being scared half to death."

"I don't. This is very interesting."

"Interesting? Is that all you can say? It's not interesting. It's terrifying. I don't want these Gifts. They're not even gifts. A gift is a nice sweater or a good book. This is a curse."

"Gifts or curse, you have them. Now what are you going to do about them?"

I took a deep breath and tried to calm down, although, God knows, Judy was calm enough for both of us. "That's what I called you about. Chris made me see today that I really have to get training for these...whatever. Or at the very least understand them better."

"It's about time you came to that conclusion. Good for Chris. Who is he?"

"She, not he. Novak lined her up to help me out in DC since I don't know the city. She said I should look at this as just another tool to use in my line of work, and to do that I need to figure out how to take advantage of them."

"I like this Chris. Although you probably shouldn't think of them as tools, really. They're not exactly something you can actually control. There's no on-and-off switch. However, she's right in that, if you understand them, you'll be able to make better use of what they tell you."

"So will you help me?"

"I can't."

"What?" Surely, I misunderstood her.

"I can't."

I hadn't misheard. "Why not?" I was completely flabbergasted.

"Your Gifts aren't like mine. I struggle to even sense Amalie, while for you it's natural. My strongest Gifts lie in the future and sometimes in the present. Yours are obviously tied to the past. That's why it's so easy for you to sense the dead."

"Lucky me."

She shrugged.

"So you can't help me at all?"

"I didn't say that."

"Can you help me or not?"

"I can't exactly, but I might know someone who can."

"Who?" I was struggling to keep my patience.

"Well, now, don't get your hopes up. He doesn't live here."

"Who?"

"It all depends on whether I can talk him into coming here." She frowned. "That won't be easy. He's a little...eccentric."

"Who's eccentric? And where is he?"

"And the soonest he could come would probably be this summer. Unless I can convince him it's an emergency — which I suppose it could be."

"Judy, if you don't tell me right now who you're talking about, there will be an emergency."

She laughed. "Sorry, Killian. I was thinking out loud. The man I have in mind is Hector Huang. He's an old friend from back in California."

I blinked. "California?"

"Yes. I know it isn't ideal."

"How can he teach me if he's on the other side of the country? Do they have correspondence courses for psychic powers?"

Judy sighed. "Drink your tea, dear."

I obediently took a sip of tea and realized I hadn't added any sugar. I made a face, then quickly spooned in a few scoops and stirred it in. I liked my tea very sweet.

Judy seemed lost in thought, so I decided to nudge her with a question. "Besides being an old friend, who is this Hector? Why do you think he could help me?"

"He's a shaman. His Gifts are closer to yours."

"When you say his Gifts are closer to mine, does that mean they're not exactly the same?"

"No, not exactly. His are more closely related to the spirit world. I'll ask him when I talk to him next if he thinks he'll be able to help you."

"Isn't what I'm dealing with the spirit world?"

"Not in the same way. The spirits Hector senses and communicates with are not now, nor have they ever been, human. They're not deceased people. There's a whole spirit world out there that most people never know about."

This was all a little much for me. I felt slightly shell-shocked. "You mean like angels?"

"Among other things."

"I don't even want to know."

She smiled and reached over to pat my hand. "It's really not all that bad, sweetie. You'll get used to them eventually."

I sighed. "I don't guess I have any choice. No matter how hard I try to ignore them, they won't go away."

She stood up and gave me a hug. "It'll be okay, Killian. I promise." Ruffling my hair playfully she added, "I only have one question."

"What's that?"

"While you were chatting with Paul, why didn't you just ask who killed him?"

My mouth flew open, and for a second nothing came out, while several thoughts ran through my mind in rapid fire. Then everything tried to tumble out at one time. "We didn't... I didn't... He... Could I have done that?"

Judy threw her head back and laughed heartily at my expense. When she'd pulled herself together, she patted my cheek. "I was just kidding." She wiped a tear from her eye. "Even if you had thought to ask him, he probably wouldn't have told you. It's never that easy."

"Why not?"

She shrugged again. "Who knows? It just doesn't seem to work like that. Now, I'd better go. Will you be okay?" I nodded, and she gave me a quick kiss on the cheek. I started to rise to walk her to the door, but she waved me back down. "I can let myself out. Stay put and drink that tea. Don't let it go to waste."

I nodded, only half-listening. My mind was already picking at her comment about how it didn't work like that. I remembered Seth's saying he had rules about what he could say and do. Was it the same with all ghosts? I'd gotten the impression that Seth occupied some sort of special category in the echelon of the dearly departed, but what did I know?

I absently picked up the mug and took a sip.

"It's about time you came to your senses," someone said, and I almost spit my mouthful of tea across the table.

"I hate it when you do that," I said.

"I know," Seth said smugly. He slid into the chair across from me and propped his feet on the table. I started to protest, until I realized it was just a little silly to care whether an insubstantial being had his feet on the table.

"Just for the record," he said, "you were never in any real danger today, at least not from ghosts. Snooping around a sealed crime scene is a danger of another type entirely."

I sat up excitedly. "Was that Paul? Was he there?"

He shrugged. "I don't know. I wasn't there."

"Then how do you know I wasn't in any danger?"

"I was listening to what you told Judy."

"You were eavesdropping."

"No, I just hadn't made myself known yet."

"You were eavesdropping."

"If you'll stop interrupting me, I'll get to my point." He glared at me. "From what you told Judy, if whoever or whatever was guiding you had wanted to hurt you, there was plenty of opportunity."

"What do you mean whoever or whatever?" I asked uneasily.

"Just what I said. You heard Judy. There are other things in the spirit world besides what you call ghosts."

"Are any of them unfriendly?"

"You bet your sweet booty."

"Great."

"Don't worry. If I had to make a guess as to what was guiding you in the apartment, I'd say it was Paul, or at least some essence of Paul."

"Huh?"

"It doesn't necessarily have to be Paul himself. Your personality leaves an imprint of itself on any place where you spend a great deal of time. That impression isn't exactly sentient, but if you have a strong enough Gift, it can respond to direct questions."

"But what about feeling like someone was strangling me? And the sense that I was being drawn to the bedroom?"

"Both of those could just be aspects of your Gifts: sensitivity to strong emotional imprints. Death is a pretty strong imprint, especially a violent death. I'm not surprised you picked up on that. And if you were going to be drawn anywhere, it would be to the bedroom, where the strongest impression was."

"So you don't think Paul's ghost is really in the apartment? It's just this impression?"

He shrugged. "I don't know. He could be. I'm just throwing out some other options."

"You're not a big help, you know that?"

"Hey, I can stop coming."

"No! Don't!"

"Then quit your whining."

I stuck my tongue out at him. He quickly returned the favor before vanishing into thin air.

"You always have to have the last word, don't you?" I said to the now-empty room.

I had classes the next morning, so I didn't arrive at the office until the afternoon. I found Novak sitting at my desk.

"I've got good news," he said before I was even all the way through the door.

"What's happened to manners in this society?" I said theatrically. "Doesn't anyone say hello anymore?"

"I thought you'd be more interested in my news."

"I am. Still, it would have been nice to get some sort of greeting. I have news for you, too. Actually, I want to fill you in on what I did yesterday."

"I'm eager to hear all about it. Who should go first?"

"You."

"I got you tickets to the AIDS Ball."

"Yes! You're a miracle worker, Novak."

"Yeah, yeah. I know. Actually, I just happened to know someone who had a couple of extra tickets."

"Are you going with me?"

"No, you're going with Micah."

That brought me up short. "What? I am? Why?"

"I want someone with you. I don't think I'm the best choice, because you're bound to run into Jake while you're there, and you couldn't very well explain my presence. You and Micah, on the other hand, could conceivably be there — Micah in his role as a reporter and you as his date."

"But..." I started to argue. I wasn't sure I was ready to go on a date with Micah just yet, even a work date.

"No buts. Either you go with Micah or not at all."

I was almost beginning to think Novak was playing a bit of the matchmaker. "When is it?"

"Next Friday, Halloween night. It's a masquerade ball."

"Great. So now I have to find a costume, too."

"Not exactly. This isn't your average costume party. You can't go dressed as a mummy. It's a formal masquerade ball — tuxedos with masks are the normal attire."

"You're kidding."

"I assure you, I'm not. You might want to let Micah know too, so he can come up with something."

"But how are we supposed to know who anyone is if everyone is wearing masks?"

"People seldom leave the masks on the whole time at soirées like this. The whole purpose of going in the first place is to see and be seen."

I sighed. "Nothing is ever simple, is it?"

"What would be the fun in that? Now tell me what you accomplished yesterday. How did the first day of your new investigation go?"

I gave him a brief rundown, omitting the more supernatural and illegal elements of the adventure. He was quiet for a minute when I finished, then said, "That was a good report. Now give me your impressions so far, what you actually feel rather than a blow-by-blow of what happened."

"Well," I began slowly, "I don't like Razi. I instinctively don't trust him, but somehow I don't really believe he's the killer."

"You know by now not to go on instinct alone. You've been fooled before."

"You're right. I think a lot of my dislike for Razi might be based on the situation with Tad. I don't feel at all comfortable with that."

"Nor do I, but it's a side issue at the moment. Don't let it distract you. Once the case is over, if nothing has changed, you can revisit the situation. If it continues to bother you, turn it over to the police. Anything else?"

"Everyone I've talked to mentions Paul's secretive behavior the last few weeks before he was killed. I'm wondering if that could possibly be connected somehow."

"Good thinking. What's your next step?"

"I want to interview his family and the guy who owns the agency."

He smiled. "You're doing great, kid. That's exactly what I would've suggested. The only thing I would add is that I'd suggest making the agency your higher priority. Find this Neal person and talk to him. And to do that, I think you need to get Micah's input."

There he went, pushing me toward Micah again. Or was I just being overly sensitive? I sighed, knowing he was right. "I'll call him now. As soon as you let me have my desk back, anyway."

Novak stood up and moved in the direction of his office, only to stop in the doorway as I took the seat he had just vacated. "I know this is none of my business, but whatever's going on with you and Micah, you should work it out before it's too late."

I looked up sharply. "What do you mean, before it's too late?"

"Life is unpredictable, kiddo. You never know what tomorrow might hold. Let go of the unimportant things; hang on to the ones that matter." He shut his door with a quiet click.

I sat for a minute, thinking about what he'd said, trying to separate the important from the unimportant. It's often hard to tell the difference when you are in the thick of it. I knew one thing for certain, however, even if my heart wasn't quite ready to admit it: Micah was important to me. I took a deep breath, picked up the phone, and dialed his number.

Chapter 16

I sat alone at Micah's favorite diner, anxiously waiting for him to arrive. I'd managed to snag a corner booth, so at least we'd have some measure of privacy when we had the conversation I'd been rehearsing over and over in my head. Despite our having agreed to meet at five, I'd been such a nervous wreck I'd left work well before the appointed time.

I slouched there, playing out what I planned to say while mutilating sugar packet after sugar packet. Although Novak's advice had set me off on a path of self-examination that ended with some very clear decisions, I was still worried about how Micah would react. I don't know why I chose the diner for our meeting, since we didn't have the best memories of the place. The previous time we'd been there, Micah had broken up with me.

I destroyed the last sugar packet and was about to move on to the Sweet-n-Low when Micah slid into the seat across from me.

"Hey," he said easily. His dark-blue pullover looked a bit rumpled, and his hair was mussed up a little, but he somehow looked better than ever.

"Hi," I said softly.

"How did things go yesterday?"

"Okay, but I need to talk to you about something else first, if you don't mind."

An odd expression flickered through his eyes, but it was gone too quickly for me to read. I fought a sigh as I wondered what the point was in having all my Gifts if they didn't help me out when I really needed to know what was going on right across the table from me. Before I could say a word, however, a waitress appeared to take our order. I tried not to grit my teeth.

Once she'd gone, Micah turned the full weight of his attention on me, causing my stomach to suddenly curl itself into the fetal position. "Yeah. So, uh, Novak said something this morning that really got me thinking about us." I took a deep breath. "He told me to let go of the unimportant things and hold on to those that matter. As I thought about what he said, I realized you matter to me...and I don't want to lose you."

Micah opened his mouth to respond, but I held up a hand to stop him. "Please, just let me finish. I've been rehearsing this all afternoon, and if I don't say everything now, I may never do it."

He nodded, and I continued. "I know I reacted very badly when I found out about your past. I could make a lot of excuses — it caught me by surprise, I found out in a rotten way — but the truth is I overreacted. Who am I to judge your past? I have no right to do that. Even if it wasn't what I would have chosen, it's just not my place. I've never been in the same situation, so I don't know what I would have done.

"The important thing is that I love you. I love who you are, and who you are is a direct result of your past, so how can I have a problem with it? These last few months together with you have been wonderful. That morning in DC when we made love...I've never been so happy or felt so right. I don't want to lose you. I...I guess what I'm saying is, I hope you can forgive me and we can start over. I would understand if—"

"May I speak yet?" Micah said, catching me by surprise.

I nodded mutely.

"There's nothing to forgive," he said gently. "The way you found out was crappy. I should have told you sooner. You needed time to process everything, and you got it. Now you're ready to move on, and that's just what we'll do: move on...together. There's no need to start over. So we both come with baggage. Who doesn't these days? The important thing is we love each other and want to be together."

I breathed a huge sigh of relief and realized I was grinning like an idiot. An answering grin lit up Micah's face. "Damn, Kill, I was afraid you were here to tell me to go jump in a lake."

"Not a chance, Mr. Gerber. You're stuck with me."

"Suits me just fine, Mr. Kendall. So now that's settled, what happened yesterday?"

I quickly took him through my conversations with Tad, Razi, and Sabrina, and my search of Paul's apartment. "At this point, I need to get in touch with Paul's family and with Neal," I said. "I was hoping you'd be able to help me."

"I can maybe help you with Neal," he said thoughtfully, "but I have no idea how to locate Paul's family. I never met them, and he rarely talked about them." He paused for a moment. "Do you have the key with you?"

I nodded. I'd slipped it into my pocket, just in case. I slid it across the table.

Micah picked it up and examined it. "It looks like a safe-deposit-box key."

I frowned. "Do you know if he had one of those?"

"Not while I was with him, at least as far as I was aware."

"I guess that doesn't mean anything. He had plenty of time to rent one after you left and no real reason to mention it when you were together. There aren't any markings on the key. How do I know where the safe-deposit box is?"

"Hey, you're the detective. That's your job. Even if you find out, though, you can't just waltz in and pop it open."

"What do you mean?"

"There are two keys to a safe-deposit box — the one you have and one that stays with the bank. Both are required to open the box, and you'd need proof of identity to get the second key."

I sighed. "So I took it for nothing?"

"I didn't say that. I'm sure something will occur to you."

I smiled at Micah's vote of confidence. "You think so?"

"Absolutely. Okay, what's next? You want to know how to find Neal."

"Right."

The waitress brought us our sandwiches just then, and we took a minute for a bite. Then Micah frowned. "I don't think I have his number anymore. I didn't save much of the stuff from that life. I wanted to make a fresh start here." I must have looked disappointed because he smiled. "I didn't say I couldn't get it, though."

"How?"

"Well, it might take another trip to Michelangelo. I didn't keep in touch with anyone who worked for Neal, but if they're still in the DC area, that would be the best place to run into them."

"Razi said most guys don't stay with an agency for very long. Paul was an exception to the rule."

"He's right about that, at least, but even if they don't work for Neal anymore they might know how to get in touch with him. I can't come up with a better idea right now. I never knew his last name, and I never met him in person. All my contact with him was by phone or email. I think that's pretty much his usual M.O."

"How soon can we go?"

"Well, I can't do it right away. I have to get my story finished pronto or my editor's going to birth a calf. There's always a big crowd at the club on Halloween weekend, we could go that night."

"Oh! I almost forgot. I have tickets to the AIDS Benefit Ball for Halloween night."

"You what?"

"I have tickets for the Ball."

"How in God's name did you get them? Those things are almost impossible to come by."

"Novak did it for me. I wanted them in connection with another case I'm working on."

"What other case?"

Realizing I'd never mentioned I was investigating Jake, I explained about Judy's request and how I found his ticket to the ball in his room. "So, you wanna go to the ball with me? You can be my Prince Charming."

"Does that make you Cinderella?" I stuck my tongue out at him, causing him to laugh. "Of course I'll go. You think I'd pass up the chance to see you in a ball gown?"

"You're too funny. Actually, though, we do have to dress up. Novak said tuxedos and a mask."

"Let me take care of it. I might be able to get the paper to swing for the tux rentals. They ought to be thrilled that one of their reporters will actually be attending this thing."

"Didn't they plan on sending anyone?"

"Not that I know of, which gives me another leg up on old Walters."

Walters, one of the senior reporters at the paper, had been in the business since Ben Franklin started printing and resented the younger reporters like Micah. After Walters sabotaged some of Micah's early assignments, their relationship became especially acrimonious, leading Micah to relish every chance he got to upstage the older man.

"So when can we go to the club?"

"Um, how about this weekend?"

I thought a moment but couldn't recall anything to interfere with that plan. "Sounds good to me. The sooner I'm able to contact Neal the better. Can you tell me anything about the agency itself?"

"Like what?"

"Well, how does it work? How long have they been around? Isn't this kind of activity illegal?"

"Technically, it is illegal, but they operate pretty much underground. I don't know how Neal handles everything, but I imagine he has some sort of cover business to launder the money. As I told you before, I was approached by a guy who worked for the agency. It's called recruitment. He thought I might be interested, so he took a risk and mentioned it. Like I said, I never met Neal personally. I don't know if anyone else has either. The closest I ever got to him was talking on the phone or an occasional carefully worded email. Usually, he communicated by text messages. When he had a job for me, I'd get either a call or a text. I deposited the payment, minus my share, into an account at the bank if it was cash, and he deposited my share directly into my account if it was charged."

"You took credit cards?" I asked incredulously. For some reason, that blew my mind.

"Yeah. Anyway, the agency's been around for about five years, I guess. It has a good reputation as a safe and reliable service."

"It's like another world."

"It is, in a way."

"How many guys work for the agency?"

"I don't know. I didn't have a lot of contact with other escorts unless there were some sort of special circumstances."

My sandwich stopped halfway to my mouth. I didn't like the sound of that. "What kind of special circumstances?"

Micah suddenly looked shifty. "Um, well, every once in awhile someone would request two guys."

Feeling a little queasy at the idea, I dropped the sandwich on my plate. "I see. Is that how you met Razi and Paul?"

His face colored. "That's how I met Razi. He introduced me to Paul."

"Oh." Time to change the subject. "What was Neal like?"

"He seemed nice enough on the phone. He never got mad if you couldn't make an appointment, as long as you had a valid excuse. He was a little controlling, maybe. He wanted to be able to contact you at all times. You were never supposed to turn your phone off, and you had to call him back within half an hour if you couldn't answer when he called."

"Or what?"

"I don't think he ever did anything physical. The first time, you'd get yelled at. The second time, he'd dock your pay. If it happened too often, he'd stop using you altogether."

"Couldn't the guys just go out on their own if they were fired?"

"Yeah, and as Razi told you, most of them do eventually anyway if they intend to keep on being escorts."

"How did Neal get into the business in the first place? I can't imagine it's the kind of thing you grow up dreaming about. 'What do you want to be when you grow up, little boy?' 'I want to be a pimp!'"

Micah laughed. "He's not exactly a pimp. Well, I guess he is in a way, but sex isn't necessarily the only thing people want from an escort. To answer your question, though, if what I was told is true, Neal retired from a very successful dot.com business just before everything went bust. He made out like a champ while his former colleagues took the dive with the rest of the Internet. I guess he got bored with retirement, and — *voila* — he decided to open an agency."

"Just like that?"

"I heard he'd used an agency before and thought he could do a better job running one. Maybe he worked for one when he was younger. It was all just rumors, so who knows what the real story is?"

"How old is he?"

"I don't know."

We ate in silence while I digested all I'd learned. After a few minutes, I asked, "What are you doing tonight?"

He made a face. "I have to work. The story."

"Oh yeah, I forgot. I was hoping we could hang out."

"Wish I could. Besides, I figured you'd be going to the GSA meeting on campus."

"Another thing that slipped my mind. I seem to be forgetting everything lately. I'd better start writing my appointments down."

"Get an organizer."

"I'm not that busy. Maybe I will go to Haven, though, now that you mention it. I enjoyed it last week. Was it just last week? So much has happened since then."

"I'm glad you're going. It's good for you to have more friends."

I gave him a curious look. "What do you mean?"

"Just that you seem to get a little too involved in your work sometimes, and it might be good for you to spend more time just hanging out."

"You really think I get too caught up in my job?"

"You're only eighteen, Killian. You should be partying and having fun, not spending all your time following cheating husbands."

"I have fun. We go dancing and..." I couldn't think of anything else I did simply for fun. "I do have fun," said lamely. "I'm just not a party person."

Micah tried not to smile but his twitching lips gave him away. "Well, all I'm saying is, it never hurts to have more friends."

I shrugged. "They seemed nice."

"Then why are you arguing with me?"

"I'm not."

He grinned.

"Okay, maybe a little. I think I'm just getting annoyed with how everyone's always telling me what to do with my life...even when they're right."

"Who else is telling you what to do?"

"Just about every living person I know, plus a few who aren't."

"Huh?"

"Long story."

Micah glanced at his watch. "I have another half hour before I really need to get back. What's going on?"

I tried to figure out where to start. Micah knew about Amalie. He'd been present for most of what happened with her the last time, so he was aware of my Gifts. We'd even talked about my being sensitive to supernatural things. Still, I'd never gone into much detail, and I wasn't sure how he'd handle it.

I finally came to the conclusion that it was best to get everything out in the open. I'd learned my lesson the hard way about keeping secrets in a relationship. I quickly filled him in on what had been going on and my decision to seek some sort of training, if there was such a thing.

Micah sat quietly for a minute after I finished.

"I'm glad you want training," he said at last. "You need to understand what's going on so you aren't so freaked out."

"You mean you aren't freaked out?"

"Not really. After all, I was there for Amalie, remember?"

"Yeah, but..."

"If seeing dead people didn't freak me out, why would this? Give me a little credit."

I sighed. "You're right. I'm sorry. It's just that I've had such a hard time dealing with all this, I figured everyone else would, too."

"Not everyone has as difficult a time accepting new things as you do, Kill."

"You really think I'm like that?" I was a little offended. His only answer was a raised eyebrow. "Am I?" I asked again, almost to myself.

He smiled and patted my hand. The waitress brought the check over, and Micah grabbed it before I could. "This'll be on me," he said, pulling out his wallet. "I have to get back to work now, but I'll call you tonight, okay?"

I nodded and smiled up at him. I was glad things were returning to normal between us — or at least as normal as anything ever got with me. He smiled back, then suddenly leaned down and gave me a quick kiss on the lips. I felt my eyes fly open wide, and I darted a look around to see if anyone had caught it. It was the first time he'd ever kissed me in a public place.

A waitress at the counter was smirking in our direction. When her eye caught mine, she winked and disappeared into the kitchen. I felt a blush creep up my face as I turned back to find Micah grinning down at me. "You going to survive that?"

I nodded and giggled.

"Good. Get used to it. I'm tired of sneaking around like we're doing something dirty." With that, he turned and walked briskly out of the diner.

I giggled again, feeling like a schoolgirl on her first date. I pulled myself together as best I could and started to follow him out.

Just as I was passing by, the waitress reappeared and gave me another wink. "You've got a cute one there, hon. Better hang on to him."

I blushed all the way to my car.

Later that night, after Haven, I once again came home to an empty house. I was beginning to think everyone else moved out and forgot to tell me. It had been a couple of days since I'd even seen Adam or Steve. Micah called me later that night as he'd promised, and we talked about nothing in particular — just chatted. It was a nice change of pace.

I was still on the phone with him when I heard the doorbell. Quickly saying goodbye, I dashed downstairs. When I peeked through the side window, I was surprised to see Judy standing in the yellow glow cast by the bug light on the porch.

"Judy, hi. What are you doing here?"

"I came to get you."

My heart leaped into my throat. "What's wrong?"

"Don't panic. Nothing is seriously wrong — at least nothing that hasn't been going on for some time now. Amalie is on the prowl again. Steve called me. Apparently she woke up a couple who was staying there. Their screaming brought the whole place running, and all but one couple checked out."

"Oh, my God!"

"It's time to start learning how to use your Gifts, Killian." Her grim expression didn't leave any room for arguing. That didn't stop me from trying.

"What? Now?"

"No time like the present."

I tensed up. "But I don't know anything yet."

"Haven't you ever heard of on-the-job training? Besides, what do you need to know how to do? You've seen Amalie before. You've even spoken to her."

"She didn't answer back."

"Not verbally, but she did lead us to the basement where we found her baby."

"I'm not ready for this."

"Yes, you are. More importantly, Steve needs you. So does Adam. Amalie has been getting worse and worse. Steve and Adam have hardly slept the last two nights."

I sighed, and my body slowly released some of the tension as I accepted the inevitable. "What will I have to do?"

"Talk to her again. Try to find out what's wrong. We have to get her to stop."

"Why can't you just have an exorcism?"

"Steve doesn't want to. He wants to lay her to rest somehow, not just drive her out."

"What if we can't?"

"We'll cross that bridge if and when we come to it. Are you going to join me or stand there and argue all night?"

"I'm coming, but I don't like this at all."

"I'm not asking you to like it."

We drove to the bed and breakfast in almost complete silence. As Judy pulled into the drive, her headlights washed across the beautifully painted sign that Adam had surprised Steve with just before the grand opening. It was a large oval about three feet across, hand-carved with a picture of the house on one side, the creek running across the bottom, and the name Amalie's House above.

It occurred to me how appropriate the name was. Even though she'd been dead for a century and a half, without a doubt the house was still hers.

Judy parked by the front door, since guests weren't exactly an issue at that point. Steve and Adam looked surprised when I followed Judy inside.

"Killian!" Steve exclaimed.

"I'm glad you came," Adam said with a tired smile.

My dads both seemed to have aged since I'd last seen them. They were haggard and worn, with dark circles under their eyes. A sudden flash of self-realization made me understand how selfish I'd been by not wanting to come. After all Adam had done for me, how could I not do this for him? I felt deeply ashamed and almost burst into tears.

I humbly turned to Judy. "What do you want me to do?"

I read approval in her eyes. "We're going to try to contact her."

"And do what?" Adam asked.

"I want Killian to ask her why she's still here now the baby is gone. I'm hoping she'll communicate in some way."

"And if she doesn't?" Steve asked.

"Are you still opposed to an exorcism?"

He sighed. "Not as opposed as I was before tonight, but if we can find some other way..."

"I'll try," I said, sounding more confident than I felt. "How are we going to do this? In the cupola again?"

Judy shrugged. "It's as good a place as any."

"Can we come?" someone asked from the stairs, causing us all to jump and turn toward the voice. The couple standing there appeared to be in their early to mid-thirties, fit and lean. They looked enough alike that they could have been siblings, but the way she had her hand resting on his shoulder seemed more intimate than a sister and brother. They both had short brown hair and dark eyes, and I thought they were roughly the same height, although it was a little hard to tell since she was standing on a higher step than he was.

"I'd forgotten you were still here," Adam said in a surprised voice.

"We're Alan and Carla Moss." They came down the rest of the way to join our little group in the foyer. "I guess you could call us ghost hunters. A friend of ours was told this house was haunted, so we came as soon as we could both take off work. We were really excited when we heard about the sighting tonight, but disappointed we weren't the ones the entity appeared to."

I couldn't believe what I was hearing. Were these people for real? I looked around at everyone else, and judging by Adam's and Steve's expressions, they at least were having the same doubts.

"Well, I guess that explains why you didn't join the exodus when the others left," Adam said dryly.

"I appreciate your interest," Judy said politely, "but I don't think it would be a good idea for you to come with us."

"Why not?" Alan asked, disappointment written clearly on his face.

"First off, you might not be sensitives. Have you ever actually seen a ghost?"

The couple looked at each other. "Well, no," Carla said after a moment.

"Amalie is unpredictable. She might not want to perform for an audience, and we really need to make contact with her right away."

Alan frowned. "Why the rush? You're not going to get rid of her, are you?"

"She's not exactly good for business," Adam said.

Carla beamed. "Hey, we're here."

Steve pointed out the obvious. "No one else is, though."

"I'm sorry," Adam said, "but it would be best if you just returned to your room. Maybe she'll feel like dropping by for a visit later tonight."

Looking unhappy, the couple turned and went back upstairs.

"Weirdos," Adam muttered under his breath.

"Are you ready?" Judy asked me.

"As I'll ever be."

"Then let's go."

I dutifully followed her up the stairs to the third floor. The house was quite old by American standards — pre-Civil War, in fact. A wealthy sea captain, who had married late in life, built it for his wife, one Amalie Marnien. Its style was hard to categorize, since the architect seemed to have blended several together to form a rather unusual result. It was three stories, with a flat roof, lots of intricate trim, and a wrap-around porch. Perched in the middle of the roof was a small room the Captain had built so his bride could watch for his return. He left the young woman alone in the house for months at a time while he was out to sea. Although she'd died a long time ago, her spirit had never departed.

Our resident ghost might have gone unnamed had I not found a painting of her stored in one of the rooms when Steve bought the house. I'd let Judy talk me into contacting Amalie once before, during the renovations. That time she led us to the basement.

Judy and I had both experienced strange dreams while sleeping in the house. They involved Amalie burying a baby, we assumed to be hers, in the basement. When the dirt floor was excavated, sure enough, a tiny skeleton was found with the silver brooch Amalie wore in her portrait placed with the body. We reburied the baby next to its mother in the small private cemetery on the grounds, but for whatever reason, Amalie's spirit hadn't been laid to rest with the child.

It had been a few months since I'd last climbed up the narrow steps to the cupola, but as I followed Judy, the same sense of loss and despair I'd felt the other times washed over me again. We believed the baby might have died when Amalie fell down those very stairs. I tried to ignore the way every hair on my body was standing on end.

When I reached the top, a small scuffing sound came from behind me. I spun around but didn't see anything...or anyone. A strange sensation started to creep over me, not quite dizziness, but as if I was almost disconnected from my body.

"Killian?" Judy's voice seemed to come from far away.

I started to turn toward her, but the feeling suddenly intensified. It was much more defined than the vague sense of dread I'd had on the staircase. My vision flickered, and the already ill-lit room seemed to become even dimmer. The stairs darkened until I could no longer see the bottom riser. The steps directly in front of me were illuminated by a flickering, wan light.

My feet were rooted in place, yet at the same time, I felt a terrible, almost overpowering fear. I wanted to run away. I wanted to throw myself headlong down the stairs, but I couldn't. It was as if I was frozen in time. I somehow knew, without being told, that I was Amalie, and just as surely, I knew I clutched a small baby to my chest. There was someone or something behind me, someone I was afraid of, someone I desperately wished to escape. Suddenly, I was shoved violently from behind. For a few seconds, it was as if I was suspended in midair, before I fell into the inky blackness of the stairwell.

Chapter 17

"Should I call an ambulance?" I heard someone ask in a tense, strained voice that sounded like Adam's.

"I don't know," Judy said. "Wait...I think he's coming around."

I opened my eyes to find myself lying at the bottom of the stairs on the hall floor. Steve, Judy, Adam, and the strange ghost-hunting couple were standing around me in a football huddle. Everyone looked a little fuzzy.

"Killian, are you okay?" Adam asked anxiously.

"I was pushed," I mumbled.

"What?" Steve, Judy, and Adam demanded in chorus. Steve and Adam turned disbelieving stares on Judy, who looked stunned and a little afraid. I'd never seen that expression on her face before, and I found it rather disconcerting.

"There was no one up there except me and Killian," she said quickly.

"The ghost pushed him?" Carla the ghost hunter asked.

"No," I said as things began to come into focus and my thoughts cleared along with my vision. "Amalie was pushed. Not me. I think I fell."

Everyone stared at me as if I'd lost my mind. Maybe I had, but the excitement of the scenario forming in my head overcame any thoughts of insanity.

When I struggled to get off the floor, Steve quickly pushed me back down. "Lie still, Killian. You might have a concussion."

"I'm fine," I insisted, nudging him aside and sitting up. Although my head spun for a moment, it quickly settled into its proper place. "Don't you see? Amalie didn't fall with the baby. She was pushed."

"Baby?" the couple asked in unison. Adam and Steve seemed to remember they were there and turned twin glares in their direction. They took the hint and quickly excused themselves, leaving us alone.

"Are you sure she was pushed?" Judy asked as soon as they were gone.

"Yes. It was like..." I broke off and glanced at Steve and Adam, who both looked confused. "It was like what happened with Paul in DC."

I saw realization light up Judy's eyes. "You experienced it yourself?" I was surprised by the intensity in her voice.

I threw a meaningful glance at Adam and Steve, but it was too late. "What do you mean?" Adam demanded.

"Like an out-of-body experience?" Steve asked, excitement coloring his words.

I paused and then sighed. "It seems like one of my other so-called Gifts is to experience the emotions and certain events of another person's life as if they were actually happening to me."

Adam shook his head. "I don't understand."

"It has to have already happened," Judy said. "From what I can tell, Killian's strongest Gifts all pertain to the past. Somehow, he can feel and experience things that have happened to other people. I would say the things he perceives will almost always be connected to either death or some sort of very strong emotion. They would leave the strongest imprints for him to pick up on."

"So you're saying he felt Amalie being pushed down the stairs?"

"No, I felt like I was Amalie being pushed down the stairs. I knew I was Amalie. I can't explain how, but I did. I also knew I was holding the baby, even though I couldn't see it. It was like I was actually there, inside her body. I couldn't move, I was frozen, but I was aware of someone else in the cupola with me, someone I was afraid of. And then it felt like I was shoved from behind and was falling. The next thing I knew, I was down here with all of you standing over me."

Adam turned his attention to Judy. "You never said these Gifts could be dangerous," he said.

"As far I as I know, they aren't. If Killian had been on solid ground he probably wouldn't have fallen."

"Well, he wasn't on solid ground. He was standing at the top of a very steep staircase. He could've been killed. And what do you mean, as far as you know? Are you saying you don't really know how dangerous this stuff is? And you've been encouraging Killian to pursue it?"

"Adam, calm down," Steve said, laying his hand on his arm. Adam shook it off angrily.

Judy was all business again. "Nobody knows everything about the Gifts, and anyone who tells you otherwise is either a liar or a fool — and probably both. Every person's experience is unique to them. No one can say that this or that will definitely happen, or that this is the way it works for sure. The Gifts come in different strengths and combinations, not to mention God only knows how many variations. I'm not an expert, and I've never pretended to be."

"She's right, Adam," I said as I stood up shakily. I felt like one of those newborn giraffes you see on TV, all wobbly and unsteady, not quite sure where to put their feet. Steve moved quickly to support me, and I leaned against him gratefully. "She never promised me anything, and it's not like she gave me the Gifts. I already had them. All she's ever done is try to help me understand them and encourage me to learn more about them. If I have them and don't understand them, that will be truly dangerous. I'm sure many people have driven themselves insane because they didn't realize what their Gifts were. I've wondered more than once if I was losing my mind, and I knew what was happening — well, for the most part."

Adam sighed as his rush of adrenaline slowly drained away, leaving him looking even more tired than he had before. "It's just that I've never thought about all this as really being risky."

"We still don't know if it is," Judy said. "It might have been a coincidence this particular time because of where Killian was standing when it happened. We don't know that his...experience was the cause of his fall."

"Maybe I was just disoriented and lost my balance," I said, but I don't even think I convinced myself. Still, the white lie was preferable to believing something pushed me.

Adam clearly wasn't satisfied with that explanation. Before he could argue further, however, Judy began to question me about the experience. "What exactly did you see?"

"Not much of anything, really. I thought I heard a noise behind me on the stairs so I looked, but there was nothing there. Then, just as I was about to turn back around, it was like time stopped. I couldn't move or speak. The stairs got darker and darker until the only light came from behind me and seemed to be cast by a candle. Somehow, I knew I was Amalie and I was holding a baby. And I knew I was in danger, that there was someone behind me I was trying to get away from...but I didn't know who it was."

"You didn't know, or Amalie didn't know?" Judy said.

I shrugged. "I seemed to be thinking separately from Amalie. The thoughts were my own, but I understood certain things, like in a dream. You know how you don't always need to have things explained, you just...know somehow?" Everyone nodded. "All I can tell you for sure is that I wanted to get away so badly, but I couldn't move. Then, all of a sudden I was shoved really roughly. That seemed to break the spell, because the next thing I knew I was falling."

"It sounds to me like you were pushed," Adam said.

"I might have just been dizzy. Actually, I was dizzy after the last time it happened, too."

"The last time?" Adam said. "It's happened before?"

"Once."

"And you didn't tell me?"

"I didn't really have a chance. I haven't seen you since it happened."

Adam flushed, looking a little ashamed. A phone rang somewhere downstairs, and Steve reluctantly left to answer it. Judy excused herself as well, giving us a little time alone.

"I wasn't saying that to make you feel bad. I know you've been busy here with Steve."

"It doesn't change the fact that I haven't been home in three days," Adam said wearily. He sat down on the staircase. "I haven't seen Kane since Tuesday, and here it is Thursday. Since I hadn't heard anything from you boys, I just assumed everything was fine."

"Everything is fine," I said. I sat down next to him on the step. "We're making out okay. It won't be like this forever."

"Is everything really fine? You're having these...these experiences. What happened with the other one?"

"It had to do with a case I'm working," I said simply. The less Adam knew about my cases, the less he worried.

He shook his head. "Honestly, how is Kane holding up through all this?"

"He'll be okay. He was upset the other night, though. He felt the family was falling apart. We agreed to try and spend more time together, which seemed to cheer him up. He's a good kid. Don't worry about him too much."

"I'm a dad. That's what I do. I worry. I worry about you, too."

"I'm going to get training for these Gifts. Once I understand them..."

"The Gifts are only part of the reason I'm concerned about you."

"What else is there?"

"I'm afraid you're working too hard. You juggle school, a job that's hazardous by nature, and a serious relationship. I'm afraid you're going to get hurt, that you don't get out enough, that you're not happy..."

"Okay, okay. I get the picture. You have a lot of fears. I'm a big boy now, Adam. I can take care of myself."

He sighed. "I know you think you are...and that worries me too."

"Micah is good to me," I said gently. "He would never hurt me."

"Not on purpose, maybe..."

"Listen to me. Please. We just went through a rough patch that could have been the end of us, but instead I think we've come out of it stronger. I love Micah, and he loves me. We both have baggage to deal with, and we realize it now.

"I'm doing fine at school — as far as I know, anyway. My job is my job. I don't think it's really more hazardous than any other. Most of the time it's actually pretty boring. It could be worse. What if I were a cop? Or it might have been much worse. I could have been..." I dropped my voice to a dramatic whisper, "...a lawyer."

That at least brought a smile to his face. "You said Kane is a good kid, but actually I have two good — no, two great kids."

I leaned in and hugged him. "And we have a great dad."

He pulled me tight into his shoulder and wrapped his arms around me. It had been a long time since he'd held me like that. He sighed. "I'm beginning to think this whole thing was a bad idea."

I pulled away gently. "What whole thing?"

"This..." He made an expansive gesture that took in his surroundings. "The bed and breakfast."

"But it was Steve's dream."

"Maybe some dreams aren't meant to be realized."

"Do you actually believe that?"

"I'm not sure anymore. I do know it's not worth losing my family over."

"You've not lost anyone."

"Yet. It's causing a lot of strain on my relationship with Steve, too."

I looked at him closely. "How much strain? You're not going to break up, are you?"

"It's not that bad, but it seems like all we do is fight these days. He's so stressed out I'm beginning to worry he's going to have a breakdown."

"If Amalie were gone, a lot of the stress would be relieved, right?"

"It would help. It might not be a magical cure, but it would go a long way."

"Then I just have to get her to go away."

"How? We don't even know why she's hasn't left. We found the baby and moved it out next to her grave, and she's still here. Now it seems as if someone pushed her down the stairs. What does she want, justice for the person who killed her baby?"

"I don't know what she wants. But I intend to find out."

"Just don't do anything stupid."

"I promise."

"I'm going to go see who was on the phone. If it wasn't Kane, I think I'll drive home and spend the evening with him. Since the Munsters are the only guests staying here, Steve doesn't really need me. You want to ride back with me?"

"Um, actually, I think I'll stay here and see if I can find out anything else."

I could tell he didn't like the idea. He seemed to struggle inwardly for a few moments, then stood up and dropped a hand to my shoulder. "Be careful, Son."

I smiled up at him. "I will, Dad." I saw a tear form in his eye before he turned and walked quickly away. I rarely called Adam Dad, and whenever I did, he had a pretty emotional reaction.

I slowly pulled myself to my feet, using the doorframe for leverage. I had several very sore spots that I had a hunch would be bruises later, if they weren't already. I decided to take stock of my injuries another time.

I turned to face the stairs to the cupola and tried to summon the courage to go up there alone. Taking a deep breath, I started the climb, leaving the light off because it somehow seemed appropriate. I took one step at a time, waiting for the sense of horror to hit me again, but it never did. The feeling of old pain and death still lingered, but the overwhelming horror was gone. Now that I knew what happened there, had it faded?

I reached the top of the stairs without incident and peered around the small room. It was lined with windows on every side. During the day, it had a spectacular view of the surrounding woodlands and the creek that wound its way along the side of the property. In the dark, all I could see was the thick blackness that lay over the house like a blanket.

"What do you want, Amalie?" I whispered.

I heard a creak from the hall below. The hairs stood up on the back of my neck as the soft brush of a footfall followed on the stairs. I found myself backing away from them. A figure began to come into view, looking eerily as if it was rising directly from the floor. My breath caught in my throat, and I fought the urge to cry out. Why did I do this alone?

"Killian?" the figure asked in Judy's voice.

"Judy?" I released my pent-up fear in a whoosh of relief.

"What are you doing up here in the dark?"

"You scared the hell out of me!"

She chuckled. "Sorry. Adam said you were still up here, so I thought I'd come check on you."

I attempted to gather my scattered wits. "Did you notice anything as you climbed the stairs?"

"I wasn't paying—" She broke off.

"No horrible feeling?"

"It's never as strong for me as it is for you, so I didn't really notice, but you're right. Now that you mention it, I didn't feel anything. What do you think it means?"

"Maybe we're done with this room, now that we know what happened here."

"Where do we go now?"

"If you don't know, I'm sure I don't."

I looked over to the stairs and remembered the fear I felt just before falling. "Who do you suppose pushed her?"

"I've been wondering about that. Do we have any proof that the story the real-estate agent told Steve was true?"

"What kind of proof? And what part do you suspect might not be true."

"I don't know exactly. It's just a feeling I have. Maybe some research is in order."

"Research?"

"I'd like to know if all the dates of death add up."

"What are you thinking?"

"Remember your dream? The man you saw running from the creek towards the house? We never knew who he was. I'd like to be able to rule out the Captain."

"But I thought he was lost at sea."

"That's where the veracity of the real-estate agent's story comes into play. What if she didn't have all the facts straight? Or maybe she simply was recounting the version of the story she'd heard. Facts have a way of getting changed over time."

"How would you do the research? This all happened so long ago."

"I'll try the library. They have an extensive genealogy and local history research room. They have all the old tax records, vital statistics records, censuses, and so on. Hopefully, I'll be able to find something about the Marniens. The Captain must have been a fairly prominent citizen of the area, so the old newspapers may have published something, too. I think they have most of those on microfilm."

"Have you done this sort of thing before?"

"A friend of mine back in California was a genealogist, and sometimes she'd get me to help with research. It's actually not all that hard. It just takes a lot of patience."

"Sounds like detective work."

Judy laughed. "It's the same thing, really. Anyway, it doesn't seem likely that Amalie is going to make another appearance tonight. Why don't I take you home?"

"Well, since they have a few spare rooms at the moment, I think I'll stay here. That way I'll be on hand in case she does decide to show up again. Besides, I'm closer to work and school here. Steve or Adam can drop me off."

"What about clothes?"

I shrugged. "I'll just wear these again tomorrow. I'm not that dirty. Someone can run me home tomorrow night and I can grab some clothes and pick up my car."

"You're really serious about getting to the bottom of this, aren't you?"

"Yeah, I am. I've been totally selfish about all this. After everything Adam has done for me, it's the least I can do. For that matter, Steve's probably done just as much. It would be wrong for me to be able to do something and not do it."

"You know, I was a little worried for a while, but you're turning out alright." She chuckled. "You're an amazing kid, Killian. Adam should be proud to have a son like you."

I blushed, but her comments made me think about Jake. Although it was too dark to make out her expression, I couldn't help wondering if she was feeling as lucky. "I'm sorry I haven't been able to do more about Jake lately."

She waved her hand dismissively. "Don't worry about it. I know you haven't forgotten, and you've had enough other things going on."

"But I made a commitment to you..."

"And I have no doubt you'll live up to it. Shane told me he managed to get you tickets to the AIDS Ball. That's good. Maybe you'll be able to figure out what Jake is doing there."

"I hope so. I still feel really lost on this one. I have no idea what's going on."

"You'll figure it out. Come on. Let's go downstairs. I'll help you make up a bed before I leave. Steve should just try to take what little rest he can before he has to get up and start breakfast."

We found Steve downstairs sitting on the settee in the foyer, half asleep. When I told him I was spending the night, he said I could stay in one of the rooms that hadn't been occupied, so the sheets would be clean. He gave me the key and gratefully dragged himself off to bed. I saw Judy out and locked the door behind her before going to find what would be my bed for the next few nights.

The room was beautiful, just like every other one in the house. Adam and Steve had furnished the entire place with 19th Century antiques. This particular room was done in shades of blue with white accents. Very soothing. Rich, heavy, blue velvet curtains hung at the window over sheer white drapes. A large, comfy-looking chair with carved wooden arms and legs had been upholstered in the same material. A tall mahogany dresser stood against one wall with an oil lamp and a silver-framed mirror on its top. Framed watercolors hung on the wall, and a beautiful hand-painted glass shade covered the overhead light bulb.

Despite the beautiful decor, there was only one piece of furniture I was interested in at that particular moment: the bed. It had a mahogany frame with carved spindle-posts and a mattress that came up almost as high as my waist. I barely registered any of those details, however, as exhaustion suddenly overtook me. It had been a stressful night, and it was beginning to take its toll. I turned off the light, pulled my clothes off, and tumbled into bed. As I drifted into the dream world, I wondered again if it was simply too late to help Amalie. I could only hope it wasn't too late to help Adam and Steve.

Chapter 18

I was relieved when I woke up the next morning without having been roused during the night by anyone, alive or otherwise. Despite my determination to see things through, I wasn't looking forward to dealing with Amalie again.

I took a break from my cases that day, went to class, and, after picking my car up from home, caught up on routine stuff at the office. It was a nice change of pace.

That night, Micah invited me out to dinner. We avoided discussing the case while we ate. Afterward, as we walked along the river that ran by the restaurant, I could no longer resist bringing it up. I'd been working on a plan to find Neal, but I needed some questions answered first.

"What's the name of the agency you and Paul worked for?" I asked.

He looked at me as if gauging my feelings on the subject. "Are you sure you want to talk about this?"

I shrugged. "I'm doing better with it. I'm trying not to be so judgmental."

He gave me a lopsided smile. "I thought I'd told you the name already. Not that it will help much. They're not exactly listed in the yellow pages. It's called Top to Bottom."

I blinked for a second, thinking he must be joking. When I realized he was serious, I couldn't help bursting into laughter. "No. You definitely didn't tell me the name before. I would not have forgotten that."

Micah waited for the giggles to wear off before asking, "Why did you want to know? Are we still on for Michelangelo's tomorrow night?"

"Yeah, we're still on, but I have an idea. If it works, it might mean we can just have fun at the club and not worry about business." I gave him a smile to soften my next words. "Our last trip there didn't turn out so well. I wouldn't mind exorcizing those memories."

He grimaced. "True. I'd ask what your plan is, but the fact of the matter is I don't want to talk business right now."

"Oh?" I gave him a coy look through my lashes. "And what do you want to talk about?"

He stopped and caught my arm, swinging me around into his embrace. "I don't want to talk about anything," he said in a husky voice before kissing me tenderly on the lips. I melted into him, slipping one arm around his waist and running my other hand through his hair. It didn't take long for the kiss to grow heated. We came up for air a few minutes later, both of us breathing heavily.

"I've missed you," he whispered, holding me tightly to his chest.

"I've missed you too."

"Do you want to come back to my place tonight?"

I knew what he was asking, and I did want it. I was surprised at how desperately I wanted it. "I wish I could, but I need to stay at the bed and breakfast. I'm on Amalie Watch."

Micah pulled back wearing a startled expression. "Since when?"

"Since last night. It's a long story, but to make it short, I'm trying not to be so selfish. Steve and Adam need help with this, and I'm going to do my best."

"To get rid of Amalie?"

"Something like that."

"I'm proud of you."

"You shouldn't be. I'm still scared spitless."

"What does that have to do with anything? Who wouldn't be scared? The important thing is you're doing it anyway. How about if I stay over with you, then? You have your own room, right?"

"You'd be willing to do that?"

He laughed. "Do what? Would I be willing to sleep with you? That's a silly question."

"I meant sleep in that house, goof."

"It wouldn't be the first time, remember? Besides, I'm not sensitive the way you are. She could show up and do a Mexican-hat-dance in the middle of the bed and I doubt I'd notice."

I snorted at the mental image. "Oh, you'd notice alright. She can make herself known to just about anyone — sensitive or not — if she wants to. If you're serious about staying with me tonight, though, I'd like that."

"I'm very serious." He pulled me close again and showed me just how serious he was.

I'd picked up some clothes and toiletries from home when I'd picked up my car, so we ran by Micah's place so he could pack a bag. Despite almost getting sidetracked there, we finally made it out the door. Since we'd left my car at his apartment when we went out to eat, I drove from there with him following.

Steve gave me a surprised look when I showed up with Micah and we both went upstairs carrying duffle bags, but he didn't comment. Although Micah was still feeling quite amorous, I tried to convince him we should restrain ourselves for the moment and go back down to be sociable. He agreed only after I promised him we wouldn't stay long.

When the ballroom on the first floor wasn't being used for parties, Steve and Adam arranged a comfortable sitting area around the large fireplace. It wasn't quite chilly enough yet to need a fire, but Steve had lit one anyway for purely aesthetic reasons. Then again, there is something comforting and inviting about a crackling fire, so maybe there was more to it than I first thought. Steve served drinks from the wet bar in the corner every night, and often the guests would gather and socialize with one another and their host.

Although another couple was scheduled to arrive the following day, the ghost-hunters were the only other people staying that night. Conversation with Alan and Carla was awkward at best. All they wanted to talk about was supernatural phenomena in general, and ghosts in particular. Whenever we tried to steer the conversation to other topics, they always managed to turn it back to Amalie. They did their best to grill me about my experiences. My reticence only seemed to inflame their curiosity all the more. They were beginning to give me a headache when I guess Micah realized how much they were annoying me.

"We'd better go soon," he said suddenly, cutting off Alan's diatribe on the importance of understanding the living impaired in midsentence. "I have to get up early in the morning and finish that story. They want it for Sunday's edition."

The couple blinked at Micah in surprise. I couldn't tell if they had simply forgotten he was there, or if they were caught off guard by the implication that we were retiring to bed together. I took advantage of their moment of silence to jump to my feet and offer a quick, polite good night.

"Killian," Steve called just as we made it to the doorway. "Can I speak to you a second?"

"Sure." I paused as he started across the room.

"I'll meet you upstairs," Micah said, thoughtfully giving Steve and me privacy to talk.

Steve stared after him. "Killian," he said, sounding slightly uncomfortable. I suddenly grew a little uneasy. "I don't know if this is my place or not. I mean, I'm not your father..."

"What is it, Steve?" I tried to keep my voice neutral. "And you may not be my father, but for all intents and purposes you've been like a second father to me. Or maybe that would be a third father. I don't really count my dad, though." I was babbling. I had a feeling I knew what Steve wanted to talk to me about, and I'd rather have avoided it if at all possible.

"It's just that...well...I guess I didn't realize your relationship with Micah had progressed to the point of sleeping together." He rubbed his face and sighed. "Which I admit was probably pretty naïve of me. I know I haven't been around much the last couple of months. I've been so busy with this place I don't suppose I'd have noticed if you'd suddenly gone straight and started dating girls."

I grinned. "I think we're all safe on that score."

Steve chuckled, but sobered quickly. "I just want you to be safe on every score."

"What do you mean?"

"You're eighteen so you can make your own choices. Adam and I both respect that. But I know if he were here he'd want to tell you to be careful."

"I've done a lot of thinking about Micah and me. I'm sure this is right for us."

"That's not quite what I meant," Steve said with a slight blush.

My blush was more than slight as I realized what he was talking about. "Oh. Oh! You mean..."

"Are you having safe sex?" he asked bluntly.

At that moment, I would have actually welcomed a visit from Amalie, but of course, there's never a ghost around when you need one. I felt as if my face would burst into flame at any moment.

"I... We... I mean... We've only... I..." I stammered to a stop, took a deep breath, and managed to get a coherent answer out. "Yes."

Steve looked eminently relieved. "That's all I needed to know." He pulled me into a sudden hug that caught me by surprise. "I'm sorry that was so...ghastly," he said, releasing me. "I've never had kids, and I don't exactly know what I'm doing. It really shows at times like this."

I kissed his cheek. "If you ask me, you've done a great job."

His face creased into a grin. "Liar." He ruffled my hair and gave me a gentle shove towards the stairs. "Now get on up to your man before he falls asleep without you."

"Not much chance of that," I said with a wicked smirk. "He's been promised something, and he isn't likely to forget it." With that bit of payback, I left a blushing Steve and took the stairs two at a time. Revenge is sweet.

After all my assertions to the contrary, had Amalie decided to show up and do that Mexican-hat-dance in the middle of our bed, I think I just might not have heard it. I was so exhausted after I fulfilled my promise that I slept quite soundly.

Waking up in Micah's arms and feeling his body pressed close against mine was wonderful. In fact, it was something I could get used to very quickly. I stayed as still as possible for a while, reveling in the unfamiliar comfort, afraid to move for fear of breaking the spell. When he started to nuzzle my neck, I realized he was awake as well. I rolled over to face him, tossing a leg casually across his body as I did.

He gave me a warm smile. "Good morning, love."

"A very good morning," I said. "I wish I could wake up like this every morning."

Micah studied me for a minute, his eyes searching mine, before he broke into a wide smile, his eyes twinkling. "If you think this is good, then you're just going to love what comes next." With that, he ducked under the sheet.

By the time we both showered, which took a lot longer than usual, and finally went downstairs, I was just about ready to go back to sleep. Steve was checking in the new couple, two women in their mid-forties, as we passed by the reception desk. He gave me a knowing smile before returning his attention to his guests.

"What was that about?" Micah asked me. As usual, his sharp reporter's instinct hadn't missed a thing.

"Oh, nothing..." I felt the heat rise in my cheeks, belying my attempt at a casual tone.

Micah smirked, but accepted my evasion and moved on. "Okay, so, I'm going to go finish this story and make sure my editor gets it. Do you want me to pick you up at the office or here?"

"Call my cell when you're ready, and we'll just see where I am then."

"Okay. Makes sense. You're still not going to tell me this plan of yours?"

"If it works, I'll tell you all about it. If not, you'll never know."

He laughed and gave me a quick kiss before opening the door. I nabbed a leftover blueberry muffin and followed him out.

My plan wasn't anything elaborate. The only reason I was avoiding Micah's questions was because it was a little embarrassing to admit I even knew about these sources. I was planning to log on to the gay.com chat rooms in the DC area and ask if anyone knew how to get in touch with the Top to Bottom Escort Agency. The rooms were nothing more than pickup joints, places for freelance escorts, horny guys, and dirty old men to score sex. I'd gone to the rooms a few times when Asher and I were having problems, thinking I might be able to meet someone nice, but each time I'd just ended up leaving feeling slightly dirty.

Once in the office, I answered my email, then signed into my gay.com account and pulled up the list of chat rooms. I joined the DC room and tossed out my question about the agency. All I got were a few lewd and suggestive comments along the lines of, "Why pay for it, sweetie, when I can give it to you for free?" I was about to admit defeat when an IM window popped up on my screen.

"Why are you looking for Top to Bottom?" someone with the screen name DCHawtBoi asked me.

I tried to decide how to play it. Should I pretend to be someone looking for an escort, which is what everyone else in the chat room had assumed, or just be honest? It seemed that most escorts were a little wary, so I decided I was in the market for an escort.

"Someone recommended them to me," I typed.

"So you're looking for an escort?"

"Yes."

"I work for T2B. My name is Brady."

"Hi, Brady." I wondered what the protocol was for something like this. Did you make small talk or get right to the details?

"What's your name?" he asked after an awkward pause.

"Travers." I gave him my middle name. For some reason, I was hesitant to use my real name.

"Have you ever been with an escort before?"

"Yes," I answered. It was a partial truth.

"So you know the drill. What do you like?"

Uh oh. I was getting in over my head. "The usual." I tried to bluff my way out of it.

"You'll have to be more specific than that. Do you like smooth or hairy? Younger or older? Top or bottom? Do you like it rough? Are you into dungeons?"

Dungeons? I shuddered at the thought. "I'm definitely not into dungeons," I typed. "Just nice, normal..." I couldn't bring myself to say it. "Just nice and normal," I finished up.

"Vanilla."

That sounded safe so I agreed. You can't go wrong with vanilla, right?

"Top or bottom?" he asked again.

"It doesn't matter." This was getting a little more involved than I had planned.

"Versatile, huh? I think I'd be a good match for you."

"Great!" I jumped at the chance to get out of the question-and-answer portion of our program. "How do I make an appointment?"

"You have to make it with the person who handles the scheduling. His name is Neal. You can ask for me."

I was relieved that, after all the rigmarole, I was going to get what I was after.

"How do I contact Neal?"

"I can give you an email address or a phone number."

"Both?" I asked hopefully.

"No problem." He provided me with the information, which I jotted down in my trusty notepad. Then, thanking Brady, I closed the IM window. I wrote Neal a quick email, telling him who I was and requesting an appointment to talk to him about Paul. I wasn't confident I'd get an answer, but figured I'd try that first and hold the phone number to use as Plan B.

Micah called me much earlier than I had expected. "I have a surprise for you before we head for DC. Can I come by now?"

"What is it?" I asked suspiciously.

"I'm not saying. You'll see. So, is it okay if I come by now?"

"No, I want you to tell me," I insisted. I don't really like surprises. I prefer to know what I'm doing and what's expected of me. If someone says there is a surprise, predictably, I obsess over it until I find out what is going on. Blame it on my insatiable curiosity. That's why I'm an investigator.

"If you cooperate you'll find out a lot quicker," he reasoned.

"Just hurry up and bring it here."

"I'll be there before you know it."

Despite his promise, it felt like forever until he came through the office door. I jumped to my feet and noted his empty hands. "So what's this surprise?"

"You have to come with me to find out."

"Go with you where?"

"The sooner you stop asking questions and just do what I say, the sooner you'll find out."

I crossed my arms obstinately. "I'm not moving until you tell me what's going on."

"Fine, we'll do it the hard way." He was grinning as he said it, so I knew he was enjoying every second of our little standoff. He walked calmly around my desk and before I knew what he was doing, he'd grabbed me around the waist and tossed me over his shoulder like a sack of potatoes. Have I mentioned that Micah is a lot stronger than he looks? I struggled, but it was cursory at best, my laughter betraying how much fun I was having. He carried me through the door just as Novak was coming in.

"I won't even ask," my boss commented coolly as he squeezed by and went into the office without so much as a look back.

"It's nice to know I can count on you if I'm ever in trouble," I yelled after him, mustering as much dignity as one can while hanging over a man's shoulder with one's rump in the air.

"I didn't ask to be included in your sexual peccadilloes," I heard him call back.

"What?" I gasped. "What did he say?"

Micah just laughed and carried me outside.

"Now," he said, setting me down in the parking lot next to his car, "we can either do this the easy way — namely, you get in the car and quit being a pain — or I can stuff you in the trunk."

I had a feeling he would do it, too. I made a show of smoothing my clothes, then turned calmly and climbed in.

"There now, that wasn't so bad, was it?" he asked.

"Just drive," I replied.

Chuckling, he took us a short distance to one of those small strip malls that are scattered abundantly around any good-size community. This one boasted a Chinese restaurant, a sporting-goods store, a Kenpo studio, a framing gallery, and a bridal-wear shop. It was an eclectic assortment — and one that told me nothing about why we were there.

"So, are we going to take self-defense classes or have some moo goo gai pan?" I asked.

"Neither," he answered. "Follow me." He strode purposefully to the bridal shop. I had to give him props — he had certainly succeeded in surprising me. I trailed after him, wondering the whole time what the heck was going on.

He ushered me inside with the grave dignity of an English butler. The clerk, a small, rather effeminate-looking man with a receding hairline and twinkling blue eyes, seemed to be in on whatever Micah had up his sleeve. He was positively beaming at us, which only served to increase my unease.

"Okay, I'm here. Now what's going on?" Then a terrifying thought occurred to me. "This better not be another surprise wedding," I yelped. The bewildered expression on both of their faces was almost enough to make me laugh. Almost.

"Surprise wedding?" Micah asked in confusion.

"Whoever heard of such a thing," the clerk added with a dismissive wave of his limp wrist.

"Will someone please just tell me what the hell is going on?" I interrupted, a bit louder than I had intended.

"The ball," Micah replied quickly, apparently deciding he had pushed his little game far enough.

"Huh?" I responded cleverly.

"I told you I would take care of the tuxedos for the ball," Micah explained. "We're here to get fitted."

I looked at him blankly. "You mean to tell me all of that was just to get fitted for a tux?"

"Yes."

"That was my surprise?"

"Well, it is a ball. I wanted it to be special and exciting."

"You kidnapped me to take me to a tux fitting?" I was struggling to keep a straight face. I wasn't really upset, but revenge, as I may have noted before, is sweet.

"I didn't kidnap you. Well, not exactly."

His expression was finally too much for me, and I burst out laughing. It didn't take him long to do the same.

The clerk just stood by looking even more befuddled. "If we could...?" he asked after a moment. He whipped a tape measure from his pocket and unfurled it with a flourish. I had a feeling he'd practiced the maneuver in front of a mirror.

"Sorry." I submitted to the process of being measured from every possible angle. Then it was Micah's turn. After that we looked through the tuxedos on hand. We tried several of them on to get an idea of the style, and finally decided on ones we liked. They would have to be altered to fit.

We ended up eating dinner at the Chinese restaurant. I did not order moo goo gai pan, but rather double-cooked sliced pork. Micah had Hunan chicken. Both were excellent.

After retrieving my car and stopping to pack an overnight bag, we were off for DC. Micah had planned the whole trip, so I didn't know where we were staying after we went clubbing.

During the drive, I told Micah how I'd managed to get Neal's email address and phone number.

He gave me a look of respect. "Smart move. I don't know if I would have thought of it, and I knew about those chat rooms. I used to go there to drum up business when things got slow. Well, then tonight is all about us."

It sounded good to me. After being told by several people that I was too serious and didn't have enough fun, I was determined to just relax and enjoy myself for once. When I'd mentioned to Adam and Steve that we were going to DC for the night, and it was strictly a pleasure trip, they'd actually seemed relieved. It was both funny and sobering to think they were worrying that much about me.

"So what did you mean about a surprise wedding?" he asked after a few minutes.

"Oh, nothing." I was a little embarrassed that my mind had gone there straight away.

"It had to come from somewhere," he persisted.

I sighed. It would be easier to tell him outright than go through the third degree. "You know Will Keegan?"

"Yeah, he's a friend of yours, right? He was involved in those murders about a year ago? I think I've met him."

"Yeah, well, he was dating my cousin at the time, Aidan."

"The one who...?"

"Yes. They stunned all their friends with a surprise wedding, planned by none other than Adam. No one had any idea why we were invited over to their house — I just figured it was a holiday party — but when we arrived, everything was all set up and they got married."

"Oh wow, how romantic...and tragic."

"Yeah. It was beautiful, though."

"If Adam was in charge, I'm sure it was. And you thought I was throwing you a surprise wedding?"

"No! I mean...maybe. I didn't..."

He chuckled. "There was one big difference you should have seen right away. Aidan and Will wanted to get married. They were just surprising their guests. It would be a different thing altogether to surprise one of the grooms!"

I laughed too. "I didn't really expect a ceremony. It just went through my mind, and I blurted it out."

"Well, you can relax. I don't plan on getting married," he paused, and then added, "yet."

We fell into silence as I thought about that "yet" and all its implications.

The hotel Micah had chosen wasn't quite as nice as the one we'd stayed in the last time we were in DC, but it was clean, and would be more than sufficient for the brief time we'd be there. We left our bags in the room and took the Metro to the Dupont area, where we browsed through some of the shops. Another short Metro ride brought us to the Mall and the Washington Monument, with the moonlight shimmering beautifully in the reflecting pool. By then, it was time to head over to Michelangelo.

The club was every bit as packed as it had been the last time we were there. Bodies writhed and wriggled wherever you looked. Most were male, but not all. It was just as exhilarating as I remembered. I let the music sink into my body and the beat take over. We danced until I was completely exhausted, stopping only to drink the bottled water Micah kept pushing on me.

"I don't want you to dehydrate," he yelled over the din.

We left at three in the morning, tired, relaxed, and happy. We caught a cab — expensive at that time of night, but the Metro had stopped running by then. When we got back to the hotel room, we both shed our clothes and collapsed into bed.

The night wasn't over, though. We made love until the sun was just starting to brighten the sky. I watched through half-closed eyes as Micah got up to pull the curtains closed all the way, and was almost asleep before he crawled back in bed. He wrapped me in his arms, and that was the last thing I remembered for a while.

It had been a long day, but it had been satisfying too. It felt good to be back with Micah, and it seemed like things were beginning to go right for a change. I should have suspected it was nothing but the calm before the storm.

Chapter 19

Waking in Micah's arms for the second morning in a row was just as pleasant as the first time. I squirmed around until I was facing him, somehow managing not to disturb him in the process. I watched him for a few minutes, marveling that he was mine and wanted to be with me. Finally, unable to stand it any longer, I leaned forward and began to tickle his ear with my tongue.

He twitched and rubbed the spot but still didn't wake up, so I tried again. This time he jerked away and blinked, giving me a confused look for a moment. As his bleary eyes focused on me, I was rewarded with a huge smile.

"Good morning," I purred, pressing my body against his.

He trailed a hand lazily down my side, his fingertips barely grazing my skin, causing a chill to snake its way deliciously through my body. "Waking up to you makes it a good morning." He gave me soft kiss, which I returned with enthusiasm. "Am I mistaken," he asked, pulling away, "or is someone a bit horny this morning?"

"You must be mistaken." I smiled innocently despite my obvious state of arousal jabbing him in his side.

"Really? Then you won't mind if I go take a shower." He started to get up, but I quickly pulled him back down on the bed.

"You are not going anywhere, mister," I growled, throwing a leg across him.

He chuckled and wrapped his arms around me. "You're insatiable."

"Are you complaining?"

"Not in the least. Just making an observation."

"Well, quit observing and start acting. If you don't do something soon, I might just doze off."

With a devilish grin, he flipped me onto my back, then slowly brushed his lips across my stomach. I couldn't hold back a gasp as my tummy did a little somersault.

"Oh, I think I can keep you awake," he said in a husky voice.

I didn't doubt him for a second.

Adam was actually home when I pulled into the driveway later that day. Micah had dropped me off at the office a little earlier, and I had decided to pick up some more clothes before returning to the bed and breakfast.

"Micah has made the big leagues," Adam said as I walked through the door. "I hope you're ready for the flak that's going to come out of this."

"Huh?"

"His article. Didn't you see it yet?"

"No, we went to DC last night. We just got back."

He made a face. "He may wish he'd stayed there before this is over."

"Why? What's going on?" I was suddenly concerned at the tone of Adam's voice.

"I think you'd better take a look at the article." I followed him into the living room, where he handed me the first section of the Sunday paper. "At least he made the front page."

I read the main headline. "COUNTY COUNCIL CORRUPTION," it screamed in a large, bold font, and under that, in smaller print, "Payoffs, Bribes, and Cover-ups Abound in Local Government." I glanced at the byline, and there was Micah's name.

"I knew he was working on this," I said. "Is it a big deal?"

Adam snorted. "You'd better believe it's a big deal. He's stirring up a hornets' nest, and some of these hornets pack a mean sting. He'd be well advised to lie low for the next few days. There are bound to be some people out for blood over this."

"Do you mean that literally or figuratively?"

"I hope figuratively, but you never know. According to the article, some of these people were involved in illegal deals worth millions of dollars. They're not going to be very happy about losing that kind of money, which is probably the very least of what's about to happen to them. There'll be official investigations, fines, and possibly even indictments. We're talking about influential people in local government. You know better than anyone what happens when you mess with the good old boys club."

He was referring to my biological father, who had been a State's Attorney before an investigation into the mishandling of a murder investigation brought down his own little empire of corruption. In Dad's case, the corruption wasn't as widespread as the neighboring county's council — at least according to Micah's article — and most of the blame landed squarely in my father's lap. He was currently serving a five-year prison sentence.

"I'd better go call Micah." I ran up the stairs to my room. I dialed Micah's cell phone first, but only got his message service. I tried his desk phone next, but that was busy, so I called his cell again and left a message. While I waited for him to get back to me, I signed online to check my email.

The first one was from Noah. He was inviting me to attend the gay/straight Halloween dance Haven was sponsoring that Thursday night. He said there would be awards for the best costume and I was welcome to bring friends. At the last meeting, I'd heard everyone talking about the dance but hadn't really considered going. Suddenly, it seemed it might be a good idea to invite Micah. That would be one place no one would really care about his article. It might give him a chance to relax and get away from all the attention Adam seemed to think the scandal would bring him.

At the bottom of my inbox, buried beneath a mountain of spam mail, was a response from Neal. My heart started pounding as I opened it and read over his brief note: "I would be willing to speak with you regarding the unfortunate death of Paul Flynn. However, the nature of my business being what it is, I'm afraid I will need some sort of verification that you are who you say you are. If I'm satisfied, we can meet and I will answer your questions. Please call me at my office, and we'll see if we can work things out."

Cautious, but accommodating, I thought. *Almost as if he's afraid I might know something.* Or maybe he just wanted to find out what I knew. At the same time, he couldn't be sure I wasn't a cop on the vice squad.

I was reaching for the phone when it rang in my hand. It was Micah.

"Hey, I saw the paper," I said after we'd exchanged greetings. "Adam seems to think you'll be catching hell."

"Adam would be correct," he said without inflection.

"Is it bad?"

"Not yet, but it could be. We've already had several very angry phone calls from local bigwigs, all of them outraged over the paper's printing 'something like that', and most of them wishing me bodily harm. Some of calls were threatening lawsuits, so I'm guessing this is going to be a lot bigger than even I expected. These guys are in so many pockets, and they in turn have guys in their own pockets. Let's just say this looks like it's going to have fallout far beyond the county. It could reach State level."

"Let me guess..." My voice was heavy with irony. "The consensus is you should have let sleeping dogs lie."

"Yes. I can't believe this. They'd rather allow these guys to get away with everything than hold them accountable."

I gave a short bark of humorless laughter. "This is the Eastern Shore, Micah. That's how it works. The good old boys protect each other. Lesson number one in backwoods politics."

"That's just it. Maybe the Shore used to be backwoods, but times are changing. We can't let people continue to get away with stuff like this."

"They might be changing, but change comes slowly to the Shore. These guys play hardball, Micah. You said some people are wishing you bodily harm. Have there been any actual threats against you? Do you think you're in any danger?"

"No, there haven't been any overt threats. The people involved are too smart for that, but they have been making threatening noises, if you know what I mean. I hadn't taken them too seriously before now, though."

"I think you should. You need to be careful. Maybe you should ease off for a little while, keep a low profile."

"No way. I need to be out there doing follow-up articles, interviews—"

"I need you alive. Please, can't you let someone else take it from here? You broke the big story."

"This is huge, Killian. I can't just hand it over to someone else at this point. It's my job. It's what I do, and I love it. I'd never ask you to give up an investigation just because it turned dangerous."

"You're right. I'm sorry. I shouldn't have asked that."

"It's okay. I understand. Trust me, I definitely understand. You're scared. Sometimes I'm scared for you too. But I need to do this."

"Just...promise me you'll be careful."

"That's a promise I can make. It's not like I want to get hurt. Tell you what, I'll keep as low a profile as I possibly can and still get the job done. Okay?"

"Okay."

"You do realize you probably won't be seeing much of me for the next few days, don't you?"

"I know. It sucks, but I have a lot to do as well. Oh, wait. What about Thursday night? Do you think you'd be free to go with me to a Halloween dance at Pemberton?"

"Halloween dance?" I could hear the doubt in his voice.

"It's sponsored by Haven."

"Oh, um, yeah. I guess we could do that."

"Come on, you'll need to get away and have some fun by then. Remember what you said to me about working too hard?"

He laughed. "Oh sure, throw my own words back in my face. We are going to a Ball the very next night, you know, but okay, let's plan on attending the Halloween dance, too. Do I have to wear a costume?"

"Yes," I said firmly.

"Okay, okay." I heard some voices in the background. "Hang on a sec, Kill." I could hear him talking to someone, but he must have put his hand over the phone because I couldn't understand what was being said.

A few seconds later, he came back on the line. "Hey, something's come up. I have to go. I'll talk to you later, 'k? Love you. Bye."

Before I could answer, he'd hung up.

I stared at the phone for a minute, hoping I'd get through the next few days without Micah. *Just when I was really getting used to waking up next to him,* I thought wistfully.

I shook my head to clear it, then dialed Neal. I might as well get to work. It would help keep my mind off how much I'd miss Micah in my bed.

Neal answered on the second ring. "Hello, Top to Bottom Escorts. Neal speaking. How can I be of service?"

"Neal, this is Killian Kendall. I sent you an email yesterday regarding Paul Flynn, and you sent me a response asking me to call you."

"Yes, I did. I'm sure you understand that, before I can meet with you, I need to be sure you are who you say you are."

"And not a cop?"

He laughed. His voice was smooth and cultured; he sounded well-educated. "You cut right to the point, don't you, Mr. Kendall?"

"Please, call me Killian. And, yes, I do like to get to the point. I'm sure you're a busy man, and I don't want to take up any more of your time than I have to."

"I appreciate that. You said in your email that you're a private investigator hired to look into Paul's murder?"

"Yes, sir."

"May I ask who hired you, or is that confidential?"

I thought for moment but didn't see any harm in telling him who had hired me. "Actually, I believe you know my client. His name is Micah Gerber. He used to work for your agency."

"Micah?" His surprise came through clearly in his voice. "I thought he and Paul went their separate ways ages ago."

"They did, but Mr. Gerber would still like to know what happened to his old friend." I was trying to sound as professional as possible, and I certainly wouldn't let on that Micah and I were dating.

"Of course, I can understand that, although I'm not sure how you think I can help."

"I'm talking to everyone who had anything to do with Paul, even marginally."

"You realize we never met face to face. All our business was done either on the phone or by email."

"Mr. Gerber explained to me how the business works."

"Good, then I don't need to go into all those details. Is there any way I can verify that you are a private investigator? Can I check your license with the State?"

I didn't need him to know I wasn't licensed yet, either. "Would calling my office in the morning and speaking to the agency owner, Shane Novak, be sufficient?"

"Could I call him today? If I can verify all this, I'd like to meet with you tomorrow. I'm leaving town on Tuesday for an extended vacation. I'll be gone for the better part of November."

"Florida?"

"Cancun. So, can I call this...what was his name?"

"Novak, Shane Novak. He's not in the office right now. Why don't I see if I can get in touch with him and have him give you a call?"

"How do I know you aren't just getting someone to call me and pretend to be the owner?"

Good point. "What if I have Mr. Gerber call you? Would that be verification enough?"

"That would be alright, I suppose. I haven't spoken to Micah since he left the agency. He said he was taking a job at a newspaper in the middle of nowhere on the Shore, but I always suspected he was just going out on his own. Is he still in the business?"

I bristled a little at the question before realizing how silly I was being. "Actually, he's the star reporter on the paper that covers the entire Shore." So I embellished a little? I was sure it wouldn't be long before he was the star reporter.

"Really? Well, good for him. Yes, please have Micah call me. I'll work things out with him. If all goes well — which I'm sure it will — meet me at noon tomorrow at Union Station at the Center Café. Just ask for Neal, and they'll bring you to my table."

"That sounds fine. I appreciate your help."

"Don't think it's entirely altruistic, Killian," he said with a dry chuckle. "I suspect it's in my best interest to meet with you as well. After all, I can't have you making assumptions or, worse yet, going to the police with half-formed ideas. I'll be looking forward to hearing from Micah."

"I'll have him call you as soon as I can," I said.

I hung up and called Micah right away, holding my breath while it rang. *Please be there, please pick up,* I silently begged.

"Hello?" he answered, seeming a little annoyed at the interruption.

"Micah, I'm sorry to interrupt you again, but I need you to do something for me."

"Is it important?" He sounded distracted.

"It's about Paul."

"Paul?" I suddenly had his full attention and tried not to be peeved that Paul rated more concern than I did.

"Yeah, I need you to call Neal and verify that I'm a private investigator hired by you to look into Paul's murder."

"Paranoia is the name of the game when you're doing something illegal," he said and laughed. "God, I'm glad I don't have to worry about that anymore. Yeah, I'll call him. You'll have to give me his number. When does he want me to call?"

"If you can, call him now — or at least as soon as possible."

"Okay, I'll call him now before I get back to work. What's his number?"

I read it off to him, and he repeated it back.

"That's it," I said. "Thanks, Micah. I love you." I was determined to get that in before he hung up this time.

"I love you too."

As soon as we disconnected, I dialed the phone once more, this time to call Chris. I filled her in on my appointment with Neal, and she agreed to accompany me.

"Welcome back to the Big City," Chris said as I stepped off the train at Metro Center and narrowly missed being run over by a boy on a bike.

I snorted. "With all the time I've been spending here lately, maybe I should have the post office just forward my mail. They allow bikes down here?"

"Sort of, but you're supposed to walk them. Come on, we need to get on the Red Line to go to Union." She set off briskly, and I hurried to keep up with her. As we walked, I took a moment to look her over. Today, she was wearing black jeans and a red t-shirt that read, "Warning: Hanging out with me will greatly damage your reputation." Not exactly camouflage, but I hoped she wouldn't stand out too much.

After boarding the train, we chatted for the next few minutes about the case in general, throwing ideas back and forth. We agreed that I really needed to talk to the family and find out what the key unlocked. I had a feeling it would turn out to be, well, the key to the whole case.

Once we reached the station, we laid out our game plan for my meeting with Neal. "Do you know where this restaurant is that he was talking about?" I asked.

"Yeah, the Center Café. It's in the middle of the main concourse. You know, this used to be a real train station. When it opened, it was the largest rail terminal in the world and probably the most ornate. The ceiling was actually covered in gold leaf."

"You sound like a tour guide."

She flipped me the bird, accompanied by a dirty look. "This is one of my favorite places in the city. I love to shop here."

I was surprised at that revelation, but then scolded myself for stereotyping. *You should know better*, I thought fiercely. *Just because Chris doesn't look like your typical mall rat doesn't mean she doesn't enjoy shopping.*

"Well, maybe we'll have time to browse after I talk to Neal." The offer was an attempt to atone, even though she had no idea what I'd been thinking. I glanced down at my watch. "You can give me the history lesson later, though. Right now, we need to get moving. I want you to follow me from a discreet distance. I'm supposed to go to the restaurant and ask for Neal. They'll show me to his table. Keep me in sight just in case he does something weird, although I doubt he would in a public place like this."

"Still, it's better to be safe, right?"

"Exactly."

We went up to the main level of the train station *cum* mall, where Chris escorted me to the restaurant. I took a deep breath and muttered, "Here goes nothing," before striding purposefully across the floor. As implied by its name, the restaurant was in the middle of the large open area that had once been the main concourse. It was two floors high, with the second level enclosed only by a rail going around its edge.

I approached the well-dressed young man standing at the greeter's podium. "I'm here to meet with Neal."

He looked me over from head to toe, making me feel a little like a prize bitch at a dog show. "Are you Killian Kendall?"

"Yes."

"Follow me."

He led me up the flight of stairs toward a table set off by itself in a corner. At first, I couldn't see the person I was meeting because the waiter was in my line of vision. When he finally shifted to one side, I stopped in midstep. Sitting at the table waiting for me with a pleasantly bland expression was someone I'd seen before. Not in person, and only once, but I recognized him immediately. He was the man from the newspaper clipping I'd seen in Jake's room. It was suddenly looking as if my two cases might be connected.

Chapter 20

I stood frozen in shock as my brain tried to make sense of what I was seeing. The man in the newspaper clipping from Jake's room and the man smiling genially while he waited for me at the table were definitely one and the same. What that meant exactly I wasn't sure, but any attempt to puzzle it out would have to wait for another time.

Trying to arrange some sort of pleasant expression on my face, I forced my body to move forward again. As I approached the table, the man stood in greeting.

"Hello, you must be Killian," he said in a cultured and slightly accented voice as we shook hands. I tried to place the accent, but it was too faint to be identifiable. I hadn't even noticed it on the phone.

"Yes, and you must be Neal. Thank you for meeting with me."

"Believe me, it's always my pleasure to share a meal with such an attractive young man."

I smiled in acknowledgment of his compliment. It was a measure of the shock I was still reeling from that I didn't blush. A waiter approached just then to take my drink order and refill Neal's water glass.

I seized the opportunity to examine Neal. The newspaper photo hadn't done him justice. He was strikingly handsome, deeply tanned, with flashing black eyes, strong patrician features, and smartly styled dark hair liberally shot through with silver. I would have been hard-pressed to assign him an age — he could have been anywhere from forty to sixty. He was well-dressed in clothes of the latest fashion that eloquently bespoke wealth without being ostentatious. His jewelry — a gold watch on his wrist, a slim chain at his throat, a couple of rings on each hand — were equally understated but beautifully crafted. He wasn't at all what I'd expected.

"I'm not what you expected," he stated more than asked. I was startled at the way his words echoed my thoughts. "The way you took pause when you first saw me," he said. "You looked surprised, even a little unsettled." He chuckled.

I forced a pleasant smile. "I'm not sure what I was expecting, sir, but you're right, it wasn't you."

He studied me deliberately, while I struggled not to squirm under his gaze. I picked up the stemmed glass and took a sip of the ice water, more to give me something to do than because I was actually thirsty.

"I must admit you're not what I was expecting, either," he said lightly after a long, awkward moment — awkward on my end, anyway.

I raised an eyebrow questioningly. "My age?"

"Partly that...and partly your beauty."

This time I did blush.

"When I think of a private investigator, I immediately associate him with the Philip Marlowe type, but I suppose that's my age telling on me." He smiled charmingly. "At any rate, you're nothing like Mr. Marlowe, and I find the reality much more pleasing than my imagination. Now, on to business. We're both busy men."

"Yes, I want to thank you again for taking the time to meet with me," I said formally, glad to be returning to more familiar ground.

He gave a little shrug. "To be honest, I didn't feel you gave me much choice. I'm in a rather precarious spot and thought it best to do what I could to help you. You, however, are in the rather envious position of being the only person who would associate me with the agency ever to meet me in person."

"You're very careful."

"I do what I must. It was good to talk to Micah again. To be honest, he was always one of my very favorite boys. Such a promising young man. I'm glad to hear he made good on his potential. After meeting you, however, I have to wonder if your relationship with him is more than just business...?"

I chose to ignore the rather personal question and asked one of my own instead. "What can you tell me about Paul Flynn?"

A tiny smile played around the corners of Neal's lips, as if something I said amused him in some way. "What would you like me to tell you about Paul Flynn?" His voice wasn't quite mocking, but closer than I appreciated. It made me want to make him squirm. He'd taken control since my arrival, and it was time I took back the reins.

"Let's start with how long he worked for you at the agency."

"A little under three years."

"That's a long time for an escort to work for an agency, isn't it?"

"Perhaps. The arrangement seemed to meet his needs. It was not for me to question."

"What kind of employee was he?"

He cocked his head slightly. "You must understand: it's not as if I'm the manager of a supermarket and Paul was the bag boy. He was a popular escort. He had a look not unlike yours: blond hair and blue eyes — young, fresh...pretty. That look is very much in demand. Paul was honest. He always gave me what was due and never tried to deceive me. I never had any problems or complaints from the clients. In fact, they invariably seemed quite satisfied with his services. In all these ways, I would say he was a very good employee. A model employee, really."

"Did you ever meet him personally?"

"No, I make it a point to never meet my escorts in person."

"Then how do you know what he looked like?"

"Pardon?"

"You just said he resembled me. If you never met him, how do you know what he looked like?"

"Do you think I hire my boys sight unseen? They have to submit photos, measurements, get physicals, and have a clean bill of health, and then they go for regular HIV and STD testing. I run a tight ship, Mr. Kendall. I even do background checks."

Micah hadn't mentioned any of that in my briefing. A little more familiarity with Neal's hiring practices would have been helpful. "I see. And you never had any problems with Paul?"

"None that I can recall."

"Did he seem any different the last few months?"

"Different? No, but then, I'm not sure I would have noticed. We weren't close. Our contact was minimal and always by telephone or email. The only way I'd have known if he had changed would be if his clients noticed a remarkable-enough difference that they felt compelled to report it to me, which as you can imagine is not very likely."

"You said his clients were, ah, very satisfied by his services." I tried not to blush. That would have been most unprofessional.

"Is that a question?"

"No, I was just wondering if he had any repeat customers."

Neal raised an eyebrow. "Paul tried not to encourage repeat clients, at least none that came back over a long period of time. They have a way of forming attachments, which can become rather bothersome."

"But did he have any?"

"I believe he had a few, yes."

"Do you keep records of your clients?"

"Do I keep records of the clients?"

"Yes, sir. That's what I asked."

His eyes narrowed slightly. He still wasn't squirming, but I had a feeling this was a man who never squirmed. Slightly peeved might be as close as he got.

"Even if I did, they would be held in the utmost confidence. It would be the only way I could maintain my reputation for discretion."

"So you do have records."

"I didn't say—"

"You're a little too defensive there, Neal. It's a dead giveaway. But if it'll make you feel any better, we'll refer to them as the alleged files for the sake of this conversation. Now, since I don't plan on making these alleged records public, I don't see where it would be a problem for me to have a look at them. And while we're discussing your filing system, I'd also like to see Paul's records."

Neal's face lost all traces of humor. I got the impression he was taking me very seriously now.

"I agreed to meet with you as a courtesy, Mr. Kendall." His voice had taken on an ice-cold-steel quality that sent a shiver down my spine, but I kept my expression carefully nonchalant. "I don't see how viewing these confidential files could be at all advantageous to you, and I have no intention of just handing them over."

I leaned across the table with a sudden intensity. "In case you've forgotten, this is a murder investigation, not a social visit. Someone strangled Paul to death in his own apartment. I intend to find out the identity of that someone. Whether or not I look like Philip Marlowe, I'm the PI here, and I say I need to see those files. Must I remind you that you're not exactly in a position to argue with me about this? If you give me the files, that's as far as they go. If I have to call in the police to obtain them — and believe me, I will — a lot more people get involved, people who may not be so understanding about your particular business venture. Do you see where I'm going with this, Neal?"

"Oh, I see it quite clearly, Mr. Kendall. I also see that I underestimated you — something I don't often make the mistake of doing." He sat back in his chair and studied me as if seeing me for the first time. Suddenly, he broke into a beaming smile. I wasn't surprised to notice that his teeth were blindingly white and even. "If the situation were not quite so serious, I think I'd quite enjoy being bested by such a disarmingly beautiful opponent. If I produce these alleged files, as we have agreed to call them, can you guarantee me that you'll make every effort to keep them confidential?"

"I promise to do what I can."

"You're cautious: an admirable trait. I suppose that will have to do, since as you pointed out, I'm not in a position to quibble over details. I said when we spoke on the phone that I'm going out of town indefinitely—"

"I need the records before you leave."

"Of course. I was going to suggest that I send them to you by overnight delivery, with return receipt required. Would that be acceptable?"

"That would be ideal. Just be sure all the files are there. If I even suspect you've held back on me, I'll call in the authorities."

"Somehow, I don't doubt that, my young friend. Is our business concluded?"

"I have a couple more quick questions."

"Ask away."

"Micah told me you deposited funds directly into his account when a client paid by credit card. Did you have the same arrangement with Paul?"

"I have that arrangement with all my employees."

"Do you know what bank Paul used?"

"I don't remember off the top of my head, but I'm sure I could find out for you."

"I'd appreciate that. Last question: do you have any ideas about who might have killed Paul?"

"None," he said without hesitation. "I've given the subject much consideration, and haven't thought of anyone. Paul was a good person. I can't imagine who would want to hurt him, let alone kill him."

"Then I guess we're finished. Please, don't forget to include Paul's file and banking information with the clients' files." I pulled out a business card that had our address printed on it and slid it across the table.

He slid the card into his jacket pocket without even glancing at it. "Oh, I wouldn't dare." The mocking tone was back as he stood. "You know, Killian, if this private investigator business doesn't work out for you, I have a feeling you'd make a fine escort."

"Thanks, but no thanks. I'll be looking for those files."

"You can expect them tomorrow. It was a pleasure." He sketched a slight bow, turned crisply on his heel, and walked away, never once looking back. I sat at the table for a second, collecting my thoughts. I suspected I had just taunted a very powerful — and possibly dangerous — man. I should probably be glad he found me amusing, but somehow I was still pissed. Then there was the fact that Jake had a picture in his room of the man I knew as Neal.

I was still sitting at the table when Chris slid into the seat recently vacated by Neal. "So...how'd it go?" she asked.

"It went."

"Is this fill-in-the-blanks? I couldn't really see you guys up here, so I had to content myself with loitering around at the bottom of the stairs. They almost escorted me out a few times, until I told them I was waiting for my aunt, Senator Sampson. They left me alone after that."

"Is Senator Sampson really your aunt?" I asked, momentarily distracted.

"No, but they don't know that. Why are you looking so concerned? Did the interview go badly?"

"Not really."

"Did you find out anything interesting?"

"Not really."

"So it was a total waste of time?"

"Not—"

"—really," she finished for me. "Would you care to elaborate on any of this?"

"He didn't exactly tell me anything useful. He's sending me the files I was hoping to get, however, so it wasn't a total bust. He was very...cautious. He admires caution."

"Does he? Hmm. Well, caution is very admirable, especially when crossing the street. So is that it? Are we done? I have a class at two, and if we get moving now I won't have to miss it."

Shaking my head in an attempt to clear it, I pushed away from the table and stood up. "Yeah, we're done. Let's go."

As we walked back down to the Metro, Chris was rattling on about something, but I couldn't tell you what if my life depended on it. My thoughts were completely caught up with the questions I had pushed aside earlier. Why did Jake have a newspaper clipping of Neal stashed away in his room? Was there some sort of connection to the wad of cash? I didn't like where that thought took me. Judy would like it even less.

I worried about it all the way back to my car, then continued to do so during the drive home. I hadn't come to any conclusions by the time I pulled into the driveway.

The only vehicle there belonged to Kane, which suited my purposes just fine. I wanted to talk to him about Jake. I couldn't do any more on Paul's case until I received the files from Neal, but I'd put off dealing with Jake long enough. Since it seemed the two cases might be connected, it was more important than ever for me to get back to work on Jake's. Kane was going to be my first stop.

I found him in our room, typing away at the computer. "Homework?" I asked.

He jumped a little and spun around. "Killian!" he gasped. "I didn't hear you come in. When did you get home?"

"Just now. Sorry, I didn't mean to startle you. Can I interrupt you for a minute?"

"Please interrupt me. Take as long as you want. I hate Shakespeare."

"How can you hate Shakespeare?" I forgot for the moment why I had come looking for him.

"Not everyone loves *Hamlet*, Kill. Besides, it's not even so much Shakespeare as having to write a paper about him. Why'd he have to be so damn prolific anyway? But enough about the dead guy. I need a break from him. What's up?"

"I'd like to ask you some questions if you have a minute."

Kane frowned. "That sounds sort of official."

"It is."

"So shoot."

"Who are Jake's friends at school?"

Kane rolled his eyes. "You mean who were his friends. He doesn't have any now, and that seems to be just the way he wants it."

"What happened? What drove his friends away?"

"I don't know. We weren't exactly in the same circles. He's pretty much a loner these days. He doesn't really hang out with anyone."

"But he used to?"

"Yeah."

"Who with?"

"Um, Danielle and Craig, I guess."

"What are their last names?"

"Why?"

"I want to talk to them, see if I can find out if they have any ideas about what's going on with Jake. If they were his friends, they might be able to tell me more than anyone else."

Kane shrugged. "You can try, but I get the impression that nobody really knows what's going on with Jake. It's Danielle Lewis and Craig Martin."

"And they were close friends?"

"I don't know how close they were. Danielle was like Jake's fag hag. I think Craig had a crush on him, because he always followed Jake around like a puppy dog. Craig's not out or anything, but everybody knows he's gay."

I frowned. "How do they know?"

"He's just really obvious — flamey, you know? And you should've seen the way he used to look at Jake."

"That's so stereotypical. Just because someone acts flamey, it doesn't necessarily mean he's gay."

Kane cut me off before I could work myself into a full self-righteous rant. "Don't go getting all preachy with me. I know better than to stereotype people. I'm the freaking president of the GSA, remember? Don't you think I can recognize a gay guy when I see one? I live with three gay men and my brother was gay. I believe I'm exceptionally well qualified. I probably know who's gay in my school before they do, and trust me, Craig is gay whether he knows it yet or not."

"Okay, okay. I'm sorry. You're right. You wouldn't happen to have their phone numbers or anything, would you?"

"Nope, you'll hafta work for those, Nancy Drew."

"Ha ha. You're a riot. No, really. Just for that, I won't help you with your homework. I was going to offer, but not now."

He grinned. "So when are we going to hang out? You said we should spend more time together, and I've hardly seen you since."

"I'm sorry, Kane. I've been too busy with this damn case. Hey, you like to dance, right?"

"Um, I guess so," he said suspiciously. "Why?"

"You want to go to a dance with me?"

"Wouldn't that be a bit weird? I mean you're my brother and all..."

"Oh stop. You're nowhere near as funny as you think you are. I'm going with Micah, but you can come along. It'll be fun. It's a Halloween dance at Pemberton, sponsored by Haven."

"What's Haven?"

"It's the gay/straight alliance on campus."

He looked skeptical. "No offense, but is it going to be like all gay guys and lesbians?"

I laughed. "A lot of straight girls go too, just like the GSA in high school. Think about it: you'll probably be the only straight guy there. Easy pickings."

He leered. "It's starting to sound better and better all the time."

"Are you dating anyone these days?"

"No." He sighed. "I seem to be going through a dry spell right now. Maybe a change of pace is exactly what I need. College women sound about right. So, when is this dance?"

"Thursday night. You hafta wear a costume."

"A costume? How...juvenile."

"Oh come on, it'll be fun."

"What are you going as?"

"I don't know yet. Any ideas?"

"Waiting till the last minute, are we? Hmm. Let me think about it. Remember the last costume party we went to together?"

I did. It was a huge, elaborate affair at Jake's old house. Kane had just moved in with Adam and me, so he came along. It was an unmitigated disaster from start to finish, culminating with a shattered windshield, a death threat, and a murder.

"Let's hope this one ends a little differently."

"Let's," Kane said.

"Well, I'm going to run to the office and see if there are any messages for me and maybe get a start on finding those phone numbers before I go spend the night at the B&B."

"It's back to old Billy for me," he said, turning to the computer. "I'll see ya later, Kill."

"Later, Kane." I started out the door.

"Hey," he called. "How about we make our own costumes? We can come up with ideas and get the stuff we need and then put them together one day this week after school."

I was hardly the craftiest person — another gay stereotype shattered — so I didn't want to think about what a costume I made would look like. Kane's expression was so hopeful, however, there was no way I could turn him down. "Sounds great," I said cheerily. "You come up with the idea and call me with a list of materials. Okay?"

"Okay!" His smile was so huge that I was very glad I'd agreed.

I drove to my office, where I found no messages waiting for me. In fact, it didn't even look as if Novak had been in that day. The mail was still in the box, and a yellow post-it note from a delivery service was stuck to the door, saying they would be back the next day to try again, but after that, it was tough luck.

"We need a secretary," I said as I sorted the mail, making one pile to give to Novak, and one to toss in the trash. After finishing that task, I flipped open the phonebook. At four columns, calling every Martin in the book was a bit more than I wanted to take on. Lewis turned out to be almost seven columns long. It looked as though the easy way was out.

Then again, perhaps there was an even easier way. I picked up the phone and dialed Judy's number. Luckily, she answered and not Jake.

"Judy, this is Killian."

"Hi, Killian. Has Amalie shown up yet?"

"No, actually I'm calling about Jake."

"Oh, have you found something?"

"I don't know yet." I chose my words carefully. "Maybe. I need to check some details first before I say anything."

"It sounds serious."

"I don't want to go into it at this point. I don't know enough. I'm hoping you can help me, though. I'm trying to get phone numbers for Danielle Lewis and Craig Martin. They were friends of Jake's."

"I know Danielle and Craig, Danielle especially, but I don't think I have their phone numbers. Hold on a minute. Actually, I did write them in my address book just in case I needed to track down Jake some time. Hang on, I'll go get them."

While I waited, I picked up a pencil and doodled absently on the back of an envelope destined for the trash can. A few minutes later Judy came back on the line. "Found them," she said triumphantly. She read off the numbers, which I jotted down on the envelope. "You know," she said, "I don't think he's really friends with them anymore. I talked to them when I first became suspicious, and they said they didn't know any more than I did."

"What they might not be willing to tell a mom, they might not mind telling me. You know parents are like the enemy at that age. You keep your mouth shut around them." I glanced down at the envelope and stopped in midsentence.

"Killian?" Judy asked. "Are you still there?"

While I'd been waiting for Judy, I had drawn words in bubble letters. I was suddenly struck by the ones my subconscious had chosen: Escort. Jake. Money. It was the only conclusion I'd been able to come up with...and the one I'd been trying to avoid. Looking at the facts objectively, it was obvious. It would explain where Jake's cash came from. Micah had even mentioned how much money he made working as an escort. It would also explain why Jake had a picture of Neal.

Or would it? On second thought, it didn't make sense. Neal claimed he never met his escorts in person, so how could Jake have known who Neal was? Then again, how could I be sure Neal was telling me the truth? Maybe Jake was just too much to resist, and he'd made an exception. Or Jake figured it out somehow. Perhaps he was blackmailing Neal. Jake was a smart guy.

The most sensible theory, though, was that Jake was working as an escort. It explained everything: where he kept disappearing to after school until late and even occasionally overnight, the expensive clothes, the electronics, even the ticket to the Ball. One of his clients could be taking him. It all fit too perfectly. I didn't like it, but it made too much sense to simply dismiss. More importantly, I didn't have to like it. I just had to prove it. All I had so far was circumstantial evidence.

"Killian? What's wrong?" Judy asked again. I had forgotten I was still holding the phone.

"Oh, um, nothing's wrong." There was no point getting Judy all upset until I knew for certain what was going on with Jake. "I just realized I'm late meeting Micah," I fibbed.

"Oh, then I'll let you go. Tell him I said he did a great job on the big article. It's about time we shook up those fat cats."

"Yeah, thanks. Bye, Judy."

I hung up and sat staring at the envelope and those three words. Jake an escort? Was he somehow connected to Paul's death? Could he be in danger? I didn't even want to consider it, but it was too late. I was in too far. I had to know the truth.

Chapter 21

I was still brooding over Jake the next day. It was a nice change of pace from brooding about Micah, at least. The problem with any brooding, however, is that it tends to be distracting. I had even more trouble than usual paying attention in class. I couldn't keep my brain off the case for more than a few minutes at a time. I was especially wondering what I was going to do after I talked to his old friends. I wasn't expecting a lot from them, but it was a loose end that needed to be tied up. Beyond the interviews, though, I had no idea where to go. There was the Ball Friday night, so maybe I'd just wait and see what happened there.

When I arrived at work after my classes, I thought I saw Novak's mysterious client slip down the back stairs just as I came up the front ones. "Was that your client?" I asked, walking into the office.

Novak was bending over my desk looking at several photographs. He promptly scooped them up as soon as I spoke. "Yes, it was," he said casually.

"Why was she sneaking down the back way?"

"She wasn't sneaking anywhere. I told you, she's in a delicate position and needs to be extremely discreet."

"So...she was sneaking."

"She wasn't... Okay, yes, she was sneaking."

"What were those pictures?"

"If that was any of your business, I'd have shown them to you. Don't you have cases of your own to worry about?" He retreated to his office, closing the door firmly behind him, just a little shy of slamming.

I laughed. Teasing Novak was so much fun, although I was very curious about the birdlike woman.

I turned on the computer while I sorted through the mail. Novak had already taken his, so most of what was left went directly into the circular file. I set aside all but one large manila envelope to deal with later. True to his word, the envelope was from Neal. I noticed that the return address was a PO Box with no name — cautious as always. I dumped out the enclosed documents, finding Paul's file on top, with the records of his repeat customers underneath.

I picked up Paul's file first and thumbed through it. There wasn't a lot of information really. A printout of a spreadsheet showed that he'd been popular and had plenty of business. Most of the names — a first initial and last name — were different. As Neal had said, there weren't many repeats. I checked the spreadsheet carefully, ticked off the names that showed up more than once or twice, and compared them to the customer records Neal had sent. There were only seven names, and Neal had provided all of them as promised. The records listed the dates they met with Paul and the method of payment, as well as personal information such as address, phone number, and if Paul had used his own apartment or the client's place for the meeting.

I went back to Paul's file and found his banking information. A quick search online turned up the bank's phone number, which I jotted down and slipped into his file. I'd come back to that later, once I'd figured out how best to handle it.

In the meantime, I decided to tackle his clients. The first four weren't home. They were probably at work, so I'd have to call back later. The next guy hung up on me as soon as I told him why I was calling.

I actually got someone to talk to me on the sixth try. "Are you Luis Rodriguez?" I asked after getting over my initial shock that someone answered their phone and remained on the line after I identified myself as a private investigator.

"Yes, I am. May I ask what this is concerning?"

"I'm calling about Paul Flynn."

There was a pause. "Paul who?"

"Flynn. He was an escort. I believe you knew him."

"Oh, Paul. I thought I knew him very well, but he never mentioned his last name." He chuckled. "It's just not something that comes up, you know? Now, other things came up...but not last names."

"When was your most recent date with Paul?"

"It's probably been a month ago. You see, I met someone, and I haven't really needed..."

According to the records, Luis had been with Paul about five weeks before, which meant he was telling the truth. I wasn't really interested in the details of his personal life, though, so I cut him off. "Did you know that Paul died a few weeks ago?"

"Paul...died? No, I...I didn't know. How? Was it an accident?"

"Actually, he was murdered. In his apartment."

"Wha-what? Murdered? Oh my God!"

"You didn't know?"

"No, I didn't know," he said sharply. "If I had, I wouldn't have been making sick jokes and prattling on about my love life. How...how was he killed?"

"The police think he was killed in an alleged robbery?"

"If he was killed in a robbery, why are you talking to me?"

"Someone doesn't believe the official story. They hired me to find out what really happened. I'd like to ask you some questions. Would you be willing to answer them? You could help me bring Paul's killer to justice." *Assuming it's not you,* I thought to myself.

"Yes, of course. Anything to help Paul. I may not have known his last name, but he was a very nice person. He always made me feel so special. He just had a way of putting you at ease. I...I can't believe he's gone."

I rolled my eyes and glanced down at his record while he bemoaned his deep loss. The man didn't even know Paul's last name and had paid him for sex. How broken up could he be?

"How long had you been seeing Paul?" I asked when he paused to take a breath. I had the information in front of me, but I wanted to find out if his account would agree with the official records.

"Off and on for the last six months," he said after taking a second to shift gears. That jibed.

"How many times in that six months?"

"I'm not certain, maybe five?" The records said six: close enough.

"How did he act?"

"I'm not sure what you mean."

"Well, I want you to compare the way he acted early on with how he acted toward the end. Was he any different?"

He thought a minute. "Not that I could tell. He always made sure I was relaxed and satisfied. I guess you could say he was every inch a professional. Um, no pun intended."

"He never seemed afraid of something?"

"Not that I could tell."

"Are you aware of any reason someone might want to kill him?"

"No."

"Can you think of anything you feel might be important to my investigation?"

"Look, I guess I really didn't know him that well. He didn't talk about himself much. He never revealed anything personal. All I can tell you is that he always made me feel good and special. That's not an experience I'd had very often in my life before him. He made me feel good about myself, and let me tell you, it was a lot more fun than therapy."

"Okay, well thanks," I said. "If you remember anything else, please call me." I gave him my cell phone number and was about to hang up when he stopped me.

"Wait, how did you get my number? How did you know I used to see Paul?"

I'd been anticipating that question, and since Paul was gone, it wouldn't hurt to lay the blame on him, so I lied. "Paul kept a journal."

"And he mentioned me?" Luis sounded surprised and a little flattered.

"Yes," I said, and then, after a moment, I added, "He seemed fond of you."

The line was quiet for a few seconds, before he said simply, "Thank you," and hung up.

There was one number left that I hadn't tried yet, but I decided to wait until later. That last call had taken more out of me than I'd expected. I hadn't thought of an escort actually performing some sort of valuable service, but it had obviously meant a great deal to Luis. I wondered what his life had been like that he had needed someone's validation so badly. Had he been abused as a child? Told he was unattractive? Did he have a bad relationship that left emotional scars? I almost wanted to call him back and ask, but it was really none of my business and certainly had no bearing on the case.

I looked at my watch. It was still too early to call Jake's old friends, and none of Paul's former clients would be home from work for several more hours. I checked my e-mail, but there was nothing of importance. I went through the envelopes I'd set aside earlier, which didn't take long, either. There was no paperwork waiting to be done since Novak wasn't letting me touch anything having to do with his secret case. Maybe he wasn't even leaving a paper trail.

I suddenly found myself bored. It was an unfamiliar feeling. I always seemed to have something waiting to be done, either work or school related, or else I was doing something with Micah. I'd forgotten what free time was. I figured I had at least two hours to kill and not a single thing to do.

My eyes fell on Paul's file, which reminded me to ask Novak about the safe-deposit box. When he responded to my knock, I stuck my head in. "Can I ask you a quick question?"

"Of course. Come on in."

"I want to know about safe-deposit boxes."

Novak raised one eyebrow. "What about them?"

"I found out Paul had one and went to a lot of trouble to hide his key, which makes me wonder if it contains something important. Is there any way I can find out what's in it?"

"You personally?"

"Yes."

"Not that I'm aware of. The police, or next-of-kin, would most likely have to open it."

"What if I had Paul's key?"

Novak frowned at me. "Is this hypothetical?"

I nodded quickly. "Yes, purely."

He looked as if he didn't quite believe me. "Even if you had his key, you'd have to provide some proof of identification to get the bank's key in order to open the box. It requires two keys, one of which the bank—"

"Right. I know about the two keys and how that works. So, basically, what you're saying is, I'd have to talk to his family or turn the information over to the police and wait until they got around to looking into it."

"No, what I'm telling you is that you need to turn the information over to the police, period. This is an active murder investigation."

"Active is a relative term in this case."

Novak gave me an exasperated look. "Killian..."

"Can I talk to Paul's mom first, at least?"

He sighed. "I suppose, but if you turn up anything remotely relevant to the case, you'd better contact the authorities immediately."

"Yes, sir."

We sat staring at each other for a few moments. "Is there anything else?" Novak finally asked.

"Well, I don't really have anything else to do now. Do you have any work for me?"

He gawked at me with disbelief. "What?"

"Do you need anything done? Any filing, paperwork, typing?"

"You're asking me for work? Are you ill? Do you have a fever? Don't tell me you don't have anything to do."

"I just had some free time..."

"And you want me to fill it with work? Killian, you're becoming a workaholic. Go get some fresh air. Walk through the zoo, rollerblade through the park — do something outside that doesn't require you to think. For goodness sake, take a break."

"I'm not becoming a workaholic," I said weakly.

"Did it even occur to you to relax when you realized you didn't have anything that needed to be done?"

I blinked. "That's beside the point."

"No, that's exactly the point. You're working too hard. Go enjoy yourself for a few hours. That's an order."

I snapped up straight and sketched a mock salute. "Yes, sir, Novak, sir."

He gave me a dirty look. "Get the hell out of here. Go have some fun...if you haven't forgotten how."

I grinned sourly and slipped out of his office. "I know how to have fun," I said under my breath.

I decided to go to the zoo. In the middle of town, there's a large park that runs along the Wicomico River. Part of the park is a charming little zoo that's won awards as one of the best of its size in the country. I'd always enjoyed walking through it, but I hadn't been there at all in at least a year.

I wandered around for a while looking at jaguars, bears, monkeys, and alligators, doing my best not to think about anything work-related. I was a little disturbed to realize I didn't have much else to think about. Things were good with Micah, better than they'd ever been, in fact. I could do nothing further about Amalie until she decided to show up again, and besides, I wanted to keep her off my mind as much as I could — she was more stressful than work any way you measured it. School was just plain boring. I couldn't come up with a single other idea worth pursuing. Had my life been reduced to dead people, work, school, and Micah?

I need a hobby, I thought, then laughed out loud. A little girl nearby gave me a wary look and sidled up closer to her mother. When would I find time to do a hobby?

I ended up at the playground next to the zoo. It was practically deserted at that time of day except for a young woman keeping her eye on two children playing on the slide. I sat down on a swing to watch the kids enjoying themselves, totally immersed in their fun. I'd forgotten what it felt like to be that carefree.

I was still watching them when I sensed a presence behind me. Before I could react, I felt hands in the small of my back giving me a push. With a yelp I spun around in the swing, letting go of the chains and losing my balance in the process. Strong arms caught me before I could hit the ground, and I looked up into Micah's face. His expression was warring between amusement and concern.

"Are you trying to kill me?" I asked accusingly.

Amusement won out, and he laughed. "Sorry. I wanted to surprise you, not send you to the hospital."

I laughed too as I managed to get my feet under me and stand up. "You almost succeeded in doing both. How did you find me?"

"I went by the office to see you. Novak said he'd sent you out to relax and that I might find you here. I thought it was worth a shot. Sit down, and I'll push you."

I sat back down obediently and he gave me a gentle push. "Why were you looking for me?"

"I just wanted to see you. Do I have to have a reason?"

I smiled. "I guess not. What's going on with your story?"

"Ugh. What's not going on? I think I opened Pandora's box. There's hate, greed, cruelty, deception — you name it. And it seems we've only scratched the surface."

"So how far do you think it reaches?"

"We don't know yet, but we've definitely uncovered something big."

"I guess I don't understand what's going on with all this, really. I haven't taken the time to read everything."

"It's a lot to explain, and even I don't understand it all, to be honest." Micah sighed. "Basically, though, it has to do with the environmental-protection laws. It appears the commissioners and other authorities were being paid off to allow building where there shouldn't have been any development, such as in protected wetlands. That's just the tip of the iceberg. I don't really feel like talking about it now. I need a break. That's why I came looking for you. I'm going to be pretty busy for the next few days — or longer — and I wanted to see you while I actually had a little free time. I don't want to spend what few moments we have discussing work."

"Fair enough," I said, thinking about Novak's accusing me of being a workaholic. "Let's take a walk."

"That sounds nice."

We ambled through the park along the river. There weren't too many people around, so we essentially had the place to ourselves. We paused on the little arch bridge to kiss.

"I'm sorry I'll be so tied up for a while," he said, resting his forehead against mine.

"Me too. But there's nothing you can do about it. This is your job, and it's important to you."

"Thanks for understanding."

When he pressed his lips against mine again, I melted into his arms. It didn't take long before I began to get aroused.

Micah noticed immediately. "Have you ever had sex in a public place?"

"No! And I don't intend to start now."

"You have no sense of adventure," he said.

"I just have no desire to get arrested. You're supposed to write the news, not make it."

He laughed. "I miss making love to you."

"It's only been a couple days."

"That's too long. I love you, Killian."

"I love you too."

We stood for a while just holding each other until a dog walker came down the path at a brisk stroll. We pulled apart, but she just smiled at us as she passed by with her spaniel.

"I'd better get back to work," Micah said with a sigh.

I checked my watch and grimaced. "Me too."

He gave me a quick kiss before we walked hand in hand back through the park and zoo to where we'd both left our cars. After one final kiss, we drove off in our separate directions. I felt much better for my break from the grind. The fact that Micah came looking for me certainly didn't hurt, either. It made me feel as if I truly mattered to him, which is something I guess I already knew. Still, there's nothing like being reminded in such a tactile way.

When I returned to the office, the door was locked. I let myself in and found a note on my desk: "Hope you relaxed with your free time. I'll be gone for a few days. See you Friday. Novak."

I frowned as I read over it. Why hadn't he at least mentioned he wouldn't be there when I got back? Did he know, or was it a last-minute thing? Maybe he'd just been trying to avoid the inevitable questions that would have arisen if he'd told me he'd be away. Where was he going? What was he doing? Did it involve his mystery case? Was he just trying to get rid of me when he'd suggested I go to the zoo?

I grumbled to myself and tossed the note into the trashcan. My questions would go unanswered for the moment and, knowing Novak, I might never get any satisfaction.

I stood there trying to decide whether to tackle Jake's former friends or the rest of Paul's former clients. I decided to go for the local kids. I could talk to them in person, and I didn't feel like spending a lot of time on the phone. First, though, I had to make sure they were at home.

When I dialed Craig he answered immediately. He sounded a little nervous, but was agreeable to my dropping by right away. Danielle was equally available, so I told her I'd see her in an hour or so.

Craig lived in a nondescript middle-class neighborhood, the type where all the houses look like carbon copies. For the most part, only the color varied — and that only in shades of gray, blue, and tan. Occasionally, some wild and crazy person had added an overhang at the front door or a small front porch. The houses were all well-kept with neat lawns, yet the neighborhood was strangely depressing. The only bright spots came from the jack-o'-lanterns in almost every front yard. A few families had gone all out with ghosts and witches and faux cobwebs strung on tree branches.

As I pulled into Craig's driveway, the front door — adorned with a jointed, cardboard skeleton — swung open to reveal a thin boy peering out with an anxious expression. I gave him what I hoped was a nonthreatening smile and a little wave. "Are you Craig?"

He nodded.

"Thanks for agreeing to talk to me." I stopped at the steps, wondering if we were going to have our conversation through the screen door or if he would invite me in.

While I waited for him to decide, I studied Jake's former friend and, according to Kane, at least, secret admirer. Or not so secret. Craig was an attractive boy, about five-foot ten or eleven with a slim build and a narrow waist. His flawless skin was a little too dark to be Caucasian, but I couldn't quite decide on his race. His eyes were large and dark behind his glasses, his hair slightly curly and light brown. He wore a form-fitting blue t-shirt and jeans. He could have been hot with a little more confidence. As it was, he had a way of pulling into himself as if afraid of the world outside.

He eyed me for a minute. Then, seeming to decide I was safe, he pushed open the screen door and motioned for me to enter.

"We can talk in here," he said. "My parents aren't home." His voice was soft, with a slight lisp on his sibilants.

He led me into a living room that was tastefully decorated, if a little boring, in earth tones. A family portrait hung over the couch, answering my question as to his race. His father was white, and his mother was African-American. A much younger Craig sat on his mother's lap in the picture, smiling widely for the photographer.

I turned back to him and watched him fold himself into the couch, tucking his long legs under him and watching me with uncertainty. I understood what Kane meant about him. There was something decidedly feminine about this boy.

I took a seat in a chair facing the couch. "I really appreciate your talking to me." He nodded an acknowledgement, and I hoped I wasn't going to have to drag every word out of him. "I know you don't know me or anything—"

"Actually, I know who you are," he said, catching me by surprise. "Everybody in school knows who you are. You're kind of like a legend around there."

"Me?" I squeaked in a very unlegend-like manner.

"Yeah. I mean, everyone knows you caught that murderer a few years ago and killed him yourself. I wasn't even in high school yet and I heard about it. And then you were brave enough to come out and all..." He stopped abruptly and blushed.

I made a face. "Trust me, going after that psycho was not the smartest thing I've ever done. It was stupidity, not bravery. I almost got myself and people I cared about killed."

"But you saved Jake's life."

"Maybe it wouldn't have been in danger in the first place if I'd left things alone."

"But then the killer would have gotten away with it."

I was fighting a losing battle, so I moved to his other point. "Well, coming out wasn't all that brave, either. It was just something I had to do."

"It's more than a lot of people do," he said softly, looking away.

"Maybe that's because they don't have anyone to support them the way I did."

He looked up at me and gave me an odd, slightly calculating look. "What did you come to talk to me about?"

"Jake."

He frowned. "What about Jake? I don't see him much anymore. He's too good for me now."

"What do you mean?"

"Well, everything was fine, and then all of a sudden he stopped calling me to do things, and when I'd call him he'd make some lame excuse. Then he stopped hanging out with me and Danielle at school and started avoiding us — skipping lunch, stuff like that."

"Do you know why?"

"Why he stopped hanging out with us?" I nodded. "Not really. I guess it was something I did. I don't know what, though, and believe me, I've thought about it a lot." He looked as though he could start crying at any moment.

"Do you think Danielle knows?"

He shrugged. "Danielle and I are really only acquaintances. We were just friends with Jake. We don't have anything in common besides that. We don't talk much now that Jake ignores both of us."

I wasn't getting much from this poor kid, but I felt very sorry for him. It seemed as if he was the victim in all this. Jake's treatment of him just served to reaffirm his lack of worth in his own eyes.

"You know I'm a private investigator now, right?" I asked. He nodded again. "I want you to keep what I'm about to tell you just between the two of us, okay?" His eyes widened, and he nodded once more. "I think Jake is involved in something illegal. I've been asked to look into it by someone who cares about him very much. They're worried about him. The reason I'm here to talk to you is that I was hoping you'd be able to help me figure out what's going on. Do you have any ideas, no matter how wild, about what Jake's involved with?"

He thought for a minute. "It could be drugs, I guess. I don't know what else it might be. I'm sorry."

"Don't be sorry. It's not your fault. And for the record, I don't think it's your fault that Jake's being a jerk, either. I doubt you did anything wrong. I suspect Jake is the one doing something wrong."

"Really?" There was a vaguely desperate note in his voice, as if he very much needed to believe this.

"Yes. I have to go talk to Danielle now, but I want to tell you something before I go. Remember what I said earlier about having people to support you?"

He gave me a sharp look and slowly nodded. I dug a business card out of my wallet and handed it to him.

"This is none of my business really, but if you ever need someone to talk to about anything, I'm a good listener. Maybe your parents and friends are all the support you'll need, but just in case..."

I let the offer hang in the air while he studied my card as if it was the most fascinating thing he'd ever seen. When he finally looked up, I could have sworn his eyes were filled with unshed tears.

"I don't have any friends anymore," he said in a voice so soft I could barely hear him. "And my parents are too busy to be bothered with my stupid problems."

"Your problems aren't stupid," I said gently. "They matter to you, and I'll bet they would matter to your parents, too."

He shrugged, but looked unconvinced. "They wouldn't understand."

"Maybe I would."

He tucked my card carefully into his pocket and folded his hands in his lap. "Thank you," he whispered.

"You're welcome, Craig. And I meant what I said. If you need to talk to someone, please call me."

He nodded one last time, and I stood up. "I'll let myself out."

"They call me faggot," he said suddenly.

I sank back into the chair. "Who does?"

"Everybody at school."

"Why?"

He shrugged. "Isn't it obvious?"

"Not to me."

"I'm not a jock. I'm not all macho. I'm not tough. I suck at sports. I walk like a girl." He stopped his litany of perceived faults and took a ragged breath.

"There's nothing wrong with any of that."

He snorted. "Try telling that to the guys at school."

"I remember what it was like." He looked up at me with surprise in his eyes. "I wasn't always a legend," I said dryly. "My first few years of high school, I was anything but popular. I was uncoordinated when it came to sports, shy, awkward. I was lucky, though. I didn't get picked on too much because the people I hung out with were jocks. They weren't really my friends, but we'd grown up together, and everyone assumed we were close, so they left me alone for the most part. When I got to know Seth — he was the gay boy who was murdered — and started to realize I was gay, the people who everyone thought were my friends turned on me."

"Oh wow. Seriously?"

"Yes. They left that part out of the story, huh? That stuff isn't important in the long run. After high school, you'll never even see most of those idiots again. All that matters is what you think about yourself. You shouldn't let their opinions affect that."

"Easier said than done," he said.

"True, and that's why it's important to talk to people who understand. Can I ask you a very personal question?"

His eyes looked everywhere in the room but at me. I didn't think he was going to answer me at first, but he finally gave me a jerky nod.

"Do you think you're gay?"

He bit his lip and stared at the wall over my head. Again, he didn't answer right away, but then gave another nod. A tear squeezed out one eye and rolled down his cheek.

"Have you ever told anyone before?" He shook his head no. "Well, it's okay. You don't have to worry about me telling anyone else unless you say it's okay. You can trust me." His eyes slowly lowered to meet mine. "You don't have to be afraid. You're not alone. You can ask me anything, talk to me about anything."

Suddenly, he burst into tears and began to sob in earnest, covering his face with his hands. I sat helplessly in my chair for a minute, but when he didn't show any signs of calming down, I awkwardly moved to the couch next to him and placed a tentative hand on his shoulder. He twisted into my chest so quickly he almost threw me off balance. I hesitantly wrapped my arms around his quivering shoulders.

It seemed to be the right thing to do. His sobs softened, but he continued to cry for a few more minutes before pulling away. "I'm sorry." He sniffled and wiped furiously at his eyes. "I can't believe I did that."

"Don't be sorry. It's okay. I completely understand. There's just so much pressure it eventually kind of explodes, like a dam that springs a small leak and then the whole thing blows."

He giggled a little in relief and nodded. I gave him a moment to pull himself together. He looked at his watch and frowned.

"You should probably go," he said. "My parents will be home soon, and I'd rather not have to explain why I'm crying on the couch with some guy they've never seen before."

With a grin I stood up. "Are you okay?"

He smiled and jumped to his feet as well. "Yeah. I'm okay...better than I've been in months. It feels so good to tell someone, like a weight was lifted off my shoulders. Can I still talk to you?"

"Definitely. You'll probably need to talk now more than ever. My office and cell-phone numbers and email address are on the card I gave you, so you can get in touch with me no matter what. You can call me day or night, okay?"

He nodded happily then surprised me by throwing his arms around me in a big hug. "Thank you, Killian," he said as he squeezed me.

"You're very welcome, Craig."

He released me just as suddenly as he grabbed me and stepped back, seeming a little embarrassed. I followed him to the front door, where he was unable to stop himself from enfolding me in another spontaneous hug. I laughed and hugged him back. He let me out, remaining in the doorway while I drove away.

Well, I thought to myself as I glanced up at him in my rearview mirror, I may not have found much out as far as the case is concerned, but that was definitely not a wasted trip.

Chapter 22

I pulled into Danielle's driveway only a little later than expected. Her neighborhood was a step up from Craig's, in that the houses were discernibly different from their neighbors in architectural style. She lived in a light-blue, two-story Cape Cod with an attached two-car garage, whose open door revealed a matching set of late-model Audis, one dark green and one champagne. In the drive outside sat a slightly older red Saturn, which I assumed to be Danielle's.

Unlike Craig, Danielle was not waiting to greet me. I approached the front door and knocked. After a brief delay, it was opened by a dumpy, middle-aged man in the uniform of a stereotypical college professor: sweater-vest over a button-up Oxford shirt, brown slacks, and brown loafers. His hairline had long ago sounded the retreat, and what remained was turning from a mousy brown to an equally mousy gray. He peered at me over half-glasses, wearing a slightly befuddled expression as if he expected to recognize me but didn't.

"I'm here to see Danielle," I said, hoping I had the right house.

"Oh. Yes. One minute, please." His voice was a surprisingly rich baritone.

I stood waiting on the doorstep for about a minute before she appeared. She looked remarkably like her father, except she was a little heavier and lacked the receding hairline. Her hair was the same mousy brown and hung limply to her shoulders; she had the same pear-shaped body; she even peered at me over her glasses in much the same way. She wore what looked like a man's shirt with the sleeves rolled up, a pair of Capri pants, and no shoes.

She eyed me critically. "Are you the guy who called and wanted to talk to me?"

"Yes, I'm Killian Kendall."

She nodded. "I've heard of you. Jake used to talk about you, and of course, almost everybody at school knows what you did."

"Of course," I said under my breath.

"What?"

"Oh, nothing," I replied quickly. She seemed a little sullen, and I figured it would be in my best interest to keep her talking while she was still willing. "Can I ask you some questions about Jake?"

She shrugged, which I took as an affirmative. When she made no move to either come out or let me in, I asked, "Do you think I could go inside or you could come outside so we don't have to talk through the door?"

She made a face and threw open the door with a dramatic sigh. "I'll come out there," she said as if she were making a huge sacrifice for my benefit. "If we go inside, my parents will listen."

I doubted her father would be able to work up enough interest to be bothered. I didn't know him, however, and I'd never even seen her mother, so I took her word for it. She led the way across the yard to a freestanding lawn swing with just enough room for two people to sit next to each other if they didn't mind being a little intimate. I minded, but sat down gingerly anyway, as far to one side as possible.

Danielle gave me an expectant look.

"You're friends with Jake?" I asked.

"Not anymore."

"What happened?"

She picked imaginary lint off her shirt. "Who knows? He never told me."

"What do you think happened?"

"He got bored with us and moved on to greener pastures."

"Us meaning you and Craig?"

"Yeah."

"Was it always just the three of you?"

"Pretty much. Every once in a while, some guy would try to get close to Jake, if you know what I mean. He'd be around for a few days, and then we wouldn't see him much anymore. I think Jake's motto was, 'Use 'em and lose 'em.'"

"Do you know for a fact that Jake was sleeping with them?"

"Not for a fact, no, but it doesn't take a genius."

"Who were they?"

"I don't remember their names. They weren't really important, you know?"

I tried not to sigh in frustration, wondering if she was making this stuff up as she went along. She seemed like the type. "So you know Jake is gay?"

She rolled her eyes. "Duh. Everyone knows that. He's not exactly in the closet."

"Did that ever bother you?"

"Of course not," she said quickly, which probably meant that it had. I was beginning to suspect she had a crush on Jake and had resented the competition. It made me wonder how she felt about Craig, who also had a crush on Jake, one so obvious even Kane had noticed it.

"What about Craig?"

"What about him?" she asked obtusely.

"What did you think of him?"

She quirked her mouth to one side. "Craig is a little wimp. He followed Jake around like a puppy dog, mooning after him, simpering at him like some demented Scarlett O'Hara. It was sickening. That's probably why Jake quit hanging out with him in the first place."

I had to bite back asking her if that was why he'd quit hanging out with her, too. I rather doubted Jake's sudden change had anything to do with Craig or Danielle. I suspected Jake had actually enjoyed having his own private fan club. Something else must have come along to make lovesick teenagers seem paltry in comparison. Could that something have been the escort business?

It was obvious that Danielle lived in her own bitter little world. She saw only what she wanted to see, which led me to think she was unlikely to give me anything useful. To be honest, I didn't like her, and wanted to get away as quickly as I could. Still, I had one more question I needed to ask before I made my escape. "So you don't really have any idea what's going on with Jake?"

"I already said no. We don't talk anymore."

I took a deep breath and decided I was done there. "Thanks for your time, Danielle—"

She cut me off. "Wait a minute. What was that all about? Why were you asking all those questions about Jake?"

She asks that now? I marveled to myself. The logical time would have been when I started interrogating her, not when I was done and ready to leave. Although I didn't owe her anything at that point, I suspected if I didn't give her something, she'd be on the phone to Jake before I was out of the driveway. On the other hand, she seemed like the gossipy type, so I couldn't tell her too much.

"You know I'm a private investigator, right?"

"So you said on the phone. What is this so-called case, anyway? How do I know you're not just hot for Jake's ass like those other guys?"

I gritted my teeth and counted to ten. "The case is classified," I said. Her eyes narrowed, and I knew I'd said the wrong thing. For all her bluff and bluster, however, I had a feeling she was really a coward at heart, so I decided to try a little scare tactic.

"Jake may be involved in something very dangerous." I clipped off each word in my annoyance. "Lives may be at stake, including everyone he is or was close to." Her eyes widened at that. My ploy might work after all, and as far as I knew, I wasn't even lying. "I need you to stay very quiet about our talk or you could put the whole case in jeopardy. Do you understand?"

She nodded.

"Good. Thanks again for your time." I turned away quickly before she could ask anything else and strode across the yard to my car. I hoped I'd been convincing enough to keep her quiet.

I also hoped like hell I had overstated the case. I would hate to find out I'd called it all too accurately.

I walked into the office with the intention of phoning Paul's other clients. Instead, I found a message from Craig asking me to get back to him. I wondered if he was already taking me up on my offer to talk, or if he had something to add to what he'd told me earlier.

He answered on the second ring, as if he'd been waiting near the phone. "Um, thanks for returning my call." He sounded slightly surprised, as though he hadn't expected me to.

"No problem," I said. "What's up?"

"After you left, I thought I remembered something, but I wasn't sure about it, so I looked it up in my journal. Right before Jake started acting weird, he was really excited one day at school. I asked him why he was so happy, and he said he couldn't tell me, but he might have met someone totally different from the normal boys around here. He was always going on about how much better the guys were in California."

"He didn't tell you anything about this guy he'd met?"

"No, sorry."

"Craig, you don't have to apologize all the time. It's not your fault. There's nothing to be sorry for. You've just given me some information I didn't know before. That's extremely helpful."

"Seriously?"

"Absolutely. Thank you."

"Um, you're welcome."

"I have another question for you. Danielle said Jake dated a lot of guys, but none of them stuck around for very long. Is that how you saw it?"

"I guess. Jake always said the guys here were too boring. I got the impression he missed living in California."

"But he told you the new guy he'd met was different?"

"Yeah."

"Any idea what he meant by that? Even a guess?"

"I don't know."

"Did he have any specific complaints about the guys here other than they were boring?"

"He said they didn't know how to party. And, um...he sometimes tried to get me to do drugs with him, but I never would. I don't know where he got them from. He complained no one here knew how to have fun. He always said that when I told him I didn't want to get high with him."

"What kind of drugs did he use?"

"I have no idea. I don't know much about drugs. I've never done anything. I don't even drink."

"Was it pills? Powder? Needles?"

"Pills mostly."

"Mostly?"

"I mean that's all I ever saw."

"But you don't know what kind of pills they were?"

"No, sorry. Er...I mean...sorry. I'm sorry I said sorry again."

I stifled a giggle. "It's okay. Thanks, Craig, you've been a big help."

"I have?"

"Definitely."

"Cool. Um, well, I'll let you get back to work or whatever."

"Okay. Thanks again, Craig."

"Yeah, you're welcome. Oh, and um, thank you. For, uh, talking to me and stuff."

"You're welcome. And don't forget to call me anytime you want or need to talk."

"Okay," he said softly. "Bye."

"Bye, Craig."

I hung up and thought about the difference between him and Danielle. One was sweet and gentle, while the other had the grace of a bulldozer. Jake couldn't have chosen two hangers-on who were more at odds. The only thing they had in common was their fascination with Jake Sheridan.

I took out my notebook and jotted down the little bit of information I'd managed to glean from Craig and Danielle, most of which came from Craig. That done, I retrieved the papers Neal sent me. I set aside both the guy who had hung up on me and Luis, whom I'd already talked to. That left five.

I called the first one. After a brief conversation, it became obvious he wouldn't have much to add. His visits with Paul had been out-calls, meaning Paul went to him. He was amazingly unobservant and only recalled Paul's name because he had it written down so he would remember whom to ask for when he contacted the agency.

The second person still wasn't home, or at least wasn't answering. The guy after that said he didn't know anything about Paul, that Paul never mentioned personal matters and always kept everything focused on giving as much pleasure as possible. "We never talked all that much, if you know what I mean."

I was beginning to think the clients were going to be a complete waste of time. It seemed Paul didn't talk very much about himself. He obviously didn't let anyone inside the emotional walls he'd built around himself. Maybe it was self-preservation. In a business like escorting, you'd have to keep some sort of distance between yourself and the clients; you couldn't very well get emotionally involved with all of them. And that's what it was — a business.

I decided to keep calling, though. Another one of Novak's little mottos: "Perseverance pays off." He always insisted you never knew when you might strike gold.

I thought I'd hit a nugget with my fourth call, but it turned out to be pyrite, better known as fool's gold. The guy started out as if he knew

Paul well, but I quickly realized he was only interested in keeping me on the line so he could talk dirty to me. I finally hung up on the pervert.

I almost didn't call the last number back, but figured I might as well be thorough. The phone rang for so long I was about to hang up when a young-sounding male voice answered. "Hello?"

"Oh, hi..." I was caught off guard. "Is this, um..." I scanned the page in front of me for his name. "...Howard Rich?"

"Are you trying to sell me something?" he asked politely.

"No, I just have a few questions to ask you. I won't take much of your time."

"So this is like a survey?"

"No, I—"

"Do you want money from me?"

"No."

"Well, in that case, it's Howie, please. I hate the name Howard."

"Um, okay, Howie. My name is Killian Kendall. I'm a private investigator."

"Really? How interesting. And you want to talk to me?"

"Yes." I wondered if he would ever allow me to get more than one sentence out at a time.

"About what?"

An opening. I didn't waste any time taking it. "Paul Flynn. He was an escort. I think you were acquainted? He was—"

"Murdered," he said sadly.

"You knew?"

"I saw it on the news. Actually, can I take this in my office? I'll be able to talk to you more freely there."

"Yes, of course. I'll wait."

I heard him call someone named Eileen to the phone and ask her to hang up after he took it in his office.

While I waited, I glanced down at the page of notes on Howie and raised an eyebrow in surprise. It appeared he'd been a client of Paul's for much longer than any of the others.

"Okay, Eileen, I'm back. You can hang up now." He waited until she had done as he'd requested before he continued. "Yes, I knew Paul. I was shocked to hear about his death. To be honest, I've been having a hard time dealing with it. He was a good person."

"You'd been seeing Paul for quite a while. In fact, considerably longer than any of his other clients." Howie refused to rise to the bait. When the silence had stretched out a little longer than was comfortable, I asked, "How well did you know Paul?"

"How well do you ever know anyone?"

I wasn't about to get drawn into an existential conversation. "It would be very helpful if you could answer my questions."

"Why? What are you looking for? Who are you working for? Why are you concerned with Paul's death?"

"I'm afraid I can't tell you who I'm working for — that's confidential — but I can say I've been retained to look into Paul's death by someone who cared about him. They hired me because the police don't seem to be putting much effort into finding his killer."

"So you're trying to find Paul's killer?"

"Yes."

"Sounds dangerous."

"Possibly."

"What's in it for you?"

"What?"

"What do you get out of it?"

"It's my job."

"Okay, if that's what blows your skirt up, but what does any of that have to do with how well I knew Paul?"

I felt like pounding my head against the desk. First Danielle, then the pervert, and now this guy. Had I been a bad boy recently? Was I being punished for something? I took a deep breath and tried again.

"I'm trying to get a grasp on what was going on in Paul's life the last few months. His friends have told me he became distant and secretive, but no one knows why. What little I've managed to uncover has only muddied the waters. I'm hoping to find someone who might be able to clear things up for me. If you knew him well, I was hoping you could help. If you didn't know him well, just let me know now and save us both some time."

He was quiet for so long that I began to wonder if he'd hung up.

"Howie?"

"Yeah, I'm here. I guess you could say I knew Paul pretty well. We'd become friends. He did see me longer than his other clients because he was doing me a favor. Paul's the only man I've ever had sex with. You see, I'm married to a wonderful woman. I was in denial for much of my life, and I had a family before I finally realized I was gay. I've never told my wife. She's an incredible person and the best friend I could ever ask for. I would never leave her or my children. She deserves better than that, but I still had a need to be with men...so I hired Paul. He took care of my needs very well. He knew all of this when he agreed to allow me to keep seeing him."

I didn't know what to say, so I didn't say anything.

After a moment, Howie went on. "Paul was perhaps the sweetest, most gentle man I've ever met. He gave of himself completely, and I don't just mean that sexually. I like to think we became friends. I know I cared for him very deeply."

"Did you...did you ever talk about Paul's personal life?"

"To some degree, yes."

"Did you notice any change in him over the last few months before his death?"

"Yes."

"Do you know what was causing that change?"

"Yes."

My heart caught in my throat. Could this be the answers to all my questions?

"Let me clarify that," Howie said quickly. "I knew some of what was going on but by no means everything. Paul was too much the professional to name names or give too many details, but I know vaguely what was troubling him."

"Can you tell me what you know?"

"Paul and I did a lot more than just have sex. I'd take him to dinner at nice restaurants we knew to be discreet. We'd take walks along the river; we'd talk for hours after sex. It was while we were talking that I learned he suspected someone he knew of being involved in something illegal, something serious. He didn't specify what, and I didn't press him. Those were the unspoken rules of our conversations. He asked me what I thought he should do. I told him it would depend on what this person was to him. If it was just a casual acquaintance, then maybe he should go straight to the authorities. If it was someone he respected or cared about, I suggested he go to the person and speak to him or her directly."

"Did he indicate what he was planning to do?"

"No. As I said, that wasn't how it worked. But you know, ever since I heard he was murdered, I've worried it might have been my advice that got him killed."

It was a very real possibility, but I wasn't about to tell him that. He already sounded upset as it was. "You have no way of knowing," I said truthfully enough. "You don't know if Paul took your advice or not. Even if he did, it might not have had anything to do with his murder. That's what I'm trying to figure out. He didn't give you any indication as to who this person was?"

"No. None."

"And you never saw him again after that conversation?"

"No."

"This was about a month ago?"

"About a week before he was killed."

"Can you think of anything else that might be helpful or important to the case?"

He was quiet for a second. "I believe Paul might have met someone."

"What do you mean by 'met someone'?"

"Just what I said. I suspect he'd met someone he really liked. The last couple of times I saw him, he was different somehow — happier and more relaxed. That was before he wanted my advice. I asked him what was going on to put a smile on his face, but he just smiled all the more and shook his head. When I asked him if he'd met someone special, his smile grew even wider, if possible. I said the new person must be someone very special indeed to bring about such a big smile. Then I said, whoever he was, he was a very lucky guy. Paul changed the subject after that. He never really liked talking about personal things, at least not when it was his own life being discussed. He was perfectly content to limit his role to being my confessor, counselor, and adviser."

I fought a sigh. Paul's reticence certainly didn't make investigating him any easier. It would have been so much simpler if he'd just been a little gabbier.

"Well, thank you, Howie. You've really helped a lot."

"I'm glad. I hope you catch the bastard who did this. Paul was a... He was a good person."

I hung up and sat back in my chair, propping my feet up on the desk. I had so many questions about the cases swimming around in my head that I was having trouble making sense of it all. I was rubbing my chin when I realized I was unconsciously imitating Novak. With a snap of chair springs, I yanked my feet off the desk and sat up straight, chuckling at myself. I guess there are worse things than discovering you're becoming like your teacher.

Chapter 23

I sat at my desk, tapping my pen against my spiral pad, which I took everywhere I went, filling it with notes on my cases. I was making a to-do list, but I'd gotten stuck on what to do about Jake.

Paul's list was finished. There were only three items, all of them important. I flipped back a page and read it over, hoping for inspiration.

1. Find out what's in the safe-deposit box.
2. Contact Paul's family.
3. Was Paul dating someone as Howie suspected?

The third item was very much a question. While I wasn't sure how I could find out, I figured the reminder might be helpful.

I returned to Jake's page and stared at the blank sheet. I found myself completely stumped as to where to go next. My best idea so far was to just show up at the AIDS Ball Friday night and hope for inspiration. Not exactly an aggressive attack, but maybe simple observation would serve me well in this case.

Thinking about the ball reminded me of Haven's Halloween dance scheduled for tomorrow night and of my promise to Kane to work on our costumes together. I made a mental note to be there when Kane got home from school that afternoon so I could live up to my commitment.

I picked up the phone and dialed Chris's cell phone number. Getting her voice mail, I left a message asking her to make an appointment for me to talk to the officer in charge of Paul's murder investigation.

That done, I forced myself to contemplate Jake's empty page once again. Why was this so hard? Was it because I was afraid of what I'd find out? Despite the distance that had grown between us, I still cared about him. I'd had strong feelings for him once upon a time, or at least I'd thought so. I'd even risked my life to save his. There was a part of me that insisted the experience had to have been worthwhile. I didn't want to think I had only saved him so he could become some sort of criminal. Of course, that was unbelievably selfish of me. It was Jake's life to do with as he pleased.

Who said being an escort was actually that bad? Micah had been an escort. So had Paul, who by all accounts had been a stand-up guy, respected by everyone — a model friend and lover.

Lover. Micah's lover. *Former lover*, I reminded myself. I couldn't let that begin to cloud my judgment at this stage of the game. So far, I thought I'd done a pretty decent job at keeping things on a purely professional level. Besides, their relationship had been over long before I came into the picture. They had both moved on: Micah to be with me and Paul perhaps to find a new lover as well. More importantly — let's face it — Paul wasn't exactly a threat anymore.

I realized how my thoughts on one case kept leading naturally back to the other. The two cases had so many similarities that they almost seemed intertwined. I couldn't help wondering if there was more of a connection than just the picture of Neal that Jake had in his bedroom. I suspected Jake of being an escort, and I knew Paul had been one. Paul worked for Neal. Who did Jake work for, if anyone? Did he work for Neal too? If so, he seemed a little far away from the Top to Bottom Agency's operational base. Maybe it was a satellite business. Did they have those for escort agencies? Maybe Neal was franchising. I giggled at the thought. He could have branches all around the country: over one million served.

I finally had something to write on Jake's to-do list.

1. Who is Jake working for?

The money had to be coming from somewhere. I just had to find out where.

Of course, if I found out, I'd still have to figure out how to tell Judy. I wasn't looking forward to breaking that news: "Well, Judy, it seems Jake is selling his body to buy electronics and clothes." Then again, knowing Judy, she'd probably say something like, "Oh, thank God, I was afraid he was in some awful business like selling used cars." She was pretty free-spirited when it came to things like drugs and sex. A lot of people would probably call her a hippie, but she really wasn't. She was just very open-minded.

Having at least one item on Jake's to-do list gave me a feeling of accomplishment, so I flipped the notebook closed and slid it into my pocket. My work was done for the day. I stood up and took a quick look around. Things had been way too quiet since Novak disappeared. I had no idea when he'd be back, but my curiosity about his mystery case was killing me. I decided to slip into his office to see if I could find anything on top of his desk. *After all*, I reasoned, *if he left it in plain sight, it can't be confidential, right?*

I pushed open his door and slithered inside, eying the hump-backed couch warily. I knew Novak was extremely unlikely to leave anything on his desk. It would be very much out of character for him. I wasn't surprised to find the surface completely clear except for his computer. He'd even put the phone away in the top drawer. He was meticulously neat with his space and just as scrupulous about the facts of his cases.

His eye lit up with a wicked gleam. "Settle? That just might be even better. How about Batman and Robin?"

I shuddered as I sat on my bed and Kane flopped down across his. "No thanks. I haven't felt the same about Batman since Jake's Halloween dance that first year you moved here."

"Oh yeah. Sorry, I forgot. Well, um...what other superhero duos are there?"

"Do we absolutely have to be superheroes? We'd still have to wear tights, and besides, who would be the hero and who would be the sidekick?"

"I don't mind being the sidekick. I'm younger, so it's only fair. And I know I have the body to pull off spandex. Are you a little worried there, big bro?"

"Not exactly worried. It's just that I don't especially like showing off all my goods for free. Ya know?"

"Wimp."

"Exhibitionist."

We laughed.

"Okay, so no superheroes?" Kane asked.

"If you're really set on it, I guess I can live with it."

"Well, there are other choices."

"Like what?"

"Um...you could always be a Hobbit, Kill."

"Are you trying to say I'm short?"

"I plead the fifth."

I threw a pillow at him, which he easily dodged.

"We could be hippies."

"Come on, Kane, that's not very creative."

"Hey, you be creative. I'm the one coming up with all the ideas while you just shoot them down. Are you sure you even want to go?"

"Yes," I said quickly, "I do want to go. Let's see...well, I could go as a mental patient. I wouldn't even have to wear a costume." Kane shot me a dirty look. "No? Okay, how about gangsters? No, not creative. Um...maybe we should just be pirates."

"This is a lot harder than I thought it would be."

"Tell me about it."

"Oh, wait! I have it!"

"What?"

"This is so perfect. Why didn't I think of it sooner?"

"What is it?"

"Sherlock Holmes and Watson. How perfect is that? You're a detective and everything."

I blinked. "That's actually a good idea. At least for me. It wouldn't be that great for you, though. I mean, what did Watson wear? A gray suit? Not exactly sexy."

"Then I'll go as a superhero."

"I thought you wanted to go as a duo."

"I did, but this is getting to be more work than it's worth."

"Boys?" Adam called from downstairs.

"Maybe Dad will have some ideas," Kane said and darted out of the room before I could even respond. He returned a few minutes later with Adam in tow.

Kane explained to him our idea, and Adam thought for a few minutes.

"What about salt and pepper or ketchup and mustard?" he said.

Kane rolled his eyes. "That's not very sexy, Dad."

Adam raised an eyebrow. "You didn't specify sexy."

"It goes without saying. How am I supposed to meet girls if I'm dressed as a bottle of ketchup?"

"Who said you'd get to be ketchup?" I said.

"Nobody's going to be ketchup."

"What about the Ambiguously Gay Duo?" Adam said before an argument could ensue.

"Who?" Kane asked.

"They're characters from a Saturday Night Live sketch." We stared blankly at Adam. He sighed. "You guys are too young." We all thought for a few more minutes, then he perked up. "How about Greek gods?"

"That's not too bad," Kane said. "I think I'd look pretty good in a toga."

"Only the Romans wore togas," Adam said.

Kane rolled his eyes. "Fine. What did Greeks wear?"

"They wore tunics, or chitons, under cloaks called himations. That would be a little much, though, so I suggest we simplify it quite a bit and just make skimpy, sexy tunics."

"Togas, tunics, whatever...isn't the whole thing a little cliché?" I asked.

"It doesn't have to be," Adam said. "You can decide on specific gods, and we can tailor the costumes. For instance, if you were Zeus you could carry a thunderbolt. Or Hermes could have winged sandals and helmet. Ares would have a shield, spear, and helmet. Apollo, a harp or bow and arrow. You get the point. Best of all, we could sew the tunics from old bed sheets, so we'd only have to buy a few accessories."

"Wow, you mean we'd actually be doing something together as a family?" Kane said dryly.

I saw a hurt look flash across Adam's face, although it was gone quickly. "Not quite the whole family. Steve won't be here. But yeah, the rest of us will be."

We jumped on the computer and looked up images of various Greek gods. I eventually settled on Hermes, and Kane picked Ares.

Kane and I ran to the costume store to get the props we needed while Adam started dinner. Later that night, we worked together to make our outfits. They were cut rather high, since Kane insisted they be as sexy as possible. I thought they turned out really well...until I went to put mine on the next night.

I started having second thoughts as I stood in front of the full-length mirror in our bedroom. "I don't know," I said doubtfully.

"Oh come on, Killian." Exasperation was clear in Kane's voice. "We have to leave in less than half an hour. What do you mean you don't know?"

"It's awfully...short."

"It's supposed to be short," Adam said, trying to suppress a snicker and not quite succeeding. "Kane kept insisting we go shorter yet."

"I mean, I know. There's just...less of it than I expected. I should have tried it on last night."

"You look great," Kane said. "Besides, it's too late now. Can we just go?"

I continued staring at my reflection. At eighteen, I still looked pretty much the same as I had two years earlier: short and thin. My chest was maybe not quite as scrawny as it used to be, but I was still feeling awfully exposed. My entire costume amounted to a white miniskirt, a winged helmet, and winged sandals, with a leather messenger bag slung over my shoulder.

I turned to check out Kane. His Ares costume was equally skimpy, but he was more built than I was, the result of a different body type and some weightlifting. Besides a skirt almost identical to mine, he simply carried a fake spear, a round shield, and wore a war helmet. "Easy for you to say. You look fantastic."

"You both look great, and after all the work I put into those costumes, you're damn well going to wear them." Adam softened his proclamation with a warm smile, his face glowing with fatherly pride. "You'll be the two most handsome boys there."

"I feel like I'm on display," I said weakly.

"Oh come on," Adam said. "You're young. Flaunt it while you can. My days of running around like that are long over."

"Ugh." Kane pretended to gag. "Thanks for that mental image."

Adam ignored him. "Besides, you'll be having so much fun you won't even think about it."

I sighed. "I hope so. I just wish Micah was going."

Kane squeezed by me to take one last look at himself in the mirror. "Are you done complaining yet?" he asked, his eyes never straying from his image.

I took a deep breath. "Yes."

"Good. Then let's go."

"We'll be early if we leave now," I said.

"Why don't you stop by the B&B?" Adam said. "I know it's out of the way, but Steve would love to see you in your costumes."

"It's not too much out of the way," I said. "And it'll allow us to be fashionably late."

"I guess that's okay," Kane said. "At least it will let us make an entrance."

"My thoughts exactly," I said sarcastically. "Are we going to have to pry you away from the mirror?"

"What? I'm not that bad."

"You haven't stopped admiring yourself since you put your costume on."

"So? I look good. And so do you, so don't start. Let's go." He jogged off down the stairs.

I gave Adam a long-suffering look as I stuffed my wallet in my messenger bag.

He patted me on the shoulder. "I know you wanted Micah to go, but try to have fun without him. Just not too much fun. Don't forget you're taken."

"As much as I've seen him this week, I might as well be single."

"This is a critical moment in his career. It won't last forever. Things will be back to normal before you know it."

"I can't wait."

"Come on!" Kane called from downstairs.

Adam grinned. "You'd better go before he wets himself."

I laughed and headed out the door.

"Oh, and Killian?"

I paused.

"Keep an eye on Kane, please."

Steve got a kick out of our costumes, as did the middle-aged gay couple who had checked in that day. They practically drooled over the two of us before we escaped out the door. The stop took longer than planned since both Steve and the couple insisted on taking pictures. I'm sure I was bright red in all of them.

The party was in full swing when we arrived. It was being held in the same building in which Haven met, although the room was larger. We found it by following the thumping sound of the dance music. Everett and the plump blonde from the first meeting were sitting at the door selling tickets. Everett was wearing a pink bunny costume. The girl, whose name escaped me, was dressed all in black with huge black wings. She looked like an overgrown crow, but I was pretty sure that wasn't the effect she was going for.

"Hey, Killian. Wow, you guys look great," Everett said. "You remember Tanya, right?"

"Of course." I handed him the money for our tickets, and Tanya stamped our hands.

Everett eyed Kane. "Is this your boyfriend?" he asked finally, his curiosity getting the better of him.

Kane choked, and I bit back a giggle. "No, this is my little brother, Kane."

"Oh. Hi, Kane. I'm Everett. Are you gay?" Everett batted his lashes.

Kane grinned. "Nope, one hundred percent straight, but I'm gay-friendly. Just not that friendly."

"Damn. I knew it would be too much to hope there'd be two guys that hot in the same family who were both gay."

"Actually, I'm the only person in my family who isn't gay, but that's another story. Right now, I just need to know if there are any hot girls here who aren't just into other girls."

Everett hooted a huge booming laugh. "I like this kid. To be honest with you, I don't know who's here. I just arrived and took over for Tony. He wanted to dance so bad I thought he was going to have a heart attack before I got here."

"He was dancing out here," Tanya said. "I've been on the door the whole time and quite a few straight girls and several who are bi have come in."

"Thanks," Kane said, flashing her his most dazzling smile.

Everett chuckled. "It's wasted on her, buddy. She's only into girls."

Tanya elbowed him in the side, and he laughed again.

"Well, I guess we'd better go on in," I said.

"Wait, let me get a picture." Tanya grabbed a camera and hopped up in a flurry of feathers. "Who are you supposed to be?"

"They're Ares and Hermes," someone said from behind me.

I spun around to find Noah giving me an admiring look. My mouth dropped open when I saw what he was wearing — or maybe I should say not wearing. All he had on was a leopard-print loincloth and a white shell necklace with a matching anklet on one foot.

He gave me a sexy smile. "Or is it Mars and Mercury?"

I licked my lips. "Um, you had it right the first time."

"I know my gods." He cocked his head to one side. "So, you like my costume?"

"Tarzan?"

"Yup."

"Picture," Tanya reminded me. I posed with Kane while she snapped a couple of photos. By the time she was done, Noah had paid and been stamped. He followed us into the room, which was surprisingly full.

Haven had hired a DJ, who had the music pumped up. The lights were low, and a disco ball threw tiny spotlights all over the room.

"Hey, guys," Val said, bouncing up in a cheerleader uniform. I had to laugh when I saw the letters FU across her chest. "Nice costumes," she said. Then she noticed Kane. "And who is this?"

"This is—" I started but Kane quickly interrupted.

"I'm Kane, Killian's brother. And you are?"

"I'm Valora, you can call me Val."

"Hello, Val."

"Kane is straight," I said rather unnecessarily.

"Well, I hate to disappoint anyone, but I'm not," Val said with a laugh. "However, I can introduce you to some girls who are."

"That would be great." Kane jumped on her offer like a starving dog on a bone. He turned to me with a pleading look. "Is that okay?"

"Sure, go have fun. Just be careful. And you'd better not drink anything or Adam will kill me."

"There's no alcohol here," Val said. "At least officially. Come on, Kane. I'll introduce you to everyone."

The two of them went off into the crowd, leaving me alone with Noah.

"You really look great," he said after a moment.

"You look pretty good yourself." I was trying hard not to stare at his body. It was a lot more defined than I'd expected, complete with pecs and a lightly sculpted six-pack.

"Where's your boyfriend?"

"He couldn't come tonight. He was too busy with work."

"That sucks. I have to meet this guy. I'm beginning to wonder if he really exists."

I glanced over to see if he was serious or joking, but it was impossible to read his expression. "Oh, he's real," I said. An awkward silence fell between us. I spotted the drink table. "I'm going to go get a drink. You want anything?"

"Um, yeah, thanks." He sounded as if I had interrupted his thoughts. "A Dr. Pepper, if they have it."

I grabbed two cans out of the ice, poured them into clear plastic glasses, and carried them back to Noah.

"Thanks," he said, taking one of them from my hand. A chill went up my spine as his finger brushed mine. "It was nice of you to bring your little brother. I hope he doesn't get hit on too much."

"You think he will?"

"Probably. He's a cutie, and the guys will be all over a fresh piece of meat like that."

"Kane can take care of himself."

"How about you?"

"What about me?"

"Can you take care of yourself?"

"I like to think so." I was getting nervous. "What do you mean?"

"Come on, you have to know you look really hot in that costume. Every guy here is staring at you."

"They might be staring at you, you know," I said in an attempt to shift the attention off of me. "After all, you are half-naked."

"You're not wearing much more. Trust me. It was you they were watching as you walked across the room."

I glanced around and noticed several guys looking over in our direction. It was impossible to tell which of us they were checking out, although a few nodded when I made eye contact. I hoped the dim lighting would hide the blush I felt creeping up my cheeks.

"It was nice of you to notice that I'm half-naked, though," he said with a grin. "I was beginning to think I was invisible."

"Oh, I noticed. I'm just trying to behave."

"Behaving is never any fun." He shifted a little closer. I could feel the heat from his bare skin.

"I need another drink," I said.

"You haven't drunk that one yet."

I looked down at the almost-full cup in my hand. "Oh."

"Come on, let's dance." He took my drink and placed it with his on the floor against the wall, then pulled me onto the floor. Once he'd pointed it out, I noticed more than a few sets of eyes following us. I had to admit we made a pretty hot couple.

The song playing was a sexy remake of Donna Summer's "Love to Love You Baby". At first, I was very uncomfortable dancing with Noah — we were practically nude, and my attraction for him was stronger than ever — but it wasn't too long before the music took over and I loosened up. Before I knew it, I had almost forgotten I was even dancing with Noah; I just moved into my own little zone.

"You're a great dancer," Noah whispered into my ear, startling me out of the slightly hypnotized state into which I'd slipped.

"Uh, thanks," I said, surprised how intertwined I'd become with Noah's body. I tried to pull away without being too obvious, but he drew me close again. I gave up. *It's just one dance*, I told myself.

That one dance turned into two, which turned into three. Before I knew it, an hour had passed and I was still dancing with Noah.

"I need a drink," I said, escaping from his arms at last. "Water, preferably."

"I'll get it," he said. "Wait over there." He pointed to a metal door on the far wall.

As I made my way in that direction, a few guys asked me to dance, and one of them, smelling strongly of alcohol, groped me a little. I pushed him roughly away and finally reached my destination. I was only there a second before Kane was at my side.

"Hey, are you having fun?" I asked him.

"Yeah, actually I am. And from the look of things, so are you."

"What? I'm only dancing." I sounded defensive even to myself.

Kane cocked an eyebrow at me.

"Oh, put your eyebrow back where it belongs," I said. "It's just dancing. What was I supposed to do, stand against the wall all night?"

"No, but you could dance with a few other guys. You've been with the same one for the last hour. He's hot for you."

"He's just a friend."

"Killian, I saw the way he was looking at you. He wants you bad."

I chose to ignore his observations and change the subject. "Have you met anyone?"

He tried to look stern, but couldn't resist grinning. "Actually, yeah. She's really cool. She's my age and everything. Her name is Lila, she's Val's cousin, and she's just as hot as Val."

"And she's straight?"

"Not exactly. She's bi, but she's with me, which is all that matters."

I laughed. "Well, where is she?"

He turned around and scanned the dancers. Across the room, a tall, slender girl with long, dark hair fluttered her fingers at him. He waved her over. She was wearing a short buckskin dress that revealed long, tanned legs. Her shell necklace was the twin to the one Noah was wearing. It seemed to be a popular accessory that evening. I guessed she was supposed to be Pocahontas or some other Indian maiden.

Kane beckoned to her and she approached us.

"Lila, this is my brother, Killian."

"Good looks run in your family," she said flirtatiously.

"The same could be said for your family," I returned the compliment, even though Kane and I weren't technically related.

She looked a bit confused for a second, then her face cleared. "You mean, Val? Yeah, she's gorgeous. If she wasn't my cousin..." She waggled her eyebrows suggestively, and I laughed again.

Kane has his hands full with this one, I thought. Speaking of Kane, he was grinning like the proverbial cat that ate the canary, but I had a feeling he was the one about to get eaten.

Out of the corner of my eye, I noticed Noah approaching with the water I'd asked for. Kane followed my gaze and frowned.

"Be careful," he said under his breath. "Don't forget how much you love Micah." With that he turned back to Lila and offered his arm. "Shall we dance?"

"Why, thank you, sir, yes," she said with a little curtsy, and they melted back onto the dance floor.

"Your little brother met someone?" Noah asked as he handed me my bottle of water.

"Yeah, she's Val's cousin. He seems to like her, but she looks like a handful."

"If she's Val's cousin then she really is a handful, from what I hear."

"What do you mean?"

"Never mind. It might not even be the same cousin. Is it hot in here or is it just you?"

I groaned. "That was awful. Can't you come up with something better?"

He grinned. "Actually, I'm serious. I'm really hot. I could use some fresh air. Come outside with me?"

A little fresh air sounded nice. "Sure."

He pushed open the door, and we slipped out into the cool night. A few other couples had the same idea, several of them busy making out in the shadows.

"The moon is almost full," Noah said.

I glanced up at the bright yellow orb hanging low in the sky. "A full moon for Halloween? The goblins and ghouls will love that."

"It's beautiful, though, don't you think?"

"Yeah, it is."

He moved a little closer to me. I shifted away as nonchalantly as I could.

"You really look great tonight, Killian."

"So you've mentioned a few times," I said teasingly. "You look great too. I suspect we're going to get cold quickly, though."

"It is a little chilly, now that you mention it." He scooted closer again, and once more I moved away. At that point, he nearly had me pinned against the wall. Another foot and I wouldn't have anywhere to retreat. "You could keep me warm," he said when I failed to pick up on his hints.

"Or we could go back inside." I liked Noah, but things were quickly getting out of hand.

"I'm not ready to go back inside just yet." He turned to look at me, the moonlight reflecting off his face making him almost seem to glow. His eyes locked onto mine as his full, red lips parted.

He really has amazing lips, I found myself thinking. *I wonder what it would be like to kiss them...*

He moved a little closer, and my back hit the wall. He lifted his hand to softly stroke my cheek. "I've wanted to do this since the first time I saw you," he whispered, leaning in quickly to press his lips against mine.

Chapter 24

For one shocked, confused moment, I actually returned the kiss, instinct and lust taking over to make my lips respond of their own accord. Then my brain caught up, and I reacted. I twisted my face away, planted my hands firmly against his chest, and shoved with all my strength. Noah stumbled back and, tripping on an uneven paving stone, sprawled on his ass. He stared up at me with an expression of disbelief.

"Noah, I have a boyfriend," I said softly. I reached out a hand to help him up.

He stared at my hand for a few seconds before purposefully ignoring it and standing without my assistance. "You know," he said in a low, tense voice as he brushed off his bottom, "I'll admit I'm not blameless here, but let's get one thing very clear: neither are you. You've been sending out mixed signals to me since the day we met. You were staring at me that day in the bookstore, you flirt with me, you've been dancing with me all night, you came out here alone with me, and I know damn well you kissed me back just now."

"You're right, and I'm sorry. I have been sending out mixed signals. The truth is I am attracted to you. I can't deny that. I like you. If I wasn't already dating someone, I'd probably want to date you. But I am dating someone, someone I care about very much. I'm sorry if I confused you or hurt you, but I can't do anything to risk losing Micah. He means too much to me."

Noah slumped against the wall and slowly slid down to a crouching position on the ground. I winced as I thought about his bare back against the rough brick, but he didn't even seem to notice. Without looking up, he asked, "How much does he mean to you?"

"Everything."

"What does that mean?"

"It means...I want to be with him. I can't stand the thought of losing him, and I really want to try and make our relationship work. It means...it means I love him." I sank down Indian style to the ground a few feet away facing him. "It's taken a lot to get us to the point we're at now. I don't know if it's a forever thing, but it feels like it could be. Do you understand?"

"Not really. I've wanted that for so long, but I've never experienced anything like it. Most guys don't seem to be looking for a relationship. All they want is a quick screw or maybe a fuck buddy. I want more. I'd hoped I could have it with you. Maybe I'll never have it. Maybe I'm not meant to have it."

"Don't say that. You have to believe you'll find someone. You're so young still. How can you give up?"

"I never really knew any other gay people until I started college. When I got here, I became involved with Haven, and suddenly I had friends who understood, who were like me. But we're all single most of the time. You're the only person I know with a serious boyfriend. The longest anyone in Haven has been in a relationship is a couple of months."

"You're in college. How many straight couples do you know who've been together longer than that? And they have more of a selection to choose from. We're what? Ten percent, at best? How many of those are even out of the closet?"

He shrugged. "I guess you're right. Intellectually, I know you are. Emotionally, I'm just tired of being alone."

"Well, I can't be your boyfriend, but I'd like us to be friends, if we can."

He smiled a sad smile. "If I can keep from jumping you, you mean?"

"No. That's not—"

"I was trying to make a joke, Killian. I'd like us to be friends too. I realize I've said that before, but I mean it. Now I know where the boundaries are. I accept that I don't have a chance with you as anything more than friends — at least, as long as Micah is in the picture. Not that I'm wishing you'd break up or anything."

I laughed. "At least not too much?"

He smiled, a real smile this time. "I still have to meet this guy. He really must be something special to have won your heart so completely. I just hope I can keep from being too jealous."

At that moment the door opened and Kane came out, obviously looking for me or, perhaps I should say, checking up on me.

"Over here, Kane," I called softly so as not to disturb the amorous couples.

He turned in our direction, eying the distance between us with undisguised approval. "I hadn't seen you in a while, so I thought I'd look for you, make sure you were staying out of trouble."

I laughed at his bluntness. "You know, I was supposed to be the one keeping an eye on you."

"Just goes to show that Father doesn't always know best," Kane said dryly.

I grinned up at him, then turned my attention back to Noah. "You ready to go back in?"

"Might as well, I'm pretty chilly."

"Maybe if you weren't naked..." Kane said under his breath, just loud enough for me to hear.

I snorted, but turned it into a cough. "You'll warm up quickly enough once you start dancing again."

The three of us walked back into the building, where it seemed even more people had arrived while we were outside.

"It's a really good turnout," I said. "I have to admit I'm a little surprised so many people would come out for a dance put on by a gay/straight alliance."

"It's not just our school," Noah said while Kane scanned the crowd — for Lila, I assumed. "We went in with the other two colleges in this area and several of the other large schools on the Shore. Some high school groups showed up too. Plus, everyone knows that gays throw the best parties, so people come to these things. Probably fewer than half those here even have gay tendencies."

I laughed. I noticed several guys who definitely had gay tendencies, judging by the way they were eying Noah hungrily. "Well, with this many people here, you shouldn't stay with me the whole night. Mr. Right might be out there while we speak."

"And if not Mr. Right, then at least maybe Mr. Right Now," he said morosely.

"Go have fun." I gave him a little push, and he flashed me a crooked smile in return.

"I'm sorry," he said.

"Don't apologize. It's over, forgotten."

"I hope it's not forgotten. I'd like to think I'm not that forgettable."

I winked and shooed him away, then moved off to one side and sat on the edge of a bench. Several guys and a couple of girls approached to ask me to dance, but I wasn't in the mood anymore. What I really wanted to do was find Micah. Kane was still dancing with Lila, though, so it was obvious he wasn't ready to go.

"Why the long face?" Val said, appearing beside me.

"Just missing my man." I shifted over to let her sit down.

"Did he have to work?"

"Yeah. He's a reporter, and he's working on a big story."

"He's not the one who broke the big scandal with the council, is he?"

"Actually, yeah. Micah Gerber."

"I saw him on TV. He's pretty hunky."

I giggled like a schoolgirl. "I agree."

We sat in silence for a minute, then she cleared her throat. "I know this is probably none of my business," she said, "but I couldn't help noticing you seemed pretty, um, close to Noah tonight."

"It's not—"

"Hey, like I said, it's none of my business. It's just that Noah's a good friend, and I'd hate to see him get hurt, so if you're just playing around..."

"Val, really, it's not like that. We talked earlier tonight, and we're fine now. We're just friends. Things got a little confusing for a while, but we got it all worked out."

"Yeah?"

"Yeah."

"Good. I'm glad to hear that. So, you want to go see your boyfriend?"

"Yeah, but Kane's having such a good time with your cousin I don't want to ask him to leave."

"They do seem to be hitting it off, don't they? Your brother seems like a nice kid."

"He is. He's a great kid." I paused then added to be polite, "I only met her for a second, but Lila seems nice too."

"Lila...well, Lila's been through a lot," Val said slowly.

When she didn't elaborate, I asked, "Like what?"

"Oh, I'd rather not go into it right now. Family stuff, you know? It's just not been easy for her. She came to live with us this summer. She doesn't really know many people yet, and she's bi, so I invited her to the dance. I'm glad she met Kane. Look, if you want to leave, why don't you go ahead? I'll keep an eye on the kids, and I can drive Kane home afterwards."

"I don't want you to go to all that trouble," I said.

"No, really. It's no trouble. I'm going to be here anyway. I have to keep an eye on Lila, and it's not like they've been more than a few feet apart all evening. It's no extra work."

"You really don't mind?"

"I really don't mind. Go. See your boyfriend." She smiled and gave me a little push.

"Thanks, Val. I really appreciate it."

She shrugged. "*De nada.*"

I stood up, then bent to give her an impulsive hug that seemed to catch her by surprise. I interrupted Kane and Lila's slow dance long enough to let him know what the new arrangements were. Predictably, he was quite agreeable to the change. I started to say good night to Noah, but he seemed pretty busy with a tall redhead who looked like a slutty Howdy Doody — denim shorts, suspenders over a bare chest, red scarf around his neck, and some drawn-on freckles — so I left him alone and slipped out of the party.

A short time later, I pulled into the parking lot of the *Times*. Micah's car was still there, along with several others. Since I'd never been to the offices at night before, I had no idea how to get in. I was pretty sure the doors would be locked, and I doubted there was a receptionist at the desk at that hour. I could have just called Micah on my cell, but that would ruin the surprise.

I was standing next to my car trying to decide what to do when a side door opened and a black woman in her late thirties stepped out to light up a cigarette. She didn't notice me, and jumped as I approached. Her eyes grew wide as she took in my costume.

"Hi, is Micah working?" I asked in as normal a voice as I could manage, as if I always walked around in a winged helmet and a mini skirt.

"Uh, yeah," she said without taking her eyes off of me. I was beginning to feel like a piece of meat the way she was blatantly ogling my body.

"Could you please tell him Killian is here to see him?"

She blinked and looked at my face for the first time, her eyes widening even more, if that was possible. "You're Killian? As in Micah's boyfriend?"

It was my turn to be surprised. "He talks about me?" I hadn't even known Micah was out at work.

"Not to everyone," she said, taking me in again from head to toe as she sucked on the cigarette and slowly blew out a stream of smoke. "Damn. Micah said you were cute, but he never mentioned you were a god."

"Hermes, actually." I fought a blush and lost, suddenly glad for the dim lighting. She stared at me blankly. "The costume. I'm supposed to be Hermes, the messenger of the gods. I, uh, just came from a costume party." I have a bad tendency to ramble when I'm nervous.

"You mean you don't dress like this all the time?" She smirked. "Too bad." She took a final drag from her cigarette and flicked it away with a practiced gesture. "Come on in: I'll show you to his desk."

"Sorry for interrupting your smoke break," I said, following her down a hallway.

She stopped and turned back, hand on her hip, to give me one more lascivious inspection. "Honey, looking like that, you can interrupt me any day." She winked and started walking once more.

We came into a large, open office space divided into cubicles. I spotted Micah right away at his desk on the far side of the room. He was bent intently over his laptop, his fingers flying over the keys.

"Micah, there's a messenger here to see you," my guide announced.

Micah's head popped up as he glanced absently in our direction, his mind clearly still on his project. When he saw me, however, his eyes grew wide, and a delighted grin spread across his face. He jumped up and quickly crossed the room. For a moment, I thought he was going to kiss me right there, but at the last second he seemed to remember we weren't alone and stopped just inches from me.

"Mmm. Don't let me stop you," the woman said.

Micah laughed. "You'd like that too much, Tina."

Tina grinned. "Didn't say I wouldn't. I'll give you two some privacy. I need to go check in with pagination." She winked at me as she left us alone in the office.

Micah quickly swooped in for the delayed kiss. "What are you doing here?" he asked as he pulled away.

"I just wanted to see you."

"Hold still, I've got to take this in." He walked around me in a slow circle, looking at me from every angle. "Wow! You look... Wow!"

I laughed. "Micah Gerber at a loss for words? You do know Hermes was the patron god of orators and writers, don't you?"

"Wasn't he also the protector of thieves? I think you're stealing all my rational thoughts." He grabbed me and pulled me against him for a tight hug, knocking off my hat. "Do you have any idea how hot you look?"

"Um, no, but if you keep telling me, maybe I'll buy it." My snappy retort came out somewhat muffled since my face was mashed against his shoulder.

"I'm serious," he said, pushing me away and holding me at arms' length. "I really wish I could have been there tonight."

"Me too."

He glanced down at his watch and frowned. "It can't be over already. Where's Kane?"

"No, things were really just getting going when I left. Kane is still there. He met a girl, and I hated to drag him away."

"Then why are you here?"

"I told you. I just wanted to see you."

He pulled me against him again for another, much gentler hug.

I enjoyed just having him hold me for a minute before saying, "I'm sorry about interrupting your work."

"Oh please. I welcome any break, especially if it involves you. So, how about if you tell me why you're really here?"

I pulled back, surprised. "What do you mean?" I sounded defensive, even to myself.

"Easy. I'm not accusing you of anything. It's just that I can tell there's more to the story than you've told me. If you don't want to talk about it, that's cool."

"It's not that I don't... It's just..." I sighed and nervously ran my hand through my hair. "You know that guy Noah from Haven?"

"Yeah, the one who invited you to go?"

"Yeah, him." I took a deep breath. "He, um...he kissed me tonight."

Micah's expression didn't change. "Did you kiss him back?" He sounded completely calm, as if he were asking about the weather.

"I don't know," I said miserably. "Maybe for a second. But then I realized what I was doing and told him to stop and that I was dating you."

"And then what happened?"

"We talked about it for a while. I told him you meant too much to me to risk losing you."

"And that's it?"

"Yeah."

He shrugged and smiled. "Okay."

"Okay?"

"Yeah. Okay. Thanks for telling me."

"You're not mad?"

"Why would I be mad? We've talked about this before. It's inevitable that we're going to be attracted to other people. What's important is how you react to that attraction. You decided we were more important than your interest in Noah. How could I be upset about that? I'm just really glad you trusted our relationship enough to tell me."

I rushed into his arms again. "Damn it! You just keep getting more and more amazing. I don't know how much of that I can take. How did I get so lucky?"

"Hey, I'm the one holding a hot Greek god. Speaking of which, now that we've got your little confession out of the way, how about if you put the hat back on? Just for me?"

I rolled my eyes but obliged.

He let out a wolf-whistle that I was sure they could hear all over the building. "Why do I have to go back to work?" he lamented.

I frowned. "How late do you have to stay?"

"I don't know. I guess I could leave it for the night. Why?" A little smile played around his lips as if he already knew the answer. "Do you have something else in mind?"

I struck a pose — fists on hips, feet splayed — and gave him my most suggestive smile. "How about you and I slip back to Mount Olympus for a little frolicking of mythical proportions?"

He broke into a grin as he adjusted himself. "I, uh, think I'll just run and let them know I'm leaving for the night. My place or yours?"

"Yours, I think. Adam wouldn't be happy if I showed up without Kane. I'll deal with that tomorrow."

"Great. I'll be right back."

While I waited, I thought about how blessed I was to have a guy like Micah. The same thought returned several more times that night and again when I woke up the next morning.

"Well, it's not that Hermes costume, but you still look pretty damn hot," Micah said from behind me. I contemplated my reflection in the full-length mirror in his bedroom. I'd never worn a tuxedo before, and still wasn't sure how I felt about it.

"I think I look like a penguin," I said.

"Babe, penguins don't turn me on. You do. Nuff said."

I laughed as I turned to admire him. "How come you're so much better looking in these things than I am?" The tuxedos were pretty much identical: after all, how different can two all-black suits be? The only difference I could detect was that Micah's lapels were plain satin while mine were embroidered with black silk thread. Somehow, though, he looked a lot better in his. I reminded myself of a little kid playing dress-up. To be honest, I hadn't felt this ridiculous in the Hermes costume.

"Oh stop," he said. "You look fantastic. Put your shoes on."

I did as he said and turned around one last doubtful time to check my reflection. "I'm not wearing one of these at our wedding," I said, following him from the room.

He stopped so suddenly I ran into him. He turned slowly around to face me. "What did you say?"

I realized what I'd said and blushed furiously.

"We're getting married?"

I opened and closed my mouth a few times but nothing came out.

"Are you proposing to me, Killian Kendall?"

"I...I...I..."

He grinned suddenly and let me off the hook. "Breathe, Killian. Inhale, exhale. I'm just kidding."

My knees buckled a bit as air rushed back into my lungs. As much as I loved Micah, I definitely wasn't ready for that level of commitment.

Micah reached out and straightened my tie. "One day, maybe we'll be there. It's not such a bad thought, is it?"

I shook my head, slipped my hand into his, and pulled him close for a kiss.

He broke away a few minutes later. "Before we get too carried away and decide to just skip the ball, I have a few more surprises for you."

"More surprises?"

He walked over to the breakfast bar and handed me a white box about twelve inches square and three inches deep. I was amazed at how light it was.

"Open it," he said.

I sat down on the couch, lifted the lid, and caught my breath. Inside was an exquisite mask covered in hundreds — maybe even thousands — of tiny, brilliantly colored glass beads in an intricate pattern.

"Micah, it's beautiful! Where did you get it?"

"I have my sources." He positively beamed at my reaction. "I was hoping you'd like it. Each bead was hand sewn onto it."

"It must have cost a fortune."

"Let's not talk about that. I can say I couldn't afford two of them, so mine's a little less...elaborate." He produced a white feathered half-mask from somewhere behind the counter and held it up to his face. It was pretty, but nothing like the one on my lap.

I lifted my mask carefully out of the box. "I'm afraid to even wear it. It's a work of art."

"Of course you're going to wear it, and yes, it is a work of art. I didn't spend that much money for something to sit in a box. After the Ball I'll have it framed, and you can hang it on the wall."

I stood up and gave him a tight hug. "Thank you," I whispered.

"You're welcome. Now, we have to go or we'll be late."

Usually, I preferred to make a fashionably late entrance, but that night I wanted to be in place before Jake got there so I could observe him — hopefully without his seeing me first. As an added bonus, we'd also get to see all the "beautiful people" arrive.

We were on our way out before I remembered that Micah had said he had a "few more" surprises. So far, I'd only seen my mask. "Hey, what are the other...?" I stopped mid-question as I caught sight of the parking lot.

Idling at the curb was an obscenely long black limousine, complete with uniformed chauffeur waiting patiently for us by the door.

The drive was incredible. I couldn't believe Micah had gone to all that trouble. "I know you're technically working, but I wanted it to be special," he said as we sipped chilled champagne in the backseat of the limo. "The AIDS Ball is one of the social events of the year, and attending, even while on a case, should be a big deal."

I leaned in for another kiss, not caring if the driver could see us.

The gala was being held in the ballroom of the Cromwell, the city's nicest hotel. I'd never been there before, but I'd heard it was spectacular. It lived up to its reputation...and then some. It was done in the opulent style of the Golden Age of Hollywood: crystal chandeliers, red carpets, dark wood polished to such a luster you could practically see your reflection in it. I fully expected to catch a glimpse of Bette Davis, Marlene Dietrich, and Cary Grant sipping martinis around every corner.

Not many people were there when we arrived, which was just the way I'd planned it. We were able to position ourselves in a fairly inconspicuous spot where we could observe both the people coming in the main doors and the rest of the room at the same time. The crowd began to arrive soon after, a veritable Who's Who of Eastern Shore society. Micah kept up a running commentary for me since I'd never seen most of them before. There were various local officials and politicians, a congressman, the mayor, the police chief, the sheriff, and some of the wealthiest — and therefore influential — residents of the lower Shore. The list went on and on until I eventually lost track of who was who.

I noticed that many of the local officials who wandered by us seemed to recognize Micah. As they did, their faces would take on rather disgusted expressions, and they would make a show of turning their backs to him. Some of the looks were downright hostile.

"Does your status as official pariah have anything to do with that article?" I asked him finally.

"Yeah. Try not to let it bother you. Just ignore them."

"You'd think they'd be grateful to have the corruption exposed," I said.

Micah snorted. "Surely you jest. First off, the ones who were exposed were popular. Some of them had been in local politics for decades. That makes me the bad guy. Secondly, corruption has a way of spreading to everyone it touches, whether they are actually involved or not. It taints everyone with a certain amount of suspicion. Since this is an election year, that once again makes me the bad guy. Are you seeing a trend here? And finally, I wouldn't be at all surprised if some of these people here are every bit as corrupt and are just better at hiding it. Like I said, this thing's a lot bigger than we originally thought, and I'm just beginning to realize how extensive it is."

"Maybe you should put your mask on so they won't recognize you." No one seemed to be wearing their masks, just carrying them around as a somewhat awkward accessory.

He laughed and was about to reply when the mayor approached us. At first I was worried he was going to tear into Micah about the article, but his warm smile immediately dispelled that thought.

He shook Micah's hand and then mine as Micah introduced us. He made polite noises in my direction before turning his attention back to Micah. "Mr. Gerber..."

"Please, Mr. Mayor, call me Micah."

"Only if you'll call me Phil," he said with a wide politician's smile that somehow managed to show all his teeth at once. It made me think of a shark. "Micah, I just wanted to congratulate you on the excellent work you're doing on this corruption case, and assure you of my full support. I know certain people may be giving you a hard time, but you're doing the right thing."

"Thank you, Mayor...er...Phil. That means a lot," Micah said sincerely.

They shook hands again, after which the mayor wandered off to glad-hand his other voting constituents.

I was just returning my attention to the doors when Micah grabbed my elbow and started to drag me off. "Where are we going?" I asked.

"I want you to meet someone." He steered me toward a distinguished gentleman talking to a group of elegant men and women. The man looked vaguely familiar, although I couldn't place where I'd seen him before. The first thing I noticed was that he was very tall, towering over almost everyone else present. He wasn't, however, one of those tall, thin, stick people. He was more like a tree, maybe a sequoia. He was just plain large. His short hair was iron gray, and not a strand of it was out of place. Somehow, even with his considerable bulk — or perhaps because of it — he carried himself with an effortless grace.

"Dr. Mason," Micah said.

The man turned and smiled. "Micah," he said in a surprisingly soft, cultured voice. He excused himself from the group of people with whom he'd been talking and moved a few feet away with us. "So good to see you." He looked to me, and his eyes twinkled. Where had I seen him before? "And who is this?"

When Micah smirked, I wondered what was going on. "This is my boyfriend, Killian Kendall. Killian, this is Dr. Hiram Mason."

His name clicked into place as I reached out to shake his hand. "You're the president of Pemberton University," I said, quite unnecessarily since I'm sure he knew who he was.

"That would be correct. It's a pleasure to meet you, Killian. Are you a student?"

"Yes, sir. In my first year."

"None of this 'sir' business." His eyes sparkled again, and I felt I was missing out on some great joke. "This is quite a party, isn't it? Although, I have to say I've seen better. The music is somewhat dull." He tilted his head towards the live jazz band playing at one end of the room.

"You'd rather they played a little techno?" Micah asked. I was surprised at his familiar tone. I hadn't been aware Micah knew the president of Pemberton.

"Disco was more my era, Micah," he said with a chuckle. "But I'm afraid my dancing days are over."

Micah laughed. "Oh, I believe you could still dance circles around anyone here."

His comment pulled up a memory, and suddenly my brain made the connection with a jolt like an electric shock. I felt my mouth drop open and my eyes grow wide as I stared rudely at Dr. Mason. Micah leaned over casually and placed a finger under my chin to shut my mouth.

Dr. Mason, obviously trying to hide a smile, patted me on the shoulder. "Our little secret, Killian."

I nodded mutely as one of the women from the group of people he'd been with when we approached disengaged herself and took his arm. She looked to be a little younger than he was, with dyed-blonde hair and slightly too much makeup for her age. Her dress was one size too small for her figure, and her jewelry could only be described as ostentatious. They made a decidedly mismatched pair.

"Dear, this is an old friend, Micah Gerber, and his companion, Killian Kendall," Dr. Mason introduced us. "This is my wife, Lenore."

Before Micah or I could say a word — assuming I was yet capable of speech — her face took on a pouty expression. "I'm thirsty. Hi," she said as if we weren't even there.

"Then we'll get a drink. Boys, if you'll excuse me..."

"Of course," Micah said.

"It was nice meeting you, Killian," Dr. Mason said. I nodded again. He gave me a surreptitious wink as they moved off.

"Charming lady, isn't she?" Micah said when they were out of earshot.

"That..."

"Hmm?"

"He..."

"Spit it out, Killian."

"He's married?"

"Yep. Thirty-five blissful years, I think it is."

"But..."

"But what?"

I shook my head silently. I'd have to think on that one for a while.

It was turning out to be a night of surprises, and I hadn't even found Jake yet. I scanned the room as we started back toward our observation spot. I suddenly froze in my tracks. On the far side of the room was the biggest surprise of the evening. I'd spotted Jake, but that wasn't the shocking part. I'd come specifically to find him, after all. It wasn't even all that unexpected that he'd gotten in without our seeing him. He could easily have slipped in while we were talking to the mayor or Dr. Mason. The thing that astonished me was whose arm he was clutching.

Micah realized I had stopped and followed my gaze. "Well, I'll be damned," he said. "I didn't expect to see him here."

"You know him?"

"Not personally, but I know of him. Every reporter in the tri-state area — and possibly farther — knows who he is. That's Fenton Black."

"No it isn't," I blurted out. "That's Neal!"

Chapter 25

Micah blinked at me in astonishment. He looked at the man I knew as Neal and then back at me. "What did you say?" He'd obviously decided he had misheard me.

"That's Neal," I said, tugging at his arm. I wanted to get out of Neal's line of sight before he or Jake spotted me.

Suddenly becoming a stubborn mule, Micah planted his feet firmly against my pull. "Neal as in...?"

"As in your old boss. As in the guy in the newspaper clipping in Jake's room. As in the guy I was sitting across the table from in DC earlier this week. Now move before they see us."

He reluctantly allowed me to drag him behind a large column. "I don't understand. That's Fenton Black. I know it is. I've never met him personally, but I've been in his presence before. I recognize him when I see him."

"Who is Fenton Black?"

"You've never heard of Fenton Black?"

"If I had, would I be asking you who he is?"

"He's probably the richest man on the Eastern Shore, possibly one of the richest in the country. No one knows exactly how much money he has or how he got it in the first place, just that it's an obscene amount. He's originally from Colombia, South America. He's known to be a bit eccentric, and if I said there are a lot of rumors about him, it would be a gross understatement."

"What kind of rumors?"

"Well, while no one's ever been able to prove anything, it's whispered he has pretty much every politician in the area in his pocket, and the ones he hasn't bought off are in his debt in some way. Officially, he's in the import/export business. That's pretty vague, but it's said all his imports aren't entirely legal. Drugs, for instance. A few people have suggested he's the kingpin in some sort of large-scale organized crime society."

"Like a mafia?"

"Something along those lines."

"But nothing can be proved?"

"Not so far. Anyone who ever even hinted to the authorities that they have hard evidence on him seems to wind up dead in some unfortunate accident. To be honest, I don't know if catching him is a big priority on anyone's list. The guy's sharp. He gives enormous amounts of money to worthy causes. I think he single-handedly sustains several local charities. In some people's minds, his money pays expiation for his sins."

I peeked around the edge of the column. "Well, you can add running an escort agency to that list of sins, because he's definitely the man I met on Monday who introduced himself to me as Neal."

"This is just unbelievable," Micah said, peering over my shoulder. "Well, at least I finally know what Neal looks like."

"You're sure you never met him the entire time you worked for him?"

"Yes, Killian. I think I'd remember that. As far as I know, no one who's worked for him ever has."

That gave me just a glimmer of hope that maybe Jake wasn't an escort — unless Neal had changed his policy of never meeting his employees. The question was if Jake wasn't an escort, then how did he know Neal? So many things just didn't make sense.

"You have to give him one thing, he's got balls," Micah said almost admiringly.

I ducked back behind the column and glared at Micah. "What do you mean?"

"I mean meeting you and then showing up here."

"He had no reason to think I'd be here." I considered the situation. "Still, his picture could have wound up in the paper again."

"Actually, he's notoriously freakish about having his picture taken. Usually he won't allow it for any reason, and if someone takes one without his permission, he'll demand the entire roll of film."

"Well, someone got away with it at least once. Jake has the clipping."

"You know, I remember when that was taken. It was earlier this year at a fundraiser for a children's hospital, I think. It was taken and published in some small local paper without his knowledge. The paper mysteriously went under a few weeks later. I remember one of the other reporters joking that it was because they printed Fenton Black's photo, and everyone laughed uncomfortably the way you do when you suspect the joke might actually be true."

"But the chance is still there that I could see him and recognize him somewhere, somehow. That makes it a risk. He doesn't sound like the kind of guy who takes risks. Why would he meet with me?"

"Probably because he didn't take you seriously. He thought it would be better to simply get you off his back. He never expected to run into you again. Or maybe he's getting cocky."

"Oh jeez. Something you said just clicked. You're right, he seemed to underestimate me at first, but I don't think he was making that mistake by the end of our meeting. I could very well be on his hit list now."

Micah paled. "So what do we do next? Somehow, I have a feeling it would be unhealthy for you to let him see you here."

"I can't leave, if that's what you're suggesting."

"Why not?"

"I don't know why Jake is here with him. That's the whole reason I came tonight. Remember? Novak pulled a lot of strings to get me these tickets. He'd kick my ass if I wasted this opportunity."

"Not if you didn't have an ass to kick. Killian, this guy is dangerous. Deadly dangerous. You're really playing with fire here. We should leave."

"Micah," I said calmly. "Think about what you're saying. Didn't we just have this conversation a few days ago — except it was me worrying about your job? Do you remember what you told me?"

He grimaced. "Yeah, I remember."

"And?"

"I said it was my job and I had to do it."

"Right, and then you said you would never ask me to give up an investigation."

"I'm not asking you to give up on your investigation."

"You might as well be. You're asking me to compromise it. What's the difference? If he's already decided I'm a liability, then there isn't much I can do to make it worse. If he's still underestimating me, it could work to my advantage. That's all beside the point, though, because I don't intend to let him see me."

"And just how do you plan to avoid that?"

I pulled the mask out of my jacket pocket and slipped it on. Most people still weren't wearing their masks, but enough were that I wouldn't draw too much attention if I wore mine. "I've only met him once, he doesn't expect to see me here, and I have a mask on."

He sighed. "Just be careful. Guys in his line of work can't afford to be unobservant."

"I'm always careful. I don't think we should stay together, though. Even if you never met him, I imagine he knows what you look like. If he sees me with you, he might put two and two together."

He opened his mouth to argue, then nodded. He wasn't happy about it, but he was willing to admit I was right. "Okay, we'll split up."

"I'll let you know when I'm ready to leave."

He nodded. Turning sharply on his heel he started to walk away, then stopped and came back. "I just remembered another rumor about Mr. Black that might be important."

"What's that?"

"They say he likes young boys."

"He's a pedophile?"

"Maybe not quite that young. But Jake would probably be just about right."

I looked around the column again. Now that he'd put the idea in my head, it did seem as if Jake was his date. Jake was wearing an expensive-looking tux that appeared to have been custom tailored for him. He didn't have a mask, so his expression was easy to read: utter boredom. Fenton/Neal, dressed in an equally expensive white tuxedo, was speaking quite earnestly with someone I knew I'd seen before but couldn't place.

"Who's he talking to?"

"Who? Black? That's Ronald Humphrey, one of the other commissioners. One of the people not implicated in the big scandal."

"Where would I have seen him?"

"On the news, possibly. He's been the most outspoken critic of the article I wrote, calling it irresponsible journalism. Chances are he's protesting so loudly because he has something to hide."

"Do you think it means anything that he's talking to Neal — I mean Fenton Black?"

"It might, although it doesn't have to mean anything. Everyone wants to talk to Fenton Black. He's like a celebrity in these parts. He has a lot of money to throw around."

"I want to get closer."

"How are you going to do that without attracting his attention?"

"Um...maybe you could create some kind of distraction..."

"Like what?"

"I don't know, do something outrageous. Pretend to fall down or choke or something."

"Killian, I have to think about my professional reputation. I might have to interview some of these people, and I don't want them to remember me as the klutz at the ball."

"Yeah, okay. You're right. How about if you just walk up to them and start a conversation. You can just pretend to be a reporter asking that Humphrey guy some questions."

"First off, I wouldn't have to pretend to be a reporter. I am one. Secondly, there are certain rules you follow at a bash like this. You don't just walk up to people and start interrogating them. Not unless you want to be thrown out on your keister, and trust me, Humphrey would do it. He dislikes me that much."

"Okay, we don't want that. Forget the distraction. I'll just move around the outside edge of the room and try to work my way up behind them."

"Sounds like a plan. I'll mingle. Good luck."

I stuck my tongue out at his retreating back, before slipping through the crowd as inconspicuously as possible. Once I reached the wall, I began to slowly sidle toward the spot where Black and Jake had stationed themselves. Black didn't mingle so much as people came to pay homage. While I was attempting to get into position, Humphrey had gone elsewhere, and already two more people had approached, spoken briefly, and then moved reluctantly off. I could have sworn he was dismissing them like royalty. A third person was speaking to him, and another waited to one side.

At last I reached a point directly behind them. Keeping a careful eye on Jake — who wasn't paying any attention to the people approaching Black and was busy looking around the room — I started to ease up nearer to where the two of them stood. Finally, I was close enough to eavesdrop. Or I would have been if not for a small group nearby that seemed to have already imbibed a bit too much and were a little on the loud side. They were party laughing — frantic, with a slightly hysterical edge, the kind that says I'm going to have fun even if it kills me.

They quieted down for a moment as a short, fat guy began to tell a joke — something about an airplane and a pilot who leaves the intercom on by mistake. I was finally able to hear Black and Jake.

"Again, thank you so much for your generous donation," a woman was finishing up whatever conversation she'd been having with Black. She was quite an imposing sight. To say she was top heavy would be misleading. She was heavy everywhere and still managed to look top heavy. Her bosom was easily large enough to serve tea from. Altogether, she rather resembled a cruise ship.

"You're very welcome," Black said. "Now, if you'll excuse me." The behemoth accepted his dismissal and retreated. "Tiresome woman," he said as soon as she was out of earshot.

"They're all tiresome," Jake said. "I hate these things."

"Jacob, we've been through this before."

"Yeah, I know. It's part of the bargain."

I couldn't hear what was said next because the rowdy group burst into raucous laughter as Dumpy delivered the punch line. When I could make out what Black was saying again, he was placing a drink order. It only took me a second to remember that the closest bar was directly behind me. Before I could react, Jake turned around and started in my direction. For just a moment, I panicked. Then, remembering I was wearing a mask, I turned casually — I hoped — to the side, as if I was with the band of merry jokesters.

Stupid! That was way too close. I had to be more careful. Out of the corner of my eye, I watched Jake approach the bar and place Black's drink order. He returned to Black's side without so much as glancing in my direction, and a moment later a waiter brought the drink over. I was just about to break cover when he leaned in and whispered something in Black's ear. Black nodded, and then to my stunned horror, Jake walked right up to me.

"Can I have a word with you in the hall, please?" He spoke in a civil-enough tone, but his eyes were flashing with anger.

"Of course," I said quickly. What else could I do without causing a scene?

Jake spun on his heel and marched stiffly toward an inconspicuous door behind the bar that I had completely failed to notice earlier. I followed him out into a deserted but brightly lit, if sterile, hallway. Jake kindly waited for the door to close before ripping into me.

"What the fuck do you think you're doing?" he said as soon as the door snicked shut.

"Huh?" No one can ever say I don't think quickly on my feet.

"Damn it, Killian. I know you've been snooping around, talking to my old friends. Danielle called me in a panic and wanted to know what was going on, that you'd told her she was in danger because she knew me, or some shit like that." I'd expected that would come back to bite me in the ass. "What kind of fucked-up shit is this, Killian? I thought you were my friend."

"Calm down, Jake," I said, which is, of course, always the worst thing to say to someone who's upset.

"Calm down? You want me to calm down? After I find out you're sneaking around talking to people about me behind my back? And then I catch you following me around here at the AIDS Ball and eavesdropping on my conversation? And you want me to calm down?" His voice had been steadily climbing throughout that whole tirade, but it reached a crescendo on the last question that I thought would bring security running. I decided a judicious fib was in order.

"I'm not following you," I said in what I hoped was a completely believable voice. I pulled off the mask and tried to arrange an expression of righteous indignation on my face, but I was feeling so guilty that I'm not sure I pulled it off. "I'm here with Micah."

"Bullshit." I opened my mouth to argue but he cut me off. "Oh, I know you're here with Micah. I saw you both hiding behind that damn column, peeking out at us every few minutes. And then you come creeping up behind us. And I know you've been following me for a while now. I've seen you behind me in traffic and at the mall once. At the time, I just thought it was a coincidence, and I wondered why you didn't say anything. Now I know it's because you're...you're...investigating me!" He spat out the last two words as if they tasted nasty, which they probably did. He stomped back and forth a few paces while I tried to decide what to say.

"Jake, listen—" I tried, but he wheeled around and silenced me with an angry slash of his hand.

"So far, Fenton doesn't know you're here. He's too busy playing benevolent king to the greedy peasants." So I wasn't the only one who'd made that comparison. "But all I have to do is make a scene and he'll have your ass in jail so fast you won't know what hit you. I'll say you're harassing me or that you tried to force yourself on me here in the hall."

My mouth fell open in shock. "You wouldn't do that to me."

"Really? Well, I didn't think you'd stoop to sneaking around behind my back, either." There was genuine hurt in his eyes, and it killed me to see it.

"It's only because we care about you," I said.

"Oh please. Spare me."

"Really. Everyone is worried about you. You stop talking to your friends, you don't come home at night, and then you suddenly start throwing around a huge amount of cash that you won't explain where it came from."

"Judy's behind this, isn't she? God. I should have known. I knew someone had been through my stuff. That settles it. I'm moving out."

"You're only seventeen."

"I'm almost eighteen."

"You're still underage. What are you doing with this Fenton Black guy? He's bad news, Jake."

"What do you mean? You don't even know him."

"We've met."

That stopped him. "You've met?" There was a hint of jealousy in his voice. "Where? How?"

"Through another case."

He waved it away. "Well, you don't know him. I'm old enough to make my own decisions."

"And what decisions are you making? To throw away your family and friends? For what?"

"For what? I'll tell you for what. For a life I could never have with my so-called family and friends. Fenton gives me anything I need or want. He takes care of me."

"Does he love you? And what's your end of the bargain?"

"What good is love? What has love ever gotten me? My whole family is dead, and my own brother killed them. And tried to kill me. Then, before I even had time for that to sink in, I was yanked away from the only people alive that I still knew and cared about. I go off to live with complete strangers on the other side of the country, and everyone expects me to be just fine.

"And then, once I finally start to make friends and enjoy life again, Auntie Judy decides it will be good for me to move back here. Good for her is more like it. My old friends? Where to start? No one gave a damn about me. No one ever once asked me how I was doing or if I was okay. No one ever cared about me until I started throwing a little money around, and then suddenly everyone is so concerned for me. Give me a fucking break.

"And you. The person I thought was my closest friend. You were too busy following me around and asking people about me to actually talk to me. If you were so damn concerned for my wellbeing, why didn't you just fucking walk up to me and ask what was going on?" He paused to wipe angry tears from his eyes.

I was reeling from his revelations and his accusations. I'd had no idea he felt like that. After everything he'd been through, why hadn't it ever occurred to me that he'd be having a hard time dealing with it all? Because I'd been too caught up in my own life to think about anyone else's. I'd talked — really talked — to Jake only once since he'd been back. He was right. I'd done a piss-poor job of being a friend.

"Jake, I'm—"

"Sorry? Well guess what, Killian? It's too late for that now. Do you know how many nights I've lain awake in bed for hours wishing you'd just let Todd finish me off? At least that way I wouldn't have been feeling all this shit. But you know what? I finally found a way to make the pain go away, at least for a little while. So I don't need you, and I don't need Judy, and I don't need my supposed friends, who never really cared about me, either. The only reason they ever hung out with me was because they wanted something from me. They wanted me but not for me. They didn't even know me. They just thought I was hot."

I didn't even try to argue with him. I couldn't. He was right.

"So save your apologies for someone else. I don't need them. I'm fine. I have everything I need. You can quit following me around, and you can stop asking questions, and you can tell Judy to fuck off, because I don't need her anymore, either."

"Jake, please, just listen to me. Judy loves you. She really does. She's tried to do what she thought was best for you."

"Then why didn't she ever ask me what I wanted? She got stuck with me, and that's all it is. Let's not pretend there's anything more to it than that. I barely knew her before. She's not my mom. She can't expect me to do whatever she wants just because she thinks it's right for me. It's my goddamned life, and I'll do whatever I want."

"It's not like that."

"How would you know? If she really cared so much about me, wouldn't you think she'd at least have asked me if I wanted to move back to Maryland, instead of just springing it on me one day when I come home?"

"Did you ever try to talk to her about it?"

"Why bother? She does what she wants when she wants. She can't even handle this like a normal person. She has to hire a private detective. I don't know why she didn't just get her boyfriend to do her dirty work for her. Why'd she have to drag you into it? Or maybe you volunteered for the job of snooping on me. You always did seem to like watching me when you thought I wasn't looking." I flinched. "I was good enough to stare at but not good enough to love. Even then, you chose Asher over me. I guess you got tired of him too, huh? Maybe Micah had better watch out."

He was baiting me, trying to get me to lash out in some way, and I could feel my temper rising. I wanted to defend myself. I wanted to tell him that wasn't how it happened, and he knew it. I would have been playing into his hands, though. He wanted a real screaming match. It's hard to fight when only one person is angry.

Stay calm, I told myself. If you lose it, you'll just give him more ammunition.

I took a deep breath. "Jake, I'm sorry I hurt you. I don't know what else to say. I'm sorry I've been such a shitty friend since you've been back. You're right. I haven't been there for you. But this isn't the answer. Can't we try to start over?"

All the fight suddenly seemed to drain out of him. He almost seemed to collapse in on himself. "No." His voice was suddenly soft and broken. "No, we can't. It's far too late now. Too much has happened. I'm in too deep. I can't start over."

"Too deep into what? It's never too late. I can help."

He laughed in a hollow-sounding way. This new, withered Jake was much scarier than the angry, overblown one from just a few seconds ago. "No one can help. I'm beyond help. Can't you see? Just give up. Go back to your happy little life. It's too late."

"Jake—"

"It's too late," he screamed. "It's too fucking late!" He slumped back against the wall and slowly slid to the floor. I rushed over and knelt at his side, but he shoved me away with surprising strength. I landed hard on my tailbone with an "oof" of surprise and pain. That was going to hurt in the morning.

"Just go," he said, beginning to sob. "Get out before I call security."

"Jake, please let me help."

"I told you, you can't help. Get out. Now."

"But—"

"Get out! Get out! Get out!"

The door we'd come through earlier — had it really just been a matter of minutes? — swung open and Fenton Black stepped into the hall. It only took a moment for his gaze to fall on the two of us. His eyes swept over Jake with a look of annoyance.

His expression when he took me in was harder to read. There was clearly surprise there — and recognition. The other emotion was less definitive, but I didn't need to know what it was to recognize that it was dangerous.

"Go!" Jake said in a voice so low only I could hear him.

I didn't need to be told again. I was on my feet and racing down the hall before the word was off his lips. I heard Black yelling angrily behind me, but he wasn't pursuing. It only took a few more seconds for his words to sink in. He wouldn't need to chase me. He had the entire security staff at his beck and call. I risked a glance back to see him screaming into a small walkie-talkie.

I started looking frantically for an exit. I spotted one up ahead just as a door to my left burst open and a burly security guard blinked at me in surprise. For a guy his size, his reflexes were quick. He made a lunge for me, but I was quicker. For once, size was on my side. I slipped under his arm and bolted down the hall.

Another guard, shorter and thinner than the first one, came around a corner in front of me. Fortunately, the exit was between him and me. I slammed into the door with my full weight and was gratified to feel it fly open. Some small part of my brain had been worried it might be locked. I didn't take the time to breathe a sigh of relief, however. The chase was still on.

I sprinted across the parking lot and ducked behind a car. I tried to control my breathing as the door exploded open again and the guards raced through it. They had been joined by one more. All three stopped just outside and looked around. I stayed very still, trying not to make any sounds.

"Should we look for him?" the shorter one asked.

"He's gone by now," the tall one said. "Why'd we want him anyway? Was he a gate-crasher?"

"You got me. All I know is that Mr. Black told us to catch him," the burly guy said.

Shorty snorted. "Well, we can guess why Black wanted him, a pretty boy like that."

"Yeah, we shoulda just let him go even if we had caught him," Stretch said with a snicker. "Poor kid. He probably just didn't want to play with Mr. Black."

Burly elbowed him in the side. "Why don't you both shut up?" He lifted his radio to his mouth and reported that they'd lost me. A burst of static mixed with curses was their response. Mr. Black was not happy.

Neither was I. I might have just escaped from an immediate danger, but I knew Black had recognized me. I was still very much at risk. Probably even more so now. And what if I'd put Jake in danger? My heart was racing.

I waited until the guards retreated into the building, tails between their legs, before quickly digging out my cell phone and dialing Micah's number.

"Where are you?" he asked. "I looked all around, and you and Jake were both gone. Now I can't find Black either."

"I'm in the parking lot behind the hotel."

"What are you doing there?"

"It's a long story. Go get the car as quickly as you can and come pick me up."

"Killian, what happened?"

"I'll tell you later. For now, let's just say I'm in big trouble."

Chapter 26

I stayed hidden, crouching behind a bright red Firebird, until the limo came around the corner. It was a tense wait, because I expected the security guards to return with reinforcements at any moment. I tried to remember if they carried guns.

As soon as the limo appeared, I ran to the passenger side, yanked open the door, and leaped in. "Go!" I shouted.

"Go where? What's happening?"

"Just drive. I'll tell you when we get away from here."

I slumped down in the seat as he pulled off. Micah was silent until we were a distance from the hotel, then, "Killian, what the hell is this all about?"

I sighed and chose my words carefully. "I may have messed things up a bit."

"Messed them up how? You said you were in trouble. What did you mean?"

"Okay, well, Jake saw us at the Ball, and he's noticed me following him a few times. Apparently, I'm not as good at this whole detective thing as I thought."

"So he saw you. How'd you get into trouble? Did he confront you?"

"Yeah, you could say that. We had a huge argument in the hall behind the ballroom. He ripped me a new one, told me I'd been a shitty friend, and had no right to care about him now when I didn't before."

"Ouch."

"Yeah...and the worst part is..." I stopped and swallowed a few times. "He's right."

"Killian..."

"No, he is. I wasn't there for him as much as I should have been. I knew he'd had a hard time in California — we talked a couple of times right after he got back — and I still wasn't there for him. I was too caught up in my own problems. I was a shitty friend."

"Okay, so maybe you could have been a better friend. What's done is done. How did that get you in trouble?"

"Well, it seems Jake is dating Fenton Black...or at least he's Black's kept boy."

"Oh. Oh! So that's where all his money is coming from. And the gifts and clothes. How did he get tangled up with Fenton Black?"

"I don't know. But while we were arguing, Black came looking for Jake."

"Shit."

"My thoughts exactly. Jake told me to go so I did. Black called security, and three guards showed up and chased me. Not that they tried very hard to catch me once they were out of Black's sight. I managed to get away from them and hid in the parking lot."

"So Black now knows that you've identified him and you were talking to Jake, but maybe not that you two are acquainted. Let's hope, for both your sakes, that Jake is quick on his feet. You're still a target either way, though. Black will probably assume you're investigating him instead of Jake, which makes you a very real threat."

"As I said, I'm in trouble."

"Trouble? Killian, that doesn't begin to cover it. You're in danger, serious danger."

"Yes, I know. I just need to figure out what to do next. Should I go to the police?"

"Are you listening to me? You're in big-time, serious danger!"

"Yeah, I got that, Micah. I don't really need you to keep telling me."

"Then act like you understand what that means."

"And how am I supposed to act? Scared? Well, I am, but what do you expect me to do? Cry on your shoulder? I don't have time for that right now. I can't let my fear get in the way of the investigation. I'm sure I'm right on the edge of figuring this whole thing out."

"I don't want you to cry on my shoulder, but Fenton Black is a very deadly man. He's killed before, and I seriously doubt he'll hesitate to have you killed."

"Then we have to stop him before he gets a chance."

"How are we supposed to do that? You're not a superhero, Killian."

"I never said I was. Do you think I should go to the police?"

"And tell them what? That Fenton Black is a bad, bad man? I'm sure they'll jump right on it."

"I can tell them he runs a prostitution ring."

"Why should they believe you? Just because you say so?"

"I have contacts in the police department." At least I hoped I did. Sergeant Hank Kaplan had helped out a lot in the Caleb Cohen case.

"Even if you could pull strings and get them to not only believe you but actually do something about it, they'd still have to investigate on their own. You'd be dead long before they found anything concrete. This guy is smart. He knows how to hide his tracks. He's gotten away with worse than prostitution in the past."

"So I'll have to think of something else. Just stop yelling at me. You're not helping."

We fell into a heavy, tension-filled silence. I understood Micah was overreacting because he was terrified for me — I could feel the fear rolling off of him in almost physical waves — but it definitely wasn't helping my own rising panic. I tried to force my mind to go over everything I'd learned that night from Micah and Jake. I knew I was missing something...and it was important.

"Where are we going?" Micah asked after a few minutes.

I thought about it for a minute. "The bed and breakfast. I'll be safest there, I think. I don't want to go home. It would take him less than five minutes to find out where I live. I can't go back with you. Jake knows we're dating, and he might tell Black. It would take him longer to find out that Steve is Adam's partner and that he owns a B&B. Even if he found out, he wouldn't know which room I was in, and he couldn't very well just start breaking into one after another."

"I don't know if I'd put anything past him, but you're probably right: the bed and breakfast would be the safest place for tonight."

"You should stay there too. You might not be safe at your apartment."

"I think I'll sleep at the office — if I sleep at all. I want to get back to work on this story. It occurred to me earlier that Black, quite possibly, could be involved with the whole county-council scandal. It would be right up his alley and, as I said, he already has most of the officials in his pocket. At the very least, he would've known about it, even if he wasn't directly involved."

"Well, one thing is clear. It's more important than ever that I talk to Paul's family and the detective in charge of his murder investigation." I dug my cell phone out of my pocket.

"Who are you calling?" Micah asked.

"Chris." Her brother answered. "Kevin, this is Killian Kendall. Is Chris there?"

"Yeah, hang on."

He set the phone down with a clunk, and I heard him yell, "Chris, it's your boyfriend."

A few seconds later Chris was on the line. "Hello?"

"Chris, it's Killian."

"Hey, what's up?"

"A lot, but I'll have to fill you in later. Were you able to get me an appointment with the detective in charge of Paul's murder investigation?"

"Well, yes and no. I talked to him. His name is Owen Evans. My dad says he's a good cop. Evans is willing to talk to you, but he's really busy with another case right now."

"Can you call him back in the morning and tell him it's urgent that I speak to him immediately? It could be a matter of life and death."

"I doubt he'll be able to resist that. What's going on? What did you find out?"

"I can't go into it now. I'd rather tell you in person."

"Okay, but you're killing me here."

"Poor choice of words. Look, try your best to get me in with him tomorrow afternoon. I'll drive up in the morning."

"You're pretty confident you'll get in to see him."

"Just determined."

"Okay, then I'll see you tomorrow. And I'll be expecting a full briefing."

"I promise."

We hung up, and Micah looked over at me. "I wish I could go with you to DC, but I know you'll be safer there than here."

"It's okay. You have your job to do, and I have mine."

"I just..." He drew a shaky breath. "I don't want to lose you."

I reached over and grasped his hand. "I'll be okay, Micah. I'm not going anywhere."

"I wish I knew that for sure." He bit down on his lip and stared straight ahead.

A few minutes later we pulled into the circular drive in front of Amalie's House. Micah walked me in and waited while I called Adam and Kane at home to tell them I thought it would be better if they came and stayed at the B&B. Of course, Adam demanded to know why. I told him I couldn't go into details, but it was possible they could be in danger at the house because of one of my cases. That sent Steve and Adam into almost identical panic attacks. By the time Adam and Kane arrived and I got everyone calmed down enough to go to bed — Steve, armed with a small pistol I didn't even know he owned — it was almost one a.m.

I tossed and turned fitfully under the covers, my mind refusing to shut off. I was still full of energy even though I was dead tired. I ran the case over and over in my mind, looking at it from every angle I could imagine.

Once that bone had been thoroughly gnawed, I moved on to what Jake had said. I was riddled with guilt for the way I'd neglected him. The worst part was that he wasn't the only friend I'd been neglecting. I couldn't remember the last time I'd talked to Asher's cousin Will.

After what seemed like an eternity — but what the clock said was only about an hour — I finally fell into an uneasy sleep filled with strange, foreboding dreams I couldn't recall when I woke up a short while later. They just left me feeling very unsettled.

I was lying in the dark with my eyes open when I suddenly felt another presence in the room. I sat up with a jolt to find Seth standing at the foot of my bed.

"My God, you scared the hell out of me," I said.

"You're in grave danger." His words were filled with an intensity I'd never heard before in his voice.

"Tell me something I don't know."

"You have to be careful, Killian. I helped you once in the past. I won't be allowed to do it again. You're on your own this time."

"Do you know what's going to happen?"

"No. I've told you before, I'm not omniscient. All I know is that you've set certain events into motion, and by doing so, you've put yourself at risk. There are many ways this could go — and more than one of them ends with you either hurt or killed. The choices you make from here on out will be crucial to the outcome."

"Isn't that true of everything? Every choice we make has an effect, like dropping a stone into a pond. No matter how tiny the pebble or huge the boulder, there is some effect."

"I don't have time to get existential with you. Just be very careful."

"I will. I promise."

"Good. I...I don't want to lose you."

A shiver went down my spine at his words that so eerily echoed Micah's from earlier. "How can you lose me? Won't I be with you no matter what?"

"Oh, Killian. You can't understand, and I can't explain. I gave up so much to be able to come back...and all for you."

"What do you mean?"

"I can't explain it. It's against the rules..." For once, his smart-assed manner was completely absent. Pain filled his voice.

"Fuck the rules. What do you mean?"

"I can't, Killian. I can't."

"I don't understand."

"I love you." With that, he vanished, leaving his final words hanging in the air like the scent of someone's perfume after they pass by.

"Great. Just what I needed," I said to the empty room. "One more thing to worry over."

I flopped down onto the bed and tried to will myself back to sleep. That never works. Finally, I gave my mind full rein and allowed it to wander where it wished. I thought about Seth and our brief friendship while he was still alive. I'd known him longer as a ghost than I had as a living, breathing person. I'd never really thought about what it meant that he could come speak to me whenever he wanted. He'd mentioned the rules before, but always in vague terms, never anything concrete. I knew so little about what made it possible to see and talk to him. I'm sure it must have been made easier by my Gifts.

Thinking about my Gifts made me remember Judy's promise to find me a teacher. While I wasn't necessarily eager to deal with all that, in some ways I was looking forward to finally understanding things a little better. I wondered who my teacher would be.

Eventually, my mind wore itself out, and I began to drift back to sleep. I was just at the threshold of slumber when I once again felt the tingly awareness that told me there was another presence in the room.

"Seth..." I said as I pushed myself into a sitting position. "Aren't you going to let me get any sleep tonight?"

266 ❖ Josh Aterovis

I froze. It wasn't Seth. It was Amalie, standing right where I'd last seen him. My mouth dropped open as the hairs stood up on the back of my neck.

I'd never been able to understand why seeing Seth was so much easier for me than seeing Amalie. Every time I came face to face with her, I felt terror wash over me like ice water. There was just a very different quality about her, a different aura, one of despair and pain.

She looked exactly the same as the first time I'd seen her: all in black, her hair pulled back, an undeniable air of sadness about her. She stood staring at me with a pleading expression on her incorporeal face.

"What?" I couldn't help responding to her expression. "What do you want?"

For a moment, she seemed almost surprised I'd spoken to her. Then she turned and took a few quick steps toward the door. I noticed there was no sound accompanying her footsteps, yet we'd heard her walking around before. Maybe they weren't needed at the moment. She paused at the door, turned back, motioning me to follow her. Without hesitating, I slid from the bed. She turned once again and walked through the door...without opening it. Unable to do the same, what with being solid and all, I had to open it to exit the room. She was standing in the hall, waiting expectantly.

As soon as she saw me, she moved silently down the hall to the stairs. I hurried to keep up. On the first floor, she went directly to the cellar door, where she'd led me the last time I'd followed her.

"We've been down there before," I said, coming to a stop. I wasn't keen on entering the cellar alone. It was dark, dirty, and spooky — not to mention cold — and I was only wearing a pair of boxer-briefs. Until that moment, it hadn't occurred to me that Seth's warning could have applied to anything except my cases involving Fenton Black. Suddenly, I wondered if he might have been referring to Amalie instead. He had warned me about her before, telling me to be careful because she wasn't like him.

When she realized I was no longer trailing her, she stopped and emphatically motioned me to follow her again.

I sighed. I'd made a promise to find out what was happening, and if that meant risking my life entering the cellar in the middle of the night alone in my underwear with a ghost, then so be it. I'd have to take the risk. I started forward and Amalie melted through the door.

I unlatched the safety catch and opened the door to reveal the pitch-black stairwell stretching out before me like the throat of some giant monster, waiting to swallow me whole. I was reluctant to plunge into the inky darkness. At least so far, I'd had enough moonlight and a few nightlights to illuminate the way. Beyond where I stood there was no light apart from a bulb that turned on with a pull chain at the bottom of the stairs. Steve had intended to have an actual switch installed at the top since before the place opened, but it just wasn't high on his list of priorities. Hardly anyone ever went down there anymore.

I gritted my teeth and started down the wooden steps, carefully feeling my way along, and hoping with all my heart that Amalie stayed well ahead of me. I'd never come into contact with her and didn't want to start then. My progress could best be described as a snail's pace. At last, my bare feet felt cold, slightly slimy dirt under them instead of the rough planks of the stairs. I began waving my hands about in the dark, searching for the chain that turned the light on. I must have looked quite a sight, flailing my arms around like a blind man in a cave full of bats. I was glad it was dark so Amalie couldn't see me — although why I thought she couldn't see perfectly well in the dark or, more importantly, why I cared if a dead woman saw me was beyond me.

I found the chain and gave it a tug, gasping as the cellar was flooded with light. It was very dim, barely illuminating the small room, yet it was enough to blind me temporarily. When I'd blinked away the sunspots, Amalie stood waiting for me by the far wall.

The space was actually an old-fashioned root cellar, with a plain dirt floor and brick walls covered with moss. It stank of musty rot. Along one wall was a wooden bench-like structure that had once held vegetables and other perishables in the days before refrigeration. Overhead, pipes and wires ran between the rough-hewn joists that supported the floor of the house above.

As soon as she was certain she had my attention, Amalie turned and walked directly through the wall.

"Now what am I supposed to do?" I asked no one in particular. Somehow, I knew Amalie was gone. The feeling of her presence vanished as soon as she went through the wall. "You know," I said to her anyway, "there's no door in that wall. I can't follow you. I'm not a ghost."

Maybe I should have enlisted Seth, I thought. *He could walk through walls if he wanted.*

I waited a few minutes, but it soon became obvious she wasn't returning. Whatever she'd led me there to see, she'd shown me. I decided it was time to wake Steve up — after I put on some more clothes. I realized I was freezing in just my underwear. I slipped back up the stairs, leaving the light on at the bottom, and went to my room where I pulled on jeans, a t-shirt, and shoes. Then I tapped softly on Steve and Adam's bedroom door. They must have been sleeping as lightly as I had been, because they answered almost immediately.

"What's wrong?" Adam asked in a tight voice.

"I need to talk to Steve," I whispered.

"What's going on?" Steve echoed, appearing over Adam's shoulder.

"Amalie came back."

"Should we call Judy?" Adam asked.

"It's after three o'clock in the morning," Steve said.

"I think we should call her," I said. "If we don't, she'll be very unhappy when she finds out."

Adam picked up the phone and dialed her number.

"What happened?" Steve asked me while Adam talked to Judy.

"I'll explain to everyone at once when Judy gets here," I said.

Adam hung up. "She's on her way. I don't think I even woke her up. Maybe she knew something was going to happen tonight."

That was possible, or maybe Jake just hadn't gone home.

Judy must have broken land-speed records driving to the B&B. She was there before Adam and Steve barely had time to get dressed and meet me downstairs in the lobby.

I quickly filled everyone in on Amalie's appearance and my subsequent adventure in the cellar.

"You went down there alone?" Adam said in horror.

"I didn't see where I had much choice. Besides, she was pretty insistent."

"I'm really proud of you, Killian," Judy said in a soft voice. It was obvious she was only half there with us.

"Proud of him for risking his life?"

"How did he risk his life?" Steve asked. "Amalie's never had a history of hurting anyone."

"There's a first time for everything. Have you all forgotten how he fell down the stairs?"

"Why don't I show you the wall she went through," I said, in an attempt to head off any hysterics. We went down to the cellar, where I pointed to the place Amalie had made her dramatic exit.

"Why would she walk through there?" Steve asked. "What could she be trying to tell us?"

"Maybe it wasn't a wall when she was alive," Judy said.

We all turned to stare at her in surprise.

She walked over and scraped at the moss growing on the bricks.

"What do you mean there was no wall here?" Steve asked.

"Just what I said. If she walked through this wall, she did it for a reason. There's something on the other side she wants us to know about. Maybe the baby was never the reason for leading us down here in the first place — or at least not the only reason."

"But why would that make you think there wasn't a wall there when she was alive?"

"Just a hunch. Aha. See?"

"See what?" Steve and I said in unison.

"The outline of a door," Adam answered for her.

"So you see it too?" Judy asked.

"Yes, it must have been bricked up sometime after the wall was built. Notice how the pattern of the bricks inside the outline is different from that outside."

When he spoke, something shifted inside me. For a moment I felt disoriented, as though the ground had dropped out from underneath me, but before I even had time to stumble, everything stabilized. Only, instead of the cellar as it looked a few seconds before, I was seeing it as it must have appeared in the 1850s.

The wall we had been studying was suddenly partially covered by floor-to-ceiling shelves full of preserved vegetables in glass jars. Without being told, I somehow knew the shelves were a door cleverly disguised to hide an opening behind them. I blinked, and the shelves were gone, replaced with the blank brick wall once more.

"It was part of the underground railroad," I said.

It was my turn to have everyone stare at me in surprise. "Did you see that?" Judy asked with a quiet intensity.

I nodded. "Just now."

"See what? How?" Adam said.

"It's another one of his Gifts," Judy said. "Sometimes he can see things from the past."

"There were shelves there." I waved toward the wall. "Almost like a big bookcase filled with canned foods, but not like what we have today. They were in the kind of glass jars used to can food at home."

A slightly amused smile flickered across Judy's face. "I still do it that way."

"I have no idea how I knew it," I said, "but the shelves were really a door, and behind them was a secret room or something."

"My house?" Steve said almost reverently. "Part of the underground railroad?"

"It still doesn't tell us why it was bricked up," I said. "Or why Amalie wanted us to know it was there."

Steve walked over and ran his hand over the bricks. "We'll have to open it."

"Are you sure that's a good idea?" Adam asked.

"It's a historic landmark," Steve said with a frown.

"Who knows what we'll find in there."

"Amalie knows," Judy pointed out. "And she wants us to know, too."

Adam pursed his lips. "Well, we're not going to find out tonight. I say we all go back to bed and try to get some sleep."

Steve nodded. "Adam's right. We can't do anything about this now, and a little sleep sounds like a good idea."

I had to admit some rest would be awfully nice. I'd gotten precious little that night. Judy nodded her agreement. We all climbed the stairs, Steve coming last after he'd turned off the light.

"I need to speak to Killian for a moment," Judy said, once Steve had latched the door. I suspected I knew what the subject would be. I agreed to see her out after we were done.

As soon as Adam and Steve went upstairs to bed, Judy turned to me with a concerned expression. "I barely know where to start."

"Let me guess. I'm in danger?"

She raised one eyebrow. "Yes."

"You're only the third person to tell me that tonight, and I knew it already on my own."

Her lips pulled down sharply into a frown. "Don't be flippant about this, Killian."

"I'm not, really. Trust me, I have a healthy amount of fear about the situation. I'm just trying not to let it paralyze me."

"It has something to do with your investigations, including the one I asked you to do on Jake." It was a statement, not a question, but I nodded anyway. "Jake is in danger too. I can feel it. It terrifies me because there's nothing I can do about it. He...he didn't come home tonight."

I held a silent debate in my head about whether to tell her what I'd discovered, finally deciding to just give her a capsulated version. "I saw Jake tonight at the Ball. He was with Fenton Black. Do you know who that is?"

"I've heard of him." From her monotone voice and the look on her face, I thought it safe to assume that what she'd heard wasn't good.

"Apparently, Jake's been — for lack of a better word — dating Black." Judy cringed. I took a deep breath. "It gets worse. Jake saw me at the Ball and dragged me into a hallway, where he proceeded to tear me limb from limb for investigating him behind his back. It seems I left a trail wide enough to drive an eighteen-wheeler through. He figured out it was you who hired me. He's furious."

She sighed heavily. "I was afraid it was something like that."

"I'm sorry I messed things up so badly."

She patted my cheek. "You didn't mess anything up. I'm the one who hired you. And who knows, maybe something good will come out of this yet." She didn't sound very convinced.

She gave me a hug and started to leave, then stopped with her back to me. "You know," she said slowly, in a tired, worn voice, "there are times when I wish I wasn't Gifted, when I think it would be better not to know certain things. It would be nice to just live my life as ignorantly as everyone else for a change."

Turning deliberately, she looked me in the eye. "There's death in the air, Killian. I don't know who, but someone's going to die...and soon."

Chapter 27

Between my ghostly visitors and all the accompanying excitement, I didn't fall asleep until the sun was crowning the horizon. It seemed I'd barely closed my eyes before I found myself wide awake again and inexplicably alert. A quick glance at the clock told me I'd received a grand total of two hours of rest. I tried to will myself back to sleep, but it was useless. I finally gave up and climbed wearily out of bed. Although my mind might have been bright-eyed and bushy-tailed, my body was anything but.

I took a shower, hoping it would revive me, but it failed miserably to achieve that goal. I dragged myself downstairs, ate a light breakfast, then took a walk by the creek in the brisk fall air. It was a morning designed to make you feel energized and alive, yet I was still drained and weary.

Considering how tired I was and how much sleep I'd had the night before — or, rather, didn't have — I thought about not attempting the trip to DC. Intellectually, I knew driving there alone wasn't the best idea, but I felt so close to discovering the truth that I couldn't simply sit at home and do nothing. A pressing urgency had come over me that I couldn't ignore.

I forced myself to wait until nine, downed an energy drink, and set out for Washington. My car could just about make the trip on autopilot at that point, which was a good thing with the way I was feeling. I would be glad when the case was over so I wouldn't have to do it so often.

I made good time and arrived at Chris's just before noon. She answered the door at my knock.

"Were you able to get me in to see the detective?" I asked before she even had time to say hello.

"It's nice to see you too," she said sarcastically, stepping aside to allow me in. A small black-and-white dog came barreling down the hallway and skidded to a halt at my feet, looking up at me with enormous, expressive brown eyes. "Have you met Janie?" Chris asked.

"I don't believe so," I said, momentarily distracted.

"She's a Boston Terrier," Chris said with all the pride of a dog owner, almost as if she were the parent of a newborn child.

"She's beautiful." I knelt down to rub her ears. Janie wriggled with pleasure. "Why'd you name her Janie?"

Chris blushed slightly. "It's short for Janeway, as in Captain Janeway."

"I didn't know you were a Trekkie."

"I'm really not, but I had a huge crush on Captain Janeway when I was a kid."

Just then, Janie leaped into my arms, knocking me off balance. I tumbled backwards onto the floor with the dog happily bouncing on my chest and giving me kisses. I laughed and played with her for a few more seconds before returning to business. "You never said if you were able to get me an appointment with the detective."

"Ye-e-e-s." Chris managed to drag the word out to impossible lengths.

I looked up at her suspiciously. "That doesn't sound good."

"I did manage to get you in." She glanced at her watch, a big sporty affair. "Your meeting is later this afternoon."

"I sense a 'but' coming..."

"Well, I may have had to stretch the facts a little to do it. I mean, it is a Saturday."

"Stretch the facts how?"

"I...uh...I may have told him you knew who the murderer was and had proof."

I gasped. "You what?"

"It was the only way I could get him to agree to meet you."

"But, Chris, I don't have any proof. I don't even have a real suspect. What am I supposed to do when I get in there and he expects me to have solid proof? When he finds out I probably know less than he does, he'll be so pissed he won't help me at all."

"Then hold off on telling him that for as long as possible."

"Oh great. Then he'll lock me up for...for...something."

"For what?"

"Obstructing justice. I don't know. He'll make something up."

"Calm down. You're awful high-strung today."

I sighed. "I didn't get much sleep last night."

"Long night?"

"You could say that."

"Well, then, don't keep me in the dark. You promised when you got here you'd give me all the details."

"Okay."

"Can we do it in the living room? I'm getting tired of standing in the foyer."

I made a face at her, and she pulled me to my feet. Janie trotted along beside us as we went into the living room, where I gave Chris the rundown on everything that had happened since we'd last seen each other.

She thought for a minute. "Wow. You weren't kidding. So why do you want to see Detective Owens?"

"I was hoping he could fill in some blanks, tell me if they've gotten anywhere on the case. What's he like?"

"He sounded busy, mostly. The cops here in the city are overworked and underpaid. This isn't his only case, you know."

"I never said it was. It would be nice, however, if he didn't have to be bribed into working on this one."

"I didn't bribe... Well, okay, maybe I did. Look, it's only natural for me to side with the cops on this — my dad is one, after all — but that doesn't mean I don't see your point of view, too."

"I know. I'm just grouchy. You've been a huge help. I couldn't have done this without you."

"Sure you could have. I've just made it easier."

"When do I have to go see Evans?"

"Not till five."

I frowned. "That's a while off. I'll have to kill some time until then."

"Is there anybody else you could interview while you wait?"

"Just Paul's family, and I don't know how to get in touch with them. That's part of the reason I wanted to talk to the detective."

"Oh. Isn't there any other way you could get up with them?"

"If there is, I haven't thought of it yet."

"What about Sabrina? Did you ask her about his family?"

I stared at Chris dumbly. Had I? I wasn't sure. I whipped out my notebook and flipped through to my notes from my conversation with Sabrina. There was no mention of Paul's family. "It, uh, seems like I may have overlooked that."

Chris shrugged. "It's worth a shot."

I found Sabrina's number and called her, but she didn't answer. I figured she was at work or screening her calls — maybe both — so I left a message asking her to call me back.

Chris and I talked for a few more minutes about the case before we were interrupted by the buzzing of my phone. "Killian? It's Sabrina. I got your message. Has there been a break in the case?"

"Not exactly. I just thought of something I forgot to ask you when we talked last. Do you know how to get in touch with Paul's family?"

"His family? No. Like I said— Wait! Actually, I think he did give me his mom's number once in case of an emergency. Let me check to see if I copied it over when I changed address books last year." The line was silent for a couple of minutes, then she returned. "It's your lucky day. I found the number."

Silently thanking the patron saint of private investigators — assuming there is such a thing — I jotted it down. I thanked her and hung up.

"Did she give you anything useful?" Chris asked.

"Yeah, I got lucky. Sabrina had his mom's phone number."

"Where does she live?"

"I'm not sure. Do you recognize the exchange?" I showed her the number.

"It's a 301 area code, so it's Maryland, but that's all I can tell you. We can look it up on the computer, though. We may even be able to find the address using a reverse directory."

I stared at her in admiration. "Good thinking!"

She grinned. "Maybe you'll make a detective out of me yet."

A few minutes later, we had the information we needed. Paul's mother lives in Laurel, Maryland. "That's about half an hour from here by car," Chris said. "The MARC train goes to Laurel and would be much faster as long as she's close to the station."

"Let's just hope she'll agree to see me."

I dialed the number, and the phone rang three times before someone picked up. The woman on the other end had a pleasant, sunny voice.

"Mrs. Flynn?" I said.

"Yes. May I ask who's calling?"

"My name is Killian Kendall, Mrs. Flynn. I'd like to ask you some questions about your son, Paul."

"Paul?" she asked, the brightness suddenly fading from her voice. "Why do you want to talk to me about Paul? You do know he's dead, don't you?"

"Yes, ma'am. That's what I wanted to speak to you about, actually. I'm so sorry to intrude, but I'm a private investigator, and I've been hired to find out who killed him."

There was no response. "Mrs. Flynn?"

"It's very hard to lose a child," she said at last.

"I can't even imagine your pain."

"I lost him twice. I got him back after the first time, but nothing can return him to me now."

"You don't think his killer should be brought to justice?"

"It's not that. It's just...my older son, James, he doesn't want me to even talk about Paul. He wouldn't like it if he knew we were having this conversation. We're a very religious family. My husband and James could never accept...they couldn't understand..."

"That Paul was gay?"

"You know?"

"Yes, ma'am."

"My husband is dead now, but James still won't even speak of Paul."

"Is James there now?"

"No, he's at work. He won't be home until after five."

"Could I come to your house and talk to you before that? He wouldn't have to know."

"I don't like to lie..."

"You wouldn't have to lie."

"I suppose if it will help you catch Paul's killer, it would be okay."

"Thank you. I'll be there in about an hour," I said, allowing myself some wiggle room.

"I'll be looking for you," Mrs. Flynn said.

I hung up and turned to Chris. "Should I drive or take the train?"

She jumped back online and looked up a map of Laurel. "I think you should drive. It's not very close to the station. Actually, maybe I should drive. I know how to get there, and you look really tired."

When she said that, I realized just how tired I was. I was running on adrenaline, and when that was used up, I had a feeling I would crash. Still, the urgency I'd felt earlier was even more intense. I had to keep going. "I am tired, but I'm okay. Besides, what about your brother? Can you leave him here alone?"

"Crap! I forgot about Kevin. He has a two-o'clock appointment with the orthodontist. I guess I can't take you."

"I'll be fine. Besides, Mrs. Flynn might be uncomfortable if two of us appeared on her doorstep."

I set off to make my way through the confusing maze of DC area streets, beltways, and highways. Thankfully, I had my GPS in the car. Even with its assistance, however, it took me half an hour longer than it should have, thanks to several wrong turns on my part.

Mrs. Flynn lived on an attractive, if crowded, street with well-cared-for homes that looked as if they'd been built during the post World War II housing boom. Large, old trees lined the road, keeping everything shaded. The lawns were immaculately groomed with neat, color-filled flowerbeds.

Mrs. Flynn's house was a small cottage, part brick and part white clapboard, with a chimney on each end. Enormous mums exploded with autumn color along the brick path leading to the door and against the foundations. Dark-green ivy climbed up one chimney. It made for an idyllic scene.

I walked up the path, breathing deeply the smell of fall — a pleasingly earthy, spicy scent. When I knocked, the door was quickly answered by a small, plump woman wearing white cotton pants and a blowsy, emerald-green top: Mrs. Flynn, I presumed. I was surprised to see she was older than I'd expected. She had short, permed, brown hair, shot liberally with gray. Her round face was relatively smooth, but deep creases cut into the skin at the corners of her mouth and eyes. She looked like a woman who smiled often, though she wasn't doing so at that moment.

"Yes?" she asked cautiously, as if she suspected I was selling something.

"Mrs. Flynn? I'm Killian Kendall. We spoke on the phone?"

Her eyes widened. "Oh! I didn't expect—"

"Someone so young?" I gave her my most winning smile. "I get that a lot."

She smiled tentatively and opened the screen door. "Please, come in."

"Thank you for seeing me, Mrs. Flynn."

She led me into a cozy living room decorated with an eclectic mix of antiques and modern furniture. Knickknacks, photographs, and souvenirs covered every available surface: the evidence of a lifetime only family members could decipher. The pictures seemed to be of several different children. Over the fireplace, in a place of honor, was a huge portrait of Jesus. Although he wore a benign smile, I had the creepiest feeling his eyes were following me as I moved.

I was relieved when she offered me a seat on an oversize armchair that was turned slightly away from the fireplace, which kept me from having to look Jesus in the eye. Mrs. Flynn took the sofa.

I decided to start off with some easy questions to put her at ease. "How many children do you have, Mrs. Flynn?"

"We had six: three boys and three girls. My husband and I were married for forty years before he passed away."

"I'm sorry for your loss."

"We had a good life together. He's in a better place now."

I paused a moment at the nonchalance in her voice as she talked about the death of her husband. I couldn't imagine being that blasé about Micah's dying, and we hadn't been together anywhere near forty years. "Where did Paul fit in?"

"He was the youngest. I always called him my surprise package. I was forty when I found out I was expecting for the sixth time. My next-youngest was almost ten by then. After five children, I knew what was happening as soon as the morning sickness started. I didn't even need to go to the doctor, but of course I did. They assumed I'd want an abortion. It wasn't safe to have a baby at that age then, not like it is now. Women can have babies at almost any age these days. Then it was dangerous. I wouldn't even hear about an abortion, of course. It was never an option."

"One of your sons lives with you now?"

"Yes, James. He's the youngest one after Paul. He moved in after his father passed away."

"I understand Paul was estranged from the family for a while, but reconciled with you after his father...passed away."

"Yes, when he told us he was...well, you know, his father said we couldn't accept that. Unless he was willing to get help, we couldn't have anything to do with him. Oh, how it broke my heart, but there was nothing I could do. My husband was the man of the house, he was an elder of the church, and it was what he felt was right."

"Did anyone from your family stay in touch with Paul?" I tried to mask my horror at the matter-of-fact tone in which she spoke of how they had turned their backs on their own child.

"Not that I know of. As far as I can remember, my husband's funeral was the first time any of us had seen Paul in years."

"And after the funeral, he began to visit you?"

"Yes. Always while James was at work. It was wonderful to see him again. He'd grown into such a handsome young man." She cocked her head slightly to one side. "He looked a bit like you, actually." She stood up, went to the mantel over the fireplace, and picked up a small, silver-framed photograph, which she handed to me. "That's Paul."

It was strange to realize it was the first time I'd seen a photograph of him. I'd been poking into his life and investigating his death for weeks and had never known what he looked like. The picture had been taken at his high-school graduation. He was wearing a blue robe and holding his mortarboard hat in his hands, posing in front of the ivy-covered chimney. There was indeed a certain air of resemblance between us. He was, as he'd been described, small and blond. Beyond the superficial similarity, however, we really didn't look all that much alike. His face was shaped differently, his eyes smaller, his nose thinner and longer, and his ears larger. His hair was lighter than mine and straight. He wore glasses, while I had contacts. He was cute in a quiet, unassuming way.

"Do you know who might have wanted to harm Paul?"

"No, I have no idea. I really didn't know much about his life. He almost never spoke of personal things. I didn't even know what he did for a living until the newspaper articles came out with it. I don't know why they feel they have to smear that sort of thing all over the pages like a trashy novel."

I felt my hopes take a nosedive. "Then you wouldn't know much about his personal life?" I asked without much optimism.

"No, not really. I did meet his...friend once, though."

My heart skipped a beat. "His boyfriend?"

"Yes. He brought him to meet me a few months ago. I asked Paul if he had anyone special in his life, and he told me yes. At first, it was enough to know he was happy, but a mother wants to meet the person in their child's life, so I finally told him that on his next visit he should bring his...friend."

"Can you tell me about him?"

"He was a very nice young man. He was tall with dark hair. It was obvious, even to me, that he cared very much about Paul. I've thought of him often since Paul was killed, but I didn't know how to get in touch with him."

"Do you remember his name?"

"Of course. His name was Tom, Tom Jackson."

It was all I could do not to crow in exaltation at those words. That was information I hadn't even expected. I tried to keep my excitement under control, however. I had more questions to ask.

"Did Paul ever seem worried or scared during his visits?"

"No, not that I noticed."

"Did he ever mention anyone who might want to harm him?"

Mrs. Flynn shook her head firmly. "Definitely not. I would remember that for sure."

"Do you know anything about a safe-deposit box he kept?"

"No. I'm sorry. I don't seem to be very helpful."

"You've already helped me a lot, Mrs. Flynn." A kernel of an idea began to form in the back of my mind at the mention of the safe-deposit box.

"I have?"

"Yes, and there's a way you could help me even more."

"How is that?"

"The safe-deposit box I just mentioned. I have a feeling it could be very important to know what's in it."

"The police can't find out?"

"Well, they could, but they're taking their time with Paul's case. They're overworked, and it...hasn't been a high priority for them, to be honest." Mrs. Flynn looked distressed by my blunt honesty, so I hurried on. "I intend to turn everything over to them, but I'd like to know what's in it first. I have Paul's key, but I can't get into it. You could, however."

"Me?"

"Yes. They would open it for you as Paul's next of kin."

"Oh, I don't know..."

"Please, Mrs. Flynn. The two of us could go there right now. It wouldn't take long at all. I'd have you back long before James got home." I hoped I was telling the truth there.

The older woman thought for a few minutes. "You really think the contents could be important to finding Paul's killer?"

"I suspect the key to the whole case may be in there."

She nodded hesitantly. "Then okay, I'll do it."

I quickly called the bank and asked to speak to the branch manager. I didn't want to make a trip all the way there, only to find out they wouldn't open it for us. After I explained the situation, the manager checked Paul's record and discovered he had listed his mother as his emergency contact. The manager said as long as she had a photo ID on her, she would be able to open the box. I got directions and hung up, my excitement building with every development. My earlier weariness was all but forgotten.

I loaded Mrs. Flynn into my car, suddenly very grateful I'd driven, and we set off for the bank. We didn't speak much on the way, each of us lost in our own thoughts.

The manager met us personally and, after expressing his condolences to Mrs. Flynn, led us to the vault. Mrs. Flynn inserted Paul's key into the lock and turned it, then the manager did the same with his key. He slid the long, narrow box from the wall and carried it to a nearby table before leaving us to open it in private.

Mrs. Flynn lifted the top with shaking hands while I peered over her shoulder. At first glance, all I saw were individual coins encased in plastic sleeves, which I figured must have been the more valuable pieces in his collection. When Mrs. Flynn slid them to one side, a thick envelope appeared. She pulled it out, and we read the scrawled handwriting together: "Open in the event of my death."

Mrs. Flynn gave a shuddering sigh and handed the envelope to me. "I don't think I want to read it."

I debated whether to read it there or wait until later, but my curiosity got the better of me. I lifted the flap, which wasn't sealed, and removed the contents: several sheets of paper folded together. I flattened them out and picked up the top letter, dated a week before his death.

To whom it may concern:

I don't know who will find this, but I will more than likely be dead if you're reading it, so I suppose it doesn't really matter. I recently found out some information that I've come to believe may have put my life in danger. To explain, I'll have to go back a while, though.

I was hired by the Top to Bottom Escort Agency several years ago. Not long after I started working there, I was assigned a repeat client I later learned was the man I knew as Neal, the owner of the agency. I only found out because he wanted me to be his boyfriend. I told him that, while flattered, I wasn't interested since I was already dating someone. He seemed to take the news in stride and stopped seeing me. Our business relationship remained cordial, although he did offer me a larger cut of my earnings in exchange for my silence. He didn't want the other escorts to know we'd met in person. I agreed.

A few months ago, I was attending a symphony concert with a client when we ran into Neal. My client also knew him and proceeded to introduce the two of us. We pretended not to know each other, but my client introduced Neal as Fenton Black. As soon as I got home, I looked up Fenton Black on the Internet. Most of what I could find online made him sound like a wealthy philanthropist. One site, however, claimed to "out" criminals who had gone unprosecuted. The site alleged the man was a murderer and involved in drug smuggling and all sorts of other illegal activities, yet had somehow remained above the law. It said pictures of him were very rare, but they'd managed to get a photo of him from a newspaper. Sure enough, it was Neal. I saved the picture to my computer and printed it out. I'm glad I did, because the next time I tried to go to the site, it no longer existed.

I didn't know what to do with my knowledge that the infamous Fenton Black owned an escort agency. Should I tell him I'd stumbled across his true identity? Go to the police? The site had said no one had ever managed to bring him down. What if I could help? After talking to some friends, I finally decided I couldn't ignore what I knew, although I felt I owed it to him to at least talk to him about it first. Maybe it was all just some sort of misunderstanding.

I wrote him an email, making it seem like a funny joke that the client had introduced him as Fenton Black. I played ignorant, like I didn't know it was really him. He responded almost immediately, saying he didn't know what I was talking about, that he hadn't been at the symphony at all that night. I knew he was lying. I'd looked him right in the eye and shaken his hand.

I still don't know what I'll do with this information, but if Fenton Black is as dangerous as everyone seems to think he is, then I could be at risk. I'm placing this letter in a safe place along with the other information I collected and printed out.

If anything suspicious happens to me, please take this information to the police.

Signed,

Paul Flynn

My heart was pounding as I flipped through the other pages. The first sheet was a blown-up, grainy copy of the same Fenton Black newspaper photo I'd seen in Jake's room. It had been printed out on computer paper, and at the bottom in Paul's handwriting were the words, "Fenton Black = Neal". The next few sheets were, as Paul had said, printouts of web pages. I didn't take the time to read them.

I looked up at Mrs. Flynn, who was staring down at her hands clasped in her lap. "I think I need to take these to the police," I said softly.

She looked up and me. "Does it...does it explain Paul's murder?"

I hesitated, not wanting to make promises when I wasn't sure. The letter certainly seemed to imply Fenton Black was behind Paul's death, but I couldn't be positive. I shrugged. "It seems to, but I don't know. I have an appointment with the detective in charge of Paul's case later this afternoon. Is it okay if I take this to him?"

She nodded. "Yes, of course."

We quickly finished up at the bank, and I drove Mrs. Flynn back home. After seeing her inside and thanking her profusely for her help, I flew back to Chris's. She and Kevin weren't back yet, so I sat on the doorstep to wait. When they eventually showed up, Kevin looked cranky and Chris frazzled.

"Hey," she said, catching sight of me. "How'd it go?"

"Very well. How was the orthodontist appointment?"

Kevin glowered at me.

"Don't ask," Chris said. She unlocked the door, and we all filed inside. Kevin immediately disappeared to his room. "He hates having his braces tightened, and I hate being his mother."

"You could always move out," I said.

She sighed. "Nah. Dad needs me. Maybe someday when Kevin's a little older. So anyway, what happened with Mrs. Flynn?"

"Well, I think I may have gotten enough information that your promise to Detective Evans won't be a complete fabrication."

"What? That's great! What did you find out?"

I quickly outlined everything I'd learned at Mrs. Flynn's and what I'd discovered in the safe-deposit box.

"So you think Fenton Black killed Paul because Paul discovered who he was?"

"I think it's possible, at least. It's the first solid clue I've come up with. I'm going to turn the letter over to the detective when I see him."

"I think that's a good idea. It sounds like you could be in danger, and your friend Jake, too."

"I knew that already. What I still can't quite figure out is the connection to Jake. How did Jake meet this guy? It sounds like Jake is totally Black's type, though. He went after Paul, flirted with me... He clearly likes them young and blond."

We tossed around more ideas for a while until Chris glanced at her watch. "You'd better leave if you're going to meet Detective Evans on time."

"You're not coming?"

"No, I'd better stay here with Kevin. It'll be dark soon, and I don't like to leave him alone at night."

"Oh. Okay." I was disappointed and a bit nervous at the prospect of seeing Evans alone. "You'll at least give me directions, right?"

She laughed. "No, I thought I'd let you find it for yourself. By the way, you're not meeting him at the station. He said, and I quote, 'If I have to waste time with some amateur sleuth, he can talk while I'm eating dinner.'" She gave me the directions to the place where I would find him.

The restaurant turned out to be a little hole-in-the-wall Irish pub. A neon sign in the window proudly proclaimed that they served — what else? — Killian's Irish Red. I pushed open the door and stepped into a dimly lit room. Round tables sat in the middle of the floor, while old-fashioned, red, leather-upholstered booths lined the walls. The place was doing a brisk business, with almost every table full. It only took one look around to see I was the youngest person there by at least a couple of decades.

A geriatric waitress carrying an empty tray stopped near me. "Can I help ya, sugar?"

"I'm here to meet with Detective Owen Evans," I said.

She pointed out a man sitting alone in a corner booth at the far back of the restaurant. He was intent on his hamburger and wasn't looking up.

As I approached, I took him in. He was on the far side of middle-aged and had to be nearing retirement, but he appeared to be in pretty good shape physically. He was just starting to expand a little in the middle, and meals like that greasy burger and mountain of fries weren't going to help any. He had salt-and-pepper hair that was a little on the shaggy side, as if he'd missed a haircut or two. Although his face was lined, it didn't make him look old, just interesting. He was wearing a slightly rumpled suit with a fresh ketchup stain on the lapel.

"Detective Evans?" I asked when I reached his table.

He looked up at me with startlingly green eyes. "That's me. You Kendall?"

I nodded, and he inclined his head towards the seat across from him. "Have a seat."

I sat down and opened my mouth to tell him I didn't have proof of anything when he asked, "So you're a friend of Chrissie Silver's, huh?"

"Chrissie..." I had to struggle not to laugh. I wondered how long it had been since he'd seen Chris. She definitely wasn't the Chrissie type. "Yes," I finally managed. "Thank you so much for agreeing to meet with me. As Chris...sie may have explained to you: I'm a private investigator and I've been hired to look into Paul Flynn's murder."

He gave me a very unimpressed stare before taking a bite of his hamburger. I waited while he chewed and swallowed. "I hear you think you know who the killer is," he finally said, before taking another bite.

"Well, I have a strong suspicion. I think a man named Fenton Black may be involved. I believe he uses the name Neal to run the escort agency Paul worked for."

Evans swallowed and chased it down with a gulp of his soda. He eyed me for a moment then said, "You think. You believe. You suspect. You got any proof, or you just wasting my time?"

I pulled out Paul's letter. "Paul left this in a safe-deposit box. His mother opened it today and gave it to me to pass on to you." I was stretching the truth a little there, but I hoped he wouldn't find that out.

He reluctantly set his burger on the plate and wiped his hands before picking up the letter. He read it over slowly while I fidgeted impatiently in my seat. When he finished, he drummed his fingers a few times on the table, then went back to his sandwich again.

"So, um, what do you think?" I finally asked.

He stared across the table at me while he chewed slowly and deliberately. "I think it's interesting but circumstantial at best. For all I know, you typed that letter up. Flynn didn't even sign it. It's just his name printed at the bottom."

I blinked. It hadn't even occurred to me that the detective wouldn't believe me. "You can ask Mrs. Flynn. We went to the bank a few hours ago. The letter was in a safe-deposit box."

"How'd you know about the box?"

"I found a letter Paul had written that mentioned it. I just had a hunch there might be something important in it."

"A hunch, huh? And you found the letter this afternoon?" I nodded. "So what proof did you have yesterday when your friend called me and badgered me into agreeing to this little tête-à-tête?"

"Well, she may have overstated my case when she said that..."

"So, essentially, you're wasting my time."

"No! I mean, the letter—"

"The letter proves nothing."

"Why don't you just let me tell you everything I've found out? Then you can decide if there's anything to it or not. You're not losing anything, since you have to finish eating anyway. If you still think I'm wasting your time when you're done, I'll pay for your burger and leave you alone."

He took a huge bite of his sandwich, making about half of what was left disappear in one gulp. "Deal," he said. Or at least that's what I thought he said, his mouth being a little full.

Since he wasn't leaving me much time to talk, I didn't want to waste any of it. I outlined my investigation to date as succinctly as possible, leaving out such trivial details as breaking and entering, and tampering with evidence. Even without those particulars, it added up nicely — or so I thought. What really mattered, however, was what the detective thought.

When I finished my recital, he swallowed the last of his burger and signaled the waitress over. I held my breath as she approached. I was certain he was going to tell her to give me the check and walk out, leaving me with nothing more than I'd arrived with.

He surprised me by ordering a chocolate milkshake and a cup of regular coffee. "You look like a chocolate kind of guy," he said after she'd left. I nodded my agreement, still too surprised to know what to say. "I have to give it to you; you've done a good job on the investigation. I suspect you left out a few things, but that's neither here nor there. Unfortunately, you've also left out the most important part. You don't have any evidence. So you suspect this Fenton Black character? So what? What do you want me to do about it? I can't go after this guy just because you say so."

"The letter—" I tried again, but he broke in.

"The letter doesn't prove anything. So Flynn thought his pimp was also a drug lord? Not a big shock there, if you ask me. It doesn't necessarily mean the guy had anything to do with Flynn's murder."

"I...I know Black is involved..."

"How? Another hunch?"

I frowned. "I know I can get the proof. I just need more information."

"What kind of information?"

"Do you know who Paul was dating?"

"I didn't know he was dating anyone. Everyone we spoke to said he was single."

"You didn't speak to his clients."

"His clients? You make it sound like he was a dry-cleaner. He was a prostitute."

The waitress came to pour his coffee, and I waited until she left to continue. "I know what he was, and I really don't see how that makes any difference. Why does it matter what he did for a living? He was a nice guy, a good person. Everyone that knew him loved and respected him."

"Obviously not everyone."

I was annoyed that I'd walked into that one. I'd made the same point several times myself. "One of his clients told me Paul was dating someone, but he didn't know who. Then, when I spoke to Paul's mother today, she told me she'd met his boyfriend and said his name was Tom Jackson."

"That's great. I'll look into it."

"I'd like to talk to him myself."

"I'm sure you would. I'd like a 1967 Ford Mustang. Too bad we'll both be disappointed."

I decided to change tactics slightly. "What about Paul's cell phone?"

"What about it?"

"Maybe the boyfriend's number was in it."

He shrugged. "It's possible."

"Any chance you could give me the number?"

"Absolutely not."

"Why not? What if it helped solve the case?"

"It could also help me lose my job. I can't just run around handing over key evidence to everybody who asks."

"How is Paul's boyfriend's phone number key evidence?"

"The cell phone was taken from the murder scene, that makes it — and its contents — evidence in a homicide investigation."

"Have you at least contacted everyone in it?"

He gasped melodramatically. "Gee golly! You know what? We didn't even think of that. It's a good thing you came along to remind us how to do our job."

I gritted my teeth in frustration. I jumped as the waitress dropped a large glass of chocolate milkshake in front of me with a loud thunk. I hadn't even seen her coming that time.

"You don't have to get all snotty about it," I said when she'd gone. "I was just asking. It didn't lead anywhere?"

"Nobody knew nothin'."

"Can you at least tell me if Tom Jackson's number was in it?"

He sighed. "You don't give up, do you, kid?"

"Nope."

"Even if his number is in there, we've already talked to him."

"You've already talked to a lot of the people I have, and I found out much more than you did."

He didn't look too pleased at that reminder, but he couldn't argue with its validity.

"I won't tell him where I got the information, I promise."

He pressed his lips together and silently whipped out a small notebook from his inside jacket pocket. The notebook was almost identical to the one I carried. I felt a little thrill to see that a professional police detective used the same notebook I did. Then I realized how childish it was to get excited by something like that. I pulled out my pad while he flipped through his pages. Wanting to be ready, I waited with pen poised over paper.

"There was no Tom Jackson in the cell phone," he said. I felt my heart drop. "But there was a TJ. Damn, you are one lucky son of a bitch. We did talk to him, and his full name was Thomas Jackson. He claimed he was just an acquaintance of Flynn's and didn't really know him." He rattled off a phone number, and the notebook vanished back into his pocket. "Just one more thing: we're going to have to question him again. I could order you to leave him alone until after we've had our crack at him, but to be honest, I have a feeling you'll get more out of him than we would. Chances are he'll be a lot cagier getting questioned for a second time by the police and confronted for being less than truthful the first time around. You haven't spoken to him before, you're in an unofficial capacity, and you're closer to his age — all of which makes you very nonthreatening."

"What are you saying? You'd like me to talk to him first?"

"I didn't say that...officially. However, if you do talk to him before I can get in touch with him — which probably won't be until tomorrow at this point — I would expect you to fill me in on your conversation afterward."

"Of course. I'll tell you everything I find out."

"You'd better." He threw back the last of his coffee and signaled the waitress. "He's picking up the check," he told her as he stood up.

I gaped at him. "The deal was I would pick it up if you thought I didn't have anything to offer."

"And you didn't. All you gave me was some speculation and allegations without anything to back them up..." He belched. "...and a bad case of heartburn. Thanks for lunch." He nodded at the waitress, who was busy keeping a professionally bland smile on her face, and walked out.

Chapter 28

As soon as the detective was gone, the waitress's fake smile fell. "Don't let him get to you, hon," she said softly. "He's a real hard ass. From what I overheard, he's just mad because you've done a better job on this case. For a guy who's been at this game for as long as he has, that's a real kick in the gut. The other guys on the force are always ragging on him about losing his edge. He's trying to hold out a few more years till he can retire."

"You know him?"

"I ought to. He's my ex."

"You were married?"

"Yep. It wasn't one of those messy divorces, you know? It's pretty hard being a cop's wife. I just wasn't cut out for it. We're still friends, though, which is why he eats here all the time."

"Oh. Well, I guess I'll take that check now."

"Don't worry about it," she said. "Owen eats on the house. He was only giving you a hard time."

"Can I at least pay for the shake?"

"That one's on me. Think of it as an apology."

I smiled. "Thanks, but you don't have to do that."

"I know, but I want to."

"Well, thank you."

"Any time, cutie." She moved off to check on her other customers. I finished my milkshake, left a couple dollars on the table, and slipped out before she could notice the money.

Once in my car, I quickly dialed Tom Jackson's phone number and held my breath while it rang. Detective Evans was giving me an awfully narrow window of opportunity. If I couldn't get up with Tom that night, I'd lose my chance.

He answered on the fifth ring.

"Tom Jackson?"

"Speaking."

"This is Killian Kendall. I'm a private investigator looking into the death of Paul Flynn."

There was a long silence. I allowed it to stretch out, determined not to be the one to break it. "I already told the police I didn't know Paul Flynn that well," he said at last.

"I'm not the police, Mr. Jackson. I'm aware you and Paul were lovers. I spoke to his mother, who confirmed she'd met you." Silence. "I'm trying to find Paul's killer. I think I know who it is, but I need your help to catch him." More silence. "Mr. Jackson?"

"What do you want?"

"I'd like to talk to you face-to-face. I promise you I don't mean you any harm."

"Who hired you? Why are you investigating Paul's death?"

"I was hired by a friend of Paul's, his ex-lover."

"What does he have to do with this?"

"He still cares for Paul. He was very upset when he heard about the murder and even more so when he found out the police weren't pursuing the case with much fervor."

Jackson snorted. "They're hardly pursuing it at all."

"That's why he hired me."

"You know who did it?"

"I have a suspicion."

"And you think I can help?"

"I'm hoping so."

"Okay. I'll meet you, but it has to be somewhere public. For all I know, you could be the killer and you're afraid I know something, so you're coming after me, too."

"Is that why you didn't talk to the police? You were afraid?"

"Wouldn't you be in my position?"

"I probably would be. Where can we meet?"

"I live in Annapolis. How about you meet me here in about an hour? I can give you directions to a restaurant I know where we can talk privately."

"I don't really know the area well. I'm in DC now. How long will it take me to get there?"

"An hour should be plenty of time." He gave me directions to the restaurant, and we disconnected.

I realized as I pulled out into traffic that I was doing a lot of driving around for this case. The trip was a simple one, for which I was grateful. While I drove, I tried to keep my mind busy with facts about Annapolis to avoid falling asleep. Aside from being Maryland's capital, I knew it was also the home of the United States Naval Academy — which meant lots of hot guys wandering around in Navy uniforms. The city had even briefly served as the capital of the United States.

It didn't take me long to run out of trivia. Letting my mind wander, I went through several topics quickly — Amalie, Jake, Fenton Black, Tom Jackson — before finally settling on Paul. After seeing the picture of him, he'd become more real to me somehow. It was almost as if, before I'd seen it, he was just an abstract concept, a puzzle to unravel. He'd been Micah's ex. The escort. The murder victim. Now he was an actual person, someone who had loved and been loved, someone gone forever. I had a sudden urge to cry but fought off the tears. It wouldn't do to show up for my meeting with Tom Jackson with red-rimmed eyes and a case of the sniffles — not a very professional image. I knew I was getting overly emotional due to my exhaustion.

I located the restaurant easily enough, but parking proved to be more difficult. I finally found a spot on a side street and had to backtrack to our meeting place. It was on the first floor of a two-story brick building, just one in a block-long stretch that could have easily dated back to the nineteenth century. On either side was a small, upscale boutique. Further down the road I saw antique stores, art galleries, coffee shops, bars, and restaurants. It appeared as if the second floors had been converted into offices, or perhaps apartments, one of which might be Tom's. I thought it wouldn't be a bad place to live at all. The neighborhood had a bustling, cozy feel.

I walked into the restaurant and looked for someone sitting by himself. The place wasn't crowded, and most of the people were there in pairs or groups. Alone at a table off to the side was an attractive, light-skinned black man in his early 30s, well dressed with close-cropped hair and a clean-shaven face. I approached his table cautiously, unsure if he was the one I was supposed to meet.

"Tom Jackson?" I asked in a low voice.

He looked up, and surprise registered on his face. "Are you the detective?"

"Private investigator. My name is Killian Kendall." I held out a hand for him to shake, which he did somewhat hesitantly.

"I expected—" He cut himself off.

"Someone older?" I finished. "I get that a lot, but I can assure you, Mr. Jackson, I know what I'm doing."

"Call me TJ." He had a soft, lyrical voice that would lend itself well to jazz. "I didn't mean to insult you. I realized as I was speaking that it was a stupid thing to say. I don't even know how old you are."

I smiled. "I'm almost as young as I look. I appreciate your talking to me."

"It's the least I could do."

"I don't want to take up a lot of your time, so I'm going to jump right in. You and Paul were dating?"

"Yes."

"For how long?"

"We'd just celebrated our six-month anniversary the week before he...before he was..."

He stopped and swallowed several times, his eyes blinking rapidly.

His grief was painfully obvious. It rolled off of him in almost physical waves, washing over me and bringing those earlier tears back to the surface. I wondered why I could feel his pain so clearly and decided it must have just been because I was so tired. Before meeting him, I'd half wondered if my suspicions about Black could be wrong and the boyfriend might be the killer. Having met him, I no longer thought that. Every ounce of my intuition said he was innocent and had loved Paul very much. I hated to continue to dredge up these painful memories but knew I had to.

"When and how did you meet?"

"It was last year. I teach music at a school in the city."

"DC?"

"Baltimore. The school was holding a benefit concert, and Paul was there with a client. He approached me afterwards to tell me how much he'd enjoyed the performance and to congratulate me on my work with the students. He was so sweet. We hit it off right away. We talked for a while, but when he left, that was it. I didn't know his name or anything.

"A few months later, we ran into each other at a jazz concert on the Mall in DC." I smiled to myself about the jazz reference and my earlier guess. "He wasn't working that time, and I was there with a couple of friends who wouldn't miss me at all, so we hung out for the rest of the night. That led to a few more dates, and things just grew from there."

"You knew he was an escort?"

"Yes, Paul was totally upfront about that right from the start."

"And it didn't bother you?" I admit that question was more for my benefit than relevant to the case.

"Not really. It was his job. He had it before I met him. Who am I to judge anyone else? He was a good person. I knew that instinctively from the very first." He shrugged. "That was all I needed to know."

His words sank into me like rain into parched earth. I sat quiet for so long that TJ finally waved a hand in front of my face. "You still there?"

"Sorry," I said, blushing. "My mind wandered for a second. I didn't get much sleep last night." I shook my head to clear it. "Why all the secrecy? Why lie about knowing him when the police called?"

"Two reasons. First, as I told you earlier, I was scared. Second, the school I work for isn't the most liberal institution. It's private, with a religious affiliation, and the administration doesn't know I'm gay. I'm out to a few people on the faculty, but they're all very protective of me. State law would prevent me from being fired if the powers-that-be found out, but the working conditions would no longer be pleasant. I love my job, Mr. Kendall."

"Call me Killian."

"Okay, Killian. I admit it was cowardly of me, but I was scared and trying to cover my ass."

"What about bringing Paul's killer to justice?"

"That's why I'm talking to you now. I've had some time to calm down and look at things rationally. I realized I was wrong. I'd made up my mind to go back to the police with what I know, but just hadn't worked up the courage yet."

"What were you going to tell them?"

He drew in a shaky breath. "I think I know who may have murdered Paul, or at least who might have been behind it."

I leaned in intently. "Who?"

"His boss."

"Neal? At the escort agency?"

"Yeah."

"Do you have any proof?"

"No, but I know Paul found something out about him a month or two before he was killed."

I slumped back, disappointed. I knew that much already. "Yeah, we found a letter he'd written explaining all that in his safe-deposit box. He knew that Neal was really Fenton Black."

TJ rubbed his face. "God, he became consumed with the whole thing. He didn't know what to do about it, or if he should do anything. We were both stressed out from the idea that he could be in danger. I wanted him to just drop it, pretend it never happened. That wasn't his nature, though. He was the type of person who couldn't stand to see injustice go unchallenged."

"Do you know if Paul ever confronted Neal directly about his real identity?"

TJ shook his head. "I'm not sure. Not that I know of, but it had become such a sore spot for us that, over the last few weeks, we just avoided talking about it altogether."

"What was Paul hoping to accomplish? Was he trying to get Black to do the right thing? Turn himself in? Was he really that naïve?"

"In many ways, yes. It wasn't really so much that he was naïve, he was just very idealistic. He had this view of the way he thought the world should be, and he expected everything to fit that outlook — even after all he'd been through, with his family abandoning him and his lover leaving. He wasn't stupid, though. He'd started gathering proof that Black was involved in the agency — emails, phone records, bank records — all stuff that could be traced back to Black."

"There was nothing like that in the safe-deposit box. Just some stuff he'd printed off the Internet."

"That's because it was never in the safe. He kept it somewhere else, as a precaution."

"Where?"

"I...I don't know."

"TJ, Black is a ruthless criminal," I said, urgency filling my voice. "You have to tell me what you know. Paul isn't the first person he's killed, but we can make sure he's the last."

He stared at me for a moment, then stood up abruptly and walked out. At first, I thought he'd simply abandoned the interview. I was a little miffed about being stiffed with the check for the second time that day — even though he'd only ordered a soda and I hadn't ordered anything — but a few minutes later he returned carrying a file folder.

He sat back down and slid the file across the table. "I haven't even looked inside it, but I had a feeling you'd want to see this, so I brought it. I just didn't know if I'd have the courage to give it to you."

"Why wouldn't you have the courage?"

"It makes me more involved than I already was. If Black decides to take revenge, now he has a reason to come after me."

"How would he even know who you are?"

"You found me. If he's half the master criminal Paul and you have made him out to be, he'll be able to find me, too."

"If this information accomplishes what I hope it will, he'll be behind bars."

"People like him have ways of reaching beyond those bars."

"I think you've been watching too many mob movies." I wanted to insert a little levity into the conversation, because I could tell TJ really was terrified. He was still eying the folder as if he was thinking about snatching it away and running. I quickly flipped it open and began to read.

I immediately felt my eyes bulge as I thumbed through the contents, amazed and excited by what I saw. If Paul hadn't been murdered, he would have made one hell of an investigator. He had somehow amassed a dossier documenting Black's illegal activities, complete with the much-needed proof. As TJ had said, he had managed to conclusively connect Fenton Black to the alias of Neal Parsons, owner and operator of the Top to Bottom Escort Agency. There were several photographs of Black talking with various men, all taken outdoors. On the back of each one, Paul had carefully printed the date, time, and location, along with the identity of the men with Fenton Black. I didn't recognize any of the names, but I had no doubt the police would. How on earth had he gotten them?

It was the last few pages that really blew my mind, however. They were deeds for large plots of land, all on the Eastern Shore. Each piece of property was originally zoned as protected wetlands, but I was pretty sure a little research would show they had recently been rezoned for development, thanks to certain corrupt politicians — the very same ones Micah had recently exposed. Pieces began to fall into place. I was suddenly very afraid for Micah.

"You haven't read this?" I asked TJ, my heart pounding in my chest.

"No. I told you, I wanted as little to do with all this as possible."

"I need you to go with me to the police, immediately."

He began shaking his head. "No way," he said. "You don't need me, you've got the file. I've done my part."

"I may need you to verify that Paul gathered this data, that this is what he was killed for."

"I can't do it. I'm sorry, but I'm just not a brave person."

"Yes, you can. You have to. Look, the police know you were Paul's boyfriend. I'm not operating on my own in this investigation. I'm cooperating with the police. I'm going to tell them exactly where I got this from and everything you told me. If you don't come forward now, they may assume you have something to hide. And you can be guaranteed they'll come looking for you."

He was the picture of absolutely misery. I only hoped my little speech wouldn't spook him, as Evans had warned me might happen. If TJ bolted, Evans would have my neck for sure.

"Fine, I'll go with you," he said at last, after several long seconds of tense silence.

"Good. I have to make a couple of quick phone calls. Wait here." I jumped up and practically ran out of the restaurant. I had to call Micah and warn him.

I stayed near the front door so I'd see TJ if he tried to escape. Micah answered quickly.

"It's Killian," I said somewhat breathlessly.

"Are you okay?"

"It's been a long day, but I just found out some things you need to know. Listen carefully. I don't have a lot of time. I've got a skittish witness waiting inside that I need to get to the police, pronto."

"Killian, what's going on?"

"I found Paul's boyfriend. Paul knew that Neal was Fenton Black, and Black was aware that Paul knew. Before he was killed, Paul gave his boyfriend a file containing evidence that Black was the same person as Neal Parsons and that he was associated with drug lords."

"That's great! Solid evidence? It's the proof you needed to show he had a motive for killing Paul."

"Micah, there's more. Black was also involved in the wetlands scandal there on the Shore. He was the real owner of the properties that were rezoned."

"What? But his name isn't on any of the deeds."

"Dig back and you'll find it. I have copies of the deeds in my hand right now. He probably sold them to some dummy corporation or to fake names, but I'm betting he's at the core of the corruption."

"Whoa. This is an even bigger story than I ever imagined."

"Weren't you listening? That means you're in as much danger as I am."

"I've been in danger of one sort or another since I broke this story. I'm not worried."

I sighed. "You'll at least be careful?"

"Of course I'll be careful, as long as you promise to be careful, too."

"I promise. Now I've got to run. I have to make photocopies of all these papers, then see the detective and give him the originals."

"Okay. Killian, I love you."

"I love you too."

Next I called Detective Evans to tell him I was coming in with an important witness and the evidence he'd been waiting for.

"This had better be good, Kendall. I was supposed to get off in 15 minutes," he said.

"It'll be worth the overtime, sir. I think you'll be very interested in what I have to show you."

I hung up and rushed back into the restaurant. TJ was still waiting at the table, although he'd shredded his napkin into confetti.

"Are you ready?" I asked.

"No, but I'm as ready as I'm going to get."

I smiled encouragingly. "Can I trust you to drive yourself or should we go in my car?"

He stood up and drew his shoulders back, as if bracing for a storm. "I'll follow you, I promise. I need to do this...for Paul."

"Great. Let's go stop a killer."

After all his growling about having to work overtime, Evans kept us cooling in the waiting room forever. Or maybe it only felt that way because I was still wondering if TJ might have second thoughts and bolt.

Finally, Evans seemed to feel he'd made his point. He stuck his head into the cramped sitting area and motioned us back with a jerk of his head. I practically had to drag TJ behind me. Since it was my first time in a police detective's office, I took a quick glance around. I'm not sure what I'd been expecting, but it wasn't this impeccably neat shrine to the Baltimore Ravens football team. Not so much as a pencil was out of place on the faux-wood-grained top of his standard metal desk. The guest chairs were also standard office issue — hard, upholstered, maroon seats with wooden arms and legs.

Nothing else was standard issue. It seemed as if every other item in the room was either purple or black. Glass-fronted display cases housed autographed footballs, helmets, photographs, stuffed animals wearing the Ravens uniform, caps with the team logo, even a mini-reproduction of the stadium. A framed shirt with scrawled autographs of the entire winning Super Bowl team hung on the wall over his desk. It was a little overwhelming, rather like walking into a museum.

"I would have pegged you for a Redskins fan," I said as I sat down.

A look of disgust passed over Evans' stoic face. "Please, just because I live in DC? I'm originally from Baltimore. But we're not here to talk football. You said on the phone you had some important news for me. I'm assuming that news has something to do with your friend here?"

"Yes, excuse me for not introducing you. Detective Owen Evans, this is Thomas Jackson, who goes by TJ." TJ flinched at his introduction. I plowed on doggedly. "He was dating Paul. He knew a lot about what was going on, and the best part is, he has proof."

Evans held up his hand as if to stop traffic. "Let's get right to the good part. What's this proof?"

I handed the file to Evans, who carefully flipped through it, his expression never changing. When he'd finished, he laid the file carefully on the desk and looked up at TJ.

"You had this all along?" he asked in a deadly calm voice. A slight shudder rippled though my body. I'd heard someone else use a voice like that whenever he was furious — my father. I moved quickly to head him off.

"He was scared and grieving. His lover had just been murdered and he was afraid the killer would try to get him too if he came forward with the information."

"So he was going to let his lover's killer just walk away?"

"He wasn't exactly in a condition to be making solid judgment calls."

"If he'd come to us in the first place, the killer would be behind bars and he'd be safe."

"We both know it doesn't always work that way. Good lawyers can get even the guiltiest clients off scot-free, and Black can afford the best in the country. Besides, if Black has mob ties, and there is evidence here that he does, then he could take revenge even from behind bars."

"Hello?" TJ said. "I'm sitting right here, and this isn't exactly making me feel any better."

"Feel any better?" Evans snapped. "Why should you feel any better about anything? This isn't about making you feel good. It's about catching a murderer and bringing him to justice."

"So you do believe Black is the killer now?"

"I think it's probable he was behind it at the very least, although it would be more likely that his type would hire it done."

"The crime didn't show any signs of a professional hit. Everyone said it seemed more like a crime of passion."

"Black is smart," Evans said. "After our conversation earlier I made a few calls about this guy. He's a very wanted man. They've been trying to get him for years, but he's like Teflon: they can never make anything stick. He's suspected of being behind no fewer than six deaths — five murders and one suspicious suicide — and that's just in the US alone. It's long been common knowledge that he's involved in the drug trade, and as you pointed out, he's rumored to have mob ties. The man is scum, but they've never been able to prove anything. He's very careful. I doubt he'd be so foolish as to hire a killer who would make this look like a professional hit. They'd want to confuse things as much as possible."

"Or maybe Black went to talk to Paul, perhaps to try and scare him off, and it got out of hand."

"Why the hell does it matter whether it was a professional or an amateur?" TJ suddenly blurted out.

"You're right, Mr. Jackson." I was shocked to see a compassionate expression on Evans' face. "It doesn't matter. We have more than enough reason to bring Fenton Black in for questioning. In fact, thanks to the contents of this folder, it's likely we'll be able to do a lot more than just question him. I have to be honest with you: there's a good chance you'll have to testify at the trial, but there's no reason your name should ever come up before then. If it would make you feel better, we can place you in protective custody in the meantime. I'm sure the FBI will be involved in this before it's over, so I can even say it's a safe bet you could be offered the witness-protection program."

TJ shook his head. "None of that. Whatever happens will happen. I'd like to stay out of the media as much as possible, to protect my job. If that can't be done, then I guess I'll just have to face the consequences."

"You've certainly changed your tune since you walked in here," Evans said thoughtfully.

"Listening to you made me realize that this is a lot bigger than me. This man has to be stopped."

Evans nodded and turned his attention to me. "Mr. Kendall, on behalf of the police department of Washington DC, I want to thank you for your help in bringing this evidence to our attention. Now, your part is finished. You've done a fine job. We'll take it from here."

"Hey, you'll get no argument from me," I said. "I'm not some maverick who wants to bring this guy down on his own. I only have one request to make."

Evans rolled his eyes and heaved a monumental sigh. "Here we go," he muttered.

"It's not that big a deal. I just want a little time before you move on this, maybe one day at the most."

He narrowed his eyes. "A little time for what?"

"I'm afraid that's private," I said quietly. I suspected Jake was at Fenton Black's house, and I wanted time to get him out of there before the SWAT team burst through the door. I couldn't very well tell Evans that, however. I didn't know how I was going to contact Jake if he was holed up with Black, but I had to try. I owed him that much at least.

Evans stared at me a while longer, then shrugged. "It's going to take between twelve and twenty-four hours to get the warrants in order. You have however long that takes. I can't give you any more time and I can't nail it down any closer. When the team and the warrants are ready, we'll move in. Simple as that."

"It's something," I said.

"It's a damn sight more than you had any reason to expect," Evans said.

I nodded. When you're right, you're right.

The detective stood up, and TJ and I quickly followed his lead. We both shook his hand, and then we were led out.

Standing in front of the police station, I turned and gave TJ a careful once-over. "Are you going to be okay?" I asked.

He cast me a bleak look. "Only time will tell. I don't really expect them to be able to keep it from the news forever. Eventually it will come out, and so will I — out of the closet that is. And then I'll have problems with my job...and quite possibly lose my life."

"You could always take them up on their offer of the witness-protection program."

"And spend the rest of my life pretending to be someone I'm not? I've done that for the first half of my life. I'd rather not have to do it for the remainder. No, I'll just take things as they happen."

"Maybe it won't be all bad. Things seldom are, you know. You could find another great job at a more accepting school."

He shrugged. "There's always hope." He stuck out his hand and we shook. "Thank you, Killian."

"For what?" I asked, confused.

"For forcing me to take action. That file had been eating away at me ever since Paul died, but I seemed paralyzed to make the first move. You took the decision away from me...and it was actually a relief. Come to think of it, I'm half hoping the papers will get wind of this and out me. It would save me the trouble." He flashed me a feeble grin. "I guess that makes me a coward, huh?"

I impulsively reached out and hugged him. He returned it, clinging to me for several seconds as if I were a lifeline. Then he released me all at once and stepped back as if embarrassed.

"For the record, I don't think you're a coward," I said. "Take care of yourself, TJ."

"I will. And you take care of yourself. You're the one with the dangerous job."

"Really, it's not usually this dangerous."

"If you say so." He waved and walked away to his car.

With all the excitement over, I suddenly felt my remaining energy drain out of me as if someone had pulled the plug. My vision blurred, and I swayed a bit. Shaking my head and forcing my feet to walk to my car, I climbed inside and rested my head against the steering wheel. *I'll just close my eyes for a few seconds...*

Chapter 29

A sharp knock jerked me awake. I jumped upright, briefly disoriented, not knowing where I was. Then I focused on Evans' sour mug glaring at me through the car window and realized what had happened. Glancing at my watch as I opened the door, I saw I'd been asleep for almost half an hour.

"I hope you weren't waiting to bug me some more," he said.

"No, actually I was just resting my eyes. I haven't been sleeping very much lately."

"If you're that tired, are you sure you're okay to drive?" He sounded almost concerned.

"Yeah, I'll be fine after my power nap," I said with a cheeky grin.

"Then get going," he said, slapping the roof.

"Yes, sir." I sketched a salute and pulled the door shut.

He tapped on the window again, but this time I just rolled it down. "One more thing." He leaned down to look in at me. "You be careful. You're one of the good guys. It'd be a shame to lose an investigator of your caliber. That was some fine detective work you did. I'd be proud to have you on the force."

"Thank you, Detective Evans," I said, sincerely moved. He walked quickly away across the parking lot. I watched him go, then started for Chris's house. I owed her an explanation.

Chris's father, Louis, insisted I stay for dinner so I could tell the three of them what had happened. Their reactions to my account were all a storyteller could hope for: Louis was impressed, Chris hung on every word, and Kevin was in awe.

"Man, you're like the Hardy Boys or something," he said when I'd brought them up to date. "Both of them rolled into one."

I laughed. "At least you didn't say Nancy Drew. That would have to be Chris. I couldn't have done it without her."

Chris actually blushed a little. "So that's it, then?" she said, in an effort to shift the attention away from herself. "The case is closed? Fenton Black killed Paul Flynn?"

"Well, the case won't be officially closed until they arrest Black, but yeah, all the evidence points to Black as the killer."

"But our part is finished?"

"Your part is finished. I still have one more thing I have to do."

"What would that be?"

I shook my head. "It'd be better if you didn't know."

"It's not something illegal, is it?" Louis asked.

"No, nothing like that."

"Then what did you mean it would be better if I didn't know?" Chris asked.

"If you knew you'd probably try to talk me out of it, which would be pointless because it's something I have to do."

"So it's something stupid or dangerous," she muttered darkly.

"Or both," Louis said jokingly.

"Killian..." Chris started.

"Chris, really. You don't even know what I'm going to do, so why try to talk me out of it?"

"Listen to him, Christina," Louis said before our difference of opinion could degenerate into an argument. "Sometimes there are things on a case that aren't part of the official investigation but still need to be taken care of for closure. God knows we don't often get it, so if we have the chance, we go for it."

I practically glowed under the inclusion implied in his statement. This veteran cop considered me to be an investigator. I was still basking in the warmth his words gave me when Chris sighed. "Well, at least you're spending the night here."

"Actually no, I can't do that. I have to get back tonight."

Chris frowned. "Why? What's the rush?"

"I...I just have to get back as quickly as possible."

"Does this have to do with your closure?"

"Yes."

"Killian, I'm going to have to side with Chris on this one," Louis said. "It's obvious you're tired. If you hadn't been telling us about the investigation, I think you'd have been asleep in your plate by now. It's not safe to drive when you're that tired. Whatever it is you have to do will wait until morning."

I shook my head vehemently. "That's just it. What I have to do can't wait. I have a very narrow window of opportunity, so I have to take advantage of it tonight. It could be too late by tomorrow."

Everyone sat in tense silence for a few seconds while Kevin looked back and forth between the three of us, all equally stubborn and determined.

Louis finally broke the deadlock. "Okay."

"Okay?" Chris demanded.

"Yes, okay. Killian isn't my child. In fact, he isn't a child at all. He can make his own decisions. He knows the risks. If he says he has to drive back tonight, then that's the way it has to be. I can't stop him."

"Thank you," I said quietly. "I'd better head back soon, though, so I'll be that much less tired." He nodded while Chris scowled. "I have a few phone calls to make first. I'll use my cell phone outside."

"You don't have to do that...unless you need the privacy."

"Well, that and I get better reception. I'll say goodbye before I leave." I excused myself from the table and slipped out the door to dial

Judy's house. She answered on the first ring as if she'd been sitting right next to the phone waiting.

"Judy, it's Killian."

"Oh, hi, Killian." Her voice was filled with disappointment, which pretty much confirmed my reason for calling.

"You haven't heard from Jake?"

"Nothing. Not a word since he left for the AIDS Ball."

"That's what I figured. Well, try not to worry. I think I know where he is, and I'm going to try to go get him."

"Killian...be careful." Her voice carried much more weight than I thought those simple words could convey.

"Do I have reason to be?" I asked carefully.

"Yes."

"Does this have anything to do with your...Gift? What you told me about the other night?"

"Yes. The feeling of death has gotten stronger. I...I'm scared."

I took a deep breath as the hairs on the back of my neck stood up. "I'll be careful."

"I just hope it isn't too late."

With those dire words echoing in my mind, I hung up and called Micah.

"Hello?" he answered.

"Hey, it's me."

"What's happening? How are things going?"

"Very well. I'll tell you everything, but you have to be quiet until I'm finished. I need to hurry."

"What's the rush?"

"I'll get to that." I quickly filled him in on everything that had happened since I'd talked to him last. I finished up with, "So Evans told me I only have twelve to twenty-four hours before they move to arrest Black. I have to get Jake out of there before then."

"Considering how badly the Feds want Black, I'd say you're probably closer to the twelve-hour estimate, maybe even less."

"That's what I figured. So what I need from you now is Fenton Black's address."

"Why do you need to know that?"

"I just told you, I have to try and get Jake out before the police show up."

"Killian, you're not going to be able to just waltz in. Black lives on a gated estate, and I'd be willing to bet he has security guards. You could be walking right into their hands."

"It's a risk I have to take. I can't just leave Jake in there."

"Killian, this is nuts. Do you have a death wish?"

"No," I said between clenched teeth, trying not to think about Judy's premonition. "I do not have a death wish. If you're not going to help me, I'll figure it out another way, but I'm doing this with or without your help."

Micah sighed. "Okay, fine. I'll help, but only on one condition."

"What's that?"

"That you wait for me."

"Huh?"

"Black's house is only about twenty minutes on this side of the bridge. He's closer to you than to me, so I want you to wait for me."

"You're not coming," I said firmly.

"It's the only way you'll get the address from me."

I stewed and argued for a few minutes but eventually gave in.

Micah looked up the address and gave it to me. "Hang on. I'm pulling it up on Google Earth so we know what we're up against." I listened to his keystrokes for a few seconds before he continued. "His place is on a secondary road and sits well away from the street. There aren't any other houses nearby. A fence runs around the perimeter of the property, which backs up to a river. The only way in seems to be the front gate. If you pass the house, the road ends in another half mile in a little cul-de-sac where you can turn around. On its left side is a small dirt lane that I think was a logging access road at one time. It looks to be mostly overgrown now, but there should be enough room for you to hide your car. Pull in as far as you can to let me get in behind you. Wait for me there."

"When can you leave?" I asked.

"I'm at work, so I'll need a few minutes to get everything squared away. I can't just walk out. It'll take me an hour and a half at least to drive up, so expect me in about two hours. From DC, it shouldn't take you more than an hour to an hour and a half, depending on traffic and how fast you drive."

"I'll wait for you there."

I let myself back in to find Kevin smirking at me by the door. "Chris went upstairs. She said she wasn't going to speak to you. Want me to show you to her room anyway?"

I stifled a smile. "Yes, please." Occasionally, a bratty younger brother can prove useful.

He led me up the stairs to Chris's door, which was closed. I tapped on it hesitantly. "Chris? It's me. Can we talk?"

She opened it and stood glaring at me. I managed to get a peek around her at the room beyond, which was pretty much what I'd expected: organized and neat as a pin. A few black-and-white photographs in simple black frames hung on plain white walls. A state-of-the-art computer center shared the wall I could see with a floor-to-ceiling bookcase that was filled to overflowing. The only semi-feminine touch in the entire room was an ornate brass bed covered with a pure white coverlet.

"I thought you were in a hurry," she said peevishly.

"I sorta am, but I didn't want to leave until we'd talked."

"What's there to talk about? I thought we were partners, and here you go running off to do something stupid and/or dangerous, and you won't even tell me what it is."

"Is that what this is really about? That you're not included?"

She frowned. "Maybe."

"If I tell you what I'm doing, will you ease up on me?"

"Maybe."

"Look, Chris. I meant what I said at dinner. It's true I could have never done this without you. I've really enjoyed working with you, and I'd like to think we became friends as well as partners in this investigation. It would be great if we could work together again someday if I have a case that leads me up this way."

"Yeah, I'd like that too," she said. "I've learned a lot helping you. You're a good investigator, Killian."

"So are you. Friends?"

"Yeah. Now, what is it you have to do?"

I quickly gave her a rudimentary outline of what I was going to try.

She stared at me dubiously when I finished. "That sounds extremely stupid and dangerous."

I shrugged. "Maybe so, but I have to do it."

"Because this guy Jake used to be a friend of yours?"

"Yeah, and because I let him down. That's part of the reason he's in this position to begin with. I feel I owe it to him to at least try to get him out of there before the cops show up. Maybe it will start to make up for my being such an awful friend."

"I can't imagine you ever being an awful friend, Killian. It takes two people to make a friendship."

"I have to do it for my own peace of mind."

"Okay. Just...be careful."

"I will." "Be careful" was soon going to become my motto.

She stepped forward and surprised me by giving me an awkward hug. "Let me know how it turns out." She stepped back and wiped her palms nervously on her baggy corduroy pants.

"Okay."

"Wish I was going," she added with very real wistfulness in her voice.

I raised an eyebrow. "I think that would make you the stupid one here."

"What do you mean?"

"I don't want to go. It's not that I can't wait to throw myself into harm's way. It's just something I feel I have an obligation to do."

She grinned and shrugged. "I'd like a little more excitement in my life. So sue me."

I laughed and turned to let myself out.

"Hey, Killian?" I stopped in the doorway. "You've definitely made things exciting lately. Now I know for sure I want to become a cop. Thanks."

"Anytime," I said with a wink. "You'll make a good cop."

"You think so?"

"I know so."

I shut her door behind me, said my goodbyes to Louis and Kevin, and started the drive to Black's house. I had to arrive there well before Micah if my plan was going to work.

My exhaustion caught up with me as soon as I turned onto Route 50. It was a constant struggle just to keep my eyes open. My eyelids felt as though they were made of lead. After a few swerves onto the shoulder, I rolled my window down and let the crisp fall air hit me directly in the face. Although it worked for a little while, even that began to wear off before long. I turned on the radio, found an obnoxiously upbeat pop station, and cranked the volume up as loud as I could stand. It was an exercise in futility.

I began to worry that I'd never make it over the Bay Bridge. I had visions of getting halfway across before falling asleep at the wheel and plunging to my death in the waters below. Maybe that was what Judy's whole feeling of death was foretelling. I'd always been somewhat uncomfortable around water — I had an irrational fear of dying by drowning — so the anxiety actually kept me awake all the way over.

Once on the Eastern Shore, however, the weariness returned with a vengeance. I had to struggle to stay alert enough to follow Micah's directions. They really weren't that difficult, yet I still almost missed my turn twice and had to backtrack once when I passed the road Black lived on.

When I reached his house, I slowed down slightly to get a quick glimpse of the place I would have to infiltrate. It was a hulking, gothic fortress built of brick and stone, surrounded by a high metal fence that stood at least twice as high as I was tall. Security lights were placed at regular intervals around the perimeter. There was an actual guard booth at the gate, although I didn't see anyone in it as I drove by. The whole place looked as if it had been built to withstand an invasion, which come to think of it, may have been the case.

I drove a little further until I came to the cul-de-sac Micah mentioned. My headlights swept the wall of trees, illuminating the narrow path — calling it a road would be misleading — right where Micah had described. It was just wide enough for me to ease my Mustang into, but tight enough that I had nightmares of scratching my paint job. I pulled in as far as possible, although I wasn't sure if there would be enough room for Micah's car behind me. Since a tree was too close to the driver's side to permit the door to open very wide, I had to slither sideways out the small opening.

I popped the trunk to rummage through the assorted junk that had built up in there — old CDs, a sandy blanket from an impromptu beach picnic with Micah, jumper cables that Adam insisted I have with me at all times, and a lightweight doohickey that, when plugged into the cigarette lighter, could inflate your tires and flash a warning light at the same time. Somewhere in the mess, I knew I had a plastic bag containing a black shirt, black pants, gloves, and a black skull cap. Novak called it the cat-burglar ensemble. He said every good investigator needed to keep one handy in case of emergencies. He'd never expounded on what constituted an emergency, but I figured what I was about to do qualified as one. I quickly changed into the commando outfit and started back toward the house. I had no intention of waiting for Micah. I had to do this on my own.

Slipping through the shadows, staying just inside the tree line, I didn't take long to reach the corner of the fence protecting the Black estate. I contemplated climbing it, but it was too high, and the spikes at the top looked sharp, so I decided to save that route as a last resort. I'd check out my other options first.

I crossed to the opposite side of the road to stay under the cover of the trees, and made my way to the gate. I watched it for a few minutes, but there was no sign of anyone around. I saw at least one security camera mounted to the side of the guard booth, pointed at the drive. I thought I could get closer to the booth and avoid the camera pretty easily — assuming it was the only one, of course.

I darted across the road again, staying as low to the ground as possible, my heart pounding in my chest. With the rush of adrenaline coursing through my system, my earlier fatigue was all but forgotten. I crouched under the window of the guard booth for a few seconds. Surely, if there was anyone inside, he would hear the thumping of my heart. I slowly eased up until I could see into the booth — empty, although the lights were on, clearly showing the controls to open the gate. I wondered if activating the gate caused any alarm in the house. Even if it didn't, how was I going to get into the booth to push the button in the first place? The only entrance was on the wrong side of the fence, and the glass I was looking through was undoubtedly bulletproof. It was certainly thick enough to withstand anything except maybe an atomic blast.

I edged my way to the corner of the booth and peered around at the gate. To my surprise, I realized that it wasn't closed all the way. It was open by a little less than twelve inches. That wasn't much, but, for once, being small might be to my advantage. Then again, how was I to know it wasn't a trap of some sort? Maybe Black or his security team had spotted me skulking around and decided to lure the mouse into the trap before killing it. Cats like to play with their prey after all.

I was standing there fretting about what to do when I heard the distant sound of an approaching vehicle. I glanced down at my watch. It was just about time for Micah to be arriving. I had to move quickly, or in just a few seconds I would be fully caught in the headlights of the oncoming car. Should I run back to the security of the trees or risk going through the gate? I stood indecisively until the headlights began to light up the trees at the final turn. I made my decision and dove toward the gate. It was a tight fit, and there was a moment of panic when the button of my jeans snagged, but I managed to wiggle through and throw myself behind a nearby shrub just as the car zoomed past. I thought it looked like Micah's, but I wasn't positive. If it was, I knew I had to move fast.

I began to weave my way across the seemingly endless expanse of lawn, moving in a crouched run from tree to bush. It was scant cover at best, but it made me feel better if nothing else. I finally reached the house and sat panting for a moment with my back to the cool brick wall. The breathlessness was due as much to fear as to being winded from the run. I tried to calm myself. I couldn't afford to make any mistakes at that point. My life — and possibly Jake's — depended on my having all my wits about me. Unfortunately, they seemed to have scattered.

When my breathing was finally under control, I started moving again. I had no idea how to get into the house. I was sure there must be some sort of security system, an alarm at least, wired to all the windows. I'd never broken into a house before, so I wasn't even sure I would know how to get a locked window open without simply breaking it. I'd been lucky with the gate — assuming it was luck and not stupidity — but I couldn't count on that again.

The front of the house was definitely out of the question. The main entrance was lit up as if it was broad daylight. I couldn't just march up to the door and knock.

Needing a better idea of what I was up against, I half crawled, half ran toward the back of the house. To my relief, it was not as well lit. Pools of inky darkness collected between security lights spaced too far apart. After a few seconds of study, I decided the attached garage offered me my best opportunity to gain entrance. People often forgot to lock the garage door, or so I reasoned. Although getting there would involve a race through one of the well-lit areas, I didn't have a choice. With my heart in my throat, I made a mad dash, feeling as if I was in a spotlight.

I flattened myself against the wall next to the garage door and wondered if I was under surveillance the whole time. I could picture the security guards inside watching me on closed-circuit televisions, laughing as I zigged and zagged my way across the property, knowing they could snuff me out whenever they tired of the game.

I took a deep breath, grabbed the doorknob, and twisted. It yielded. I stared dumbly at the open door for a moment, too surprised to walk through. This was way too simple. I was becoming uneasy.

I inched through the door into the dark interior, illuminated only by what little light spilled in from outside. The garage held two cars with space for a third. Both vehicles looked to be brand-new, expensive models.

I cautiously made my way to the inside entrance to the house, being extra careful not to bump into anything in the gloom, and paused at the door. The way things were going, I couldn't decide whether I should wish for it be locked or unlocked. If it was locked, I'd have to find another means of entry — unless, of course, someone had conveniently left a key under the mat. If it was unlocked, I wasn't sure if I could pass that off to incredibly good fortune. Was I stupidly following crumbs of cheese right into a trap?

I turned the doorknob and heard the telltale click. It was unlocked.

I took a shaky breath. I'd come too far to chicken out. If it was an ambush, I was already well within their reach. If it wasn't, I was quite simply the luckiest guy on the face the earth. I would have to follow this investigation with a trip to Atlantic City.

I held the door closed for a few seconds while I collected myself. Assuming this had all been some sort of amazing coincidence, which I was desperately trying to do, I was now faced with what could be the trickiest part of the operation. I had to find my way through a strange house that was easily the size of a small hotel, locate Jake, persuade him to listen to me when he'd made it quite clear at our last meeting that he didn't want to talk to me anymore, and get him out of there...all without running into another soul.

Easy as pie, I told myself.

I slipped quickly inside, closing the door behind me. I was immediately struck by the utter stillness of the house. It felt eerily like a tomb. I stood statue-still, listening for a noise — any noise — but there was only total silence. Of course, as big as that place was, they could have been having a party on the third floor complete with live music and I wouldn't have heard.

I took stock of my surroundings. The door from the garage had opened into a rather large laundry room that I was pretty certain Fenton Black never used, at least not personally. Another door stood open, leading to what looked like a hallway. There were no lights on as far as I could see.

I walked slowly down the hall, stopping every few feet to listen. I passed a couple of closed doors, but there was no light showing beneath them and no sound from within. The hallway ended at a large dining room with a door on either side. I figured the one to the right opened into the kitchen, where I finally noticed a dim light burning. The one to the left, I assumed, led to the rest of the house. Deciding it would be wise to check the kitchen before moving on, I crept up to the door and peeked in.

I froze as my heart leapt into my throat again. A large man sat at the table facing away from me, backlit by a low-wattage hood light over the stove. I was afraid to move for fear he'd hear me and turn around. Suddenly, I realized he was unnaturally still. Was he listening for me to move before spinning around and shooting?

We both remained motionless. It began to remind me of the game we used to play as children where you try to go the longest without moving or speaking. I hoped the name of the game wouldn't turn out to be a portent — it had been called graveyard.

I stayed locked in position until I couldn't stand it any longer. The man at the table still hadn't moved. No one was that good at the game. I took a hesitant step into the room. When he still didn't move, I took another. And then another, until I was within a few feet of him. My feet stuck unpleasantly to the floor, as if something had been spilled. I moved around beside him and felt the air rush out of me as I began to tremble. A perfectly round hole the size of a dime punctuated his forehead, dribbling a tiny trickle of blood down his face. If it was a mob-style hit we were looking for, I had just found it.

Chapter 30

I staggered back in horror, barely making it to the trashcan before I lost the contents of my stomach. His wasn't the first dead body I'd seen, but apparently repetition didn't make it any easier. People with their brains blown out were officially not in my league. I pulled out my cell phone to call the police before I realized it might not be wise to have the call traced back to me. Still holding onto the idea that I might somehow find Jake and get him out of there before the police arrived, I located a land-line phone on the counter and dialed 911 with shaking hands, carefully keeping my back to the dead guy the entire time. I explained to the dispatcher that there'd been a murder and gave her the address. When she asked for my name, however, I hung up.

It suddenly occurred to me that I had no way of knowing whether the killer was still in the house. A chill ran up my spine as I spun around. The hallway beyond the door was pitch black. Anyone could be hiding in the shadows, aiming a gun, preparing to shoot me right where I stood. With a stifled gasp, I dropped to the floor, getting an up-close look at the gore splattered across its surface. The room began to spin as my stomach heaved again. I fought down the nausea and waited for the dizziness to pass, then pushed myself into a crouching position.

Although no one had come into the room, it was only a matter of time before the police arrived. I had to move quickly. I wasn't about to leave the kitchen without a weapon of some sort, however. Desperately wishing I had a gun, I briefly wondered if the guy at the table had been a security guard and therefore armed, but I couldn't bring myself to get close enough to find out. Remembering a knife block I'd seen on the counter when I was looking for the phone, I pulled several out, choosing the largest and leaving the rest.

Still feeling terribly vulnerable even with my new weapon, I eased back into the hallway and waited anxiously for my eyes to adjust to the darkness. The house was deadly quiet and, for the first time, I truly began to fear for Jake. I made a hurried search of the first floor as quietly as possible. My ragged breathing sounded unnaturally loud in the silence as I grew more tense with every second. I ended up at the bottom of a pitch-black stairway leading to the second floor, feeling as if I was staring into the maw of some great beast waiting to swallow me whole. For what seemed like an eternity, I was unable to force myself to walk blindly into its gullet. Even though there was a light switch on the wall next to me, I was afraid to turn it on. There was no point alerting anyone that I was in the house if they didn't already know.

Finally, I worked up enough nerve and slowly began to climb one step at a time, testing it for squeaks before placing my entire weight on it. My ascent remained pretty much silent until about halfway up — when, of course, a step creaked. The sound was like a car alarm in the eerie silence. I stood frozen until it became obvious no one was going to come running at me with guns blazing, then took the remaining steps quickly, feeling at a disadvantage as long as I was on them.

At the top, I found myself once again in a hallway, which stretched a short distance both ways. Four doors opened off it, two on one side, and two on the other. One of the doors on my left stood open. I moved cautiously toward it, wanting to get that one out of the way first. As I edged closer, however, I noticed a light at the bottom of the door on the other side of the hall. I stopped and listened, but didn't hear a sound from either side.

The room with the open door was brightly lit by a security light outside. A quick glance showed it to be empty, with no place to hide. It was clearly a home office, sparsely furnished with a simple but elegant antique desk and chair. Built-in shelves lined the walls, holding not just books but also various exotic and ancient-looking artifacts that would have been more at home in a museum. I had a hunch they had not been obtained by entirely legal means.

I turned back to the door with the light showing under it, approaching it slowly until I could press my ear against it — not a sound. I touched the knob hesitantly, gripping the knife handle so tightly my fingers ached. I took a deep breath, twisted the knob and threw the door open in one sudden movement, jumping back into the room across the hall as I did so.

Nothing happened. No one yelled out. All was just as quiet as before.

I peeked around the corner. The door now stood open, spilling warm, yellow light into the hall. A pair of feet were plainly visible splayed on the floor. Trembling, I stepped closer. The feet belonged to another dead body, this one shot as well, at least twice in the chest from what I could see. He'd knocked over a table as he'd fallen.

I appeared to be in a sitting room of some sort. There was a fireplace at one end with two chairs arranged in a conversational grouping. Another door stood partly open on my right. I edged around the body, trying hard not to look too closely. Approaching the door, I kicked it fully open, brandishing my knife — as if it would stop a bullet. Although no lights were on, the glow from the sitting room allowed me to see it was a lavishly furnished bedroom. Someone appeared to be asleep in the bed, but something was definitely wrong — no one could have slept through all that.

I fumbled clumsily for the light switch. As bright light filled the room, I found myself staring at a very naked, very dead Fenton Black sprawled across the bed. Blood splattered the white silk sheets. He, too, had been shot. I looked quickly away.

It suddenly dawned on me that everyone I'd found looked as if they'd been caught by surprise. It was a big house, but they still should have heard the gunshots — unless the killer was using a silencer.

I took a quick look around the spacious room. The king-size bed occupied a large part of the floor space. An enormous armoire sat opposite, its front doors open to reveal a large television set. A leather sofa and armchair sat in front of another fireplace, the back side of the one in the sitting room. The walls were hung with original oil paintings that looked to my untrained eye to be old and valuable. Mirrored sliding-glass doors led to what I assumed was the closet.

I was about to go back to the hall to continue my search for Jake when I noticed a foot sticking out from behind the sofa. I crept toward it, hoping against hope that I wouldn't find Jake dead as well. A muffled sob escaped me when I got close enough to see it was indeed Jake lying naked, facedown on the floor. It took me a few seconds of panic before I realized there was no blood and he was still breathing. He was alive, but unconscious.

I dropped to his side with another sob, this one of relief. Then I discovered he had a gun gripped loosely in his hand, and felt the knife slip from my numb fingers as the implications hit me. *No, no, no, it can't be true,* my brain jabbered as I pushed away. *Why not?* another part of me argued. *After all he's been through, you had to expect him to crack eventually. His brother was a killer. Maybe it runs in the family.*

He looked so peaceful lying there, as if he were simply taking a nap. Yet only a few feet away lay a murdered man, and Jake was holding a gun. Passed out? Except for his shallow breathing, he hadn't moved a muscle since I'd found him. I took a closer look and noticed some bruising on his face and around his mouth.

"Jake?" My voice came out in a hoarse croak. "Jake?" I shook his foot hesitantly.

"Freeze! Don't move!" a loud voice suddenly shouted from behind me.

I screamed and lurched forward, throwing myself behind the couch with Jake.

"This is the police," the voice identified itself. "Come out with your hands where I can clearly see them. If you make any sudden moves, I will shoot."

"Don't shoot," I pleaded shakily. "I'm the one who called 911. My name is Killian Kendall. I work for Shane Novak. We're private investigators."

"Come out from behind the couch," the police officer repeated. "Keep your hands where I can see them."

I edged carefully out to the center of the floor, moving slowly and deliberately, holding my hands in plain sight at all times. The officer was pointing a gun right at me. If you've never had the pleasure of such an experience, let me tell you, it's very unsettling. I wasn't about to make any sudden moves.

He looked surprised when he saw me, then hid it well. "Let's see your license." He appeared to be in his mid-thirties, with dark hair, a carefully trimmed mustache, and heavy eyebrows over dark eyes.

"I don't have one. I'm still in training."

"Is there anyone else in the room with you?"

"Yes, there's another person behind the couch, but he's unconscious." I decided not to mention the gun just yet. The cop looked a little nervous as it was. "He might need medical attention."

"Guys," he called, stepping farther into the room, his gun never once wavering.

In response, two more uniformed officers entered and approached me cautiously, guns drawn. "Turn around," one of them ordered. He grabbed me roughly, pushing me to the floor with a knee in the small of my back, twisting my arms painfully behind me to snap handcuffs around my wrists. It all happened so fast I didn't have time to do more than gasp in pain. After patting me down and removing my wallet, he carefully slid my gloves off my hands and deposited them in a plastic bag, then left me on the floor with an order not to move.

The first cop, the one who seemed to be in charge, was still training his gun on me, while the other two checked Jake. "It's another kid, sarge, and this one has a gun," one of them said tightly. "He's out cold. Pulse is weak. He's not responding."

"Boyd, before you move him, go find Deacon and have him get some shots. We don't want to fuck this one up. It's high profile."

One of the officers stood and started to leave the room. "Take the other kid with you," the sergeant told him.

Boyd hauled me roughly to my feet and led me downstairs into the front room, which evidently had been taken over as a command post. The place was crawling with cops, including several CSI types. Apparently, the crime lab was already getting started. I wondered what they'd make of my bloody footprints all over the kitchen and the vomit in the trashcan. This was not turning out to be my finest hour.

My escort left me sitting awkwardly on a chair — hands still cuffed behind my back — and detailed another young cop to watch over me. The new guy wasn't very talkative, and since I wasn't exactly feeling chatty myself, we sat in uncomfortable silence while his brethren bustled around us.

I had plenty of time to study the officer they'd chosen to keep an eye on me. He couldn't have been more than a few years older than I was, probably fresh out of police academy. He had close-cut, light reddish-brown hair and hazel eyes, with a smattering of freckles across his pug nose that made him look even younger. His thin lips were pressed together nervously, making me guess this was probably his first big case. He looked almost as scared as I felt.

After about half an hour, the sergeant from upstairs came into the room and spotted me. He walked over and frowned down at the clipboard in his hand. "Killian Kendall," he said in a dark voice. "What do you know about these murders?"

"Less than you do, probably."

His frown deepened. "What were you doing here?"

"Am I under arrest?"

"Considering I found you at the site of a multiple homicide, that's a distinct possibility."

"Then maybe I should wait to talk until I have a lawyer."

"Damn kids. You've watched too many movies. You got something to hide?"

"No, sir. I just think it would be best if I wait to be questioned until I have a lawyer."

He sucked in a deep breath between clenched teeth. "Marshall," he said to my young guard. "Have him tested for residue then take him to the station and lock him up. And be sure to let him call his damned lawyer."

Marshall nodded sharply. "Yes, sir!" So he could speak. He helped me up and, after a tech swabbed my hands, led me out the front door toward the cluster of police cruisers parked on the lawn. I noticed he was being a lot gentler than the guy who'd cuffed me.

The whole thing was kind of surreal. I'd never been arrested before. I was pretty shaken, but I would have been a lot more scared if I thought there was any chance of being charged with something. I knew I hadn't done anything they could charge me with...except maybe breaking and entering...and possibly interfering with a crime scene. I was suddenly worried.

"I'm going to switch your cuffs to the front," Marshall said, stopping next to one of the cars.

"Thanks." I was unsure of how else to respond. It was a relief, though. I was very uncomfortable with my arms locked behind my back.

"You're Killian Kendall?" he asked softly, unlocking one side of the handcuffs. I gratefully dropped my arms to my side, but he quickly pulled my wrists forward and cuffed them again in front. "I've read about you in the paper."

"About me?"

"Yeah, I—"

"Killian!" a familiar voice called from the direction of the street.

I turned and spotted Micah by the front gate behind the police tape. Another officer stood nearby, arms crossed over his chest, making sure no one dared attempt to get through the line.

"The reporters are here already?" Marshall said. "They're like vultures."

"Actually, he's with me." I shouted to Micah, "Find Novak and Judy."

"You shouldn't be talking to him," Marshall said uncertainly.

"Sorry." I allowed him to push me gently into the back seat.

He buckled me in, then slid behind the wheel. A metal grill separated the front seat from the back. We didn't speak again until we were on the road.

"What did you mean you've read about me in the paper?"

"After you solved that ax-murder case. I wasn't on the force yet, but there was a big article about you. It said you'd solved another case too, when you were younger."

"Oh. Yeah. I guess." I wasn't used to being recognized, and under the circumstances, wasn't sure what the proper response should be.

"So...is that what you were doing here?"

"I probably shouldn't say anything."

"I'm not going to tell anyone. I think it's awesome that you're so young and you're out there solving crimes the police can't figure out."

"It's not always that they can't," I said, thinking about Seth and Paul. "Sometimes it's because they don't really care."

"What do you mean?"

"Not all cases seem to get the same priority. Fenton Black was a killer and a criminal, and there must be twenty to twenty-five cops crawling around his house, just because he was rich and powerful. I had a friend who was murdered for being gay, and no one cared about finding his killer. The case I'm working on now involves a young guy who was murdered in his own apartment, but since he was a gay escort, nothing was done about it for over a month."

"So you were on a case. I was right. And Black was involved?"

I sighed. "I'm not saying anything more about it."

Marshall looked disappointed. He glanced at me in the rear view mirror, his eyes catching mine. "I'm gay too," he suddenly blurted out.

I blinked in surprise. I couldn't believe this was actually happening. There I was, sitting handcuffed in the back of a police car, while the cop driving came out to me. This day kept getting more and more bizarre.

"I'm not out to many people," he said.

"Oh." I didn't know what else to say.

"Was that reporter your boyfriend?"

I nodded. "How did you know he was a reporter?"

"You start to recognize the reporters pretty quickly around here. There aren't too many of them, and he's been working on that corruption case." He was quiet for a minute. "I've never had a boyfriend."

He obviously wanted to talk about it. "How long have you known?"
I asked.

"That I'm gay? A long time. Since junior high at least."

"Why aren't you out to many people?"

"I don't know. I grew up in a small farming town, very rural. All my
friends were rednecks. I wasn't like...you know, queer acting, so I fit in.
It just seemed easier not to tell anyone. I dated a couple of girls in high
school, but it wasn't serious. I never even kissed one of them. I've only
told a couple of friends, but they're all girls. Man, it feels good to be
talking about this to someone who understands."

"Um, glad I can help."

"My dad used to be a state trooper, but he was injured in an
accident when I was a kid. He always wanted me to become a cop too,
so when I graduated from high school, I went to community college and
then into the police academy as soon as I was old enough. I've never
even kissed a guy, but I've thought about it a lot." He glanced at me in
the rearview mirror again, and I got the feeling he was thinking about it
at that very moment.

"You should, uh, meet more people. Gay people, I mean," I said
awkwardly.

"I don't know where." He blushed. "And I'd be scared. I don't think
the guys in the department would be very happy if they found out." His
eyes widened as he thought of something. "You won't tell anyone, will
you?"

"No, I won't tell anyone," I said. "I promise. It's not my place to
out someone else."

He gave me a tentative smile. "Thanks. Maybe I'll come out some
day, but not yet."

We arrived at the police station, and all gay-related conversation
was abruptly dropped. He led me inside, where the officers had
apparently been warned of my impending arrival. I was photographed
and fingerprinted — just like a real suspect — then allowed to make my
phone call. I looked up the phone number for the only lawyer I knew,
Ilana Constantino. Technically, she was a family lawyer, but I figured
she was better than nothing. I certainly didn't want to call Adam. He'd
go into cardiac arrest on the spot.

Luckily, Ilana answered and agreed to get there as quickly as
possible. She also insisted she would call Adam to let him know what
was going on. The idea of being behind bars when Adam found out
seemed almost appealing.

After my call, I was led to the holding area. My cuffs were
removed, and I was locked inside a small, featureless cell. My stomach
sank as the door swung shut with a loud clang. I sat down on the metal
bed built into one wall, and suddenly everything caught up to me at
once. The lack of sleep, the shock of finding the dead bodies, my fears

for Jake, my arrest — whatever had been holding me together completely collapsed, and tears began to fall, slowly at first, then faster as my sobs built. Eventually, I cried myself into an uneasy sleep.

I was startled awake by keys jangling outside my cell. I sat up with a jerk to find the sergeant who'd been giving orders back at Black's house. He didn't look any happier than the last time I'd seen him. "Your lawyer is here now, Kendall." He unlocked the door. "If you'd be so kind as to follow me, we'll have that little chat now."

I didn't actually follow him; he walked a few careful steps behind me, directing me where to go with terse commands. At least he didn't put the cuffs back on.

The interrogation room was a small space with a table and a few chairs. Ilana was waiting there, looking as calm and self-assured as always. She'd handled the legal proceedings when my mother gave Adam custody of me, as well as when Adam fought his ex-wife for custody of Kane. She was a close friend of the family's, and it was a comfort just to see her.

I sat down at the table and the officer sat across from me. "I'm Detective Sergeant Rosen," he said. "This will all be recorded. Please state your full name."

"Killian Travers Kendall."

"Please tell me what you were doing at the estate of Fenton Black this evening when police responded to an anonymous call that a murder had taken place at that address."

I looked over at Ilana, and she nodded. I took a deep breath. "Actually, the anonymous call was from me. I was there because I work for Shane Novak. He's a private investigator, retired from the Baltimore City PD." Rosen didn't look impressed. "I'm working on a case involving a murder in Washington DC, a strangled escort. In the course of my investigation, I learned that Fenton Black was actually the murdered escort's...er, employer. Then I discovered evidence linking him to the killing itself. I turned the evidence over to Detective Owen Evans of the DCPD this afternoon. At that time, he indicated they were planning on moving to arrest Black within the next twenty-four hours."

Rosen was scribbling furiously. He paused when I stopped. "I'm assuming this is the Reader's Digest version?" he asked dryly.

"Yes, sir."

"You still haven't explained what you were doing at Black's house."

"I was getting to that. The unconscious guy behind the couch is a friend of mine. His name is Jake Sheridan. Maybe you remember the Sheridan murders a few years ago." I could see in his eyes that he did, although he refused to comment. I continued, "I knew he was involved with Black and...well...it's a long story."

"We've got all the time in world."

I took another deep breath. "I guess I felt I owed him a favor, so I wanted to warn him to get out before the police arrived."

"Exactly what do you mean by involved."

"I don't know all the details. I've heard that Black was something of a pedophile, or at least he liked his boys young. I think Jake was his...boyfriend. I'm pretty sure he was supplying Jake with drugs."

"So you went to warn him that the police were coming?"

I nodded miserably, sure I was going to be charged with something now. I realized just how stupid I had been.

"What happened when you arrived? I want a detailed, step-by-step account of your movements so we know where you went and what you did."

"I parked up the road at a dead-end turnabout."

"How'd you know it was there?"

"A reporter friend told me." He nodded, and I went on. "I walked back and found the gate open. I was trying to decide whether to risk going in when a car came along, so I ducked inside to avoid the headlights." He quirked an eyebrow, but I ignored it. "Staying hidden as best I could, I made my way to the back of the house and entered through the garage."

"It was all unlocked?"

"Yes."

"And that didn't strike you as odd?"

"Maybe a little. To be honest, I wasn't thinking very clearly. I'm going on a serious lack of sleep. I've been functioning on adrenaline all day. All my attention was focused on finding Jake. Anyway, I went inside, and it was dark and very quiet. I, uh, found the dead guy in the kitchen." I stopped and gulped.

"What did you do when you found the body?"

"After I puked, I called the police right away."

For a moment, I saw something that almost looked like amusement flash through Rosen's eyes, but it was gone quickly. "You didn't leave your name, and then you stayed."

"I don't know why I didn't tell them my name. I guess I didn't want anyone to know I was there, especially if there was a chance I might still be able to find Jake and leave. I really wasn't thinking clearly."

"What happened next?"

"I searched the rest of the first floor and then went upstairs. The door to the sitting room was closed, but I saw a light on, so I opened it. There was one guy in the middle of the floor. He was dead too. The door to the bedroom was open, so I went in and turned the lights on. That's when I found Fenton Black. I was about to leave when I saw Jake behind the couch. And that's pretty much when you arrived."

"Do you know of any reason why someone might want to kill Fenton Black?"

I almost sighed with relief. Maybe they didn't suspect Jake after all. "I imagine people were lining up for the privilege. He was a drug dealer, he ran an escort agency, he was involved with the mafia, and he was behind the corruption with the land deals here on the Shore."

"Let me be more specific. Do you know of any reason why Jacob Sheridan would want to kill Fenton Black?"

My heart sank again. "Jake isn't a killer," I said, sounding weak even to myself.

Rosen didn't comment, just sat there staring levelly at me.

"I really don't think he did it," I said softly.

"We'll be sure to take that into consideration," the detective said, sarcasm dripping from his voice. He stood to leave, signaling the end of my interview. "Ballistics will be able to tell if the gun in his hand was the same weapon that killed the two bodyguards and Black, and we're running tests to see if he was the one who fired it. If he did, I'm afraid your opinion won't carry as much weight as the evidence."

The mention of the gun brought something to the surface of my memory. "Wait. Did the gun have a silencer on it?"

"What?" I'd clearly caught him off guard.

"The gun you found near Jake, did it have a silencer?"

"No, it didn't. Why would you ask that?"

"Think about it," I said. "Three people were shot in the same house. Two of them I assume were trained bodyguards. They all looked like they'd been caught off guard. Now, the house is huge, but you would still hear gunshots, unless maybe the sitting room and bedroom were soundproofed, which I highly doubt. The only other option is that the shooter used a silencer."

Rosen looked down on me with a new respect in his eyes. "I'm going to go verify your story. If any of it doesn't check out, you're going to be in very deep shit. I'll be back. You can wait in here."

As soon as the door closed, Ilana breathed a deep sigh. "That went a lot better than I had feared."

"Really?" Not knowing what to expect, I had no way of judging if it had gone well or not.

"Definitely. He didn't take you back to the cell, which means he probably believes you're being level with him. You are, aren't you?"

"Yes, I told him the truth."

"Good. That was definitely the best move in this situation. You could still be facing some serious charges, though, Killian. What were you thinking?"

I shrugged helplessly. "I just wanted to help Jake. I've failed him in so many ways as a friend. I felt I owed him something. If I'd been a better friend to start with, maybe he wouldn't have even been in this mess."

"Killian, you can't blame yourself for the choices other people make. Perhaps you did play a part in all of it, but he made the decision to get involved with Fenton Black. You didn't force him to do that."

I sighed, knowing she was right but feeling no less guilty. "So you think I could still get in a lot of trouble?"

"It all depends on how generous Detective Rosen is feeling. That last bit about the silencer might be helpful. If you have any other flashes of brilliance, it wouldn't hurt to share them."

"What do we do while I wait for my next genius moment?"

"We sit here patiently."

We sat patiently for about an hour, while neither brilliance nor Rosen appeared.

Finally, the detective returned. He didn't look quite as sour as he had before. Taking that as a good sign, I sat up straighter in my seat and gripped the edge of the table nervously.

"Alright, Mr. Kendall. Your story checked out, and several good men have vouched for you. I should be charging you on various counts, but since you have a clean record — and some of your friends called in some favors — we're going to let you go with a very stern warning. If I ever catch you interfering with police business again, or even hear that you've gotten in the way of an official investigation, you'll face serious charges."

"I'm free to go?" I said, barely able to believe my luck.

"You're free to go."

"Thank you, Detective Rosen," I said sincerely, holding out my hand to shake.

"You're welcome, Mr. Kendall. By all accounts, you're a good investigator, which doesn't begin to explain the monumental mess you nearly made of this case. Do you have any idea what kind of chaos you would have caused if you'd removed the Sheridan kid from the scene of the crime? Not to mention you tracked blood all over and you vomited in the trashcan. All that confusing evidence would have slowed down our investigation considerably. Besides all that, you would have made yourself a major suspect. Is any of what I'm saying getting through to you?"

"Yes, sir. I'm truly sorry. I won't be that stupid in the future, I promise."

"You'd better not, or, I repeat, I'll throw your ass in jail." He turned to leave, but I had one more question.

"Sir?"

He turned back.

"Was I right about the silencer?"

He paused for a second, and I thought he wasn't going to answer. Then he shrugged. "Let's just say the rooms aren't soundproofed. I'll send an officer to see you out."

I hugged Ilana, then she held me by the shoulders at arms' length. "Now, if you thought that was rough, you ain't seen anything yet."

"What do you mean?"

"Adam, Shane Novak, and Micah are all out in the lobby."

I gulped. I knew she was right. Detective Rosen had let me off easy. I wouldn't be so fortunate with the trio waiting for me. I squared my shoulders and lifted my chin. "Well, it's been a good life. Let's go face the firing squad."

She chuckled and slipped her arm through mine. "Any last requests?"

Chapter 31

Officer Marshall was sent to escort Ilana and me out. He offered me a small smile as he held the lobby door open for us.

Adam and Micah leaped to their feet the moment we appeared. It was a race to see who could get to me first. Adam won by a hair, enveloping me in a huge hug. He gripped me tightly for a long time, then stepped back abruptly and shook me by the arms. "Don't you ever do something that stupid again!"

After he let go of me, Micah quickly moved in for his hug. Holding me close, even longer than Adam had, he whispered fiercely in my ear, "I love you, Killian Kendall. I swear, though, if you ever do something like that to me again, I'll leave you and never look back."

I jerked away to stare into his eyes.

He was deadly serious. "I've never been so scared in my entire life," he said hoarsely as a tear rolled down his cheek. "I couldn't stand to lose you."

"I'm so sorry." I wiped away the tear, feeling as if my heart was being ripped out. "It's okay now, though. It's all over."

"I'm still furious with you. Why didn't you wait for me?"

"If I had, you would have been arrested with me."

"At least I would have known what was happening. You lied to me, Killian. You said you'd wait."

"I'm sorry."

"Can we continue this later?" Novak asked, giving me an unreadable look. I was sure I'd be hearing from him later. "I'd like to get over to the hospital to sit with Judy."

"The hospital?" I asked.

"Jake was admitted for a drug overdose," Adam said.

"Oh my God! Is he okay?" In all the confusion of being arrested and worrying about what would happen, I hadn't even thought about Jake's condition.

"He'd still not regained consciousness last I heard, but they expect him to be fine eventually," Novak said.

I turned to look at Adam and Micah. "Can we go over there, too?"

They both nodded. "Of course," Micah said.

"Are you going?" I asked Ilana.

"Well, I was really only here as a family friend. I'm not a criminal lawyer, which means I won't be much help to Jake. Still, I can give some advice, and if things look bad, I can recommend a colleague who is an excellent criminal lawyer. So, yes, I'll join you."

We all left together, then drove to the hospital separately. Adam, Novak, Ilana, and Micah had all come to the police station in their own cars.

The ride over with Micah was mostly silent. "Micah, I'm really sorry," I said. "I just felt this was something I had to do by myself. Saying I'd wait for you was the only way I could convince you to give me the address. I wish I hadn't lied to you. I promise I won't ever do it again."

"Not now, Killian," he said, turning on the radio.

At the hospital, we found a Judy I hardly recognized. She seemed completely lost sitting in the waiting room alone. I'd never seen her look so defeated and, well, old.

She brightened a bit when she saw us, however. Her eyes caught and held mine, sharing the knowledge that her vision had been fulfilled. I could see her fear that Jake would be the final loss.

There wasn't much to say. Although nothing had changed yet in Jake's condition, the doctors were still being positive. All we could do was sit and wait in an uneasy silence while sick and injured people came and went around us. I dozed fitfully, snapping awake as images of the dead bodies I'd seen floated up before my eyes over and over.

Finally, after what seemed like an eternity, a tall, thin doctor who looked as tired as we did approached Judy. "Ms. Davis?"

"Yes." She snapped to attention, her back straightening.

"Jake is awake at last. The police have been in and talked to him, and now he's asking for you. They've given their okay for you to see him."

Judy was on her feet immediately. "If you'll show me the way?"

"Of course. Just follow me." He led her off beyond the doors. The rest of us sat tight.

"Do you think they'll charge him?" I asked.

"They'll probably hold him in custody, at least," Ilana said, "but unless they have more than they've told us, they won't be able to actually charge him yet. The ballistics tests won't be done today, even with the rush they'll put on it because of who the victim is. That means we can probably get him home by tonight, assuming they set his bail."

"I can't believe this is happening."

"Believe it," Novak said shortly, and we fell back into silence.

It wasn't too long before Judy was back out. "Killian, he wants to see you."

"Me?"

"I told him what happened. He has no memory whatsoever of the killings. He can't tell the police anything, not even to say for sure he didn't do it."

"Drugs?" Novak asked.

"Possibly." Judy gave a weary shrug. "Probably. He could also be blocking the memory. Or maybe he's lying. Who knows anymore?"

"Did the police say it's okay for me to go in?" I asked after an awkward pause.

"Yes. They're hoping something will trigger his memory. They're recording everything, of course, so be careful what you say."

I nodded and stood up nervously.

"Just go through those doors and a nurse will be waiting to show you the room."

I almost turned around when I saw Jake. He looked so pitiful lying in that big hospital bed, his face pale and sunken. There was something black all around his mouth.

"Charcoal," he said in a frail voice.

I stepped closer. "Huh?"

"The black stuff. They pumped my stomach, then gave me charcoal just to be safe. It's supposed to soak up any poisons left in me, or something like that. I think it was just to torture me."

I reached out a tentative hand. He took it in his, his grip weak.

"You came for me," he whispered after a moment.

I bit my lip, not sure what to say.

"You risked your life for me...again. After everything I said to you the other night."

"Actually, it was because of everything you said to me the other night. It made me realize what a terrible friend I've been. I wanted...to make it up to you somehow. I wanted to help you." I looked down at him. "What happened, Jake?"

"I...I don't know."

"I don't even mean just tonight. I mean...what happened to you? How did you end up with Fenton Black?"

He looked away as a tear rolled down his cheek. "I told you how messed up I was in California." His voice was so soft I had to lean in to hear him. "That's part of the reason Judy wanted to move back here. I was having sex with anyone who would supply me."

"Supply you?"

"Drugs. I got into drugs. I guess Judy thought moving me back here would stop it. And it did...for a while. Even I thought things might be different...but then they weren't. I started using again. Small stuff at first — weed, maybe some pills now and then, all of it easy to get. You can score it at school.

"But it kept escalating. There was this one guy who supplied me for sex. His name was Julio or something like that. I don't even remember. Isn't that disgusting? He told me he knew someone who would like to meet me. It was Fenton."

"And Fenton offered you drugs for sex?"

"More than just drugs. He showered me with clothes, presents, cash. I felt like a prince, like someone actually cared about me for a change. He didn't, of course. He was only interested in the sex, but I could fool myself, lie to myself enough that I didn't think about how he was using me."

I squeezed his hand. "Did you kill him?" I asked softly.

His eyes welled up. "I don't know."

"What happened after I left the Ball?"

"He was furious. He screamed at me for talking to you. He accused me of ruining everything, of being a stupid, drug-addicted slut and having single-handedly brought down his empire. I told him I didn't know what he was talking about, that I hadn't said anything to you. He didn't believe me. He took me home and knocked me around a bit."

"He hit you?"

Jake nodded. "Then he gave me some drugs, I don't even know what. I didn't really care. I think he was hoping I'd OD and take care of his dirty work for him."

"You almost did."

He looked up at me. "I wish I had."

I bent over and gathered him up in a hug. "Don't say that, Jake."

"Why not? It's true."

"Because...do you know what that would have done to me? To Judy? We love you, Jake. I know I haven't done a very good job of showing it, but I do. I want to be a better friend for you."

We cried for a few minutes, with him clinging to me as if I were a life preserver and he was drowning.

"Jake," I said at last, "I don't think you killed Fenton."

"You don't?"

"No, but I don't know who did. You have to try and remember."

"I can't, Killian. I've been trying. Really I have."

"Okay, what about the case I was working? Did you ever hear Fenton mention someone named Paul Flynn?"

He thought for a minute. "No, not that I can recall."

"He was an escort in Washington DC who was murdered a little while ago. Paul knew that Fenton was involved in some illegal activities, and had been collecting evidence against him. I'm not sure what Paul intended to do with it...turn Fenton in, I guess. Unfortunately, he was a nice guy — if more than a little naïve — so he gave Fenton the chance to turn himself in first. I believe Fenton killed him instead."

"I...maybe there was something..."

"What?"

"It must have been a month ago or more. Something was really bothering Fenton. He'd been pretty edgy for a couple of weeks. We were in his bedroom one night when someone came to see him. Apparently

Fenton had asked him to come. Fenton always sent me out of the room when he talked business, so I went to the sitting room and lay down by the fireplace. Sound came clearly through it from the bedroom, and I could hear most of what they said. I got the impression that Fenton wanted this guy to kill somebody. Although he didn't spell it out, he kept hinting, saying stuff like, 'This problem has to be eliminated,' and 'I want you to take care of this for me.'"

"You think he was hiring this guy to kill Paul?"

"They never mentioned any names, so I don't know. And he wasn't exactly hiring the guy, either. They never discussed money or payment. It was more like Fenton had something he was holding over the guy's head, like blackmail."

"Did you see the guy?"

"Yeah."

"Can you remember what he looked like?"

"He was kinda small and dark skinned, might have been Middle Eastern. He had dark eyes, long black hair, and fairly sharp features. He reminded me of a hawk."

I knew someone who fit that description perfectly. "Razi!"

"You know him?" Jake asked in surprise.

"We've met." My heart was hammering in my chest, my mind racing. I sat down heavily in the single chair next to the bed.

"You think this guy may have had something to do with what happened?"

"If Fenton coerced Razi into killing Paul, or even hired him, and Razi discovered I was getting close to finding that out, he might have had reason to want Fenton dead."

"I don't understand."

"As far as Razi is concerned, with Fenton dead there's nothing left to tie him to the crime. He doesn't know you overheard his conversation with Fenton, which is probably the only thing that saved your life."

"What do you mean?"

"I think when Razi found you unconscious, he decided to try and pin the murders on you. That's why he put the gun in your hand and left you alive. If you'd died later of an overdose, it would have been all the better, as if you'd offed yourself after killing everyone else. There'd have been no one left to defend you."

"You don't have proof of any of that."

I stood up. "No, I don't, but I intend to get it."

Jake eyes widened. "How?"

"I'm going to see Razi."

"Killian, no! If he's the killer, you could be in danger."

"It's the only way to clear you of the murders."

"Let the police handle it. I'll tell them everything I've told you."

I'd forgotten about the police for a moment. "You won't have to tell them anything. I'm sure they're listening. You're right, though. They should handle it, but if that doesn't work..." I left the rest unsaid. No need to tip my hand to the police just yet.

I left to go find Ilana and a police officer. Ilana went in first for a brief conference with Jake, then she was joined by the officer, who took Jake's official statement. I sat tensely in the waiting room with Novak, Micah, and Judy. I seemed to have gotten my second wind — or was it my third or fourth by then? — and my body was aching for action. I was itching to be in on whatever the police decided to do about Razi.

Finally, Ilana came back out. I was on my feet in a flash. "What's going on?"

She shrugged. "You know about as much as I do. Jake gave them a statement regarding this Razi character, but I don't think they gave too much credence to it. They seem to be under the impression that he's making it up to draw suspicion away from himself. They want to see you now to find out what you know about Razi."

As she finished speaking, Detective Rosen came into the waiting room with a sour expression on his face. Spotting me, he signaled me over. "I didn't think I'd be having another conversation with you this soon," he said. "We've got Jake Sheridan's statement, and now we need some information from you. He doesn't know what this Razi's last name is, but he thought you might."

I flipped through my notebook until I found Razi's information. "It's Akiba, Razi Akiba." I spelled it for him.

"What do you know about him?"

"Not much. I interviewed him during my investigation, but he wasn't exactly cooperative. I know he used to work for Fenton Black's escort agency and was supposedly a friend of Paul Flynn's, the guy who was murdered."

"That it?"

"I have an address for him."

He copied it down from my notebook.

"Are you going to look into this?" I asked.

Rosen gave me a probing stare. "Not that it's any of your business, but I'll be getting in touch with the DC detective handling the case. We'll compare notes and see where it goes from there."

"Don't you think you should at least have Razi taken into custody? What if he finds out you're on to him and runs?"

"We can't just lock people up for no reason. Right now, we have no evidence that he's involved with these murders in any way. All we have is the word of some drug-addled kid who'd probably say anything at this point to save his own hide. Maybe he's telling the truth. Until we have something more to go on, however, we're assuming Jake is the killer here."

"What about the gunpowder residue tests? Did you do them on Jake?"

He raised one eyebrow. "Are you telling me how to do my job?"

"No, but—"

"We're running the test, but even if it comes up negative, that's hardly conclusive. It's not that reliable. Your friend won't be off the hook that easily. Now, I suggest you go home and stay out of this. Your involvement is finished."

I opened my mouth to object, but he ignored me and walked away.

"Killian, relax," Micah said, coming up next to me.

Realizing I had clenched my fists at my sides, I forced myself to let go. "I have to go back to DC," I said in a low voice.

"What? Now?"

"Yes, now."

"Killian, you haven't had any real sleep in almost forty-eight hours. You can't turn around and drive back to DC. Let the police handle this."

"Like they handled Paul's case? I've got to do something, Micah. I can't just sit here."

He sighed. "You're going to do this no matter what I say, aren't you?"

I nodded.

His shoulders slumped in resignation. "Then I'll drive you."

"You'll do that for me?"

"I'll go get the car."

As Micah walked out, Novak appeared at my side. "We need to talk. Let's step outside." His tone of voice implied that this would not be a fun conversation.

I followed him without a word. An older man was smoking a cigarette just beyond the door, so we moved a few feet away.

"I need to apologize to you, Killian."

I felt my mouth drop open. "Apologize to me? For what?"

"I've been very negligent in my training. You came along so quickly and you're such a good investigator, I keep forgetting you're still a rookie. I never should have vanished in the middle of your investigation."

"Novak, you don't have to apologize." I was confused and a little shaken by this sudden turn of events. "It's your job..."

"It's also my job to make sure you're properly trained as an investigator...and keep you out of trouble. This business at Fenton Black's house was reckless, and well — let's face it — stupid. First of all, if you had a license, it would probably be revoked. What you did is called illegal entry or trespassing. It was also incredibly dangerous. If the security force had been in place, or if the killer had still been on the premises, you would quite possibly be dead right now."

"I know it was stupid. I'm sorry."

He held up a hand. "But...if you hadn't done what you did, Jake would probably be dead right now from a drug overdose. Plus, it gave us a jump on the killer that we might not have had if you hadn't gotten there when you did."

"So, wait... Was it a good thing I snuck into Fenton's estate or a bad thing?"

"Both."

"I don't get it."

"You were given a lot of breaks, so everything worked out for the best. You might not be so lucky next time. I overheard you saying you're heading to DC. If you're planning on confronting Razi in some way, I would advise you not to. Somehow, though, I have a feeling I'd be wasting my time." He gave me a look that clearly invited a response of some sort.

"The police could drag this out who knows how long, if they do anything at all. The more we delay, the more chance Razi will bolt. Or he could hurt Tad."

"Tad?"

"The boy who lives with him."

"Do you have any reason to think Razi will hurt this boy?"

"He's killed at least four people so far. Isn't that reason enough?"

"You've obviously made up your mind about this. As your employer, I could forbid you to go, but you'd probably just do it on your own time." He shook his head. "And I can't say I wouldn't do the same thing if I were in your shoes. I want you to be better prepared than you are, however."

Just then, Micah drove up, reminding me I'd left my car parked in the woods. "Where's my Mustang?"

"Probably in impound," Novak said. "You'll have to go after it."

"It'll have to wait. I don't have time right now."

"Then I'll take care of it. Come on. I have something to give you," Novak said, setting out across the parking lot.

I jumped into Micah's car. "Follow Novak, please. He has something for me."

"What?"

"I don't know."

When we stopped behind Novak's beat-up old jalopy, he was leaning into the passenger's side to rummage through the glove box. "Too much crap in here," he grumbled. He pulled out a shiny black gun and laid it on the seat next to him.

"You're giving me a gun?"

He carefully turned to give me a withering glare. "Have you lost your mind? Do you honestly think I'd give you a gun? Do you have any idea how quickly they'd lift my license if you ran off and shot somebody with my gun?" He ducked back in and emerged a few seconds later brandishing a black, tube-shaped object.

"What's that?"

"Pepper spray."

"Pepper spray?" I asked disbelievingly. That was what he wanted to give me?

"Have you ever been on the receiving end of it?"

"No."

"I have. We had to when it was issued to the police department. Let me tell you something: it hurts. All you can think about is how much it hurts. It's some of the worst pain I've ever felt in my life. It's a very effective, relatively nonviolent weapon. Don't knock it. Put out your hand." I did, and he slapped the canister into my open palm. "Stick it in your pocket and don't forget it's there. If you need it, don't hesitate to use it. But for God's sake, make sure it's pointed in the right direction before you spray it. We'll talk more when you get back."

I put it in my pocket, thinking it wasn't very likely I'd be using it. I left Novak returning things to the glove box and rejoined Micah in his car.

"What did he give you?"

"Pepper spray."

Micah frowned.

"Yeah, that was pretty much my reaction too," I said. "Let's go."

"Where exactly are we going...besides DC, that is?"

"Razi's apartment."

"Do you think it's safe? Even with your trusty pepper spray?"

"No, I don't think it's safe, but what choice do I have?"

"Maybe you should call your detective friend that you worked with yesterday."

"Evans? I wouldn't exactly call him a friend."

"Still, he knows the history of the case. He might be willing to go out on a limb to help."

"I doubt that." I pulled out my cell phone anyway and dialed Evans' number.

A voice message answered. "Hi, this is Detective Owen Evans. I'm not at my desk right now, but if you leave a message at the tone, I'll get back to you as soon as possible. If this is an emergency or if you would like to speak to someone else, please press zero now." I did so.

The phone rang a few times before being answered by gruff male voice.

"I'm trying to reach Detective Evans," I said.

"Detective Evans isn't on duty right now. Would you like to leave a voicemail message or speak to the detective currently on duty?"

"No, that's okay." I disconnected. "He's not on duty," I said to Micah.

"What about Chris's dad?"

"He's not even working on this case."

"Still, he might be able to help."

"I should at least tell Chris what's going on," I said. Glancing at my watch, I realized that between jail and the hospital I'd spent another wakeful night. "It's 7:30. I hope she's an early riser."

Her little brother answered after several rings. "Hey, Kevin, this is Killian. Is Chris there?"

"Yeah, hang on." I heard him bellow for Chris, followed by their father yelling at Kevin to finish getting ready for school. The phone was set down with a thud.

A few seconds later, Chris came on the line. "Killian! What the hell is going on? We heard on the news this morning that Fenton Black is dead, along with his two bodyguards."

"I know. I'm the one who found them. I was there when the police arrived, and I spent most of the night in jail."

"What?"

I quickly gave her the whole story, including how Jake was currently under suspicion for the murders, and what he'd told me about Razi. "So we're on our way there now," I said. "I'm not sure what I'm going to do when we arrive. I guess I'll figure it out as I go along."

"Killian, this is crazy. You can't go in there alone."

"Oh, it's okay. I'm armed with pepper spray."

"Huh?"

"Chris, I have to do something. Tad could be in danger. You've met him. He's just a kid, and he's already been through so much."

"You know what, Killian Kendall? You have a savior complex."

"A what?"

"A savior complex. It's common among cops. It means you think you have a mission to save everyone. Well, guess what? You don't. You're only human. You can't be there for everyone in trouble."

"Of course I can't save everybody, but what kind of person would I be if I knew someone was in danger and didn't do anything to help them? Sure, it would be easier, safer, to just let the professionals deal with it. The problem is, they don't always want to deal with it, and when they do, they're often too late."

"That doesn't mean you can just take the law into your own hands."

"All I'm going to do is try to get Tad out of there. And maybe see if I can get Razi to admit anything."

"I just don't think it's a very good idea."

"Is there anything your dad can do?"

"Like what?"

"I don't know. Backup of some kind?"

"Backup? You're not a cop. You can't get backup."

"I just meant maybe some officers could be sent over to Razi's apartment or something."

"That would be backup. Without evidence, their hands are tied. Right now, there's absolutely nothing linking Razi to either crime, except for the testimony of your friend, who isn't the most reliable source. If someone else could corroborate his story..."

"Everyone who could have done so is dead."

"Which would be convenient if he was lying, since it also means that everyone who could disprove his story is dead."

"Except Razi."

"And, of course, all you have to do is ask him if he killed Paul and the others. I can just see him falling all over himself to admit it."

"I didn't say that."

"Then what exactly are you expecting to happen?"

"I don't know." What was I expecting? Why was I doing this?

Pausing for a second while I thought about it, I recognized the underlying feeling of pressure, which I'd pretty much grown accustomed to over the last few days, as having been my driving force through all of this. Although I couldn't identify it, I felt something bad was approaching, as if a storm was building and only I could do anything about it. "It's hard to explain, Chris. I just feel...compelled to do something. Look, I'm sorry I called and upset you. I'll handle this myself."

"Killian, does your compulsion have anything to do with those — what did you call them — Gifts you were telling me about?"

"Yeah, I'm pretty sure it does."

"Please don't do anything stupid."

"I won't." I hung up and slumped down in my seat sulkily.

Micah took his eyes off the road long enough to glance over at me. "Why don't you try to get a little sleep? I'll wake you up when we reach the city."

I shrugged. It was as good a suggestion as any, although I doubted I'd be able to fall asleep, considering how keyed up I was. Somewhat surprisingly, however, I realized I was drifting off after just a few minutes. I struggled against it for a bit longer, then finally gave in and fell asleep.

I came awake with a start when Micah gently shook my arm. "We're almost to DC. Where do we go from here?"

I drowsily pulled out my notebook and tried to focus my eyes. My little nap seemed to have done more harm than good, leaving me feeling very discombobulated. It took me a moment to find Razi's address and read it off to Micah.

"Oh, I know where that is."

"Have you been there before?" I asked with a flash of suspicion.

"No, but I'm familiar with the area. I did live here for several years, you know."

We drove in silence for a few minutes. Finally he asked, "Okay, what's the plan once we get there?"

"I don't really have one."

"Well, it might a good idea to come up with one, don't you think?"

"I work better without a plan."

"Okay. Well, what about me?"

"What about you?"

"Hey, Killian, can you stop being so hostile with me? I'm on your side, remember? I didn't have to drive you up here."

"You're right. I'm sorry," I said contritely. "I'm just so tired. Not that I'm trying to make excuses. It's just..."

"Never mind. I understand. This is something you feel you have to do. I can sympathize with that. I'm not going to try and stop you. I want to help you, but I don't know what to do. Should I go in with you, or stay outside and act as your backup?"

I rubbed my face, wishing I was more alert for this. "I don't know. Which do you think would be better?"

"Neither one is going to be a picnic," he said darkly. "If I go in and something goes wrong, I may not be able to call for help, but at least I'll know what the hell is happening. If I stay outside and something goes wrong, I may be able to call for help, but I won't know what's happening. And what if Razi isn't home?"

"Huh?" That possibility had completely escaped me.

"What if Razi isn't even there? He could be out on a job."

"Well, that would make it easier to get Tad away from him, at least."

"Have you thought ahead as to what you're going to do with Tad if he decides to leave with you?"

My silence was answer enough.

"You're really doing this on a wing and a prayer, aren't you?"

"He can stay with me until we figure out what to do with him," I said.

"I hope Adam will be okay with that."

"He will be. Besides, he isn't even at the beach house that much these days. He spends most of the time at the B&B."

"Okay. What if Razi is there?"

"Then I'll think of something."

"Kill, I know you think fast on your feet — usually, anyway — but you're awfully tired right now. You're not exactly at your peak performance."

"Do you have any ideas?"

"Not really."

"Alright then. We wing it."

Micah sighed, obviously not happy with that prospect but unable to come up with a better alternative.

We drove the last few minutes to Razi's neighborhood in tense silence. Micah parked the car, and we approached the apartment building on foot. At Razi's door, I hesitated, wondering if maybe we shouldn't form some sort of plan after all.

The question was answered for me when the door suddenly swung open and Tad stepped into the hall carrying a large trash bag. He blinked in surprise when he saw us. I quickly put my finger to my lips before he could say anything. He pulled the door shut and looked at me questioningly.

"Is Razi home?" I whispered.

He nodded uncertainly. "I have to throw this in the dumpster. If I take too long, he'll be mad. He's been in a really foul mood lately. What are you doing here?"

"Keep walking. I'll come with you and tell you on the way. Micah, you stay here and watch the door in case Razi comes out."

"And what should I do if he does?"

I shrugged. "You'll think of something."

Tad trotted off down the hall, with me matching him step for step. "Do you know why Razi has been in such a bad mood lately?" I asked him.

When he shot me a sideways glance, I noticed the fading evidence of a black eye. "No," he answered shortly.

"Was Razi home last night?"

"Yeah, why?"

That stopped me in my tracks for a second. I rushed to catch back up. "He was home? Are you sure?"

"Why? What's going on?"

"There was a murder last night, several murders in fact, and a friend of mine is being accused of them. I suspect it's all connected to Paul's murder, and Razi is involved up to his eyeballs. But if he was here last night..."

"You think Razi is the killer?"

"Yes, there's a witness who heard Razi being asked to kill Paul."

"But...but Paul was Razi's friend. Razi wouldn't kill him."

We approached the dumpsters in an alley next to the apartment building. Tad tossed the bag into one of them, and we started back at a slower pace.

"The witness said the guy who wanted the job done seemed to have something on Razi, something he was holding over Razi's head. Besides, it could have been killing two birds with one stone. Didn't you say Paul had been talking about getting in touch with your father?"

"Razi wouldn't have killed him," Tad said again, although he didn't sound so convinced this time.

"Look, I know you feel you owe Razi some sort of loyalty because he took you in, but as I said before, it could be a lot different, better. You can stay with me until we figure something out."

Tad's eyes widened. "Are you serious?"

"Yes, very serious. I don't think it's safe for you to be here anymore." I stopped and grabbed his wrist. "Listen for a minute, Tad. If I'm right, then Razi has killed at least four people, one of whom was supposed to be his best friend. Even if I'm wrong about that..." I reached out and gently touched the fading bruise. "He did this, didn't he?"

Tad nodded slightly.

"If he's hitting you, what makes this any better than living with your dad?"

"It's not always like this, only when I do something wrong."

"Nobody deserves to be treated this way, Tad. Get out while you can."

"What about Razi?"

"What about him?"

"What if he comes after me?"

"Do you think he would?"

"I don't know. Maybe. He doesn't like to lose things he thinks of as his."

"And you're his property?"

He shrugged.

"We'll have to deal with that if and when it happens. Do you have anything inside that you need?"

"I never said I was going with you."

"Tad, come on. Use your brain. You've essentially become Razi's sex slave." He winced but didn't argue. "And now you're turning into his punching bag, too. Is that what you want?" He shook his head. "I can give you a safe place to stay until we figure something out. Will you go with me?"

He nodded, although he looked more terrified than ever.

"Good. Is there anything in the apartment you need, or can we just leave?"

"The clothes Razi bought me..."

"We can get you new clothes."

"That's all I have."

"Okay. You wait by the car while I go get Micah." I pointed out the car and started back inside.

"Killian, hold on," Tad called before I reached the door. I turned back.

"I wasn't completely honest with you."

"About what?"

"When you asked me if Razi was home last night."

"He wasn't home?"

"He was, but not all night. He got a phone call yesterday afternoon that seemed to upset him. I don't know who it was or what it was about, because Razi hardly said a word. As soon as he hung up, he slammed around the apartment for a few minutes, then left. He returned after dark in a terrible mood. I did my best to avoid him for the rest of the night."

"So he could be the killer?"

Tad shrugged helplessly.

"This changes everything."

"What do you mean?"

"I need to talk to Razi."

"No! Soon he's going to notice I've been gone too long and come looking for me. We have to go. Please?"

He was right. Tad was my first priority. The police could handle Razi. "Okay, I'll go get Micah. Wait by the car."

When I reached Razi's floor, however, Micah was nowhere to be seen.

Chapter 32

I stood uncertainly in the hall, trying to force my tired mind to think logically. My brain was, however, putting up a valiant fight. When I'd left Micah there to watch out for Razi, I hadn't specifically told him what to do if Razi appeared. I'd simply hoped he'd know enough to invent a distraction. Micah wouldn't have deserted his post, so if he wasn't where I left him, it followed that he was most likely in the apartment. I shuddered at the thought.

Once I had a reasonable assumption regarding his whereabouts, I had to figure out what to do about it. I took a deep breath, boldly walked up to the door, and knocked.

A few seconds later, it swung open to reveal Razi's thin frame and frowning face. His eyes narrowed when he saw me. "I should have known."

"Is Micah in here with you?" I asked, as if it seemed perfectly natural that he might be.

"Yes, I opened my door and found him standing in the hall. He didn't mention you were with him."

"Oh, I was parking the car," I lied fluidly.

When his frown deepened, I realized he didn't believe me. I wondered frantically what pretext Micah had given him for being there. Until I knew, it would be better to avoid the issue.

"You didn't happen to see Tad while you were out there, did you?" he asked suspiciously.

"He's the boy who lives with you?"

Razi's dark eyes flicked over me. "Yes, that would be him."

"A case of lost boys seems to be sweeping through the city," I said with a smile. Razi gave me a blank stare. "I couldn't find Micah either," I explained lamely.

Razi seemed to remember that we were still standing at the door. He stepped back and motioned me in, somewhat ungraciously, I thought. He scanned the hall one last time, then shut the door firmly.

In the living room I found Micah sitting on the couch, looking somewhat lost and nervous. I was struck again by the impersonality of the room, which contained nothing at all of the man living there. It could have been an anonymous showroom apartment anywhere in the country: well furnished and tastefully decorated, but empty of soul.

"I was just telling Razi how relieved we are that this whole mess is over," Micah said a little too loudly. I blinked uncomprehendingly, my brain too exhausted to catch his hint. "You know," he went on, "with Fenton being dead, now we can finally put Paul's death behind us."

"Oh, yeah," I said, catching on at last. "It's such a relief."

Razi walked slowly past and stood facing me across the glass-topped coffee table, where several glossy, oversize photo books of nude young men were scattered. He glanced pointedly between Micah and me, then cocked his head to one side. "Shall we try that again?"

"What do you mean?" The tension in my voice was clear, even to me.

"Why are you really here?"

"I told you, now that this is all over we just wanted to see how you were," Micah said. "I mean, you were Paul's closest friend and all..."

Razi cut him off with a razor-sharp glare before turning his attention back to me. "I know you were the one who found Fenton's body."

I shook my head in confusion. How could he know that? It hadn't been released in the news. The media had been told that Fenton and his bodyguards had been discovered dead during an unrelated police raid on his estate. They had been given no further details.

Razi misinterpreted my headshake. "Don't bother denying it. I have excellent sources."

"Sources?" I asked stupidly. I was dying here. I had to clear my head. It was vitally important to my health — and Micah's — that I start thinking faster.

"It doesn't matter who they are. Let's just say I trust them completely. They've never let me down yet."

I took a seat next to Micah, who put his hand on my back, offering comfort. The slight tremble in his touch was not reassuring, however. He was as scared as I was — more so, really, since I was still too flustered to be properly panicked.

I shrugged. "Yeah, I found him, but what difference does that make? It's still over. Everything led to him. Paul found out about his criminal activities and had evidence on him. Fenton knew that, so he had Paul killed."

Razi's eyes snapped to mine. "Had him killed?"

"Or killed him himself." I tried to shrug my gaffe off. "Does it matter now? Paul is dead either way...and so is Fenton. It's finally over."

"Is it?" Razi asked with a dangerous edge to his voice. I was beginning to worry about our chances of walking out of there easily.

"Yes, it is. With Fenton dead, the case is closed as far as the police are concerned."

"What about Fenton's killer?"

"The police believe they have him in custody."

"And what about you?"

"What do you mean?"

Razi's eyes locked with mine. "Is it over as far as you're concerned? Do you believe the police have Fenton's killer in custody?"

"What difference does it make what I think?"

"It makes a big difference...to the killer."

I laughed uneasily. "Aren't you giving me too much credit?"

"Am I? You pretty much single-handedly solved Paul's murder when the police couldn't."

"When the police wouldn't," I corrected. "They could have if they'd wanted to."

"I'm not so sure. You had contacts they didn't. People would talk to you that wouldn't talk to the police. People like TJ Jackson."

My eyes widened. He did have good sources if he knew TJ's name. "Where is all this going?" I asked, tiring of our tense game of cat-and-mouse.

"Going? It's not going anywhere." Razi suddenly seemed more at ease. His shoulders slumped, and a small smile turned up the corner of his mouth. "I'm just killing time until Tad gets back."

"Where'd he go?" I asked, relieved at the break in the tension. I felt Micah relax next to me as well.

"To take out the trash," Razi said. He walked over to a long, narrow table against the wall and leaned casually against it. The top was completely barren except for a carved wooden staff lying stretched across a matching set of intricately fashioned brass stands. "He's never taken this long before. I hope he didn't run into trouble." He threw me an unreadable glance.

"You want us to go look for him?" Micah asked hopefully, no doubt seeing a chance to escape.

"No, that's quite alright. I wouldn't want to impose."

"It wouldn't be an imposition," Micah said quickly — too quickly.

Razi gave us a little smile I didn't like at all. I suddenly felt more uneasy with this relaxed Razi than I had when he was so clearly on edge.

He trailed his fingers lazily across the staff. "It's beautiful, isn't it?"

"It is," I said. And it truly was: magnificently carved with mythical creatures writhing around its entire length.

"It's one of the few things I own from my homeland." He looked up at me, his eyes heavy-lidded, almost seductive. "I didn't bring it with me, of course. I didn't have time. I bought it here." He paused and smiled creepily again.

"I never told you my story, did I?" He was speaking only to me, as if Micah wasn't even in the room.

I shook my head, my throat suddenly too tight to speak.

"The last time you were here, I said we all have stories. You asked me what mine was, but I was rude and didn't tell you. I'll rectify that now, if you'll allow me."

I nodded.

"I was born on the West Bank in a village not far from the Israeli border. My parents were considered freedom fighters by my people, terrorists by Israel and the US. Death was a daily occurrence. Killing and fighting were a part of my earliest education. I could shoot a gun by the time most American children are learning to tie their shoelaces. I can handle almost any weapon with ease, from a rifle to a knife. I can even kill with my bare hands if I have to. It didn't mean I liked killing, just that I was good at it. When I was ten years old, my mother died in a car bombing. Two years later, Israeli soldiers arrested my father, and he was never seen again. I was sent to live with my uncle and his wife."

He paused for a moment. I sat in horrified silence, watching as he gripped one end of the staff and gave it a slight twist. To my surprise, a slender steel dagger slipped from it like a sword from its sheath. The blade was no longer or wider than that of a large letter opener, but I had no doubt the glittering edge was lethal.

Glancing our way, Razi seemed pleased to see our eyes glued to the dagger. "Beautiful and useful," he said, sliding the blade back into the staff and locking it in place. "What good is beauty if it's useless?

"To continue my story, although my uncle was married, he and his wife never had children. I don't know why. Maybe because my aunt couldn't conceive, or possibly because my uncle was gay...at least, I understand that now. I didn't even know what the word meant then. All I knew was that my uncle liked to do things to me at night when everyone else was asleep. He used to tell me that if anybody ever found out, I would be killed. I accepted what he did to me as payment for living with them instead of on the street as a beggar. It got to the point where I became quite good and even rather enjoyed it. It went on for a few years, until one night his wife caught us. She was utterly horrified, as you can imagine. My uncle panicked and killed her — strangled her to death."

Razi began to pace, never moving too far from the staff and its concealed blade. "That left us with the question of what to do with her body. I suggested leaving it near the border, to appear as if an Israeli had killed her, but the border area was dangerous, and my uncle was never a fighter. Besides, soldiers didn't kill by strangulation. My uncle decided I would have to take the blame. Who was I to argue? I was barely fifteen. My uncle couldn't stand the idea of my being executed, however, so he chose to help me leave the country. He would tell the authorities I had run away. I'd be long gone by the time they came looking for me. He still knew my parents' friends, people who could arrange for me to slip over the border unnoticed. I was passed from one place to another, from person to person, until I reached Jordan.

"There, I was helped by a kind woman who reminded me much of my mother. She took pity on me, a young boy alone and afraid in a strange country. She had contacts, knew the right people, and arranged for them to supply me with false documents, including a passport, so I could travel to the United States. Today, in our post-9/11 world, I doubt I could make it past the immigration authorities. Back then, my fake passport was sufficient."

He paused his pacing and leaned against the table once more. "There I was, fifteen and alone in a foreign country. I barely spoke English, didn't know a soul. I managed to find my way to the city, where I quickly learned to survive using what my uncle had taught me — first as a street hustler, later as an escort. I've done pretty well for myself, wouldn't you say?" He gestured around the room with an all-encompassing sweep of his arm. "So there, Killian Kendall, that's my story. Are you satisfied now?"

"Yes," I managed to say.

"Good." Then, moving so quickly I barely had time to register what was happening, he suddenly leaped forward, swinging the staff like a club. I slammed myself against the back of the couch while Micah, who I'd almost forgotten was there, threw himself in front of me. The carved cane hit Micah's head with a sickening thud, the force of the blow actually knocking him off the couch and onto the floor.

I sat stunned by the sudden violence. It took me a few seconds to realize that Razi was making no move to hit me.

He stared down contemptuously at Micah. "How heroic, sacrificing himself to save his beloved. Hero — it's really just another way of saying someone did something stupid." He looked up at me with terrifyingly cold eyes. "If only the poor idiot knew he was the target all along. Now that we're alone we can talk...man to man. I told you my story, so it's time for you to tell me yours."

"What do you mean?"

"I know why you're really here. We can skip that part. Somehow, you figured out who killed Paul and Fenton and, of course, you came running right to me. Unfortunate for you, convenient for me. It saves me the trouble of hunting you down. You were my last obstacle. What I really want to know is how you figured it out, and more importantly at the moment, what have you done with Tad?"

"I haven't done anything with Tad," I said, praying the boy would be smart enough to stay by the car and not come looking for us. I'd completely lost track of how long we'd been in the apartment. "I didn't see him when I came up."

If we were going to stay alive, we had to escape — and fast — but I had no idea how to accomplish that, especially with Micah unconscious. My only chance was to get the pepper spray out without Razi noticing it and hope it really was as effective as Novak said. In order to do that, though, I had to stall and distract him, so I kept talking. "I thought Fenton killed Paul, except everyone kept saying it wasn't his style, that he'd probably hired a hit man. Either way, I knew who was behind it, so I went to the police with the evidence I had."

"Considerable evidence," Razi commented offhandedly.

I filed that away, beginning to suspect his source was a mole inside the police department.

"The police said they were going to raid Fenton's place. I had a friend who I knew was with Fenton, so I went to the estate to try and get him out before they did it. That's when I found the bodies and called the police. I guess you were tipped off and got there ahead of me?"

"You had a friend there?" Razi asked sharply, not answering my question.

"Yes. He's the one you left alive. I spoke to him last night after he came to. He told me how he'd overheard Fenton ordering you to kill Paul. It was fairly simple to put the rest together."

"I should have killed him when I had the chance," Razi said. He looked at me with narrowed eyes. "But you're here, not the police, which means they don't believe your little friend, at least not yet. I'll be long gone before they arrive. All they'll find here will be two dead bodies."

He swung the staff back. "Wait!" I screamed as I scrambled up onto the sofa, balancing precariously on the cushions. "I have one more question."

His arm stopped in midair. I took the scant opportunity before he could begin the downswing. "Why?" I asked. "Why did you agree to kill Paul?"

The staff swung down. I didn't have time to do more than flinch before it smashed across my face, sending me reeling over the back of the sofa. I hit the floor with a heavy crash, but thankfully, I was still conscious — a little stunned, but aware. I could taste blood in my mouth, metallic and warm, but I figured the damage was unimportant, all things considered. I scrambled to my knees as Razi came purposefully around the sofa.

"You want to know why I killed Paul?" He stalked slowly toward me, speaking in a chillingly calm voice, while I crab-shuffled away as quickly as I could manage. "I'll tell you why I killed Paul: for the same reason I killed Fenton and his clowns, and for the same reason I'm killing you and your boyfriend. Because I didn't have a choice."

I spit out a mouthful of blood. "You always have a choice."

"No!" he shouted, then regained control and continued. "No, I didn't. Not if I wanted to keep my freedom. That's something most of you Americans take for granted. I know the difference."

"What do you mean?" I had to keep him talking and hope he wouldn't notice me trying to get my hand in my pocket as surreptitiously as possible. "How could you lose your freedom by refusing to kill someone?"

"When I was working for Fenton as an escort, some rich, fat-cat politician tried to rape me. Apparently, he got off on taking by force what was already included in the price. I knew how to kill, remember. I'd done it before. So I killed him. A good lawyer might have argued self-defense, but it was just as likely I'd be locked up for murder. After all, he was a respectable public servant, while I was just an illegal immigrant prostitute. That's how the courts would see it anyway. Fenton helped cover it up, but what I didn't know at the time was that he carefully saved the evidence — just in case. If necessary, he wanted to be able to pin it all on me."

Razi became so caught up in his story he failed to notice my hand slip into my pocket, my fingers curling around the cool metal cylinder there. It helped that my crouching position partially hid my movements.

His tale rang a bell in my memory — a news story from a few years before. I vaguely recalled the details: the police had no leads, just the body of a well-liked family man and well-regarded politician, found in a fountain in Dupont Circle.

"Fenton used that evidence to blackmail me into killing Paul and stealing the evidence Paul had against him," he said. "I didn't want to. I tried to talk Paul into running, or at least leaving Fenton alone, but he wouldn't hear of it. He died because he was too damn stubborn." He paused, a tiny, cruel smile playing at his lips. "Kind of like you."

He made a sudden lunge toward me, whipping the staff through the air as I threw myself backwards, scrambling away from him until my back hit the wall. Yanking my hand out of my pocket, I ripped the lid off the canister. I didn't have time to aim it, only to hope I had it pointed in the right direction. I held it out in front of me, but before I could press the button, Razi caught my hand on the back swing, knocking the can out of my grip. I watched helplessly as it skittered across the floor.

I turned my horrified gaze back to Razi, who had crouched down in front of me, his face now so close I could feel his breath. If anything, he was even more terrifying than before. His eyes had taken on a crazed look that sent chills running down my spine. Any perceptible sanity that had been there in the beginning was gone, replaced now by pure hate.

"You and Micah have caused me so much trouble," he said in a low voice made rough by emotion. "No one actually cared who killed Paul until you came along. I'm really going to enjoy killing both of you." He cocked his head to one side. "I think I'll do it slowly, so you feel every second of pain."

He twisted the handle of the staff and the soft click sounded unnaturally loud in my heightened state of alert. He slowly withdrew the dagger, its razor-sharp edge eerily mirroring the glint in his eyes.

"What do you think? Should I start with your pretty face?" he asked in a breathy voice, seeming almost turned on by the prospect. "Or maybe I should start somewhere a little more personal." He flicked the blade toward my crotch, chuckling menacingly when I flinched.

I fought the rising panic in my chest, willing myself to remain still. I was deadly certain that, if I tried to move, he would forego the torture and kill me quickly and efficiently. He was clearly enjoying the smell of my fear.

He reached out a steady hand and drew the blade softly across my right cheek. There was no pain, but I immediately felt a trickle of blood spill out. I sucked in an involuntary gasp.

"Sharp, isn't it?" he asked seductively.

The cut began to sting, and I felt a tear roll down my cheek, more from fear than pain.

"Are you scared now?"

I nodded.

"Good. I want you to be scared. That makes it more fun." He was reaching out to slice my left cheek when a flash of motion caught both our attentions. Before I could turn to see what was happening, Razi had swung around to face this new adversary. With a roar of fury, Micah flew into Razi, the two of them tumbling onto the floor. The knife was lost to my sight, but I didn't waste time worrying about it. With the sounds of their struggle coming from behind me, I crawled madly in the direction I'd last seen the pepper spray rolling. I threw aside an end table, flipped over the recliner, and there was the canister. I snatched it up, leapt to my feet, and vaulted over the couch, landing next to Razi's and Micah's entwined bodies. Because their faces were only inches apart, there was no way I could spray just Razi. I hesitated a second, until I saw the missing dagger emerge from between their bodies, still in the grip of Razi's dark hand.

"I'm sorry, Micah," I whispered, letting loose with a stream of pepper spray.

Their reaction was immediate. They broke apart in a howl of feral pain that almost immediately gave way to coughing and gagging. The knife fell harmlessly to the floor as each began to claw and rub at his streaming eyes, writhing about on the floor in apparent agony.

I stood by helplessly, unsure of what to do next. "Somebody help!" I screamed, finally giving vent to my panic.

Just then the door exploded inward with a sharp crack that sent me diving to the floor. "Freeze! Police!"

Unlike the last time they shouted at me, I had never been so happy to hear those words.

It took a while to sort things out. Eventually I learned that, after I'd talked to Chris, she'd become worried and explained things to her father, Louis. He'd agreed that it sounded dangerous and called Detective Evans. Together, they decided "unofficially" to drive over to Razi's apartment. When they showed up in uniform, Tad had quickly approached them, concerned because I'd been gone so long. He had no idea they were there looking for us, assuming they were two cops who just happened to be in the neighborhood. So they were forewarned before they went in. When they got to Razi's floor, they heard Micah's scream, followed by my cry for help and, of course, they burst in.

Once they saw what was going on, I tried to explain who was who and what had happened. I'm not sure how coherent I was, but they got the gist of it. They quickly placed Razi under arrest and handcuffed him. Then they left him to cough and thrash on the floor while they attended to Micah. By this time, I was at his side and he was calmer but still in excruciating pain.

Evans rushed into the kitchen and came back a minute later with bowlful of suds. "It's just dish soap and water," he said, more to me than Micah, whose eyes were still squeezed shut in agony, streaming tears. He began carefully dabbing at Micah's red face. "Can you bring me fresh water?" he asked me. "I need it to rinse his eyes and get this soap off his skin."

Running to the kitchen, I found a glass and filled it with tap water. "Will this stop the pain?" I asked, handing it to the detective.

"Not completely, but it'll help ease it some," he said without looking up.

Meanwhile, Louis had called an ambulance, which arrived in what I thought was a surprisingly short time. Micah was handed over to the paramedics to be taken to the emergency room, where he would be treated for the pepper spray and the blow to the head, which I now saw was bleeding slightly at his temple. When they noticed that the cut on my cheek looked pretty nasty, they insisted I go too, so a doctor could decide if I needed stitches.

Miraculously, Tad had not disappeared. He arrived on the scene with the paramedics when they came up. I'd been half afraid he'd run, but he was determined to make sure we were okay. I told the officers he was with me and insisted he accompany us to the hospital. It was allowed with a minimum of questions.

"So what now?" Tad asked a few hours later as we sat in the waiting room. Micah was still in an examination room. I hadn't required stitches, for which I was very grateful, but they had bandaged the cut on my cheek with some gauze and white surgical tape.

"I guess next I'll have to talk to the police," I said wearily. "I'm sure they didn't get all their questions answered at the apartment. I doubt I was very articulate. I'm surprised they haven't shown up before now."

"That's not what I meant. I want to know what happens to me. But since you brought it up, will I have to talk to the police again?"

I glanced over at him. He looked more like a lost little kid than I'd ever seen him. "What did you tell them before?"

"Well, they were pretty busy with everything else so they really weren't paying much attention to me. When they arrived, I just told them I knew you'd gone up to talk to Razi and you hadn't come back. They took off like a light. Later, this guy asked my name and address and wrote them down, then said they'd be in touch."

"Did you tell them the truth?"

"My name and address you mean? Not exactly. I said I was Tad Young and gave them the address of another apartment in the building."

I raised an eyebrow. "Probably not the smartest thing in the world."

He shrugged. "I was scared."

"I'll talk to Detective Evans and straighten it out."

"Will he make me go back to my dad?"

"I don't know. I'll try to get him to let you come home with me."

I watched his eyes skitter toward the door and knew he was thinking about bolting.

"Don't."

"Don't what?"

"Don't run. I'm not going to abandon you, I promise. No matter what happens, I'll be there with you."

He bit down on his lip and nodded.

"So what's your real name?"

For several long seconds I thought he would refuse to answer. Then, seeming to come to some sort of decision, he drew a quavering breath. "Tad Yoder. Thaddeus."

I smiled at him and held out my hand. "Nice to meet you, Thaddeus Yoder."

He gave me a small smile back and shook my hand. "Likewise, I'm sure."

"Thank you," I added, knowing how much trust it took for him to tell me.

He left his hand in mine and we waited a bit longer in companionable silence. Finally, Micah came out through the double doors, followed closely by an attractive woman in a white coat with a stethoscope around her neck. His face was still red and a little blotchy, his eyes bloodshot, and he wore a small bandage much like my own on his temple. Other than that, he looked little the worse for wear.

"They say I'll live," he said cheerfully. A bit too cheerfully for someone who had been thwacked in the head and hit with pepper spray just a short time before.

"Luckily, he has a hard head," the doctor tacked on. She gave us all a warm smile.

"I could have told you that," I said dryly.

Just then, Detective Evans walked into the waiting room, trailed by another young officer. "Good, I see you're all here." He turned to the doctor. "If you're finished with them, I think it's my turn."

"They're all yours." She excused herself with a little half-bow.

"Lucky me," he muttered under his breath, and then louder, "Alright, kids, we're moving this party down to the station. Officer Barnes here will escort you since your car remains parked at Mr. Akiba's apartment building. I'll meet you there."

"Wait," I said and looked over at Tad. He nodded slightly. "Before we do, you need to know that Tad gave you a false name when he was questioned back at the building."

Evans gave me a surprised look. "Is that true?" he asked Tad.

"Yes, sir," Tad answered in a low voice. "My real name is Thaddeus Yoder, not Young."

"Why would you lie about that?"

Tad threw me a desperate look, and I hastened to explain. "His father abused him so he ran away. Razi took him in off the streets, but then started abusing him too. He's scared you'll send him back to his father."

Evans frowned. "Well, by law we have to report this to social services. They'll step in and do an investigation to see if there was abuse. Then he'll be placed in foster care."

Tad took on a stricken expression.

"Isn't there any way around that?" I asked. "He can stay with me."

"It's not that easy," Evans said.

"What if we talk to his dad and he gives permission?"

The detective looked at me curiously. "And bypass social services?"

"Can we do that?" He looked unsure, so I threw in a final plea. "Please? He's already been through so much."

He sighed. "Let me check into it. For now, this will stay between us." He gave Officer Barnes a meaningful look. "Let's go."

Barnes took us to a holding room at the police station. One by one, we were ushered into an interrogation room where Detective Evans sat waiting. I was last. After I gave my statement, which took the better part of an hour with all his questions, the detective shut off the tape recorder.

"Well, Kendall, as much as it pains me to say it, congratulations on a job well done — despite screwing up a few times along the way. Your visit to Fenton Black's estate and this mess with Razi Akiba were both dangerous and risky — not to mention incredibly stupid. I hope you learned from your mistakes, but you can't argue with the results."

"So what's going to happen to Razi now?"

He chuckled. "The bastard is going away for a long, long time. He's admitted to everything. Your statements are just icing on the cake."

"He admitted to it?" I asked in disbelief.

"Singing like a canary. He's hoping it'll make things go easier for him."

"Will it?"

"Not a chance, but nobody's telling him that."

I laughed.

"You've tied up quite a few loose ends. Not only do we now have all the answers about the deaths of Paul Flynn, Fenton Black, and his bodyguards, but we can also close the books on that nasty business from a few years ago."

"What about his sources? It sounded to me like there was a leak in the police department."

His face darkened. "We're working on it," was all he would say. I took the hint.

"And Tad? Have you had a chance to look into that?"

His expression lightened some. It was still burdened, but for a different reason. "Not yet. I haven't had time." My face fell, and he took pity on me. "Look, so far, he's flying under the radar. No one has paid any attention to him. That makes things a little easier. After all you've done, I'm going to return the favor. I'll look the other way on one condition."

"What?"

"I'm taking a risk here, but I don't want to see the kid stuck in foster care. There are some good people who are willing to open their homes, but it's a rough life for a boy his age. He'll be better off with you. Just...make sure you handle things correctly, okay? Go through the right legal channels. Don't let this come back to bite me in the ass."

"I won't," I said. "I know a lawyer who specializes in situations like this. She does family law."

He nodded. "The father will need to be contacted."

"I know."

Evans shook his head. "You're a remarkable young man, Mr. Kendall. I said once before that I'd be proud to have you on my force. If you ever decide to get out of the PI business and go into law enforcement, you be sure to let me know." He stood up and held out his hand.

I jumped to my feet and clasped his rough hand in mine.

"Take care, Kendall."

"I will. Thank you, Detective Evans. For everything."

He nodded and led me out to the waiting room. Micah and Tad stood up, Tad looking very nervous.

"Let's go," I said brightly.

Tad's eyes darted between Evans and me. "I can go?" he asked hopefully.

"You can go," Evans said.

The smile that slowly spread across Tad's face was like the sun rising over the horizon after a long, harrowing night. I slipped my arm through his and tugged gently.

"Come on," I said. "Let's go home."

really. If he was going to stay with people who were perfect strangers, it was to be expected that he'd be curious about us.

I answered first. "I've lived here all my life. I grew up in a small town near Ocean City."

"I'm from Montgomery County, right outside DC," Micah said. "After I graduated from college, I moved here and got a job with the newspaper."

"What was it like growing up here?" Tad asked me.

"You're from a rural area, right?"

"Yeah."

"Probably not so different than it was for you, then. I never knew anyone who was gay. If I had bothered to think about it, I guess everyone I knew seemed to be pretty homophobic. But it was never an issue for me until Adam's son Seth moved here and started going to my school. He helped me figure out I was gay."

"He's the one who was killed?"

"Yes."

"Was he your boyfriend?"

"No, I wasn't at that point yet. We were just friends."

"How was he killed?"

I didn't answer for a moment. "I'll tell you some other time, okay?" I thought I did a pretty good job of keeping my voice steady.

"I'm sorry," Tad said immediately. "I shouldn't be so nosy. It's none of my damn business."

"No, it's okay. Don't apologize. You're getting to know us better. You can ask questions if you want...I just might not answer all of them right now."

When I turned into the driveway of the bed and breakfast, all Tad's questions fell by the wayside as he caught his first glimpse of Amalie's House.

"That's it?" he asked in awe.

"That's it." I gazed up at the house, remembering how I'd felt when I saw it for the first time. It was quite grand, a real Southern plantation manor house. It looked very different from when Steve had first considered purchasing it — it had resembled the Addams family's mansion more than a country bed and breakfast — but Steve had watched over every second of the meticulous restoration, and it turned out beautifully.

"Are you sure you're not rich?" Tad said.

I laughed. "Positive."

I parked the car, and Micah and I climbed out. Tad stayed put in the back seat.

"Aren't you getting out?" I asked, leaning back into the driver's-side door.

He tore his eyes away from the house, an anxious expression on his face. "Can I talk to you alone first?" he asked in a small voice.

"I'll go on in," Micah said, overhearing Tad's request. "I want to get some Tylenol for my head anyway. I've still got a splitting headache." As if kissing my ear, he whispered, "It'll also give me a chance to warn Adam and Steve."

I waited until he was inside, then turned back to Tad. "Come on. Let's go for a walk."

He climbed out hesitantly, and we started around the house. I tried waiting for him to make the first move, but eventually my inquisitiveness got the better of me. "So what did you want to talk about?"

"It's just that..." he started, then stopped abruptly, took a deep breath, and tried again. "I don't want you to think I was eavesdropping or anything, but I wasn't completely asleep when you and Micah were talking in the car."

"Tad, look—"

"No, let me finish. Let's just forget this whole thing, okay? I don't want to cause trouble for you. You've got a good thing going. I don't want to mess it up."

"You're not—"

"I ruin everything!" he said loudly. "That's all I am, a screwup. I screwed things up with my boyfriend, so he left me. I screwed things up when I ran away, so I had to become a hustler. I couldn't even do that right. I got sick. Then I screwed things up with Razi, so he hit me."

"Oh, Tad, you couldn't help most of those things. It's not your fault your boyfriend wasn't man enough to stick by you when things got rough, or that your dad is homophobic. It's not your fault Razi abused you. Maybe becoming a hustler wasn't the best decision, but you didn't have a lot of options at that point, at least from your point of view. You were just trying to survive."

"What about you? Think about it. How did we meet? I told you Micah used to be an escort. You didn't know it before that. I remember the look on your face."

"It turned out for the best in the end. It forced us to get a lot of things out in the open where they belong. Hey, we're still together, aren't we?"

"I guess. I still don't think I should do this. I'll screw up with you too, and in the end you'll just hate me. Everybody hates me. Even my own dad hates me."

"Tad, I don't hate you."

"You don't even know me."

"Why don't you give me a chance to get to know you?"

Tad looked everywhere but at me. His eyes fell upon the old angel statue among the trees in the back corner of the lawn. He stood staring at it for a minute while I watched him. A tear slipped from his eye and rolled slowly down his cheek. Finally, he spoke, his voice so soft I had to lean forward to hear him. "Because I'm scared."

I moved without thinking, slipping my arms around him and pulling him against me in a hug. He stood stiffly in my embrace, not hugging me back but not pushing me away either. I realized how much he had lost. I, of all people, should understand what he was going through. Of course he'd be afraid — terrified to open his heart for fear we'd just turn on him and abandon him, or let him down the way everyone else in his life had.

"I know you're scared, but give us a chance. Okay?"

"What if they don't want me?"

"Then we'll figure something else out. I promised you I wouldn't leave you, and I meant what I said. Look, why worry about that yet? You're getting too far ahead of yourself. Let's go talk to Adam and see what he has to say. Maybe none of this will even be an issue."

Tad sniffed a little and nodded, pulling away to rub at his face. He followed me back to the house, where we entered through the back door.

In the hallway we ran into Steve, who quickly pulled me into a hug. "You've got to stop almost getting killed."

"Next time I'll try to get the job done right."

Steve answered that with a soft smack upside my head. "How about if there is no next time?" He turned his attention to Tad, who was hanging back uncertainly. "And you must be Tad. I'm Steve." He held out a hand, which Tad tentatively shook. "It's nice to meet you."

"Hi," Tad murmured.

Steve flashed him a warm smile. "Come on, let me show you around this huge hulk of a house."

I opened my mouth to argue, but Steve gave me a glance that quickly shut me up. "Killian, why don't you go find Adam?" Although his voice was light, I could tell there was more to it than just a simple suggestion. *Uh oh*, I thought darkly.

Leaving Steve to give Tad the history of the house, step one on the official tour, I found Adam talking to Micah in the front parlor. Adam definitely didn't look happy. I felt my stomach clench. Adam stopped speaking abruptly as I appeared in the doorway.

One look at his face and I knew this would be better off as a private conversation. "Micah, Tad is being given the grand tour of the house, and he might be more comfortable if you're along."

"No problem." He gave me an encouraging smile as he walked away, leaving Adam and me alone.

"Look, Adam—" I figured a good offense would be my best defense, but he cut me off quickly.

"I don't know what to be angriest about," he said in a voice like a whip, "the fact that you just ran off without even telling me where you were going or what you were doing, the fact that you needlessly risked your life yet again with no thought of anyone else, or the fact that you come waltzing back in here with a kid in tow — a kid, I'm told, you've already invited to live here."

I took an involuntary step back as Adam's anger washed over me. Then my own anger rose up at his accusations. "First off, I didn't know I had to ask you for permission to do my job. I was working. I didn't have time to run around asking if it was okay for me to go play with my friends. I felt it was urgent that I get to Razi quickly. I was acting on instinct, which turned out to be right. By the time the police got around to acting, assuming they ever even got that far, Razi's informants would have tipped him off, and he would have run. And maybe even killed Tad. Considering I solved a crime, caught a killer, and quite possibly saved a kid's life, I wouldn't exactly call that needlessly risking my own life.

"As for Tad, I have not invited him to live here. I told him he could stay with me until he figured out what to do. I thought you were the kind of person who would be willing to help a kid in need. His dad abused him, and he was living on the streets before Razi — a homicidal prostitute — took him in and made him his sex slave. With Razi arrested, he had nowhere to go but back to the streets. I thought we could be some sort of support for him since he's never had any his entire life."

"We don't even know him."

"You didn't know me either when you took me in."

"That was different."

"How? Because I knew Seth? Why should Tad suffer just because he didn't have the privilege of knowing Seth? He needs help, Adam."

"You can't just drag home every stray you come across, Killian."

My breath caught in my throat, and my eyes stung with the tears I was determined to hold back.

"Is that what I was?" I asked, my voice shaky with anger and hurt. "A stray?"

"Killian, no!" Adam said, all anger melting from his expression to be replaced with concern and remorse.

"Why did you take me in, Adam? Was it out of pity? Or was it just because you were so grief-stricken from Seth's death. Is that it? Was I just a replacement for Seth?"

It was Adam's turn to gasp. "Killian!"

"I'm sorry I dragged home another stray. And I'm sorry this stray has stuck around for so long, burdening you and ruining your life. You won't have to worry about either of us from now on." I turned sharply on my heel, but before I'd taken two steps, Adam caught me, both of his arms wrapping tightly around my body.

"Killian, stop. Listen to me. That was a horrible thing I said, and I didn't mean it. I was just so worried about you when you left the hospital without a word. I've been frantic ever since. I reacted badly when I saw you, all my fear and worry turned to anger, and I took it out on you. I'm sorry — so, so sorry."

I refused to look at him, keeping my back purposefully to him.

"You're not a stray. You were never a stray. You want to know why I took you in? Because I looked at you and saw a hurt, scared young man and my heart broke. You're right. I barely knew you. In that sense, maybe I did take you in out of pity, but I very quickly grew to love you. You were never a replacement for Seth. Never. Not then, not now. You've always been Killian. I love you as if you were my own son, and I've never once regretted asking you to live with me. You've never been a burden. You've only enriched my life."

I couldn't hold back the tears any longer. I burst into harsh, ragged sobs as I turned to him, his arms once more circling me in the comforting hug I'd come to take for granted.

"Doesn't Tad deserve to have that too?" I sobbed into his chest.

"Of course he does. Absolutely. I just don't know if I'm the person to give it to him."

"It could have been me."

"What?"

"It could have been me on the street if you hadn't been there to take me in. I owe it to him to be there for him the way you were for me. I can't just turn my back on him. I can't."

Adam squeezed me fiercely and was quiet for a moment. "I won't ask you to."

I pulled away, swallowing mid-sob. "What?" I asked, wiping my eyes and sniffling. "What do you mean?"

"I won't ask you to act against your conscience."

"You'll let him stay here?"

"Temporarily."

"Oh, Adam!"

He held up a hand. "I'm not promising anything, Killian. I haven't even met him yet. All I'm saying is that he can stay here while we look at his options."

"You'll help him do that too? Figure out what his options are?"

"Yes, I'll do what I can to help him, within reason."

I ignored the proviso and threw myself into Adam's arms for a hug. He held me tightly.

"I'm so sorry, Killian," he whispered into my hair. "I can't believe I said that."

"I'm sorry I left without telling you where I was going. You're right. I didn't stop to think how worried you might be. All I could think about was getting to Razi."

"That's what makes you a good investigator." He held me out at arms length and looked me over carefully, his face suddenly breaking into a grin. "You're a mess. Go wash up, then we'll tell Tad the good news."

Several weeks had passed since Razi's arrest, and it was just a few days before Thanksgiving. A lot had happened in that time. Razi was charged with the murders of Paul Flynn, Fenton Black, and both bodyguards, plus the attempted murder of Micah and me. Tad's involvement had been kept quiet, or Razi would have been facing numerous sexual-abuse charges in addition. Charges were still pending on the murder of the politician.

Jake was released on the condition that he immediately enter a drug-and-alcohol-treatment facility for rehab. He agreed unequivocally, knowing he needed help and was ready to accept it. I'd been spending as much time as possible with him, slowly mending our relationship. I'd vowed to be a better friend this time around.

Micah was the Shore's new media darling. He'd broken the corruption story, which had turned out to have greater ramifications than even he'd imagined. Charges were still being filed. Some of the wetlands had already been lost to development, but much had been saved in time. The courts issued an injunction against any further construction until things were sorted out, which could take years.

Perhaps the biggest surprise came the week before when we were all at the beach house watching a movie on TV. After it ended, the news came on. We were talking and not really paying attention when I thought I recognized someone on the screen. "Who's that?" I asked, snapping to attention.

"Who's who?" Micah asked.

"Shh!" I turned up the volume.

"After the events of the last few weeks, many of us thought we'd seen it all," the newscaster was saying, "but the latest arrest in the Wetlands Conspiracy has shocked even the most hardened among us."

"A new arrest?" Micah said sitting up.

"Shh!" I hissed again.

"The corruption surrounding the illegal sale and development of protected wetlands has reached all the way to the top," the anchor continued. They flashed a picture of a man I didn't recognize. "State Senator Tom Day was indicted today for conspiracy to commit murder, along with several other lesser charges. Police allege that Senator Day conspired with murdered businessman Fenton Black to kill Henry

Gartland, a local environmentalist who's been protesting the development of the wetlands."

"Who did you see?" Adam asked me.

"Shh!" Micah and I said together.

"Day was suspected early on in the official investigation, but police lacked sufficient evidence to formally charge him."

"I didn't know that," Micah said under his breath, low enough not to warrant another hushing.

"That needed evidence came from an unlikely source." The picture changed to the one that had caught my attention in the first place. It was the bird-lady, the woman from Novak's mystery case. "Day's own wife hired a private investigator to look into her husband's business dealings. Justine Sterner spoke with the PI earlier this evening."

The TV flashed to a close-up of an attractive young woman with close-cropped dark hair and huge doe eyes. The reporter stared into the camera for a second before beginning to speak. "I'm Justine Sterner, and I'm here with local private investigator Shane Novak." My mouth fell open as the camera panned out to show my boss standing stiffly at her side. "Mr. Novak helped police obtain the evidence they needed to bring charges against Senator Day. Mr. Novak, you were hired by Mrs. Day, were you not?"

"Yes, I was," he replied laconically. The reporter waited for more, but nothing came. Adam chuckled at Novak's terseness.

"Do you know why Mrs. Day hired you to investigate her own husband?"

"Yes, I do, but wouldn't that be something you'd be better off asking her?"

The young reporter looked a little flustered, but forged bravely onward. "What can you tell us about your investigation?"

"Very little. I'm afraid that's police business now. They'll have to decide what they want to be public knowledge."

"Is there anything you can tell us about the charges that have been brought against Senator Day?"

"Well, they're certainly very serious. If they stick, I would imagine he'll be locked up for a good long time. I'd say Tom Day's political days are over."

"How is Mrs. Day holding up through all this?"

"She's been a trooper."

The reporter waited a moment, but when it became obvious Novak had nothing more to say, she turned things back over to the newsroom. The poor girl looked as if the scoop of the century had just slipped through her fingers. If I hadn't been so shocked at seeing Novak on the news, I probably would have been laughing. As it was, Adam was laughing hard enough for both of us.

Later, I found out from Novak that Mrs. Day had overheard her husband on the phone while he was planning the murder of the environmentalist. She'd gone to Novak because she didn't have any proof other than what she'd heard, or thought she'd heard. She'd been afraid for her own life, terrified he'd somehow find out and have her killed as well. That, and the extreme delicacy of the issue, explained all the cloak-and-dagger secrecy.

Things with Tad were moving slowly. Adam took to him quickly, but Tad continued to be very reserved. I guess it was too soon to expect him to relax completely with us. I was still the person he seemed most at ease with so I made an effort to spend as much time with him as I could with my already busy schedule.

Adam consulted Ilana about Tad's situation, and she'd made overtures to his father, but so far he'd not responded. The whole situation was still too unsettled for anyone to feel comfortable enough to commit themselves entirely.

"You know, I'm still not sure if I buy this whole ghost thing," Tad said to me. We were standing in the cellar at the B&B, waiting for the contractor Steve had hired to start work on reopening the bricked-up doorway I'd seen Amalie pass through not long before.

I looked over at Tad as he watched the workman changing the blade on a masonry saw. I felt very protective of him. He reminded me a lot of myself when I was his age. Although I was trying not to get too attached to him in case he had to leave, it was becoming increasingly difficult.

He looked over at me expectantly.

"What?" I asked, defensively. I felt guilty, as if he'd heard my thoughts.

He grinned at me. "I said, I'm still not sure if I buy this whole ghost thing."

I rolled my eyes. "That's because you haven't seen her."

"Are you positive you hadn't been hitting the bottle a little too hard that night?"

"Boys," Adam said with mock weariness, "do we have to go through this again?"

Tad and I had been arguing Amalie's existence since he'd first learned of her a few days after his arrival, when Steve announced his plans to tear down the wall and hopefully put her to rest. Once that decision was made, she seemed to have settled down in anticipation — or at least that's how my overactive imagination pictured it.

Before I could respond to Adam, the contractor spoke up. "Okay, folks, we're about ready to get down to business here. You might want to step back and watch your eyes. All of you really should be wearing safety goggles, but I didn't know I was gonna have an audience."

"Just tell us if we're in the way, Bob," Steve said as our small group — Steve, Adam, Judy, Micah, Kane, Tad, and I — obediently moved to the farthest wall away from where he was going to be working.

Bob shrugged. "Hey, it's your house. You're not in my way." He started the saw and slowly eased it into the wall, which the abrasive disk cut through with surprisingly little difficulty. We watched in silence while he sliced around the outline of the old doorway. Although the loud roar would have drowned out any attempt at conversation, those of us gathered in the basement suddenly found ourselves so tense that no one would have spoken even if we could have.

When he'd finished cutting and the cloud of brick dust settled, he picked up a sledgehammer and swung it up behind him.

"Wait!" I blurted out suddenly, panic squeezing my lungs as the heavy hammer started its downswing.

The sledgehammer shuddered to a halt in midair. Everyone spun around to look at me.

"What?" Bob asked.

"You...you can't do it like that." Odd, disjointed images were shifting across my vision, confusing me. At first, I thought the lights were flickering, until I realized it was actually the small room that was wavering — between the current scene and a much darker version lit only by a single candle in a sconce on the wall. The darker room was empty except for a few wooden barrels against one wall. Floor-to-ceiling shelves filled with glass jars of canned fruits and vegetables stood where the bricked-up doorway was in the present room.

Just as suddenly as the strange flickering sensation began, it stopped, leaving me blinking owlishly at the concerned faces staring back at me.

Micah grabbed my arm. "Killian, are you okay?"

"Did you see something?" Judy asked.

I nodded.

"What did you see?"

"What does she mean?" I heard Tad ask nervously.

"The room was changing. I think I saw how it used to be. And...I don't know. I just had this feeling..." I turned to look at Bob, who was staring at me as if I'd lost my mind. "Is there some other way to open the wall?"

"Not really. If I had someone on the other side they could push it out, but since I don't, it's gotta go that way."

"Can you be gentle?"

"Gentle? It's a sledgehammer and bricks. How gentle can you be?"

"Can you just try?" Steve asked politely.

Bob shook his head as he turned back to the wall. He changed his grip on the hammer and began to use it like a battering ram. The first few bricks tumbled down on the other side with a dull thud as if hitting bare earth. I'm sure it took longer to do it that way, but the panicky feeling didn't return.

Soon he had an opening big enough to see through. He shifted one of the lights he'd brought along so that it shined through the hole. He leaned in and peered intently into whatever lay beyond the opening, then jerked back suddenly, his face going alarmingly pale.

"Do you see something?" Steve asked excitedly.

"Amalie," I muttered with inexplicable certainty.

Bob pulled a handkerchief from his pocket and mopped his face. "There's a...a skeleton in there," he said shakily. He looked over at me. "Did you know about it?"

"Not before now," I said, sounding a lot calmer than I felt.

Steve turned to me with a raised eyebrow. "How can you be sure it's Amalie?"

Judy had taken Bob's place in front of the hole. "Who else would it be?" Her voice sounded eerily hollow as she spoke into the aperture.

"What happened? How'd she get in there?" Adam asked in confusion.

Judy turned to me. "Killian?"

I shook my head.

"If we want to know what happened, only you can tell us."

"I...I can't."

"What's going on?" Tad asked, fear in his voice.

"That's what I want to know." Bob sounded a little angry now. "If you thought there was a body behind this wall, you should have told me upfront. I would've never agreed to do this. I have half a mind to call the police."

"Bob," Steve said, "if we're right, then that skeleton has been here for about a hundred and fifty years. There's nothing the police can do. We'll handle things from here. Why don't you go ahead and leave? I'll pay you for the time we agreed on."

"You don't have to tell me twice. This is all too weird for me." He grabbed up his saw and a few odd pieces of equipment, then paused. "I'll get the rest of my stuff later," he said and made his exit.

"Can we widen the hole enough to get through?" Judy asked.

"I'll do it," Micah offered quickly. He picked up the sledge hammer and began to carefully knock away more bricks.

"I think I'll go upstairs," Tad said.

"Me too," Kane added.

"If I'm not needed here, I'll go with them," Adam said. No one protested, and the three of them climbed the stairs, leaving just four of us in the cellar — five, if you counted Amalie. A shiver went up my spine at that thought. All this time she'd been entombed behind the wall instead of in the marked grave in the back yard. How had it happened?

"You have to go in there," Judy said.

"I'm scared," I said hoarsely.

"It's never hurt you before, has it?"

"What are you talking about?" Steve asked. "What's never hurt him? Amalie?"

"His Gifts. If he goes in there, he might be able to see what happened."

"Or I might not see anything at all."

"Oh, I think you will," Judy said. "You have a strong connection to Amalie. This is what she's been aiming for all along. She wants us to know what happened."

"We thought it was just the baby," Steve said almost to himself. "But there was more, that's why she didn't go away after we buried the baby next to her grave. She wasn't even there. She was here the whole time." He looked up. "But how? What happened?"

"Killian?" Judy said.

Micah stepped back and dropped the hammer, wiping sweat from his brow. "I think the hole is big enough now."

I took a deep breath. In my heart, I knew all my arguing was in vain. If I was honest, I wanted to find out what happened all those years ago as much as anyone. Maybe I even needed to know. I took a tentative step toward the enlarged opening.

Micah stepped forward to help me. "I'll be right here, Kill."

I approached the hole and took my first look at what lay beyond. The light from the lamp showed what appeared to be the beginning of a low, narrow tunnel that extended perhaps ten feet from the doorway before it ended in a pile of rubble where the roof had apparently collapsed. The walls looked to be blackened, slime-covered bricks, shored up with rough-hewn timbers. About halfway to the rubble lay a pathetic heap of bones, all that was left of Amalie. I took another deep breath and climbed over the broken bricks.

The world shifted as my feet touched the ground. Immediately, I knew on some deep level that I was no longer in my own body. I remained aware of myself while at the same time being fully integrated with my new body — Amalie's body. This was a much more intense experience than the time in Paul's apartment. I wasn't just feeling Amalie's emotions — I was Amalie.

Terror coursed through me as she/I stumbled forward. I felt a sense of movement behind me and twisted around to crouch down. Pain shot through my side as I moved, and I knew I'd been punched there. Someone was in the doorway, which now stood clear. It was a man, but it was so dark I couldn't make out his features. Again, I somehow knew that this man was Amalie's husband, Captain Marnien.

"You're nothing but a common whore," he said. He moved again, and candlelight turned his face into a horrifying mask of rage and hatred. Even distorted by the dim lighting, the part of me that remained Killian recognized him as the man from my long-ago vision, the one hurrying into the house from the boat.

A rush of foreign memories flooded into my consciousness. I was standing in the cupola. It was night outside the windows. I was cradling a crying infant in my arms. I'd gone up there because, for some reason, it usually calmed the baby. But not that night. I was so distracted with my son that I didn't hear the footsteps until they were upon me. I spun around, my heart in my throat.

"Captain!" He wasn't supposed to be there. I'd been told he was lost at sea. He couldn't be...but there he stood, water dripping from his graying hair. Astonishment suffused his face as he stared at the babe in my arms. A sense of dread washed over me, for I knew it wouldn't take long for him to calculate the months in his head, to realize the baby I held couldn't be his.

Seeing his expression start to shut down, I began speaking quickly. "I thought you were dead. They told me you were lost at sea. Your ship...they said it went down in a storm. I mourned you. Look, I'm still wearing black."

"You obviously didn't mourn me for long," he said, the first words he'd spoken since he appeared.

"I...it's not..."

"Turn to another man for comfort, did you? Even if I had drowned, I would hardly have gone under before you took another man to bed."

"Where were you? If you were alive, why didn't you send word to me?"

"Does it matter now?" He moved menacingly forward. "Let's see the little bastard. Does it take after its daddy?"

I pulled the blankets protectively over the baby's face, and his cries settled into a mere whimper. "Please no," I begged. "None of this is the child's fault."

"No, it is all your fault. You, my faithless wife." He spat the last two words, but then his voice chilled. "The child will go."

"No! Please! We can raise him as your own."

"You think I'll have some other man's child raised under my roof?" he bellowed. "You'll have me thought a fool?"

"No one else knows, except the servants."

"Servants talk. The child goes."

"Then I'll go as well," I shouted defiantly.

His hand shot out so quickly I had no time to get out of his way. His fist drove into my side, throwing me back against the windows behind me. My head hit one of the panes of glass, shattering it outward. Cold wind whipped into the room as I struggled to maintain my grip on the baby, now crying again.

"You're not going anywhere." His voice was frighteningly calm. A sudden terror gripped my heart, and instinct took over. I had to protect my baby. I had to get away. I dived past him toward the narrow stairs, a move so unexpected he barely had time to react. He lunged after me, his large hand striking between my shoulders as I took the first step. I stumbled down several more before catching my balance, but he was still right behind me, and suddenly gave me a violent shove. For a few seconds, I felt as if I was suspended in midair. Then I was falling, falling into the inky blackness of the stairwell.

For the briefest moment, I was myself again. I was crouching in the dirt of the dank passage, staring blankly at the partially opened doorway. Micah peered anxiously in at me, Judy visible just over his shoulder. "Killian, are you okay?" he asked.

Then they were gone.

I sat up with a start and looked wildly about. I was in the cellar, lying on the dirt floor. The room was lit only by a single candle. I hurt in so many places, but especially my side. The scene in the cupola came back to me in a flash. *My baby! Where is my baby?*

I spotted the little body lying a few feet away in an undignified heap, still and silent — much too still. I crawled frantically toward him, ignoring my pain, already sobbing, knowing the worst. He was dead, his tiny body growing cold. How long had I been unconscious? Could I have saved him if I'd been awake? A grief such as I'd never felt before overtook me, and for some unknown amount of time, I simply held him to my chest and rocked back and forth, weeping so deeply I didn't make a sound.

Eventually, I stopped crying. I knew I had to bury him. My husband, the Captain, wouldn't afford him that much dignity. I removed my mourning shawl and wrapped my son carefully in it, laying him tenderly aside. I quickly began to dig into the hard-packed earth floor. I didn't know how long I had, how long the Captain would leave me alone. I dug and dug with only my bare hands until my nails bled and fingers ached with the cold, and still I dug. Finally, I had a hole large enough to hold the little body. He was so small.

I once again began to cry silent tears as I lifted the tiny bundle and laid him in the hole as gently as possible. I stared down for a moment at his beautiful face. I could almost imagine that he was only asleep. He looked so peaceful I could hardly bear to cover him with the dirt, but I knew I had no choice. I fumbled with the brooch at my neck, a wedding present from my parents. Finally, the clasp gave way to my numb fingers, and the brooch dropped into my palm. Placing it lovingly on my son's chest, I leaned forward and kissed his forehead, then quickly swept the small pile of dirt over him before I could change my mind, before it was too late.

I cried while I smoothed the dirt over his grave, my tears mixing with the earth to form mud. When I had hidden the evidence of my digging to my satisfaction, I curled up in a ball over the spot and wept bitterly.

I was still crying when I heard the Captain speaking at the top of the stairs. I suddenly hated him with a depth of emotion I hadn't known I was capable of. I wanted him to suffer the way he'd caused me to suffer. I lurched to my feet and began to look madly around the room for something to use as a weapon. I had never been down there before, since the Captain had always said it was no place for the lady of the house. It didn't take me long to realize the cellar was empty except for a few wooden barrels against one wall, and a set of shelves well-stocked with the canned food the women had put up in the fall. A ham hung from the rafters in one corner.

The door at the top of the stairs opened, and the Captain descended with ominous purpose. I pressed myself against the far wall. He stood staring at me, his eyes filled with hate and disgust. Neither of us spoke for what felt like an eternity. Then he unexpectedly swung around and grasped the edge of the shelves. Even in my grief-stricken, shocked state, I was surprised to see them slowly swing away from the brick wall to reveal a dark doorway.

The Captain turned back to me, an unpleasant grin on his face. "It's a tunnel I had built for...business purposes. It comes out near the dock. If you want to leave so badly, go now."

I stared at him in disbelief. Did he actually intend to let me go? It seemed too good to be true.

"Go!" he shouted. "Get out and never return!"

I threw myself away from the wall and dashed toward the door. He pushed me as I passed him, making me stumble into the darkness. I stopped dead when I saw that the passage only went a few feet before ending in a heap of rubble. A cold laugh came from behind me.

I twisted around, crouching down into a feral position of defense as I did.

"You're nothing but a common whore," he said. His face was lost in darkness, but his voice was filled with cold hatred. "You think I would allow you to leave me? You'll never escape this house. Never! You'll die here like the dog you are, bitch!"

He started to close the camouflaged door. Belatedly, I realized he meant to lock me in the collapsed tunnel, leaving me to die. I threw myself at the door, but the Captain was quicker. It closed with a sickening thud, shutting out all light. I began to scream and claw at it, pushing against it with all my weight, but to no avail. I pounded the wood with my fists, begging for mercy, but my only answer was an unfeeling chuckle, and then silence. The utter darkness pressed in around me until I couldn't breathe. I dragged myself away from the door, crumpling to the ground where I began to will myself to die.

"Killian!" a voice shouted.

I opened my eyes and saw light. I wasn't locked in the tunnel, left to die. I moved my hand and realized that I was once again back in my own body. I was curled into the fetal position on the dirt floor of the tunnel.

"Killian, are you okay?" Micah said again. When I didn't answer, he began to scramble through the opening, which, while plenty large enough for me, was almost too small for him.

I turned my head slowly to one side and found myself staring into the empty eye sockets of Amalie's skull. One bony arm was stretched out in my direction, almost as if she was reaching for me. I slid my hand over and rested it gingerly on hers.

"I'm so sorry," I whispered.

A couple of weeks later, I stood next to Amalie's grave, watching my breath puff out into the cold air. The small funeral we'd held to give her a proper burial had been over for some time, but I couldn't bring myself to go indoors just yet. My visions, my out-of-body experience — whatever you want to call them — had affected me deeply. Ever since it happened I'd been quiet and withdrawn, which had begun to worry my family seriously. Experiencing the horribly traumatic events of Amalie's final night left me very troubled.

I looked over at the angel statue. I was somewhat comforted by the idea that the angel was there to watch over Amalie at last. It was ironic that Amalie herself had it placed there in memory of the Captain, whom she had thought lost at sea. The angel had always looked so sad. I knew how she felt.

"You're going to have to let it go, you know," a voice said from behind me, causing me to jump. I turned to find Judy leaning against a tree, watching me with a concerned expression.

"It's not so easy."

"No, I don't imagine it is." She walked slowly to my side. "It's the past, Killian. It all happened well over a hundred years ago. There's nothing now that can change it. We've done what we could, and I have to believe it's what Amalie wanted. She can rest in peace at last."

"I know in my head that it all happened a long time ago, but feeling it, living it the way I did...it's hard to convince my heart that it's ancient history. It hurts just as much as if I'd lost a close friend...again."

She took my hand. "I'm sorry, dear heart. I know so little about your sort of Gifts. I wish I could have prepared you better for what happened. I had no idea it would be such a powerful experience. We need to get you trained as quickly as possible. You must understand your Gifts if you hope to control them instead of them controlling you.

If you did, maybe they wouldn't have taken you over so completely." She looked into my eyes. "You have powerful Gifts, Killian. We're still learning just how powerful. It's not something you want to leave unchecked."

I nodded. I knew she was right.

Judy slipped her arm around my waist. "Come on. Let's go inside with everyone else."

"I'll be there in a minute."

"Okay, but don't stay too long." She kissed me softly on the cheek and walked away, leaving me alone with my thoughts once again.

I stood for another minute and then turned to leave. I'd only taken a few steps before I felt a presence behind me. It was Amalie, standing in the shade of the trees, holding the baby. The hair stood up on my arms, but I wasn't afraid. The energy was different; she felt like an old friend. She smiled at me, for the first time ever, before she and her son slowly faded away. A sense of peace suffused me, assuring me that they were together at last.

"Rest well, Amalie," I whispered. Then I returned to the house and to the living, leaving the dead and the past behind me, where they belonged.

The Truth of Yesterday is author Josh Aterovis's fourth book in the Killian Kendall mystery series. His first book, *Bleeding Hearts*, introduced gay teen sleuth Killian Kendall, and won several awards, including the Whodunit Award from the StoneWall Society. He followed up by winning the Whodunit Award again the following year for *Reap the Whirlwind*. The third book in the series, *All Lost Things*, was a finalist for the 2010 Lambda Literary Awards for Gay Mystery.

Aterovis was born and raised on the Eastern Shore of Maryland, where his books are set. He now lives in Baltimore, MD.

CPSIA information can be obtained at www.ICGtesting.com
Printed in the USA
LVOW131327250213

321598LV00001B/62/P